Praise for Shena Mackay and
Dreams of Dead Women's Handbags

"The best writer in the world today." —*Elle*

"American readers new to Mackay's stories . . . have something really special waiting for them. . . . Mackay makes most of her contemporaries seem nearly indifferent to language, and not especially good at using it." —*Publishers Weekly* (starred, boxed review)

"Shena Mackay . . . is a master of the short story."—*The Daily Telegraph*

"Novel-worthy dimensions in a few pages. . . . [Mackay's] descriptive precision and imagination are matched by a talent to surprise." —*New York Times Book Review*

"The prose style Mackay has developed . . . is a glittering one, full of highly original imagery that is often macabre and surrealistic. . . . There isn't a single [story] that doesn't attest to its author's highly original talent." —*Boston Globe*

"Funny and strikingly written sentences leap out at the reader throughout this astonishingly accomplished collection." —*Library Journal*

"The concision, economy and intensity which the [short story] genre requires in its perfect form are handled here with a startling virtuosity. . . . Shena Mackay triumphs." —*The Spectator*

"There is no suitable adjective with which to describe the work of Shena Mackay. Several come readily to mind: quirky, sharp-edged, ironic, compassionate, outraged. But none of these is adequate to convey the peculiar brilliance with which she infuses the devastating stories collected in *Dreams of Dead Women's Handbags*. . . . At a time when so much fiction, examining bland lives, is itself flat and pale, Mackay's work stands out as a vigorous and spirited testimony to the power of language to transform even the most trivial experience into something rich and strange." —*The Boston Book Review*

"The best writer we've got." —*New Statesman and Society*

"Mackay is a darkly comic writer in the tradition of Katherine Mansfield or Jane Bowles. Her lonely women characters outshine the best of Edna O'Brien. . . . The stories in this collection are without exception full of subtle shifts in tone, black humor and beautifully telling details." —*New York Newsday*

"Mackay's writing—rich, ornate, daring—sometimes halts the progress of these stories as we pause to examine the brilliant images she flings across the page." —*Fiction Magazine*

"Stylish tales of the unexpected which take off from the most commonplace things. . . . [Mackay's] work has a quality of *rightness* to its illogic that can properly be called poetic." —*The Guardian*

"*Dreams of Dead Women's Handbags* contains some gems. . . . Shena Mackay is a sharp and often funny observer of the deficiencies in ordinary life." —*London Review of Books*

"Three cheers for writers like Shena Mackay who keep British literature on its toes. Her new collection of short stories . . . pulsates with quirky originality and is written in vibrant prose that occasionally peaks towards poetry. . . . It is Mackay's gift to make us laugh even as we snivel and blow our noses." —*The Daily Telegraph*

"Remarkable." —*The Sunday Telegraph*

"[Mackay] has the ability to infuse the ordinary with the exotic. . . . These are gripping tales because of the meticulousness of the prose— a style in which every word counts, and in which she can marry psychic horror to an oddly sympathetic attitude." —*British Book News*

"A very distinguished collection." —*Financial Times*

DREAMS *of* DEAD WOMEN'S HANDBAGS

DREAMS *of* DEAD WOMEN'S HANDBAGS

Collected Stories

SHENA MACKAY

A HARVEST BOOK

HARCOURT BRACE & COMPANY

San Diego   New York   London

Requests for permission to make copies
of any part of the work should be mailed to:
Moyer Bell, Kymbolde Way, Wakefield, Rhode Island 02879.

First published by Moyer Bell in 1994.

Library of Congress Cataloging-in-Publication Data
Mackay, Shena.
Dreams of dead women's handbags:
collected stories/Shena Mackay.
p.   cm.—(A Harvest book)
ISBN 0-15-600533-6
I. Title.
[PR6063.A2425D7   1997]
823'.914—dc21 97-18477

Text set in Bembo

Printed in the United States of America
First Harvest edition 1997
A C E D B

*For Sarah, Rebecca
and Cecily*

CONTENTS

DREAMS *of* DEAD WOMEN'S HANDBAGS

THE MOST BEAUTIFUL
DRESS IN THE WORLD

There are houses which exhale unhappiness. The honesty rattling its shabby discs and dominating the weedy flower bed, the carelessly rinsed bottle still veiled in milk on the step from which a tile is missing, the crisp bag, sequinned with dewdrops, which will not rot and will not be removed, clinging to the straggly hedge, are as much manifestations of the misery within as are the gray neglected nets, respectability's ghosts, clouding the windows like ectoplasmic emanations of despair.

The woman in the back garden of such a house, although with her uncombed hair falling onto the shoulders of an old pink dressing gown belted with a twisted striped tie, she looked very much in keeping with her habitat, was not, that morning, unhappy. She was lifting a mass of honeysuckle that sprawled over the grass, trying to disengage the brittle red stems without breaking them and winding them through the almost fragile zigzags of trellis that topped the fence. The bed beneath the honeysuckle had been a herb garden and its last survivors trapping and trapped by the serpentine stems with their little ophidian heads of furled leaves, released the scent of chives. Harriet's movements were slow, with the hesitancy of one weakened by a series of blows and wounds both delivered and self-inflicted, but now, although the healing sun bathing her dressing gown and the smell of the chives on her hands could provoke weak invalidish tears, she felt convalescent, as if she had taken her first shaky steps from an asylum gate, leaving pills and bottles in a locked cabinet in a dark corridor behind her.

Other people's gardens were refulgent with sunflowers, and dahlias riddled with earwigs; the glutted trugs of Surrey bulged with late and woody runner beans. Harriet had found, at dawn, a green and yellow striped torpedo on her own step with so hard a carapace that she knew in advance how the breadknife would break as she tried to cut it and the blade would remain embedded in its shiny shell. The early October sunshine had an elegiac quality that reminded her of the slow movement of a cello concerto, still golden but foretelling full-blown autumn melancholy, the tomatoes that would never ripen, the last yellow fluted flower of the barren marrow, the falling of the leaves. The narrow lapis lazuli bracelet that rolled up and down her wrist as she worked had lost some of its stones. She had worn it for so many years that she had ceased to see it but on the rare occasions on which it had been lost, caught in a sleeve or sloughed into a shopping bag, she had been aware at once of its absence circling her arm like a bangle of air. Her daughter had played with it as a baby, had cut her teeth on it, and it had become a sort of talisman to them both.

On the underside of a curled-over leaf, cocooned so that she could not tell if it were alive or dead, lay a caterpillar. "The caterpillar on the leaf / Repeats to thee thy mother's grief," she thought as she placed the leaf gently against the trellis. As she reached up the bracelet slid down to rest above her elbow and a fly, with a bravado that suggested that it knew its days were numbered anyway, alighted on the knob of her wrist bone as if it would await its quietus grazing there among the fair down. A movement of the hand sent it flying heavily onto the silvered leaf of a blighted rose. As the glassy facets of the fly's wings sparkled she felt one of those painful flashes of joy, engendered by the natural world, which have no foundation in circumstances or power to change the lives which they illumine so briefly and which give a momentary vision, too fleeting to analyze, of the universe as benign. A long arm of honeysuckle encircled her neck in a gentle green-leaved garotte. She thought she had never known an October so golden, and that if she had not emerged from so black a pit of horrors that still writhed half-forgotten in her soul she would not have been able to appreciate the gold of the day.

As she went into the house Auden's prayer that his sleeping love might find the natural world enough came into her head. That wish, that the beloved might face the light with eyes unshielded by spectacles of alcohol or dope seemed the best that one could ask. There was only one person for whom she would ask such a gift, and that was her daughter, Miranda. She had unconsciously adapted the quotation, as she discovered when she looked up the poem in the blue book whose spine had faded to dun in the dusty bookcase: it was the mortal world which the poet hoped that his love would find enough. That would do, she thought, smiling as she replaced the book, running her finger along the shelf. Today even dust did not look like an enemy.

She felt the brush of a warm coat on her bare legs as Bruno lifted his head from his bowl and trotted past her to fling himself in a pool of sun on one of the beds. Her apparel and the state of the kitchen, strewn with breakfast debris, belied the fact that Harriet had been busy since seven o'clock that morning but the black rims of her nails, as she rinsed Bruno's bowl, and piled dishes into the sink, testified to the fact that she had repotted some houseplants; the loaf and margarine and smeary knives suggested she had made sandwiches for somebody; in fact for Miranda, who had caught an early train for the college where she was starting, that morning, her career as a fashion student. The sandwiches, though scorned, would, Harriet hoped, be welcome if they could be consumed in secret, out of the sight of fellow students posing as day-trippers and professors masquerading as ticket collectors and secretaries.

This was the first whole day that Harriet had had to herself for a long time and she determined not to waste it. She was going to paint, which was not only now the only activity which gave her any pleasure—and there was an enchanting tangle of flowers and leaves of berries hanging over an old wall down the road that she wanted to preserve on paper before it was desolated by winter—but was also the occupation which engendered the sluggish trickle of income which kept them afloat in the poverty to which they had become accustomed, of which Miranda did not always hide her resentment. The summer had been filled with Miranda's friends and alternately with Miranda's boredom and excitement, neither of which Harriet found conducive to working even on those rare occasions when the kitchen was empty; and she found that, as those who work at home know, the anticipation of arrivals and departures creates an enervating limbo peppered with frustration and irritability, and the failure of an awaited letter to arrive, or the telephone to ring can sour the day as hope curdles to despair.

She decided to wash the curtains before she started work and as she gathered the smoky clouds of net in her arms to place them in the machine she was reminded of Miranda's dress.

"Don't you think it's the most beautiful dress you've ever seen?" Miranda had said, pulling handfuls of gray tulle from the plastic carrier bag, a radiant conjuror about to produce her most brilliant trick. "Isn't it the most beautiful dress in the world?"

Harriet had stared at the crumpled greenish roses moldering on the boned bodice, with yellow stains under the arms, that rose from vapors of mothy gauze hanging over a skirt of gray tulle that time had turned to perforated zinc.

"You might be a bit more enthusiastic. . . ."

"It's perfect for the party. It'll be lovely when it's had a wash."

"I'm not going to wash it!"

Miranda beat the air from its folds and shoveled it back into the bag, and the thud of her feet on the stairs told Harriet that she had deflated and disappointed—why could she not have dredged up some spurious enthusiasm instead of flinging her own fear like a handful of gray dust over that gray dress?

The truth was, she hated the dress. It had dangled like a specter, a mocking *memento mori* against her daughter's young face; the whisk of its skirt brought a whiff of the grave, of black lips of earth and churning worms.

It was the sort of dress that Harriet had fled from in her youth, hurtling herself down the path that had led through the years to the defeated house; and in Miranda's eyes it had the charm of an antique. Later Harriet had tried to repair the damage by praising the dress exorbitantly and asking too many questions about the party for which it had been bought.

"I probably won't go," said Miranda.

Now it came to Harriet that she would wash the dress while Miranda was away, redeeming it as well as herself, and surprise her with its restored beauty when she came home. It was so delicate that it would have to be washed by hand, and she imagined a million trapped glittering bubbles irradiating its mesh as she lifted it white and virginal from the dirty water, the stains of another dancer's sweat of ecstasy or panic dissolving from the boned bodice, the mildewed roses unfurling plump petals as it waltzed with the October wind.

Whether it was her fault or not, Harriet was not a practical person. So much of the energy that might have been expended in kisses and fun had been frittered away in the foothills of mountains that other people took in their stride. She would have been perfectly happy painting, or lying in bed or in the garden all day smoking and reading detective stories, but love must be expressed in practical, financial and nutritional terms. She had never quite come to terms with the fact that a wall once painted, a room swept or dusted would not remain in that state. She regarded Hoovers and mops and dusters not as helpmeets but as enemies and symbols of her servitude; she was cruel to her household implements; their duties were not onerous or even very regular, but when they were called upon to perform they were often kicked and beaten. Sometimes in calm moments she had meant to observe herself to see if there was perhaps a pattern to her savagery, but she had never been sufficiently organized to correlate the evidence, and instead wept baffled tears as she clutched a bruised hand or toe and surveyed the broken plug or splintered handle that would add shame and self-inflicted pain to her resentment the next time she performed some hated chore.

As she turned to wash the breakfast dishes, in order to clear the sink for Miranda's dress, her eye caught the cream-colored telephone clinging like a flung vanilla blancmange to the kitchen wall.

"There is not one person in the whole world who wants to speak to me," she thought.

She was wrong. At that moment the telephone rang. It was her elderly neighbor asking, or commanding, her to go across to the shop to buy a large tin of prunes and two flat packs of soft toilet tissue. After having learned more than she wished to know about the state of the widower's intestines, and having promised to do the shopping later in the morning, she put down the phone. It rang again.

"It's only me. This is the third time I've rung. You were engaged," the voice accused.

"Oh, hi, Mo. I'm sorry, it was my neighbor—he tends to go on a bit," Harriet heard herself apologize.

"Never mind. What are you doing? I've got the car and I thought we could go out somewhere, it's such a lovely day. Are you still there?"

"Yes, it's just that I'm a bit tied up—there's something I want to do—some painting—"

"Oh well, if you don't want to—it was just a thought, as I've got the car. . . ."

"I'd love to, really, it's just that today's the first day I've had to myself for weeks so I thought I could really get down to some work."

"Couldn't you do it this evening? We needn't be back late."

"Miranda will be back. It's her first day today, and I don't want to be preoccupied . . . you know how it is. . . ."

"OK. It doesn't matter. I'll give you a ring later in the week. Happy painting!"

As Harriet stood with the dialing tone buzzing in the receiver in her hand, a young dustman passing the window, in a sleeveless vest, an empty bin on his shoulder, the hair under his raised arm flowering like the sooty stamens of an anemone against his white flesh, called something inaudible to her. She interpreted his greeting as condemnation of her slatternly state. Mo's disappointed voice had reduced her need to work to a selfish, self-important whim.

A small envelope, with a rustling and clatter inappropriate to its size, came through the letter box and landed on the mat. Harriet picked it up and saw a photograph of a little girl dressed in white, captioned "The Party Dress She'll Never See," and was at once blinded herself by trite tears and muttered, "That's all I need," as she hid it behind a stack of letters. Reminded of Miranda's party dress she finished the dishes, and was called down from halfway up the stairs by the front-door bell. The milkman, another witness to her mid-morning disarray, lounged in the doorway watching her as she wrote the check. His cheekbones were embroidered with tiny amber pustules and his nails rasped on his scalp as he pushed back his cap to scratch in his hair; she winced at the thought of those nails on the silver-foil milk bottle tops.

When he had gone she determined not to let the impulse to work dissipate and wiped the kitchen table, which was the only surface big enough, and set out paper, paints and brushes and a jam jar of water and tried to dissolve her guilt at Mo's disappointed voice in the clear water that held the faintest turquoise tinge reflected from the walls of glass that confined it and spawned spiraling strings of minuscule bubbles like glass beads. "I'll put Miranda's dress to soak," she thought, "have a quick bath and get dressed, go to the shop and have another look at the plants on that wall and then start work. I don't believe it!"

The phone was ringing again.

The voice that came through was furred-up, like an old waste pipe, with whisky.

"Dad."

"I thought you might have rung yesterday to see how I got on at the hospital."

Oh God. She had forgotten all about it.

"I did ring. All the lines to Rottingdean were busy. How did you get on?"

Her heart was banging about in the old painful way. She drummed her fingers on the marrow which lay on the table radiating vegetable calm from its green and yellow stripes.

"I didn't go!"

His triumphant crow was splattered against her ear in an eruption of wet coughing. She held the receiver at arm's length.

"Why didn't you? Did they change your appointment?"

"I was dressed and waiting for that sodding ambulance at eight o'clock. Do you know what time they turned up? Gone eleven. I told them what they could do with their bloody appointment."

"I bet that showed the bastards," said Harriet wearily, realizing that she would have to apologize, make a new appointment and accompany him.

"What? Showed the bastards, didn't I? Who do they think they are?"

"I expect some of them think they're people who are trying to do a very unpleasant job with very little money, or resources."

It didn't matter what she said, he would neither hear nor remember.

"Bloody hospitals."

"You chose not to know when I was in hospital."

"How would you know, you've never been in hospital. Except when Miranda was born, I suppose. Anyway, I just thought you'd be interested to hear how I got on."

"Fascinated."

"Has she gone back to school? You said she was coming to see me in the holidays. When's she coming?"

"I'm not sure. Soon. . . ."

"What?"

"I don't know, Dad. She's a big girl now, I can't force—"

"What do you mean, force?"—he had heard that all right. "You're just jealous of Miranda and me. Just because I'm old and ill. You'll find out one day, when you're old and ill and nobody wants to know. . . ."

and Harriet was caught by a rush of love for the body that would fill it, the bony shoulders that would rise from the stained bodice, the downy arms. "Let her be happy," she prayed, and was assaulted by the memory of a very small girl saying with such vehemence, "Mommy, when you go to Heaven, I'm going to *cling* on to you and fly up with you," that she could still feel those fingers digging into her flesh.

She gathered the dress to her, as she would have liked to embrace her daughter, and the tip of her cigarette caught a fold and a tongue of flame leaped up the gauze, and died, leaving a hideous black valley up the center of the skirt.

Her carelessness. Her carelessness that amounted to cruelty—her stupidity that might be misinterpreted as spite—she pulled the folds together as if the damage would disappear and opened them to display the blackened horror. The burn might come out when she washed it and perhaps she could mend—there was no white, or gray thread—get some when she went for the prunes and toilet paper. If only she hadn't interfered, had let well alone—Miranda hadn't wanted it washed—if she hadn't lit that stupid cigarette—it was all to prove her love—all for herself. She stood in the smell of scorched dust cradling the corpse of her attempt at redemption.

In the kitchen, the net curtains, which had not been burned, tumbled careless gouts of foam through the black outlet hose into the sink. Harriet laid the dress in the washing-up bowl and turned on the taps gently and scattered detergent like someone dropping earth on a coffin. As she watched, the stems of the roses unwound in slimy slow motion and the petals disengaged one by one as the glue dissolved, and floated separately on the surface of the water.

The door bell rang.

"Go away," she screamed.

It rang again.

"It's not *just* because you're old and ill, Dad, it's because you're also boring and disgusting and totally selfish."

Her words were lost in his coughing.

"Listen, Dad. I'll come to see you tomorrow. Can you hear me, Dad? SEE YOU TOMORROW. I'LL BRING SOME LUNCH."

"Nobody bloody cares if I go to the hospital or not. The nurses don't care, the doctors don't care, you don't care. . . ."

"If you ever looked at me, if you had the slightest interest in, or conception of what my life has been like, you would see that I had nothing left to care *with*. Why should I care? For a moment's carelessness on your part and a few miserable years I have to pay in blood for the rest of my life."

"Harriet, are you still there? Harry?"

"I said, I'LL SEE YOU TOMORROW. GOODBYE, DAD, I'VE GOT TO GO, THERE'S SOMEONE AT THE DOOR."

She went to answer it with an image in her mind of herself and her father, writhing in their separate torment, joined across the miles by an inseverable twisted plastic cord.

"Ms. James?"

A young woman in jeans and a short overall bearing the logo of a local flower shop was holding out a huge cellophane cone of flowers rosetted with yellow ribbon.

"No. I mean, I'll take them for her," Harriet lied, realizing that it would be inconceivable to the girl that anyone should send flowers to a person such as herself. But he had, and she knew who he was without reading the card.

"The last bloody straw."

She propped up the sheaf of flowers in the kitchen, lit a cigarette—the first one of the day, as she congratulated herself—and ran upstairs to Miranda's room. The dress hung from a wire hanger,

"Who is it?"

"Gas meter."

"Can't you come back later?"

"No."

"In a few minutes—" she pleaded, tearing at her hair with sudsy hands.

"I've got to—" The rest of his words were lost as she wrenched the door open. He stepped into the kitchen and smiled around at the disorder, the sun striking brassy notes in his cadmium-yellow hair.

"Caught you on the hop, did I?"

Harriet stared at him, thinking that the black tufts in his nose, contrasting so blatantly with his hair, effectively canceled out the charm that he so obviously thought he possessed, and caused the cheeky grin to lose its confidence. How could anyone be so mistaken about himself? At least she was aware of every aspect of her unkempt looks and dowdy déshabillé.

"Who's a lucky girl then?" He indicated the flowers. "Someone's birthday today?" She glared at him as if distaste would turn the bunches of hair into iron filings and choke him. She saw the stems of the flowers protruding from his mouth, his throat jammed with cellophane. She slammed on the radio.

"Mind if I use your toilet?"

She pointed silently upwards, then pushed past him and ran upstairs but had time only to claw a heap of Miranda's night things from the floor, drape a wet towel over the rail and glimpse a nailbrush and sponge stranded in the bubbles dying in the bath and retrieve a pair of espadrilles from the basin before he was standing at the lavatory, waiting for her to leave. Bruno padded in and sniffed at his ankles; Harriet shooed him away.

Downstairs, shreds of gauze came away in her hands, and as she acknowledged that the dress was disintegrating, the young man returned. He squatted down in front of the cupboard, shining his torch into the cluttered interior, then started scrabbling objects out on to the floor.

"Bit of a glory hole, innit?" he remarked, cheerfully piling up cobwebbed cake tins, a broken cup and saucer, the split plastic bag of Christmas cake decorations which scattered around him. Then, whistling along with the radio, he raked out empty bottles and stood them in a semicircle around his haunches. Harriet could have explained that they were the accumulation of past months of drinking, waiting to be taken to the bottle bank in a friend's car, that she had not in fact had a drink for weeks, but the bottles stood in a silent green hostile crowd and any defense that she offered would be contradicted by these glass perjurers. One, she saw, bore a label that said Goldener Oktober, like the golden October day that had been wrecked.

"All I wanted to do today was paint a bloody little picture," she thought. She looked at the twin shiny patches on the seat of his gray trousers. "How dare he force his way in here and rake through my life?"

All her self-hatred was directed at the slight figure in the inglorious uniform. She grabbed the marrow, lifted it high with both hands, and he received the full weight of the ruined dress, the empty bottles and the years of failure and despair on the back of his head.

She stepped back as he sprawled slowly sideways and the bottles fell like skittles around him. One rolled to her feet, almost full, splashing purple onto the floor as a bright red sticky gout dyed his yellow hair. His hand closed on a plastic reindeer. Harried picked up the bottle and as she gulped the purple vinegar sprayed her face and dressing gown and the shiny gray jacket. She forced the wine down her throat against the rising nausea. She knew she must obscure with a purple haze the enormity of what she had done; the widow and orphans and bereaved parents and siblings she had created with one mad blow. The room became darker as if the alcohol had created its own twilight. Her resistance was low and her ears were filling with purple cotton wool. A fly, like the one which had grazed on her wrist in the garden, settled on the fallen man's head as if on a luscious yellow flower oozing red nectar, and that final violation of the innocent violater was more than she could bear. She rushed from room to room getting ready to leave forever, finally grabbing her purse and tying the first thing that came to hand to Bruno's collar, finished the wine and leaving the radio buzzing away on low batteries, the washing machine throbbing in its final spin, the sheathed flowers a cone of blurred color lying across a heap of bottles, the man sprawled on the floor among the Christmas cake decorations and Miranda's dress in the washing-up bowl, slammed the front door behind her.

On her way to the station she lurched unbelievingly against the old brick wall that she had meant to paint, long ago, that morning, in an irrecoverable guiltlessness. Only yesterday it had been hung with hearts, a tangle of convolvulus, nightshade, elderberries, snowberries and ivy. Now all the white bells and berries and green hearts were gone and she traced with her fingers the fuzzy scars that laced the wall where the ivy had been ripped from the brick. At the end of the wall, through the rolled-up door, she saw a man with silver hair standing on a stepladder, whistling as he painted the interior of his garage. A rage possessed her at the sight of the neatly stacked tools and tins on his shelves, that someone's life should be so well ordered that he had to fill his time by painting the inside of a garage. The garden wall which had been so beautiful had been desecrated as she, who had once been beautiful, was ruined. She walked into the garage and kicked away the steps, hearing a scream as he fell to the concrete floor.

Bruno was dragging at his lead and she had to pick him up and carry him. As they crossed the road they passed one of Miranda's friends, a girl with long fair hair falling about her shoulders. Harriet was transfixed by the knowledge that the girl must grow old and die. " 'All her bright golden hair/Tarnished with rust,/She that was young and fair/Fallen to dust,' " she told her as a milk float screeched at her, frightening Bruno and fluttering her skirt. She couldn't remember where she was supposed to be going, only that it must be somewhere very peaceful, a haven out of the swing of the sea. "I have asked to be where no storms come. . . ." She couldn't remember. "Not Rottingdean," she said, "definitely not Rottingdean."

She swayed into the station. There were two station staff who looked so alike that they might have been brothers: one was friendly and cheerful and the other sullen. Harriet encountered one of them in the booking hall.

"Are you the nice one, or the other one?"

He did not reply.

"I want a ticket to Innisfree, to the Lake Isle. I shall find some peace there."

She wandered down the platform and sat down on a bench. She was aware that her bracelet was missing and was conscious at the time of a blacker grief but it was like trying to fit together the pieces of a grotesque jigsaw whose edges are slippery with blood, and then the darkness became absolute as she closed her eyes.

When a dream becomes unbearable the sleeper awakes. Harriet struggled through blackness, with the alarm clock shrilling like a siren in her ears, to the blessed realization that the monstrous epic which she had lived through had been only a nightmare.

"Thank God," she said as she pushed Bruno from her chest and sat up in the disoriented dawn, shaking her head to dislodge three uniformed figures on the edge of her headache, blinking away the last remnant of the dream.

They made straight for her. After all it was not difficult to spot, on a station platform, a woman in a pink toweling dressing gown splashed with wine, clutching a cat on the end of a string of bloody tinsel.

"It was an accident," she mumbled as the policewoman pulled her to her feet.

"One man is dead and another in hospital, and you're saying it was an accident?"

Harriet blinked at them in bleary bewilderment.

"The dress—it was an accident."

BANANAS

"Gin? You want cheap gin?"

In vain had she oiled her basket on wheels. The dreadful young man leaped from his doorway and was standing on the opposite pavement shouting at her.

Imogen Lemon's face swelled into one of the gross, foreign, beefsteak tomatoes sunning themselves outside his shop and such a headache hit her brow that she felt her skin would split and spill hot seeds onto her white sundress. She hurried to the safety of the supermarket, thirsting for one of the discreet little English tomatoes that had graced the shop before it fell into the hirsute hands of its present owner. The wicker basket followed at her heels like a faithful stiff old Airedale.

Two tiny veiled women in black passed in a cloud of patchouli. Imogen Lemon was a tall, slender divorcée with long hands and feet which had been much admired. Once her boss, coming upon her unexpectedly, typing in the gloaming, had momentarily mistaken her for a young girl seated at the virginals. Now she felt suddenly huge and white and freakish and half-naked in her summer frock against these scented bolts of black silk, and resented it.

On these warm evenings, after her supper and the nine o'clock news, Imogen would pour a tiny amount of gin into a tall glass and carry it, with slimline tonic brimming big rocks of ice, onto her balcony where she smoked two slow cigarettes and read the paper, the noise of the traffic blurred by the darkening leaves, and would sit in her iron garden in the sky until the leaves were black and the roses white and the glass an insubstantial rind floating at her foot.

Now, with him shouting out to the street like that about cheap gin, she felt as though his prickly face had thrust through the perfumed air, dirtying the roses.

She should never have bought gin in his shop.

The trouble was, she reflected gloomily as she trailed around the supermarket, his shop was so handy. She would often pop in after work for something quick for supper or, when Claud, her cat, declared that his breakfast smelled and was unfit for feline consumption, she could dash through the traffic for a packet of frozen fish and be back in five minutes. Lately, however, the young man's stock seemed to have deteriorated. Of course it was not his fault that they were demolishing the buildings opposite and brick dust drifted through the open door and settled in a reddish haze on everything, although she supposed that he could employ one of his mothy feather dusters to remove it, instead of lounging about exchanging gibberish with his cronies in the back of the shop. And, of course, if she should need a card of rusty hair grips or a dented tin of chick peas, a pair of tights with one leg shorter than the other, or a tub of gangrenous yogurt at midnight, a Christmas pudding in July or Easter eggs at Christmas, it was nice to know that he was there.

She would not touch his meat, however; and always avoided looking at the strange red glossy animals, peeled heads and foreshortened limbs that hinted at barbarism under their sweaty perspex cover. She left the supermarket and went into the butcher's, shouldering the English beasts of honest yeoman stock that hung in the doorway.

When she emerged, a troupe of goblins flurried around her, banging her knees, and one trod heavily on her toe. As she gasped and disengaged herself, clutching at the wall with one hand and her spinning basket on wheels with the other, she realized it was only the little girls from the preparatory school, in their distinctive red caps and lethal sandals, on their way to the swimming baths. She limped home.

That evening a storm broke on West Kensington and Imogen was quite pleased to give in to her headache and sore toe and retire early, conjuring up, as usual, an angel, in a long white nightdress not dissimilar to her own, at each corner of her bed.

In the morning, as she passed on her way to the tube, he was outside the shop unpacking a crate of bananas. He straightened and stood grinning at her through the very small white pointed teeth that glittered in his stubbly muzzle. The sun struck a gold medallion lying in the black curls that gushed from his chest and eddied around his throat, and turned the stiff fans of hair at the armholes of his blue singlet to a rusty coral. He thrust a bunch of bananas in her face.

"You want bananas? Very good today."

"No, thank you. I'm on my way to work. Perhaps later."

She forgot about him but on her way home she saw him, from the corner of her eye, on the other side of the road waving a banana at her. She steadfastly, if painfully, walked on. She did not know his name, so Bananas was what she came to call him to herself.

Later that evening she slipped out in sunglasses and plastic mac to the Victoria Wine for a bottle of tonic. Her toe was still swollen, so as well as enjoying the comfort of them, she felt that her pink slippers added the finishing touch to her disguise. On her return Claud leaped at her as if congratulating her on her cunning, and she was laughing into his fur when the telephone rang.

"Mum?"

"Hello, Jenny darling."

"You sound very cheerful."

"Yes, well. . . ."

"We thought we might come to see you on Sunday. . . ."

As she shook hands with Father Smillie on the church path and shook the scent of incense and a drifting lime flower from her hair, it came to Imogen that she should buy some limes for their pre-luncheon drinks. Fortified by the rites of the Holy Church, she decided to brave Bananas. By a small miracle he was in the back of the shop with a chum and an exquisite little boy in a long white nightshirt was standing by the fruit display outside.

"Two limes, please."

What a tragedy that Time would turn him into another Bananas. . . .

He reached for two greenish warty lemons.

"No, dear. I said limes. Those are lemons," she told him firmly.

"Two limes."

"No. Those are lemons. I asked for limes," she said very slowly and clearly. "Those small green things are limes. Could you give me two, please, I'm in rather a hurry?"

She was about to reach for them herself when Bananas hurtled into the doorway, snatched the lemons from the boy, dropped them into a paper bag and handed them to her.

"No! I don't want them. I want limes!"

"You don't want?"

"I want two limes!"

"Ah!"

He reached up, took two limes and dropped them into the bag.

"Seventy-four pence. Anything else for you today? Bananas, gin, cigarettes?"

Half-blinded and deafened by a wash of tears, she saw his little teeth moving as she put down the money and, blundering through the door, collided with a woman in black, whose beaked mask gave her cheek a sharp peck.

"You see, I was beginning to think the whole thing was an elaborate joke at my expense. An absurd pun on my name. That he had somehow found out my name—silly, really. . . ." Her voice trailed off. Obviously they found her story completely incomprehensible.

They were sitting on the balcony, the slices of lime stranded on melted ice in the bottoms of their glasses, Imogen, Jennifer and her husband Tony and Toby the baby who had a clownish red circle on each cheek and who was grizzling and banging his head on his mother's chest.

"You mean this woman deliberately attacked you with her beak?" asked Jennifer, warding off another blow from the hard head.

"No, of course not. Shall we go in and eat?"

"I'm awfully sorry, Mum," Jennifer said as she surveyed the goodies spread out on the table, "Toby won't eat anything when he's teething. Could he just have a banana?"

"A banana?" Imogen looked desperately at the blue grapes and oranges in the fruit bowl. "I suppose I could pop across the road. . . ."

"I'd go, only he screams if I put him down."

Imogen looked at Tony, but he had buried his face in *The Sunday Times*. No hope there.

The baby flung out a fist and pointed at the door.

"Of course," Imogen said weakly, picking up her purse.

Two elderly men in white robes with red and white checked tea-towels on their heads pushed past her as she went into the shop with her bunch of bananas, got into a limousine parked outside, and were driven away. She joined the queue at the checkout and a black robe fell in behind her. Bananas seemed gloomy, even morose, she was pleased to notice. Perhaps his visitors had upset him. He grabbed the bananas and bashed them, bruisingly, into the scales.

"You got no need to go to Victoria Wine for gin," he accused her, "I got cheap gin. You want any today? Any cigarettes?"

To her horror she saw that it was not a black-robed woman behind her, but Father Smillie in his soutane. And Bananas was waving a bottle of gin.

The luncheon party was not a success. The children left early, using Toby's teeth as an excuse, and Imogen was left trying to drown Bananas's voice in the washing-up water, but Father Smillie wouldn't go down the drain.

On the following Sunday she was too ashamed to face him at Mass and had to take a bus to the Brompton Oratory. When she returned she saw the limousine parked again outside the shop and the sound of angry voices came across the road.

She had resolved never to enter his shop again and to ignore him if he spoke to her, but several days later Bananas caught her as she passed with her basket on wheels.

"Good morning. What can I get you today?"

"Nothing, thank you. I'm on my way to the library," she lied.

"You like books. I got lots of books."

Imogen looked past him, at his dubious stock of literature.

"I only read the classics," she lied again.

"I got classics. You want *Lady Chatterley, The Thorn Birds, Third Term at Malory Towers*?"

Thus it happened that she was standing, a lurid-covered paperback in her hand, and Bananas calling from within, "Any gin today?" as Father Smillie passed her with a curt nod, his soutane freaked with brick dust, hurrying from some errand of mercy on the demolition site.

"Cheap gin and cigarettes. Cheap gin and cigarettes," the little girls were chanting as they skipped in the playground as she passed. Imogen tried to convince herself that they were saying something quite different, but that did it. She arranged to take a week of her holiday at once, organized a neighbor to look after Claud, and fled to a friend's cottage in Ilfracombe.

As she lay on the beach, healed by the waves and sand, she saw how absurd the whole thing had become.

On her return she strode on tanned legs into the shop to buy some special fish as a homecoming present for Claud, determined to restore Bananas to his right proportions—a foolish, over-friendly, small, foreign shopkeeper who must be politely but firmly shown his place.

A strange man, trim of beard and neat of collar and tie, stood behind the till.

"The other man, the one who used to be here, is he away?" she asked.

"He's gone."

"Gone? Isn't he coming back?"

"No."

"Why not?"

"He was losing money. He bad man. He won't be back."

"Oh."

Imogen felt a strange disappointment as she turned away. "Oh," she said again and her eye for once lingered on the meat display where a fly sat up on the perspex lid and rubbed its hands. Between two writhing heaps of mince was the boiled head of some animal, and set in its glistening jaws were two rows of tiny, very white, pointed teeth.

EVENING SURGERY

A Chopin prelude was strained through the speaker that stood on a little shelf on the surgery wall above a garish oil painting that shone in the cruel neon striplight that picked out the lines and blemishes and red-hawed eyes of the patients on the black vinyl benches. Mavis Blizzard, senior receptionist, was proud of that picture; it had been painted by one of "her" old ladies, a purblind resident of Peaceheaven House for the Elderly, which she visited regularly, cheering up the old girls, surreptitiously putting right the great holes and loops that shaky fingers made in bits of knitting, jollying them along when they grew tearful over old snap-shots that she had persuaded them to show. No matter that the picture was upside down, the artist had now lost her sight completely; it would hang as a testament to their friendship. From time to time the name of one of the four doctors flashed on a board, a buzzer sounded and a patient departed; the telephone rang, Mavis answered it, and greeted favored customers by name when they came through the door; her two minions busied themselves among files and coffee cups; although they wore blue overalls like Mavis's own, they seemed interchangeable, merged into one subdued lady in glasses, for she was the star of the surgery. Sounds of passing cars came through the glittering black panes of the window, people coughed, pages turned. The music stopped abruptly, then an orchestral selection from *South Pacific* washed softly over the surgery.

"That's better!" announced Mavis Blizzard brightly. "We'd all have been asleep in a minute. Dr. Frazer's choice. Much too highbrow for my taste."

She was leaning out of the hatch behind which she operated and enveloped her audience in a conspiratorial wink. As she opened her eye she couldn't believe that the young woman in the corner was almost glaring at her. She had a quick read of her notes before sending them into Doctor. An invisible hand had placed a cup of coffee at her elbow; she clattered the pink cup with a red waxy smear on its rim onto the saucer.

"Well, I won't be sorry to get home tonight. I've been on my feet since six o'clock this morning and my poor hubby will have to get his own tea tonight. It's his Church Lads' Band night. They're practicing some carols to entertain the old folks at my senior citizens' party, bless them," she announced to one of her sidekicks or to the surgery at large.

If there were any who thought that her husband had had a lucky reprieve, they were rifling through the *Reader's Digest* or *Woman and Home* and registered nothing.

The telephone rang.

"Hello, you're through to surgery appointments."

Her voice grew louder.

"Of course, Mr. Jackson. Is it urgent, only Doctor's very booked up tomorrow? What seems to be the trouble? Pardon? Oh, your waterworks, Mr. Jackson."

Someone sniggered behind the *Tatler*, others squirmed on the squeaky vinyl at this public shaming. It was enough to send two girls into fits; they snorted through their noses. The old man beside them moved an inch or two away from their cropped, hennaed heads, their earrings, their dark red mouths.

"You'll be old yourselves someday and it won't seem so funny then," he said. The comic they hid behind shook in disbelief. Mavis Blizzard rolled her eyes; her own daughter was a Queen's Guide.

"—well," she went on, "Doctor's got a late surgery on Thursday. We could squeeze you in then at eleven forty-five. That's eleven forty-five on Thursday then. Not at all. See you Thursday then. Byee,"—by which time the unfortunate man might be damned or drowned.

"Deaf as a post, bless him," she explained.

"Next Patient for Dr. Frazer" flashed up on the board. The woman in the corner jumped up, tossing her magazine onto the table, upsetting the neat pile. Mavis watched her disappearing jeans disapprovingly. She prided herself on getting on with all sorts, you had to in this job, but this one she definitely did not trust.

The woman walked into the consulting room. The doctor rose.

"Cathy! How've you been?"

"Bloody awful. You?"

"The same."

She sat down. He took her hand across the desk.

"It's good to see you."

"Yes."

She was staring at the desk, twisting a paper clip with her other hand. There was so much to say, and nothing. They sat in silence. Then, as if suddenly aware of the briefness of their time together, he came around to her side of the desk.

When Mrs. Blizzard had to come in to fetch a file the patient was buttoning her shirt. Dr. Frazer stood beside her. Nothing unusual about that. So why did she feel as if she was fighting her way through an electric storm? The stethoscope lay on the desk.

"Come and see me again if the pain persists," said Dr. Frazer.

"OK," she replied casually, without so much as a thank you or goodbye. Mavis rolled her eyes at the doctor, expecting a confirmatory twinkle at this rudeness, but he was grinning like a fool at the closing door.

"Well, really!" she said.

He pressed the buzzer as she went out. Nobody appeared. He was just going to buzz again when Mavis led in a frail old lady and helped her onto the chair.

"Let's make you comfy. I'll just pop this cushion behind your back."

What a kind soul she is, the doctor thought. He realized that he hated her.

"Well, Miss Weatherby, let's have a look at you." What's left of you, he almost said.

She struck the cushion to the floor with a tiny, surprisingly strong, gloved hand.

"I want you to give me a certificate, Doctor."

"What kind of certificate?"

"A certificate to confirm that I am unfit; not well enough to attend her senior citizens' party!"

He had to fumble in his desk drawer, but she had seen his face.

"You can laugh, you don't have to go!"

She was laughing too, but tears glittered in her eyes.

"Neither do you, surely?"

"She's threatening to collect me in her car. I'll have to wear a paper hat and sing carols to the accompaniment of her husband's appalling boys' band, and then her daughter will hide behind the door and shake a bell and she will say, 'Hark! What's that I hear? Can it be sleigh bells?' and her husband will leap into the room in a red plastic suit and give us bathcubes."

"Couldn't you pretend a prior engagement?"

"She's managed to ferret out that I have no family or friends. She wants me to move into Peaceheaven as soon as there's a coffin, I mean a bed."

"I'm afraid I can't really give you a certificate, but I'll have a word if you like, about the party . . ." wondering how he could.

"It wouldn't do any good. I'll just have to turn out the lights and lie in bed until she's gone."

"No you won't. Come and spend the evening with us. I can't promise any paper hats or bathcubes, but it would be nice if you did. OK?"

"OK," she managed.

As she left he saw that her legs had shrunk to two sticks around which her stockings hung in pale, deflated balloons. Time unravels us, he thought, like old, colorless silk flags in churches, which have outlasted their cause.

At home, Mary's eyes, which lately a vague unhappiness had turned a darker blue, dimmed and were brighter, as mussels washed by a little wave, when he told her of Miss Weatherby's plight.

"Of course she must come. But why does she hate Mavis? She's so kind."

"She's a ghoul. She feeds on illness and disease and death!" he burst out.

"But. . . ." Mary closed her mouth. She went to the sideboard and poured him a drink, as she gave it to him he took her hand and kissed it. "Thank you," he said.

*   *   *

When Catherine opened the gate of the little terraced house she shared with her daughter and son she saw the room as a stranger might, through the unpulled curtains, lit from within like a candle whose wick has burned down below its rim; the paper moon suspended from the ceiling, the bowl of satsumas, the old chairs, the television glowing softly like a tank of tropical fish; the familiar tenderized and made strange by the darkness.

At seven o'clock in the morning a soapy fragment of moon was dissolving in the damp sky; birds assembled in the trees to wait for their breakfast, black shapes against the blue that slowly suffused the cloud; Catherine sat on the back step. She was glad that he could not see her in the old summer dress she was wearing as a nightdress, Lucy's clogs and her ex-husband's ropey bathrobe; her eyes stung as she looked along the length of her cigarette, such a lot to get through, her mouth felt thick and dry; behind her in the kitchen the washing machine threw a last convulsion and gave a little sob, like a child who has fallen asleep crying. Paul would be back from his paper round in a minute. She went in and ran a bath. As she lay in the water, left disagreeably tepid by the washing machine's excesses, she saw how she had failed with her husband, whose robe huddled in a heap on the floor; she had never let him see that she needed him. Because she had known that he would fail her. But if she had. She recalled Hardy's poem "Had you but wept." Such watery half-thoughts as float past when people are alone and naked vanished with the bubbles down the plughole.

She put the kettle on, switched on the radio, woke Lucy, made tea, made toast, made two packed lunches, flung the washing over the line, a jumble of socks and jeans and shirts that would not dry in the damp air, tested Lucy on her Latin while she combed her hair and coaxed some moribund mascara onto her lashes; the phone rang—for Lucy; wrote a note for Paul who had been absent the day before; the phone rang again; Paul, eating the remains of yesterday's pudding from the fridge, dropped the bowl on the floor, Lucy ironed a PE shirt and the pop music on the radio crackled like an electric drill so she turned it up. No doubt, Catherine thought sourly, the Frazers are sitting down to muesli and motets. Someone called; the children left.

She found a splinter of glass on the floor near the sink and held it up to the light from the window. If one just stared at pretty glass fragments or soap bubbles or the sediment around the taps or studied the patterns left by spilled pudding on the tiles. Is that what it's like to be mad; or sane? But if everyone did there would be no glass, no iridescent bubbles in the washing-up bowl. Even as these thoughts drifted through her mind the glass splinter was in the pedal bin, a cloth was attacking the bleary taps. As she attempted to leave the house a plant pulled her back with a pale parched reproachful frond. "I'll water you tonight," she promised, but had to run back for the watering can and then run down the road, as usual, to the bookshop where she worked.

Her legs ached. With every book token, every cookery book, every DIY handbook, every copy of *Old Surrey in Pictures*, *Bygone Surrey*, *Views of Old Guildford*, *Views of Old Reigate*, *Views of Old Dorking*, every *Wine Bibber's Guide* that she sold she felt less Christmassy. How stupid and greedy the customers were, flapping check books at her and Pat, the other assistant, slapping fivers down on the counter so that they had to pick them up, taking all the change so that she had to go to the bank twice for more.

"Isn't Christmas shopping murder? Isn't it Hell?" the customers said. "I'll be glad when it's all over!"

Greetings flew from throats that sounded as if they were already engorged with mincemeat. No doubt several books were slipped into shopping bags.

"It must be lovely working here—all these lovely books!" people told them. "I could browse for hours!"

"Oh, yes!" Pat agreed mistily, not seeing the floor which muddy feet had reduced to a football pitch and which she would not clean. She was twenty-nine and wore little girl shoes, and dresses which she made herself, Cathy thought that she must be too embarrassed to take her own measurements, because they never fitted very well. She spent her lunch hours in the stockroom eating packets of pale meat sandwiches and drinking tisanes, reading children's books and lives of the saints. Mr. Hermitage, the shop's owner, who was bowing and gesticulating like a puppet in his velvet suit in the back of the shop, and who was too mean to employ a cleaner, did not like to ask Pat to wash the floor so Catherine's less spiritual hands were calloused by the mop.

When she got the chance Catherine went into the little kitchen behind the stockroom and put on the kettle and lit a cigarette. There was nowhere to sit so she leaned on the sink.

"I won't go to the surgery tonight," she told herself. "I mustn't. I know it's wrong. It's stealing. I'm not going to go."

Mr. Hermitage came in rubbing his hands.

"Coffee! That's good!"

His body contrived to brush against hers, as it always did.

"Sorry," he said, patting her as if it had been an accident, as he always did.

She carried her coffee and a cup of cowslip tea for Pat into the shop, taking a gulp on the way to drown the smell of nicotine. Six or seven people stood at the counter, impatient at the speed of the two robots behind it. Pat rolled panic-stricken eyes at her; she was up to her ankles in spoiled wrapping paper. The Scotch tape sneered and snarled. As Catherine reached into the till Pat pressed the cash total button and the drawer slammed on her fingers. She yelled and swore. The customers looked offended; shop assistants' fingers don't have feelings, especially at Christmastime. Catherine waited for her nails to turn black. Now she would have to go to the surgery. Alas, her fingers remained red and painful, but could not justify medical treatment. Her hopes abated with the swelling.

She arrived home late that evening and dumped her heavy carrier bag. It had taken ages to do the money; it had been twelve pounds short. Pat had been flustered into making several overrings; customers had asked for books and then changed their minds after they had been rung up, there was an unsigned check. Catherine's face ached with smiling at browsers and buyers; she had eaten nothing all day. There was a warm smell of cooking.

"Dinner's almost ready," said Lucy.

"I've made you a cup of tea, Mum," said Paul.

She did not let herself notice the potato peelings in the sink, the spilled sugar, the tea bag on the floor, which he had thrown at the pedal bin, and missed, the muddy rugby boots on the draining board.

"You're dear, kind children," she said. She unbent her cold fingers one by one.

"Mum? . . . Are you all right? I mean, you're not ill or anything are you?"

"Of course I'm not. Why?"

"It's just that you look so sad. You never smile. And you went to the doctor's."

"It's just the Christmas rush in the shop. You've no idea what hell it is."

Catherine felt ashamed. She saw that she was dragging them into her own abyss.

"Nobody's going out tonight, are they? And nobody's coming around? Good."

She wanted to draw them to her, to spend the sort of family evening they had enjoyed before this madness had overtaken her; the curtains closed, the gas fire blooming like a bed of lupins, the telly on; the sort of evening you thought nothing of.

Halfway through "Top of the Pops" the phone rang.

"I'll get it!" Catherine grabbed the receiver with crossed fingers.

"Hello, could I speak to Lucy, please?"

Dumbly she handed it over. They had agreed that he should not ring or come to the house. And yet. . . .

Later the doorbell rang; Catherine clamped herself to her chair.

"Door, Paul."

A male voice at the door. She stopped herself from running to the mirror and glued her eyes to her book, looking up slowly as Paul slouched back; behind him John Frazer metamorphosed into a tall boy, through a sort of grey drizzle.

"Hi. I've come to copy Paul's maths."

"Oh. How about some coffee, Paul?" Or a quadruple gin. Or a cup of hemlock.

As the boys went to the kitchen Catherine said to Lucy, "Actually I don't feel very well. I keep getting headaches. The doctor gave me something for them, but it doesn't seem to work. I think I'd better go back tomorrow . . . so don't worry if I'm a bit late. . . . Well, I suppose I'd better get on with the ironing."

"Would you like me to do it?"

"Of course, but I'd rather you did your homework."

Anyway it would kill an hour or so.

The case of a certain Dr. Randal and a Mrs. Peacock had, naturally, aroused much interest among the receptionists in the surgery. Mr. Peacock had brought an action against the doctor, accusing him of the seduction of his wife and it had become a minor *cause célèbre*, partly because there were those who thought that the rules should be changed, partly because there had been no meaty scandal of late, no politicians floundering in the soup. Dressed like their namesakes, he in flashy tie and cufflinks, she in drab brown tweed plumage, an invisible blanket of shame over her bowed head, the Peacocks strutted and scurried across evening television screens and stared greyly from the newspaper in Mavis Blizzard's hand.

"Of course, it's the woman I blame in a case like this; a doctor's in such a vunnerable position. . . . It's the children I feel sorry for. And his poor wife! What she must be going through."

Mrs. Peacock must be pecked to pieces by the rest of the flock; her brown feathers, torn by Mavis's sharp bill, drifted about the surgery.

"And she's not even pretty!"

"Must have hidden charms," came with a timid snort from behind Mavis.

"Ssh."

If their words were not, as she suspected, directed at Catherine, they nonetheless pierced the magazine she was using as a shield and managed to wound.

Mavis slotted in a cassette of Christmas carols and hummed along with it. A sickly fragrance of bathcubes emanated from her sanctum; she was wrapping them for her senior citizens' party, in between answering the phone and all her other tasks. Her daughter, Julie, who had come in to give her a hand, nudged her.

"That's Paul Richards's mother. He goes to our school. He's really horrible. This afternoon he and his friends turned on all the taps in the cloakroom and flooded it. They were having a fight with the paper towels. You never saw such a mess! Water all over the place, other people's belongings getting soaked! I wouldn't like to be in their shoes tomorrow morning!" she concluded with satisfaction.

A little boy, about two years old, was running around the table, bumping into people's knees, falling over their feet. His mother grew tired of apologizing and held him captive. He screamed and would not be pacified. She had to let him go.

"What's all this then? What's all the noise about?"

Mavis Blizzard had emerged and was advancing in a sort of crouch in her blue overall on the startled child who backed into his mother's knees.

"We can't have you disturbing all my ladies and gentlemen, can we? Let's see if I've got something in my pockets for good little boys, shall we?"

He clenched his hands behind his back. Mavis winked at his mother and dangled a sweet. The child gave a sob and flung himself on his mother banging his hard, hot head on her lip. A red weal sprang up immediately and the glassy eyes spilled over. The child joined a loud grizzling to her silent tears.

"I think we'd better let this little fellow see Doctor next, don't you?" Mavis looked around, "That is, if nobody objects?"

Nobody objected. The mother jerked to her feet a silent girl in glasses who had kept her head bent over a comic throughout, and ran the gauntlet with her and the crying boy and a heavy shopping bag.

"Poor kid," remarked Mavis as she returned to her hatch. "She does find it hard to cope, bless her. My heart bleeds for these one-parent families. Not that I'm one to make judgments, live and let live, and lend a helping hand where you can, that's my motto."

For a moment they were all bathed in her tolerance.

"Drat that phone! Blessed thing never stops, does it?" Evidently she forgot that most of her audience had been guilty. . . .

"Hello, you're through to the surgery, can I help you? Of course. I'll drop the prescription in myself on my way home. No, it's no trouble at all. Save you turning out on your poor old legs in this nasty weather. No, it's hardly out of my way at all, and I shall be late home anyway. We've got a full house tonight!" She uttered the noise which served her for a laugh.

Catherine looked at her watch; the appointments were running ten minutes late. She reached for another magazine and saw a jar of carnations on the windowsill, slender stems in the beaded water, like cranes' green delicate legs. As the bubbles streamed to the surface and clustered around the birds' knees she wished she had not come; she wished she was at home cooking the evening meal. It was absurd; it was making neither of them happy.

"You said to come back if the pain persists. It persists."

"Thank you for coming tonight. I've missed you so much."

To her dismay she was crying. He scorned the box of pink tissues provided by Mavis for patients who wept and gave her his own white handkerchief. Even as she dried her eyes she realized that it had been laundered by his wife; it didn't help.

"It's not enough," she said. "At first it was enough just to know that you were on the same planet. Then I thought, if only we could be alone for five minutes, then it was an hour, then an evening . . . it's almost worse than nothing."

The door handle squeaked. Instinctively she leaped from his arms to the couch and turned her face to the wall as Mavis came in.

"Mrs. Blizzard! I wish you wouldn't barge in when I'm with a patient!"

"You forget that I'm a trained nurse," she bridled. "Dr. MacBeth always asks me to be present when he's examining a female patient. I'm sorry to have disturbed you!"

She slammed the door behind her.

"I know it's not enough," he said quickly. "Can you get out one evening? Meet me somewhere?"

"Yes." So that was that. How easily principles, resolutions not to hurt anybody died.

He leaned over the couch and kissed her; she felt the silky hair on the back of his neck, his ear; she felt his hand run gently down her body, on her thigh.

"Don't, don't," she said, but she didn't take his hand away.

"An urgent call for you, Dr. Frazer," squawked Mavis through the intercom.

Catherine slid off the couch and found the floor with trembling legs. Her face was burning.

"Just a minute," he put his hand over the receiver. "I love you. See you tomorrow morning? About eleven? We'll arrange something."

Outside in the street she found his handkerchief in her hand and buried her face in it and looking up, saw the stars over its white edge. As she lay in bed that night she put her hand where his hand had been.

*　　*　　*

He was late. She pushed her trolley up and down the aisles of Safeways, putting in something from time to time for appearance's sake, waiting, loitering, buffeted, causing obstructions.

"I'm sorry."

She whirled around. The smile withered on her face. A little girl was seated in his trolley. He rolled his eyes toward his wife's back, at the deli counter. As Mary turned to them he said, "How are you?"

"As well as can be expected."

She blundered to the checkout with her almost empty trolley.

". . . a patient," she heard him explain, betray.

After crying for a while in the precinct she had to go to Sainsburys to finish her shopping and trudge home to transform herself from lovesick fool into mother. Loud music hit her as she opened the front door. An open biscuit tin stood on the kitchen table, seven or eight coffee cups had been placed thoughtfully in the sink; she had to wash them before she could start on the potatoes. Several pairs of muddy shoes lay about the floor. Teenage laughter came from the bedrooms. Not jealousy. Not bitterness. Just pain. Like the dull knife blade stabbing a potato. The telephone rang. Feet thudded toward it.

"She's not in."

"I am in!" She shouted and ran to the telephone.

"Cathy?" Her ex-husband.

"Oh, it's you."

She had to stop herself from hurling the receiver at the wall.

"Cathy, I was wondering about Christmas. . . ."

"Yes?"

"Well, I just . . . I mean, what are you doing?"

"Oh, this and that. One or two parties. The children have lots of things on. We're going to my parents' on Boxing Day, all the family will be there. I suppose we'll go to church on Christmas Day. Why?"

She longed to be beyond the tinsel and crackers, in the greyness of January where melancholy was the norm.

"Well, I just wondered. I mean, it's a bit of a bleak prospect—the kids and all. . . ."

"You mean you want to come here. You may as well. It makes no difference to me. Why not? It will make everything just about perfect."

She replaced the receiver, not wanting to wonder about whatever desperation had driven him to call, unable to contemplate any pain but her own.

At last the three sat down to lunch.

"Mum?"

"What?"

"We are going to get a tree, aren't we?"

She looked at her children, her babies; Lucy's long hair glittering in the electric light, Paul's pretty spikes. She determined to stop being such a pain.

"Of course we are. We always do, don't we? I thought we might go this afternoon."

"Great."

"You'll come, won't you, Paul?"

"Well, you'll need me to carry it, if we get a big one, won't you?"

At nine o'clock that night John was called to Miss Weatherby's house. A neighbor, taking his dog for a stroll, had been alarmed by her milk bottle on the step, her newspaper jutting from the door, and had found the old lady very ill. Had she had any family, John might have comforted them: she died in my arms; but she had none. He drove away feeling infinitely sad. There was only one person he wanted to tell about it; to lie in her arms and be comforted, to have wiped away the memory of the one card on Miss Weatherby's mantelpiece which said, "A Merry Xmas from Your Unigate Milkman." He stopped at an off-licence and bought a bottle of whisky. What a shabby figure he had cut, with furtive meetings in the surgery and Safeways. Why hadn't he telephoned her this morning after the fiasco in Safeways? OK, so he hadn't been alone for a minute, but he could have made some excuse to get out to a call-box, couldn't he? Why on earth did she put up with him? There could be only one reason. She loved him. He switched on the radio. Music flooded the car. He was singing as he drove into her road. Soft pink and green and yellow stars, Christmas tree lights, glowed against black windows. He was touched by these talismans in little human habitations. But when he reached her house he couldn't park. A line of cars stretched along each side of the street. He caught the poignant sparkle of her Christmas tree in a gap in the curtains. He found a space in the next road and walked back. The terraced house seemed to be jumping up and down between its neighbors, blazing with loud music. A volley of laughter hit him. He turned and walked away. He dumped the bottle in its fragile tissue paper in a litter-bin.

As Catherine cleared away the remains of last night's impromptu party from the carpet the telephone rang faintly through the hoover's noise. She switched off. Only the radio. She switched on again. The phone rang again. Nothing. At last she decided that the ringing was conjured up by her own longing or was some electrical malevolence. The phantom telephone drilled out a shameful memory; last night, among her friends, as the party wore on, alcohol sharpened her loneliness until she dialed his number. Even as she did so she told herself that she would hate herself in the morning. She did. A woman's sleepy voice had answered. She hung up. Boring into their bedroom. Disturbing pink sheets; dreams.

She couldn't read, couldn't watch television, couldn't listen to the radio. She had to admit relief when the children went out that afternoon; when you are a mother, you can't scream that you are dying of loneliness and boredom, that your soul is rotting within you. Let his shadow fall across the glass in the door. Let the telephone ring. She stood at the window for a long time staring at sodden leaves and apples, then she grabbed her coat and went to borrow a dog from a neighbor, a patchy-skinned mongrel called Blue.

Ducks pulled melancholy trails across the dingy lake. It was no better here. When she had first met John, people's faces, pavements, skies were irradiated, familiar buildings blossomed with pretty cornices and swags of flowers. Now how ugly and pointless everybody seemed, the whole of Creation a dreary mistake. Damp seeped into her boots, her coat hung open in the cold wind, her bare hands were purple and scratched from the sticks that the fawning Blue laid at her feet to be flung. She glared at the parents trundling past with their prams and tricycles, forgetting that she had been happy once doing that. She found a bench out of the wind and huddled in the corner; the wind whipped the flame from her lighter as she tried to light a cigarette. Ignited, it tasted dirty, the smoke blew into her hair. Without realizing it she was rocking slowly back and forth on the bench, head hunched between her shoulders. If only she had never gone to that party in the summer.

"Do you know Dr. Frazer?" someone had asked.

"Actually, I'm one of your patients."

"Oh, I'm sorry . . . I should have recognized you. . . ."

"It's all right, we've never met. I'm never ill."

"That's a pity."

She had not met his wife, who was at the far end of the room in a group around the fire, but now, Oh God, wasn't that them coming around the corner. There was no escape.

"Hello."

The family surrounded her bench. Blue jumped up at John; she saw him wince as the claws raked his thigh. He threw a stick; Blue bolted after it.

"I'm sorry. Your trousers. They're all muddy."

"Don't worry about those old things! I'm always trying to get him to throw them out, but somehow he always retrieves them!"

Mary gave her a wifely smile; it might as well have been a dead leaf falling or the crisp bag bowling down the path. Mary shivered.

Blue was back with the stick, grinning through frilled red gums.

"I didn't know you had a dog."

"It's not mine. He belongs to a friend."

The three children in knitted hats, and Mary, grew impatient. Catherine stood up.

"Goodbye then. Come on Blue."

John bent over the dog, stroking it inordinately. "Goodbye, Beautiful." Fondling its ears.

As Catherine walked away she heard a child's voice say, "Dad, can we have a dog?"

"Don't you think your mother has enough to do?" his voice snapped, as she had never heard it. Good. I hope your bloody afternoon's ruined. Intruding on her in her ratty fake fur coat, jeans frayed with mud, smoking a cigarette on a park bench, with a borrowed dog; flaunting his family, his wife in her neat tweed coat and matching blue woolly hat. Well, that's that then. It's over. Good. Him in that anorak of horrifying orange. They were welcome to each other. To complete the afternoon's entertainment Mavis Blizzard was bearing down the path pushing part of an old man, wrapped in a tartan rug, in a wheelchair.

When John arrived at the surgery on Monday morning Julie Blizzard was there with her mother.

"Morning, Doctor," said Mavis.

"Morning, Doctor," parroted the clone.

He searched his frosty brain for a pleasantry.

"I suppose you'll be leaving school soon, Julie? Any idea of what you want to do?"

"I'm going to work with underprivileged children."

"They will be," he muttered as he went through. Then he turned back. "By the way, Miss Weatherby died on Saturday night." Or escaped, he might have said.

"Oh dear, the poor soul," said Mavis absentmindedly. Miss Weatherby merited a small sigh then Mavis added, "It's the weather, I expect. You know what they say, a green December fills the church-yard. I've got to go over to the hospital myself this afternoon to visit an old boy, that is if he's lasted the night. I'd better check with Sister first. He's blind and his wife's. . . ."

"Doctor," called Julie after him as he turned away rudely. "You'll get a surprise when you go into your consulting room!"

Grey, rainy light filtered through white paper cut-out Santas and snowflakes pasted on the window. He punched the black couch where soon a procession of flesh in various stages of decay would stretch out for his inspection, and none of it that which he wanted to see.

Catherine ducked down behind the counter as Mavis Blizzard entered the shop with much jangling of the bell and shook sleety pearls from her plastic hood. When she emerged it was to confront Mary, who gave her a vague smile, as if she thought she ought to know her, and went distractedly from one row of books to another. A pair of wet gloves was placed over Mary's eyes. She gave a little scream. Mavis uncurled her black playful fingers.

"Oh, Mavis! You made me jump!"

As she served people and found and wrapped books Catherine managed to catch snatches of conversation.

". . . peaky. Down in the dumps."

". . . Nothing really. . . ."

"I always start my Christmas shopping in the January sales. Just a few last minute things."

". . . he's just tired, I suppose . . . so bad tempered . . . I can't seem to do anything right. . . ."

"You poor little fool," thought Catherine, "confiding in that old harridan."

She stared icily at Mavis as she paid for her book, a reduced volume of freezer recipes, putting the change down on the counter rather than into her hand, but could not kill the thought. I first liked him because he was so kind and now he is less kind because of me.

It was way past the end of Pat's lunch hour. Catherine went into the kitchen and found her, sandwich drooping in her hand, enthralled by the life of a modern saint. She lifted her eyes dreamily from the page.

"Do you know," she said dreamily, "she drank the water in which the lepers had washed their feet!"

"I think I'm going to throw up," said Catherine.

She saw that the sink was clogged with cowslip flowers. Then, at a brawling sound from the street, they both ran back into the shop. A gang of teenagers was rampaging down the pavement, school blazers inside out, garlands of tinsel around their necks and in their hair, which some of them had daubed pink or green. Catherine's eyes blurred at their youth, their faces pink with cold, the flying tinsel. One detached himself and banged on the window.

"Hello, Mum!"

She managed a weak salute.

"Disgusting! No better than animals!" said a customer's voice.

"At least they're alive!" Catherine retorted, because for the moment they *were* young animals, and not fossicking among freezer recipes and jokey books about golf and fishing.

"I thought she was such a nice girl," the customer complained to another as they went out.

"It's the other one who's a nice girl," her friend explained.

"If Blizzard answers, I'll hang up," Catherine decided as she dialed surgery appointments. One of the underlings took the call. Hers was the last appointment of the evening. She couldn't believe the little scene that was being enacted in the waiting room. Mavis evidently had caught a woman in the act of tearing a recipe from one of the magazines.

"But it is dated 1978 . . ." the culprit was quavering in her own defense.

"That's not the point. It's the principle of the thing!"

Mavis thrust a pen and a sheet torn from a notepad at her.

"Here, you can copy it out, if you like. If everybody did that. . . ."

It was impossible to see from the woman's bent head if she was writing ground almonds or ground glass, but when her turn to go in came her face was stained a deep red.

Mavis had only Catherine with whom to exchange a triumphant glance; their eyes met for an instant before she retreated to her sanctum, which, Catherine was amazed to see, was decked with Christmas cards.

"Next Patient for Dr. Frazer."

Catherine went in.

"I knew it! I knew it! I knew something was going on. What do you think I am? Stupid?"

John and Catherine were frozen together as in a freak snowstorm.

"It's disgusting! It's smutty! It's. . . ."

"I realize that's how it must seem to you, but really, I assure you. . . ."

Catherine felt his fingers slide from her breast.

"That's how it appears to me and that's how it is. What do you take me for? I'm not stupid you know." She turned on Catherine.

"You come here night after night and yet there's never anything written on your card, never any prescription. How do you explain that? Just because you couldn't hold your own husband you try to pinch someone else's! Well, you're not so clever as you think you are, or you, Dr. Frazer! Perhaps you'd care to read this?"

She flung an evening paper on the desk. The verdict in the Randal and Peacock case. The condemned pair would not look.

"Guilty, of course. It's his wife I feel sorry for. And the children. What they must be going through! I'd hate Mary to suffer what that poor woman's—"

"You wouldn't!"

"I—" She had to duck as a paperweight flew past her head and crashed into the door, then Catherine was struggling into her coat.

"Don't go," he said, but she was gone, blundering through the empty surgery in tears.

A trombone belched outside the window.

"Oh my Gawd, the mince pies!"

Mavis ran from the room as the broken notes of "Silent Night" brayed. Les Blizzard and his Church Lads' Band had mustered outside to give the doctors a carol.

Someone had rescued Mavis's mince pies, her annual surprise to the doctors, from the little oven she had installed in the office; they were only slightly blackened. The festivities took place in Dr. Macbeth's, the senior partner's, room. John looked around: the three receptionists in their blue overalls, Johnson sucking burnt sugar from a painful tooth and trying to smile, Baines eying the bottle, Macbeth, eyes moist with sweet sherry, mincemeat in his white moustache, giving a convincing performance as a lovable old family practitioner, which of course he was. The window, like his own, was decorated with white paper cut-outs. Macbeth raised his glass to Mavis.

"I have heard the Mavis singing.

His love song to the morn.

I have—"

"*Her* love song, surely," corrected Mavis, reducing his song to a gulp of sherry.

John drained his glass.

"Well, Happy Christmas, everybody. I must be off."

"But doctor, you haven't pulled your cracker! You can't break up the party yet!"

Mavis was waving the colored goad in his face. He grasped the end and pulled. "What is it?" scrabbling among their feet, "Oh, it's a lucky charm. There, put on your hat!"

She crammed a purple crown on his head; it slipped over his

eyes. As she pushed it up, to his horror, he saw a sprig of mistletoe revolving on a thread from the light.

"Ho ho ho," rumbled Macbeth.

Under cover of the crackers' explosions John muttered, "Do you think you could remove those bits of paper from my window? They block the light."

She gave no sign of having heard.

"Oh, I almost forgot! Pressies! You first, Dr. Frazer, as you've got to rush off."

She crammed his weak arms with parcels.

"Just a little something for the children. You'll love little Katy's present! It's a doll that gets nappy rash when it wets itself! Isn't that a hoot? Whatever will they think of next?"

The minions duly hooted.

Catherine watched her ex-husband's feet tangle and tear wrapping paper. He sat down heavily beside her on the floor, pushing parcels out of his way and pulled her to him. His shirt, an obvious Christmas present, perhaps from someone who wished he were with her now, burst open at the neck.

"I still fancy you, you know."

The whisky smell was like a metal gate across his mouth. She wanted to howl and weep and, failing John's, any old shirt would do, even this one, smelling so new, with a frill down the front.

"Your shirt. I'm sorry."

"It doesn't matter. I didn't like it anyway," pressing a button into her eye.

The bookshop. Mr. Hermitage. Pat. Christmas. I'll get through this one, she thought, then the next one and the next. But this will be the worst. The years ahead. Each day that she would not go to the surgery, would not pick up the phone. She saw a series of bleak victories, a lone soldier capturing pointless hills when there was no one to see.

"Do you want to watch the children opening their stockings?"

John realized that she had never had to ask this before; the Christmas tree wavered into a green glass triangle shot with lights; Mary's face, above her pink dressing gown, was pale and wary; she had sensed his absence beside her in bed and come to find him, and now excited sounds were coming from the children's rooms.

"I love you," he said.

For a moment, before he followed her upstairs, the doctor placed his hand over the pain in his heart. He knew it was incurable.

PINK CIGARETTES

As the cab dawdled down Pimlico Road Simon slithered and fretted on the polished seat. The shops, which had so recently enchanted him with glimpses of turquoise and mother-of-pearl and chandeliers sprouting jets of crystal lusters against dark glass, now threatened him with a recurrence of his old complaint, boredom. He looked neither to the left nor the right lest he see again a certain limbless torso, a gilded dodo or a headless stone lion holding out a truncated paw. Surely it would be kinder to put it out of its misery? He saw himself administering the *coupe de grâce* with a mallet and sighed, and closed his eyes but was too late to escape the sight of two Chelsea Pensioners lurking like wind-bitten unseasonal tulips among the gray graves of the Royal Hospital. He pulled off his red tie and stuffed it into his pocket. His misery was complete as they crossed Kings Road and he turned from the fortunates on the pavement in their pretty clothes to his own reflection in a small mirror; nobody, he feared, could call him yesterday's gardenia, more like yesterday's beefburger in a school blazer. He had been forced to leave the house in his uniform, and he had a cold. He had poisoned his ear with a cheap earring and it throbbed with the taxi's motor.

He thought that this was the most unpleasant cab in which he had ever ridden—a regular little home-from-home with a strip of freshly hoovered carpet on the floor, a photograph, dangling from the driver's mirror, of two cute kids daring him to violate the *Thank you for not smoking* sign, and a nosegay of plastic flowers in a little chrome vase exuding wafts of Harpic. He remembered with envy a taxi ride he had once taken with his mother; she had had no time to look out of the window or be bored. She had replenished lipstick and mascara and combed her hair and then she had taken from her bag a bottle of pungent pink liquid and a tissue and rubbed the varnish from her nails, decided against repainting them, and lit a cigarette and when she had stubbed it out on the discarded tissue, the ashtray had gone up in flames. It had been lovely.

He was thrown forward when the cab braked suddenly as the car in front pulled into a parking space.

"Woman driver!" said the cab driver.

"Or a transvestite," said Simon.

The driver did not reply, but added ten pence to the clock after he had stopped. Simon ran down the steps, hoping to avoid being spotted by the housekeeper, who had taken an unaccountable dislike to the slender blond, amanuensis of the tenant of the basement flat.

"Don't kiss me, I've got a cold," he greeted the old poet who opened the door. The cocktail cabinet was closed; that was always a bad sign. He wondered if he dared risk opening it while the old man was pottering about in the kitchen, dunking a sachet of peppermint tea in a cup of boiling water.

"Simon?"

He lounged in the doorway wasting a winning smile on his host.

"Would you like a tisane?"

"Wouldn't mind something a bit stronger. . . ."

"There's some Earl Grey in that tin," said the cruel old

buzzard who was dressed today in shades of cream, with a natty pair of sugared almonds on his feet and a dandified swirl of clotted cream loosely knotted at his throat and a circlet of gold-rimmed glass pinned with a milky ribbon to his wide lapel. Simon became conscious again of his own drab garb.

"Sorry about the clothes," he said sulkily, "my mother was around when I left so I. . . ."

"I've told you before, dear boy, it doesn't matter in the least what you wear."

Simon was not mollified. He watched him lower his accipitrine head appreciatively into the efflorescence from his cup, complacently ignoring as usual the risks Simon took on his behalf, and risks for what? He stared out of the window at a few thin early snowflakes melting on the black railings.

"Snow in the suburbs," he said.

"I should hardly call this the suburbs."

"It was a literary allusion."

"Not a very apt one, as anyway it has stopped snowing. Now, are you going to have some tea, or shall we get straight down to work? We've got a lot to get through today."

"*We,*" echoed Simon bitterly and sneezed.

"I expect that lake of yours is frozen this morning?" added the poet.

"Not quite," Simon proffered a stained shoe.

"I've got an old pair of skates somewhere. I must disinter them for you."

Simon, who thought that they were already on thin ice, drummed his nails on the windowpane. The scent that had intrigued him early in their acquaintance he knew now to be mothballs and it was coming strongly off the white suit.

"You're very edgy this morning. For goodness sake stop fidgeting and pour yourself some absinthe, as you insist on calling it."

With three boyish bounds Simon was at the cocktail cabinet smiling at himself in its mirrored back as he poured Pernod into a green glass. It was amazing how good he looked, when he had felt so ugly before. Was he really beautiful or was there a distortion in the glass, or did the poet's thinking him beautiful make him so? He could have stood for an indefinite length of time reflecting, sipping his drink, a cocktail Sobranie completing the picture but the old man came into the room casting his image over the boy's. Simon turned gracefully from the waist.

"Got any pistachios, Vivian?"

"No."

"You always used to buy me pistachios," he whined.

"It would take my entire annual income, which, as you know, is not inexhaustible, to keep you in pistachio nuts, my dear. Now, to work."

Simon gazed in despair at the round table under the window spilling the memorabilia of more than eighty years; diaries, khaki and sepia photographs, yellow reviews that broke at a touch, letters from hands all dead, all dead, with here and there a flattened spider or a fly's wing between the brittle pages, or the ghost of a flower staining the spectral ink, into boxes and files and pools of paper on the floor. Simon shuddered. His task was to help to put them into chronological order so that the poet might complete his memoirs, while the little gold clock that struck each quarter made it ever more unlikely that he would. He plunged his hand into a box and pulled out a photograph of a baby in a white frock riding on a crumpled knee, which, if it could be identified, would no doubt belong to someone very famous. He tried to smooth it with his hand.

"Do be careful, Simon! These things are very precious!"

"It's not my fault!" Simon burst out. "I don't really know what I'm supposed to be looking for, and when I do manage to put anything in order, you snatch it away from me and mess it all up again!"

"What? Listen, Simon, I want to read something to you. Go and sit down. Have a cigarette. Are you old enough to smoke, by the way? There are some by your chair. Light one for me."

Simon gloomed over the cigarettes, like pretty gold-tipped pastels in their black box, not knowing which to choose. He had expected tea at the Ritz and hock and seltzer at the Cadogan Hotel, and here he was day after day grubbing through musty old papers for a book that would never be finished, that no one would publish if it was finished, and that no one would read if it was published. . . .

"Of course it never occurs to some people that some other people are going to fail all their 'O' Levels," he muttered.

"No, we didn't have 'O' Levels when I was at school," agreed Vivian. "Listen Simon, this will interest you. . . ." The words spilled like mothballs from his mouth and rolled around the room, " 'and so I set foot for the first time on Andalusian soil, a song in my heart, a change of clothing in my knapsack, a few pesetas in my pocket, traveling light, for the youthful hopes and ideals that made up the rest of my baggage weighed but little'—you might at least pretend to be awake. . . ."

"I am. Please go on, the last bit was really poignant."

"Oh, do you think so, Simon, I'm so glad. I rather hoped it was."

Simon selected a pink cigarette, and wondering if it was possible to pretend to be awake, fell fast asleep. He woke with a little cry as the cigarette blistered his fingers.

"I thought that would startle you," chuckled the poet, "you didn't expect that of me, did you?"

"I don't know. . . ."

What deed it had been, of valor or romance, he would never know, but his reply pleased the old man.

"Come on, I'll take you out for a drink, and then we'll have some lunch."

Simon attracted some attention in his school blazer in the Coleherne Arms.

"This is a really nice pub," he told Vivian, "do you know, three people offered to buy me a drink while you were in the Gents?"

The poet stalked out, the black wings of his cloak flapping and smiting people and Simon had to scramble up from the dark corner where he had been seated and follow him.

Much later, as he ran across the concourse at Victoria and lunged at the barrier he collided with a friend of his mother, on her way to her husband's firm's annual dinner dance in a long dress and fur coat, a dab of Home Counties mud on her heels.

There was nobody in. That is to say, his parents were out. Simon made himself a sandwich and took it upstairs. His room was as he had left it; the exploded crisp bags, the used mugs and glasses, the empty can of Evo-Stik, the clothes and comics, records and cassettes on the floor untouched by human foot, for no one entered it but he. He looked out of the window, and the pond in the garden below, glittering dully in the light from the kitchen provoked an image of himself curvetting round its brackish eighteen-inch perimeter on a pair of archaic silver skates. He shivered and pulled the curtain, vowing feebly once again to extricate himself as he flopped down on the bed. When he had met the poet, not expecting the acquaintance to last more than an afternoon, he had constructed grandiose lies about his antecedents and house and garden, and had sunk a lake in its rolling lawns. He became aware of the sound of lapping wavelets; somebody next door was taking a bath, and he felt loneliness and boredom wash over him.

It was boredom that had led to his first timid ring on the poet's bell. One afternoon, in Latin, deserting from the Gallic Wars and tired of the view from the window, the distant waterworks like a gray fairground where sea gulls queued for rides on its melancholy roundabouts, he had taken from his desk a book; an anthology whose faded violet covers opened on names as mysterious as dried flowers pressed by an unknown hand. Walter Savage Landor, Thomas Lovell Beddoes and Lascelles Abercrombie, whom some wit, in memory or anticipation of school dinner, had altered to Brussels Applecrumble, Vivian Violett—Simon selected him as the purplest, and turned the pages to his poem.

"What's that you're reading, Simon?"

"It's only an old book I found in the lost property cupboard." Simon lifted tear-drenched eyes to the spectacles of the master who had oozed silently to his side.

"Let me see. My goodness, Vivian Violett! That takes me back. . . ."

"Is he good, sir?"

"I think that this is, er, what's known as a good bad poem. . . ."

He wove mistily away, adjusting his headlights, shaking his head as if to dislodge the voices of nightingales from his ears.

"Is he dead, sir?" Simon called after him.

"Oh, undoubtedly, undoubtedly. Isn't everyone? You could check in *Who's Who*, I suppose."

"You are a creep, Si," whispered the girl sitting next to him. "I got a detention for reading in class."

"Of course," said Simon.

"Poseur," she hissed.

"Moi?"

Simon, for whom the word *decadence* was rivaled in beauty only by *fin-de-siècle*, found that at the last count Vivian Violett was alive and living in London.

The next day he climbed the steps of an immense baroque biscuit hung with perilous balconies and blobs of crumbling icing, to present himself in the role of young admirer. His disappointment at being redirected to the basement by a large weevil or housekeeper in an overall was tempered when Vivian Violett opened his door, an eminently poetic Kashmir shawl slung around his velvet shoulders, and scrutinized him through a gold-rimmed monocle clamped to the side of his beak and a cloud of smoke and some other exotic perfume. The poet was charmed by his guest.

"I do enjoy the company of young people," he sighed, "especially when they're as pretty as you. . . ."

Simon reclined on faded silk, fêted with goodies, not yet knowing that he was not only the only *young* person, but almost the *only* person to have crossed the threshold for many years.

"You must tell me all about yourself," Vivian said, at once swooping and darting into his own past to peck out tarnished triumphs and ancient insults, shuffling names like dusty playing cards; a mechanical bird whose rusty key had been turned and who could not stop singing. From time to time he cocked his head politely at Simon's poor attempts, over a rising mound of pistachio shells, to attribute a little grandeur to himself before flying again at the bookcase to pull down some fluttering album of photographs or inscribed volume of verse to lay them at Simon's feet. It was then that the idea of Simon helping with the memoirs was born. A faint murmur about having to go to school was brushed aside like a moth.

"Nonsense, dear boy. You will learn so much more with me than those dullards could ever teach you. Besides, I have so little time. . . ."

Simon was struck with sadness; the figure dwindling to a skeleton in its embroidered shawl had been, by its own account, the prettiest boy in London. Already he had noticed in himself a tendency to grow a little older each year.

"You will come and see me again soon, won't you?" the poet pleaded.

"Very soon," promised Simon over the ruins of a walnut cake.

"Such a pity one can't get Fuller's walnut cake any more," mourned Vivian for the third time.

"Mmm," agreed Simon again, without knowing in the least what he was talking about.

"I hope you don't find this too cloying, Simon," resorting to a tiny ivory toothpick, a splinter of some long-departed elephant.

Simon was dribbling the last drops from his glass onto dry crumbs on his plate and licking them off his finger; the effect was agreeable, like trifle.

"Do you know that poem of mine "Sops in Wine?" Of course you must, it's in the *Collected Works*,"—a volume which Simon had claimed to possess and which he had glimpsed only on a shelf of one of the tottering bookcases which lined the room—"I'll say it to you." And he laid back his lips like an old albino mule and brayed out the verse, sing-song in a spray of crumbs.

Simon reached for the decanter of madeira as if it might drown the sound of the last plausible train pulling out of Victoria, for he had not told his parents of his proposed visit. He need not have worried because when he telephoned home they had gone out.

That had been the first of his visits, and as he lay, weeks later, on his bed wondering how he could make the next one the last, toying with the idea of a severe illness, the telephone rang. He had difficulty at first in recognizing the voice of his best friend.

"Do you want to come round to my place?" he was asking.

"Okay, I'll be round in ten minutes."

But as he was leaving the house the phone rang again.

"Oh Simon, I've just had such an unpleasant encounter with the housekeeper, complaints of playing my radio too loudly, accusations of blocking the drains with bubbles, I mean to say, have you ever heard of anything so ridiculous . . . all lies of course, you know she wants to get me out, it's all a conspiracy with the landlord so that he can re-let at a grossly inflated price. Bubbles! What would you do with such people, Simon? I know what I'd do, you must come and see me tomorrow, Simon, I'm so upset and lonely and blue. . . ."

"I really can't. I've really got to go to school."

"Well have dinner with me then at least."

"I haven't got the fare," said Simon weakly, "my building society account's all. . . ."

"Of course I shall give you some more money tomorrow, you should have reminded me."

"I've got to go. The phone's ringing. I mean, there's someone at the door!"

On his way to school the following morning Simon was overtaken by his friend Paul.

"What happened to you last night? I thought you were coming around?"

"I was, only I got depressed. . . ."

"Old Leatherbarrow's been asking about you, you know. Why haven't you been at school? Are you ill or something? You don't look too good."

Suddenly school was an impossible prospect.

"I don't think I'll come in today after all."

"Well, what shall I tell him? He keeps on at me! He'll be phoning your parents soon!" Paul's voice rose among the traffic.

"That's all right, they're never in. Tell him I'm suffering from suspected hyperaesthesia. I'm waiting the results of tests. Don't worry, I'll sort it out."

He turned and left Paul standing on the pavement exhaling clouds of worried steam.

"Simon, it was sweet of you to come!"

Simon was shocked to see him still in his dressing gown, albeit one of mauve silk with a dragon writhing up its back, and a pair of unglamorous old men's pajamas. The flat smelled stale, like a hothouse where the orchids have rotted.

"Aren't you going to get dressed?" he asked disapprovingly, being young enough to think that if a person was old or ill it was because he wanted to be so.

"I will, now that you're here," said Vivian meekly. "I wasn't feeling very bright this morning." His hand shook and a purple drop spilled to the carpet as he handed Simon a conical glass of parfait amour.

"Ah, meths," said Simon, "my favorite."

"What are you grinning at?"

"Old Leatherbarrow. The St. Lawrence Seaway. . . ." replied Simon enigmatically. The forced daffodils which he had brought on an earlier visit hung in dirty yellow tags of crêpe paper against a small grisaille.

"Why have you been so ratty lately?"

"Have I? I'm so sorry Simon if I should have appeared to be ratty towards you, of all people, the person in the world to whom I should least like to be ratty when I am so grateful to have your friendship and your help. I suppose I have been worried. A thousand small unpleasantnesses with the housekeeper, and most of all about this . . . " he waved a hand at the tower of papers on the table. "Time's winged chariot . . ." and Christmas. . . ."

"Christmas?" said Simon, "Christmas is okay—" and stopped.

"I shall go and dress now. Can you amuse yourself for a few minutes? Then perhaps we could do a little work on the memoirs. Where did we leave them?"

"You had just enlisted in the 'nth Dragoons," he said as Vivian disappeared into the bedroom. Simon entered with a drink as he was impaling a cravat with a nacreous pin.

"Ah, my little Ganymede," said the poet, smiling palely, "what should I do without you?"

It was raining when they set out that evening for the Indian restaurant round the corner.

"Oh dear, oh dear, where's my umbrella? Simon, haven't you got a hat?"

"Of course not."

"We don't want you to catch another cold. You'd better wear

this." He placed a large soft fedora on Simon's head. "Yes, it suits you very well."

Simon smiled at himself in the glass. He wondered if Vivian minded that the hat looked so much better on him.

A fake blue Christmas tree had been set in the restaurant window and cast a bluish light on the heavy white tablecloth and imparted a spurious holiness to the bowls of spoons and the candle holder by staining them the rich deep blue of church glass. Two pink cigarettes were smoking themselves in the ashtray. In an upstairs room across the street, behind a sheet looped across the window, an ayatollah or mullah was leading a congregation of men in prayer; their heads rose and fell. Simon felt suddenly the sharp happiness of knowing that, for a moment, he was perfectly happy. He smiled over his wine at Vivian. The old man gripped the handles of his blue spoon and fork.

"I don't think I can bear," he said, "to spend another Christmas alone in that flat."

"But it's a lovely flat," answered Simon inadequately and then there was silence while the waiter brought the food.

"I can't face any more unpleasantness. Days and days of not seeing you. . . ."

"Mushroom bhaji?"

"No. No. You help yourself."

Simon looked with embarrassment at his own heaped plate but was too hungry not to spear a surreptitious forkful and tried not to look as if he was chewing. He crumbled a poppadum while he tried to think of something to say.

"Do you know what I have been thinking?"

The poppadum turned to ashes in Simon's mouth.

"Why don't I spend Christmas with you?"

Simon choked on unimaginable horrors; carols round the telly, stockings suspended from a storage heater, a mournful quartet in paper hats silently pulling crackers, Vivian crushed like a leaf between his parents, in bulky, quilted body-warmers, asking for parfait amour at the bar of the local; their sheer incomprehension. . . .

"What do you think, Simon?"

When he could speak he muttered desperately, "I'm not sure that you'd get on with my parents."

"We have one thing in common anyway, so that's a good start."

"They're really boring. We never do anything much. You'd be bored out of your mind."

"I'm never bored when we're together. Besides a quiet family Christmas is just what I need, what I've missed all these years. We could do some work on the memoirs. I'm sure your parents would be interested. We could go for long walks, that would be very good for me, and you could introduce me to your friends. What do you say?"

"I—."

"It's a large house, as you've told me, so I shouldn't be in the way."

Simon had to stop him before he actually begged. Maybe his train would crash tonight, maybe his parents would have run away. . . .

"I think it's a great idea," he said, raising his glass, "I'll tell them tomorrow."

Vivian had to apply his napkin to his eye. He reached for Simon's hand and pressed it, then fell with a sudden appetite on the cold food in the silvery blue dishes.

"I wonder where those skates have got to?" he mused. "Must

be in a box somewhere, on top of a bookcase or under the bed. Ring me tomorrow when you've spoken to your parents, won't you?"

He put Simon in a taxi, and he was driven away with a despairing flourish of the black fedora through the window.

Simon could not ring him the next day, which was Saturday, because of course he had not spoken to his parents. On Sunday he woke late from a nightmare of Pickwickian revelry on the garden pond to the realization that he had left the hat on the train. He went downstairs to find a message in his mother's hand on the pad by the telephone: "Violet Somebody rang. Can you call her back?"

"They're delighted," he told Vivian on the telephone, tenderly fingering the lump on his head where he had banged it on the wall. "I can't talk now, but I'll come to see you tomorrow."

He arrived hatless, sick with guilt, a dozen excuses fighting in his brain, clutching a paper cone of freezing violets, at Vivian's house. Before he could descend the steps the housekeeper flung open the front door.

"If you want to see Mr. Violett, you're too late. They've taken him away."

"What?"

"Last night. It seems he was climbing up on some steps to get something off the bookcase. Pulled the whole lot down on top of himself. There was an almighty crash, I dashed downstairs with my passkey, in my nightie, but there was nothing I could do. It seems the actual cause of death was a blow to the head from an ice skate."

A stout woman, wearing if not actual, spiritual jodphurs, appeared on the step beside her. "This is Mr. Violett's great-niece. She's taken charge of everything."

As Simon turned and ran he thought he heard the great-niece

boom, "Of course he was always a third-rater," and the housekeeper reply, "Oh, quite."

He hailed a passing cab, and as he sat, still holding his violets, he saw that the windscreen carried the Christmas lights of Sloane Square in a little colored wreath all the way to Eaton Square. "There must be a good bad poem somewhere in that" he said to himself.

"The Headmaster would like to interview you, Simon, about your frequent absences."

Simon knocked dully on the door, stuffing his handkerchief into his trouser pocket, his heart and thoughts miles away.

"Don't kiss me, I've got a cold," he said, then saw in the mirror behind the astonished pedagogue the reflection of a red-eyed schoolboy in a blazer, whose crying had brought out spots on his nose, and as he pulled out his handkerchief again, saw a broken pink cigarette fall to the floor, and an irrecoverable past diminishing in the glass, when he had been Ganymede for a little while.

CURRY AT
THE LABURNUMS

Rain set in. The hills were hidden and the village enclosed in dull gray curtains of mist. The river threatened the supports of the bridge. Children gauged the water level, hoping, as sometimes happened, that they would be cut off from school. The playground was roofed over by umbrellas, floral patterned, transparent pagodas, under which waiting mothers complained. Little, inadequate sandbags appeared outside some houses. Fields lay under a glaze of water. Some cows were temporarily marooned and a rotten tree trunk, caught under the bridge, bobbed uncannily like the head of a drowned cow. The river continued to rise, grass and nettles disappeared and alders stood in water which poured over the sides of the bridge and reduced the road to a narrow sluice.

Commuters returning to houses draped with wet washing were bored and alienated by tales of muddy dramas, trees swept downstream, rescued water rats, coaches forcing their way through the water and taking children miles round the back roads to school. They were more interested to hear that water had got into the cellars of the pub. They became a different species from the gumbooted inhabitants of the heart of the flood, irritated by wives shut up all day with small children and felt that the trials of water in the brakes, an abandoned car rota, and a go-slow on the trains were far greater than those of the home front.

The platform was jammed. What many found hardest to bear was the unfailing cheerfulness of Lal, the ticket collector, with whom Ivor, from vague liberal principles, often made a point of speaking, exchanging comment on the weather, and last Christmas he had thrust, almost aggressively, a pound note into his hand. Since the go-slow, he somehow hadn't liked to be seen chatting at the ticket collector's box and had restricted himself to a curt nod.

Lal laughed and joked and even made mock announcements over his microphone. Many were quite indecipherable, and the packed, soaked travelers eagerly turning to gaze at the signal which still showed red, and hearing his high-pitched cackle crackling over their heads, stared angrily up the receding tracks and understood only that they had been duped. In his efforts to entertain them, Lal had brought along his own transistor radio from home and played it loud enough to cheer up those at the farthest ends of the platforms. Many of them seemed not to appreciate Radio One.

"I wonder if you know that it's illegal to play transistor radios in public places?" a lady asked, shaking a raindrop from her nose.

"Must keep my customers happy," he replied. She reported him to the Station Manager who told him to turn it off.

"Bolshie so-and-so, playing the radio while his fellow Reds hold us to ransom." A voice was heard in the aftermath.

"Blacks, more like," replied another.

Camaraderie flowered among the wet heads and shoulders as stranger muttered to stranger imprecations on Blacks and Reds. Ivor and Roger Henry, his neighbor and old school-friend, were edging along the platform to try to get some sense out of Lal. He seized his microphone and shouted:

"All passengers Wictoria and Vaterloo, you might as well go home," and cackled. Then, as the two men reached his box, he received a telephone announcement, the signal went green and he called: "All Stations Wictoria. Stopping train Wictoria!"

Twenty minutes later, the grateful commuters saw the train's round caterpillar face crawling towards them and those who could, fought their way aboard and stood steamily, agonizingly pinioned together, fainters held upright, pregnant women loathed for their bulk, dead limbs slowly filling with pins and needles, trapped ever tighter by a seemingly impossible influx at subsequent stations.

So it went on. Drivers reported late and were sent home. Rule books ruled. Trains ran spasmodically. At least the rain began to peter out and there were occasional flashes of watery sunshine.

Ivor and Roger were on the platform, at the edge of a group of older men, doyens of commuting, whose trousers were of necessity hoisted high over round bellies by braces and fell in soft cuffs onto polished shoes, whose muscles were adapted only to the hoovering of lawns with electric mowers, or hitting golf balls; electors who kept Chubleigh a safe Tory seat. At election times its windows broke out in a blue rash of posters depicting Sir John Upton, who seemed to be conjured up only then, opposed only by an occasional doomed orange placard.

". . . Harold Wilson," Ivor caught.

"Heh heh heh," laughed the old boys, products of small schools set back under the dripping beeches of Surrey. A Pekinese-faced lady, with steel-blue fur brushed up from a pink powdered forehead, bared her little teeth and laughed.

"Just let them try to treat cattle like this," said one, "and they'd soon have all the do-gooders up in arms."

Their two weeks of inconvenience led these men, holding

briefcases packed with the data of unnecessary companies, to compare themselves with Jews transported across Poland in freezing cattle trucks. One licked his livery lips, spotted like sloughed snake skins, and said:

"Did you hear about the Epsom incident? Some chaps got hold of one of those blighters and locked him in the, er, Ladies."

"Heh heh heh," laughed the old boys.

"Ha ha," laughed Ivor.

"Next train to Vaterloo approaching Platform One in about twenty minutes," broadcast Lal.

No train materialized. Some people went home. The coffee machine was jammed; a squirt of dirty water rattled into the plastic cup. Ivor and Roger trailed after the group to a little shack in the forecourt which sold such fare as sausage sandwiches, sulphurous rock cakes and tea. They blocked the doorway and jostled the taxi-drivers seated on benches around the walls, shooting spray over them as they closed their umbrellas, and brayed at the woman in broken slippers frying bacon at the stove. The kettle was shrieking; all was steam, noise and succulent wisps of smoke.

"What's yours, Tony?"

"Name your poison."

"Your shout, I believe, you old rascal."

"Heh heh heh."

The woman removed the whistle from the kettle and unfortunately the words, ". . . Bloody unhygienic, ought to be prosecuted" hung in the air.

A huge man in shirtsleeves hoisted himself up from the bench.

"Right," he said. "Everybody out. We don't want your sort here. You're all barred!"

"Now look here . . ."

"Out."

The taxi-drivers rose, a menacing semi-circle confronting former customers.

"Well really, I must say. . . ."

"Out."

"Now look here, my dear chap, it says 'ALL WELCOME' outside. Do you realize you're contravening the Trades Descriptions Act?"

"We demand to be served," said Ivor from the back.

"Berks."

The drivers stepped forward. The commuters retreated.

"If that's their attitude. . . ."

Step by step, the commuters were forced backwards into the forecourt, out of the delicious smell of bacon and hot tea into the cold drizzle.

"Good mind to call the police."

"Well, I for one shall be contacting the Inspector of Health and I suggest you all do the same."

A stomach brayed expressing everyone's disappointment.

"My wife was sold a moldy pie in the supermarket the other day," volunteered Roger and was ignored.

Ivor felt specially outraged, like a little boy who arrives late for school dinner and finds the hatches closed and his comrades wiping gravy and custard from their lips. Marian had neglected to make muesli and he had left with only a small, bitter cup of coffee. He and Roger went back through the booking hall and found themselves at Lal's box. Ivor was lightheaded and on the point of telling Roger he was giving up and going home. His mouth opened and hung open. Surely not? It couldn't be—a hot pungent drift of curry caught his nose. He stood swooning as it washed over his empty stomach. Roger caught his arm.

"The last bloody straw."

He looked. The youngest porter, a lowly boy in a too-big jacket, who swept the platforms, was crossing the line bearing foil dishes of take-away curry.

"As you say, the last straw."

Lal started across the platform through the passengers, smiling and rubbing a knife and fork in his hands, to receive the food. As he reached the edge of the platform and bent forward, Ivor and Roger exchanged a glance, each took an imperceptible step forward and thrust a foot under Lal's ankles. He swayed, the dishes in his hands, and crashed over, hitting his head on the rail; curry erupted and engulfed him. He sat up and half turned, scalding juice running down his hair, tomatoes, ladyfingers, yellow rice slipping down his face, and fell back, a knife sticking out of his striped waistcoat. Ivor and Roger were among the first to jump down. The tearful boy was sent to phone for an ambulance.

"Heh heh heh."

The old boys couldn't see the knife, and laughed away their humiliations in the café.

Lal now lay on the pile of empty mail sacks on the platform. It occurred to nobody that it wasn't an accident. The ambulance klaxon overtook the sound of the approaching train.

The incident made the evening paper; a small paragraph on the front page under the banner headline proclaiming a return to work by the railmen after the personal intervention of the Prime Minister. It seemed that Lal was comfortable in hospital with burns and a punctured lung.

Ivor rolled uneasily all night in bed, behind the window which still bore an orange shred from the last election; the quisling of the station snack bar; all his principles slithering with scalding curry down Lal's surprised face. If he could become completely evil he could forget all this, or laugh at it, continue his affair with Heather from the office, or a succession of women, refuse to attend Family Service, neglect the garden, drink himself to death, then everybody would be sorry. Would he have to use another station?

He practiced a sneer on his changed face as he shaved, but the eyes in the mirror had a puffy frightened look.

"Bye dear, have a good day," he said as he left.

An incomprehensible curse seemed to batter against the front door as he banged it. He sensed something in the atmosphere as soon as he and Roger arrived at Chubleigh station.

"Deny everything," he muttered as they squared their shoulders, the wooden floor of the booking hall resounding hollowly like the hearts in their chests. The young porter, promoted, inspected their seasons. A knot of people was down the platform, by the far seat, obviously holding some sort of conference. Roger's elbow caught Ivor painfully on the muscle of his arm. They stopped and glanced frantically back at the booking hall, but people blocked the entrance.

"Wait for the 9:12?" said Roger stepping back a pace. A patch of bristle under his nose denoted a shaky hand. Ivor shook his head. The cluster broke. A woman pointed at Ivor and Roger.

"A necktie party," said Roger.

"I am completely evil," said Ivor to himself.

His umbrella was slippery in his hand. Two students were coming down the platform towards them, his long blue jeans bent and straightened, eating up the asphalt, her skirt trailed tiny chips of grit; they heard the flap of her bare feet. The two avengers garbed in their tatty integrity moved down the platform towards them. Ivor stared at the yellow tin newspaper stand and became absorbed in a blotch of rust, dog-shaped. He scratched at it with a forefinger, to elongate its stumpy tail and a flake of rust pierced the soft skin under his nail. He stared at it. "Your nails are so neat," Heather had said, "just like haricot beans."

He felt detached pity for those polished beans, as if they were to be violated in some inquisition or boiled for soup. Meanwhile Roger was finding it necessary to search his briefcase, and not unexpectedly found only *The Guardian* within, and squinted at its sideways folded print.

"About the accident yesterday—"

"Look here," Roger started to say, but Ivor caught his sleeve.

"We're getting up a collection for Lal's family from the regulars."

A balloon burst in Ivor's chest, suffusing his veins and face with warm liquid. His leather wallet leaped to his hand and he was stuffing a fiver into the jagged slit of the improvised collection tin, around which was pasted a piece of white paper with the simple message FOR LAL, which the girl held out.

"Turrific," she uttered.

The male student scowled in silent accusation of ostentation. Roger managed fifty pence, which landed dully on Ivor's note.

"Right," said the student, taking the tin and giving it a shake, and they moved on to the next passengers.

Roger and Ivor sat at opposite ends of the compartment, as if each thought the other had behaved rather badly.

The following morning the students were waiting. The boy hovered over them, his jeans seemed to sway with self-effacement.

"Personally I think the little old lady who gave 20p out of her pension should take it, but Maggie," who had her hair in stubby pigtails today, "seems to think you genuinely love the guy, so here you are. From us all."

He thrust the heavy tin at Ivor, who stared up at him hopelessly.

"Give him the address, Maggie."

She gave him a piece of paper. As if divesting themselves of a necessary but distasteful contact with the spoils of capitalism, they loped off.

"Pompous, sentimental, young twit," said Roger.

Ivor, who had the tin, said nothing.

"You'd better go tonight," suggested Roger. "Get it over with."

"Yes, we will," said Ivor rolling the weighty embarrassing tin into his briefcase.

They met in a bar at Waterloo and fortified themselves for their task; from his seat under the red and yellow lights, above the platform, Ivor watched all the lucky commuters going home; all the fortunates who didn't have to take a tin of money to the wife and children of a man they had pushed onto the railway line for no reason.

"The more one thinks about it, the more impossible the whole thing becomes," said Roger.

Ivor grunted. Roger went to telephone Martha.

"That's settled then," he said as he came back.

"Same again?"

It struck Ivor that Roger was looking forward to the evening with cheerful or morbid curiosity. He almost told him to go home, but the thought of facing Lal's wife alone was worse.

"No thanks," he said standing up. "The woman will be busy

putting the kids to bed, maybe after visiting the hospital, we don't want to turn up stinking of booze."

Roger sighed and followed him out. It transpired, however, that they had twenty minutes to wait for a train, and they returned to the bar. Marian had hung up on him when he telephoned; too late he remembered that it was madrigal night.

Croydon was golden when they left its station. They hired one of the taxis blazing in the forecourt and gave the driver Lal's address. The street turned out to be a long hill of terraced houses, which the taxi climbed slowly looking at the numbers.

"Bet it's that one." Roger leaned forward and pointed at a blue-painted house with its brickwork picked out in pink, and windows and door, with hanging baskets of plastic flowers, pale green.

"They go in for that sort of thing. Really lowers the tone."

It was at none of the picked-out houses that the taxi finally drew up. Lal's house was a discreet cream, with only a wreath of stucco leaves above the door painted dark green and a laburnum tree trailing leaves and pods over the gate, with the name "The Laburnums."

Ivor was fumbling with the lock of his briefcase as Roger knocked. A plump dark boy in school trousers opened the door.

"Does Mr. Kharma live here?"

"My dad isn't here."

A voice called something foreign from within. The boy answered in the same language, keeping his lustrous eyes on the two strangers, standing on a hectic yellow-orange carpet which swirled up the staircase behind him like a colony of snakes. The hall glittered with dark eyes from behind doors and the spaces of the bannisters.

"Are you from the newspaper?" asked the boy.

"No, we—"

A woman came from somewhere at the back of the house and stood behind the boy, Ivor thrust the tin at her over his head.

"On behalf of the regulars at Chubleigh Station, we'd like you to accept this small token. We were all very sorry about your husband's accident. He was very popular."

He spoke slowly and loudly, feeling a flush seep up his neck from his collar. She stared at him almost with hostility. A smell of cooking came from the kitchen. The boy seemed to translate.

"Her eyes are like pansies, those dark velvety pansies," thought Ivor.

"My mother says please come inside."

"Well, that's awfully kind of you, but we really mustn't impose," began Ivor.

"Please."

The women and children moved back, the boy held the door wide.

"Well, just for a minute."

Ivor and Roger stepped in. They were led into the front room and told to sit on a black leatherette sofa backed with red, encrusted with gold thread, embossed by a bright picture of a Bengal tiger. Bamboo pictures hung on the walls and colored brass ornaments stood on the mantelpiece and windowsill. Roger shifted his feet on the blue carpet.

"Have you seen your dad? How is he getting on? That was a rotten thing to happen."

"He can talk now. His burns pain him. Did you see the accident?" answered the boy.

"Yes we were right there. We did what we could."

The woman interposed a question to her son.

"Is one of you Mr. Ivor and Mr. Roger?" asked the boy.

"No," said Ivor at once, but Roger was saying heartily, "That's us. Great pals of your dad, we are."

This was translated with some vehemence.

"All is lost," thought Ivor. He wanted to run.

Three little girls came and sat opposite them, two on chairs and one on the arm, swinging an impossibly thin brown leg and foot in a rubber flip-flop. Lal's wife said something to the boy and went out of the room. Ivor tried to remember if there was a telephone in the hall. He placed the tin, FOR LAL, on the little carved table covered with a silk cloth, beside a Monopoly game.

"My mother says please wait. She is getting you some food. She is very grateful to you."

The men exchanged a helpless glance. Ivor wondered if the plump boy was teased at school, and if his own children could cope so well with a second language. He was not really like a child, rather a small self-contained man in his white shirt, with sleeves turned back to show a heavy gold watch on his wrist. He seemed not to have inherited his father's jocularity, rather his mother's gloom. But of course they had something to be gloomy about, Ivor reminded himself.

The mother called from the kitchen and one of the girls left the room.

"Lovely kids," muttered Roger. "Beautiful eyes."

"I don't like the way they're staring at us. I think they know. Let's get out."

"Can't. Look worse."

He raised his voice to the little girls. "Do you speak English?"

"Yes."

"Jolly good."

The tallest girl returned with two thin conical glasses on a brass tray. Her hair was tied back in a long plait like her mother's and she had tiny gold stars in her ears.

"Would you like a drink?"

"I say, thank you very much."

The two assassins each lifted a glass and put their lips to the thick sweet liquor.

"Cheers."

"Cheers," said the girl, unsmiling. She held the tray behind her back; there was nowhere to put the glasses, so they drained them. She held out the tray and went out again. The younger girls were whispering and stopped when they caught Ivor's eye. He wished someone would turn on the television or the transistor with which Lal had cheered up his customers.

"Please tell your mother she mustn't go to any trouble on our account," he told the boy.

"She wants to repay your kindness."

"Mustn't offend Eastern hospitality," mumbled Roger, "besides, I could do with some nosh. Wonder what it'll be? Smells good."

The girl returned with the filigree glasses refilled. This time Ivor took a sip and set his glass on the floor.

"Good stuff," said Roger, a little thickly.

"Don't know how it mixes with Scotch though."

The mother called again from the kitchen. The little girls opened a drawer in the sideboard and took cones of incense and stood them in little brass hands and lit them. Ivor thought he heard the front door click. He reached down for his glass, the fragile stem swayed in his hand and slopped the liquor onto the floor. A child ran for a cloth and the oldest girl took his glass and brought it back brimming.

"Very clean," remarked Roger, jerking his head at the floor.

"Is your house dirty then?" retorted the child.

"Touché," he laughed.

"Would you like to come through," said the boy politely. "I'll show you the bathroom first, if you'd like to wash."

The strange drink and heavy incense swirled around in Ivor's head, he had to put his hand to the wall as he followed the children. Fresh soap and towels seemed to have been put out in the bathroom; he glanced back as he left to make sure he had left it tidy.

"Did you put the towels back?" he whispered to Roger.

"What?" He pushed past him into the kitchen. There, Ivor felt suddenly gross among these small people as he hovered at the table and sat down clumsily on the indicated chair.

"Aren't you having any?"

"We have eaten earlier, before the hospital," explained their little host.

Bowls of steaming rice and dishes of food smelling, to Ivor, of every spice of the orient were placed before them. The family grouped around the kitchen to watch the Englishmen eat. Incense was burning here too, the air was thick with it, sweet and acrid scents mingling.

"Please eat," said the girl. Lal's wife drew out a chair and sat down at the opposite end of the table from Ivor. He heaped his plate until it was swimming with beautiful colored vegetables and marbled with red and yellow juices. A full glass stood by his plate.

"It's great, it's delicious. I don't know what it is but it's great!" Roger said.

There was no need to translate this; his spoon was already digging again into a dish.

"Have some more ladyfingers, Ive."

He scooped a heap of the little pods onto Ivor's plate and took another drink.

"Everything's all right," thought Ivor, as he bit into the

delicious ladyfingers, he straightened his shoulders which were stiff with tension, and relaxed in his chair.

"I am totally evil," he thought, and sniggered a little at himself.

Roger put down his spoon and fork.

"D'you know," he said, spitting rice, "D'you know, if every immigrant family in this country was to ask one English family into their homes, just one each, for a meal like this, it would put an end to racial prejudice at one stroke. Eh, Mrs. Lal? What do you say to that? I call you Mrs. Lal," he explained, "because you people put your surnames first, in front of your Christian names."

Ivor was terrified again. If Roger was drunk would they ever escape those velvet eyes and glittering earrings, fusing, shifting, miniature watchful Lal faces, dark and golden?

"We Anglo-Saxons are a funny lot." Roger was leaning over the table. "We're very reserved, but if you people would just take the initiative, not be so standoffish, you know? We can be very nice when you get to know us, can't we Ivor?"

"For God's sake, Roger!" Surely Indians were teetotal?

"Now some people think, and I know they're wrong, that your lot are a bit stuck-up, you know, toffee-nosed, unwilling to adopt our customs, living in the past. You spread the word, Mrs. Lal, you give us an inch and we'll take a yard."

He ended abruptly and resumed shoveling. No one spoke. Ivor kept his eyes on his plate; if he stopped eating his head might crash forward into the curry; like Lal's. He blew his nose.

Roger was waving a fork at the boy; his mouth opening and shutting, trying to get the right words out. He lurched up and put his arms around two of the girls, pulling them together so that they almost kissed. The boy stepped forward to protect his sisters. Roger released them.

"These kids. Our kids. It's up to them. They're the generation that counts. You and me, Ivor, we've had our chance. They're the last chance this rotten old world's got."

He began to cry and sat down, spooning food now into his wet mouth, now down his tie. Ivor's whole head broke into bubbles of sweat; he blotted it with his handkerchief, and saw runnels under Roger's nose. He loosened his tie. He made an effort to salvage the evening and their honor.

"How did your husband seem, Mrs. Lal? In himself, I mean." He said very slowly and courteously.

"He is as well as can be expected," said the boy.

"Good. Good." Ivor nodded solemnly. His eyes were caught by Mrs. Kharma's; the pansies seemed drenched with dew; he had to shake his head to shift the image of himself unwrapping the gauzy sari, like the cellophane around a flower, to reveal the dark orchid within. He thought one of the little brass incense burners clenched and unclenched and almost felt the metal fingers on his throat. He kicked Roger and stood up.

"Mrs. Lal, my friend and I would like to thank you for a most excellent meal. We mustn't take up any more of your precious time."

He hauled Roger to his feet.

"It has been a privilege to meet Dad's friends. Please convey our thanks to all the kind people who contributed. But there is more to come."

One of the girls was taking from the fridge aluminum shells of ice cream pitted with green chips of pistachio. Roger made a clumsy move towards the table. Now or never. Ivor got him into the hall.

"Mrs. Lal, I want you to know," he heard himself saying, "I

want you to know you can count on me, as a friend of your husband. He's a good man, and I'm proud to be his friend—"

"So long Gunga Din." Roger was ruffling the boy's hair as the front door nearly clipped his fingers.

"Gloomy lot, never smiled once," he said. "Did you notice? No sense of humor."

He tangled with the laburnum.

"More like some weird ritual than a meal."

"At least one of us kept his dignity," replied Ivor.

Ivor woke, clawing his chest as if wrenching out a knife; his pajamas were sodden. He had a terrible pain; he was about to be sick. He bumped through in the dark, gagging himself with his hand, biting his palm, whooshing and whooping into the bowl, a burning poisonous volcano. At last he lay back on the floor, pressing his forehead on the cold tiles, then doubled up and vomited again where he lay.

"Are you all right?" came Marian's annoyed voice from the bedroom.

Spasm after spasm racked him; it was pouring from his mouth, down his nose, and when there was nothing left his stomach still heaved towards his raw throat. His insides felt sore and pink and mangled.

"Ivor?" She had forced herself out of bed.

"Go away," he groaned. "Just go away," trying to pull the door shut with his foot. She took one look, and fled to be sick in the sink.

"O God, O God, I'm dying, let me die, I can't bear it. Let me die," a voice was groaning over and over. He lay sweating and shivering for a long time. Then he pulled a towel over himself like a blanket and half dozed in the appalling smell. An iron band was screwed around his head.

Some time later he pulled himself, frozen, to his feet and set about cleaning up the fouled bathroom with newspaper and disinfectant and Ajax, washing its walls and floors and the interstices of the hot water pipes, specked and freckled with his guilt. Every time he bent, the burning vice tightened on his skull and his teeth clattered uncontrollably. He put his pajamas in the dirty linen basket for Marian to wash. He stood in a towel at the open window, watching the strange sky lighten over the heavy oaks. The telephone drilled.

Martha Henry's frantic voice battered against his caved-in chest. He couldn't bear to put the receiver to his ear.

"He won't die," he said, and put the phone down.

Sitting on the bath's edge, watching it fill, steam flowering up the turquoise sides, in the sour aftermath, and the draught from the open window, he thought: "You've got to hand it to them. Not a word of the pain we caused them. Not a flicker of emotion. Just a silent revenge. You've got to respect them for that."

THE LATE WASP

"Well, we've got a super day for it, Darren."

"Yes, sir," replied Cheeseman miserably.

They set off across the asphalt to run the gauntlet of the classroom windows. Mr. Glenn with his rucksack, a huge orange edifice bristling with buckles and straps, inherited from his father, bouncing on his back, and Cheeseman with a Tesco carrier bag trying to hide itself against his leg.

As they passed the sixth form common-room a girl, lying languorously half out of the window, called to someone inside.

"Glenda's wearing shorts."

Her friend appeared beside her to watch Mr. Glenn stride past on white legs that might have survived a fusillade of paprika, his peppery beard at a defiant angle.

"The saddest story ever told."

She drew deeply on a sweet cigarette and passed across a crumpled paper bag of rhubarb and custards, striped pink and yellow lozenges, provoking memories of school puddings of yesteryear before the canteen was turned into a cafeteria. The girls were due to leave school in a few days and, overcome by nostalgia from their youth, were feeding it on childish sweets and reducing the insides of their mouths to exquisitely agonizing sponges with bittersweet crystals and shards of sugar. Such was their hyperaesthesia that a shoe bag on a peg or a first-year child with name-tapes on the outside of its socks could reduce them to tears despite, or because of, the poignant knowledge that soon all this would mean nothing to them. The common-room ashtrays were spangled heaps of glossy wrappers, lollipop sticks, spent cartridges of sherbet fountains.

"Where are they going?"

"Why are we here? Where do we come from? Where are we going?" replied her friend closing the window.

Mr. Glenn and Darren Cheeseman were setting off on a Ramble on the Downs. As they crossed the tennis courts a low volley—

"Cheesey's wearing a Harrington"—smacked into the back of Darren's head.

"He can't be"—struck his ear as he turned.

"Why not?"—thud.

"Nobody wears Harringtons any more"—caught him full in the face.

Mr. Glenn seemed unaware of this rally which had left dull red marks on Darren's face under his glasses, or of the rude sign which he made behind his back. He was staring, as Darren was now, at the glittering coaches, parked at the gates, into which Mrs. Nihill, French, was counting with a clipboard the rest of the second year; girls in short vivid skirts, boys and girls with hair spiked into crests and cockades with school soap, like an officious florist bundling heaps of dahlias into a refrigerated vehicle, for export to Boulogne. On the steps of the second coach Bob Drumbell, PE, rested for a moment his brutish hand on the sparkling Bermudas of Hannah Guilfoyle, History, as she climbed aboard.

"It's not fair," thought Cheeseman.

"It's not fair," thought Mr. Glenn.

If it was anybody's fault that they were standing, in silence, together at the bus-stop that was the starting point of their outing, it was Cheeseman's. A form had been issued to each child in the second year proposing a day of Educational Visits and giving a choice of four; Boulogne, Brighton, Bodiam Castle at varying prices, and a Ramble on the Downs, free. Everybody except Darren Cheeseman, a new boy who had failed to settle, had signed up for the trip to Boulogne.

"It's quite encouraging, isn't it, that little Cheeseman has opted for the ramble?" Mr. Glenn, Geography, a new boy himself, had said in the staffroom. "Perhaps at last we've hit on something that interests him."

Mrs. Nihill snorted. She prided herself on her work on the pastoral side.

"I very much doubt if that's the case. Lives in two rooms with his Dad on the Belmont Estate—Mum's done a bunk, Dad's out of work . . ." she boasted, giving a Gallic shrug and brushing a crumb of Ryvita from her crimplene knee. Quelle know-all. No doubt already in her imagination she was heaving her haunches around the *hyper-marché* behind a heaped trolley. At her accusation of greenness Mr. Glenn felt his face turn red and buried it in his World Wildlife Fund mug. When he raised it he realized that he had been elected in a silent ballot to accompany Cheeseman to the Downs. Hannah Guilfoyle, far from showing disappointment that he would not be going to Boulogne, had laughed at his plight. In fact it was probably she who had proposed him.

Cheeseman, alone in the library at lunchtime, spotted his approach from the window.

"Darren, if it's a question of money . . . I'm sure something could be arranged—the school has a fund. . . ."

"What money? Look, sir," he pointed to a picture in the book he was reading. "Did you know that the chalk blue butterfly is occasionally found in albino form? Do you think we'll see one on our ramble?"

As the library door closed behind Mr. Glenn, Cheeseman pulled out a comic from beneath the book and resumed reading: "Dear Cathy and Claire, Please help me. Although I am only thirteen my. . . ."

"Here comes the bus," Mr. Glenn was able to say at last. He paid the fares and followed Darren to the back seat. At each stop ancients mounted slowly with their shopping bags. If buses traveled by bus, Mr. Glenn reflected, this one would take ten minutes to heave its wheels up the steps, turn to greet it cronies, have a joke with the driver, then fumble in a pocket somewhere in its metal side for its senior citizens' bus-pass. Mr. Glenn glanced around, apart from Darren he was the youngest passenger by some forty years. So old and yet they all seemed to have so much still to say. He wondered why the driver did not turn around and roar, "Silence!" and was disturbed by an image of a playground full of grey- and white-haired children leap-frogging and kicking footballs and turning skipping ropes.

He was shamed into moving his rucksack from the luggage space to make room for two shopping trolleys, beldams in faded tartan, which lurched together as the bus, meeting another in the narrow lane, had to reverse with a great scraping of twigs on the windows; and the two green gaffers hooted at each other as they passed.

It was as he was sitting down again that he saw someone enter the bus without paying his fare; elegant, narrow-waisted in black and yellow stripes. He came in by the window, and it might cost him his life. He sat unnoticed on the glass. Mr. Glenn squirmed. He saw himself rise and lunge down the aisle on his freckled legs, scoop up the wasp in his handkerchief and flap it out of the window. His face grew red, his bare skin sweated on the prickly seat, as he braced himself for ridicule.

"Wasps are early this year," he heard.

"I had two in my kitchen yesterday."

The wasp moved tantalizingly to the rim of the window. "Now," said Mr. Glenn to himself. "Quickly. Don't be such a great wet Glenn, just get up and do it. You know you should." He willed it to crawl over the edge into the air. It sat and he sat. Beside him Cheeseman was rustling about in his carrier bag. He pulled out a can and ripped it open; a few sticky drops fell onto Mr. Glenn's thigh.

"Want a drink, sir?"

"No," said Mr. Glenn sharply. "Put it away."

The wasp zoomed down the zone of the scent. A flat cap snatched from a head whipped it to the floor, a blunt toe squelched it. The early wasp was the late wasp. Mr. Glenn stared out of the window trying to think that it did not matter that something beautiful was broken; that something which should have been alive was dead.

The bus rumbled on like an old tuneless wurlitzer while the driver gave a virtuoso demonstration of its revs and groans and wheezes at every bend and hill. So that when Mr. Glenn and Cheeseman at last disengaged themselves and the rucksack, they stood on the grass verge with slight headaches, stunned by silence as the bus's green backside wobbled away in a cloud of heat, haze and exhaust.

"This way, I think. Over the level crossing and up that field and then onto the hills."

Mr. Glenn looked up at the exposed surface of chalk. He saw it as a bride and the path that led up to it as her glittering train. He didn't offer this conceit to Cheeseman as he followed him onto the level crossing. On either side of them the flashing rails raced away into the past or future. Glenn stood with a sense of being no one and nowhere, stranded in eternity on the wooden island.

"Come on, sir!"

"Yes, yes. Thank you Darren." He stumbled gratefully onto the path where thistleheads flared among the glittering dust and stones.

"You feeling OK?"

"Yes, I'm fine thanks, I just felt a bit funny there for a moment—I didn't have time for any breakfast—I was a bit late getting up."

He felt his rucksack, which contained his lunch and a copy of *Cities of The Plain,* Part I, pat him encouragingly on the back for almost achieving a conversation. He looked around for something to say to consolidate his success.

"Look," he cried, pointing into the blue.

"That bird—isn't it a kawk or a hestrel—oh, dear, you've missed it."

"Which do you think it was, sir?"

"I'm not sure. Definitely some sort of bird of prey. I expect you'd have been able to identify it."

Darren didn't respond to the flattery; he pulled a long piece of grass and stuck it in his mouth, chewed irritably, wrenched it out, threw it away and pulled another.

"Do you smoke, sir?" he spat.

"No, I don't. Why? And there's no need to call me sir today; after all we're here to enjoy ourselves."

"Oh, really?"

Mr. Glenn hoped he had misheard, but unease started to churn away again. They were now on a track evidently used by cows, balancing on the edges of deep ruts whose thick clods of dried mud crumbled like stale gingerbread under Mr. Glenn's boots and pierced the soles and sides of Darren's plimsolls. Mr. Glenn cleared his throat.

"Why don't you put your bag in my rucksack, then you'll have your hands free?"

"Sokay."

"No, go on."

Mr. Glenn crouched down on the mud offering his buckles. He squatted there until his knees cracked and sweat dripped into his eyes, feeling like a foolish frog on a dried-up river bed, fearing that Darren had sneaked away, or was going to kick him.

"Darren?"

At last he felt the straps being lifted and the carrier bag falling into the rucksack.

"Mind my thermos!"

As he straightened up he fell forward on his hands and knees. He brushed a bead of blood from his knee, which was jolly painful, a bit of grit must have got embedded, and looked at Darren for some concerned query. He saw him wipe a smirk from his mouth with the back of his hand. As schoolmaster he should have felt gratified to see a pupil taking literally that often-repeated command—"and you can wipe that silly grin off your face!" As it was he decided to risk septicaemia rather than take out his first-aid kit.

Darren seemed inclined to lounge and flop on every fence post and tree stump.

"Is it much further, sir?"

"Is what much further?"

"This place where we're going to."

"We're not going anywhere in particular. This is supposed to be a Ramble. We just ramble around and observe the wildlife and flora. . . ."

"Who's she?"

Mr. Glenn heaving a pedagogic sigh, exhaled panic and the knowledge that he would disappoint as he bowed his head to enter a green tunnel which led uphill through a little wood.

"A green thought in a green shade . . ." he said.

"No answer came the loud reply," he added silently, holding a bramble to stop it from whipping across Darren's face, and having done this once, felt obliged to hold back every branch, bramble, briar, nettle that he encountered. Unspoken words jumbled about in his head like plastic fragments in a broken kaleidoscope. From time to time he cleared his throat. Suddenly Darren had to stop short to avoid falling over Mr. Glenn's haunches, as he sank to his knees and seemed to be adoring something.

"Fly agaric," he breached, turning a face flushed with pleasure to the boy's.

Darren looked. A sort of half-eaten toadstool, curled up at the edges, red with white blotches.

"Is it poison?"

"Yes, it is. Very."

"Deadly poison?"

"It could be. Don't kick it."

"It was mouldy anyway. Do you think we'll find any Death Caps?"

"No."

After a few more minutes' silence trudging Mr. Glenn pointed to swags and garlands of green berries tinged with yellow looping the trees.

"Just imagine what it will be like in the autumn, the whole wood decked with necklaces of scarlet beads. This is white bryony, isn't it? I think it's black bryony that has the heart-shaped leaves. . . ."

"Are they poison?"

"Really Darren, anyone would think you intended to poison the whole school!"

He laughed uneasily when Darren did not reply and added quickly, "Those black berries are dogwood. They used to make arrows from it in the olden days."

"How could they make arrows from berries, sir?" Mr. Glenn sneaked a look at his watch. He reckoned lunch could be spun out for three-quarters of an hour, if he ate very slowly.

"Do you like them old-fashioned watches, sir? I've got a digital watch at home."

"Really. What's that you've found? Something interesting?" he said eagerly.

"Looks like an old pair of tights. Wonder how they got there?"

"I haven't the faintest idea," he blushed.

Darren was waving them about on the end of a stick.

"Funny place to leave a pair of tights."

"Do throw them away and come along!"

Mr. Glenn was anxious lest Darren root up something worse. Darren flung the tights into the air; they caught on a branch where they hung dangling—obscene and sinister empty legs.

"There's a little plateau just ahead where we can stop to have our lunch. I don't know about you, but I'm starving."

"I found a corset in a car park once, in Croydon."

"I say, a Roman snail!" Mr. Glenn bent gratefully over this piece of wildlife which sat obligingly in their path.

"Revolting."

"Oh, I think he's rather magnificent."

They stared at the moist granular body under the creamy swirls of shell, the glistening knobs on the ends of the horns, a tiny green leaf disappearing into its mouth.

"Revolting eating snails, I mean, I couldn't, could you, sir? I bet that's what they're doing now—eating snails and frogs' legs, and getting drunk, I bet, knocking back the old vino."

Jealous venom frothed like garlic butter through Darren's teeth. He leaped at a liana hanging from an ancient honeysuckle.

"I bet Miss Guilfoyle enjoys a drink, don't you, sir? And Mr. Dumbrell."

He swung gibbering four inches from the ground, his glasses lewd blank disks of malice.

Mr. Glenn's shorts crushed out a sharp scent of thyme as he sat down, the warm grass tickled his legs pleasantly. Behind them rose the chalk face, now more like a wedding cake with green icing than a bride and below them the valley: river, church spire, village and fields and beyond them the town.

"Magnificent view."

"It's a bit, well, rural, innit?" said Darren critically.

"For goodness sake, Cheeseman. Mind where you put your feet—you're treading on a harebell. You wanted to come on this flaming ramble."

He reached for his rucksack, his hands shaking with anger.

"Did I?"

When Darren had realized that no one else had signed on for the ramble, pride had not allowed him to admit that he did not want to go, or to apply to the school for financial help toward the trip to Boulogne on which he wanted passionately to go; it would have been pointless to ask his father for the money. He had intended not to turn up at school that morning and spend the day wandering around the town, eat his lunch in the rec., perhaps do a little shoplifting; but as ill-luck would have it, his father, on his way to buy cigarettes, had walked him to the bus-stop and several of his classmates had been on the bus. So here he was stuck halfway up a hill with this berk in shorts bleating about harebells.

"I don't believe it. I do not believe it." Mr. Glenn was scrabbling in his rucksack; out came Proust, out came a thermos flask, out came a first-aid kit, out came Darren's carrier bag.

"I seem to have forgotten my lunch," he had to admit at last, handing Darren his.

A forlorn tableau of bran rolls bulging with salad, yogurt, two apples, one red, one green and a bar of chocolate floated before his eyes. He licked his chops as he watched Darren bite into an oblong of white bread. He unscrewed his thermos, and poured a stream of clear hot water into the cup; he had forgotten to put in the tea. After a few minutes he moved closer to Darren.

"That looks tasty."

Darren pushed the bag toward him.

"May I? That's awfully kind. What's in them?"

"Those are ketchup, and those are ketchup and salad cream."

"Super," said Mr. Glenn faintly. As he sank his teeth into the flaccid, oozing bread, he noticed a little blue dot of mould on the crust.

"Can I offer you a little hot water in exchange?" he asked hoping for another sandwich.

"S'all right, thanks, I've got some shandy," said Darren and drank it. Mr. Glenn watched him pour the last few drops onto the grass as he sipped his water.

Darren stood up. "See you in a minute," he said.

"Right. Don't get lost."

Mr. Glenn went in the opposite direction. When he returned Darren was not back. He stole a sandwich and lay back luxuriating in Darren's absence and watched a bee rummaging in a knapweed's rough purple wheel and took up his book to avoid the memory of a wasp.

The shadow of a cloud fell on his page; he looked up expecting to see white sails on the sea at Balbec and was surprised to find himself on grass not sand, and realized that Darren had not returned and jumped up and pushed his way through the wayfaring trees into which the boy had disappeared. Little tracks ran in all directions. He whirled like a demented humming top, seeing Darren lying at the bottom of a crevasse, then launched himself forward, fighting twigs and brambles. Suddenly he heard very faint music ahead and burst through the bushes, half expecting to come upon Pan or some satyr or faun piping in the glade.

Darren lay stretched at ease, his head against a white rock, his eyes closed, a corkscrew of smoke spiralling into the blue from a cigarette between the fingers of one languid hand, while the other beat time to the music of a tiny radio. Mr. Glenn, calcified with rage, the frustrations of the morning whirling like furies in his brain, stood and stared. Then he tiptoed toward the erstwhile faun.

"I say!"

As he turned at the shout something heavy hurled itself at his shins and he felt a sharp pain in the seat of his shorts; he howled and danced clutching his torn shorts and rubbing his bruised, perhaps broken, legs. Two golden retrievers leaped around him barking, clawing his chest and arms, thrusting hard yellow heads into his face, while he flailed feebly at them and Darren sat laughing.

"Cindy! Bella! Down!"

With a last snap they writhed in a yellow heap at his feet. Two navy blue figures in denim skirts and T-shirts were sliding down the chalk toward them.

"Do you know this man?" one demanded of Darren, who was fondling a dog.

"Madam, do you take me for a denizen of Gomorrah?" said Mr. Glenn.

"I beg your pardon?" She bristled at a suspected insult.

"Do you know this man?" repeated her friend.

Mr. Glenn waited for Darren to say, "I've never seen him before in my life."

"Tell her, Darren."

At last Cheeseman looked up from tying the dog's ears in a bow on top of its head.

"He's my teacher," he said. "Mr. Glenn. Whitcombe School."

"Well, if you're sure. . . ."

"Funny sort of teacher, encouraging a child to smoke. . . ."

"Oh, that's the sort of thing they teach them at school these days, didn't you know? They're all Marxists and sociologists. . . ."

"We're on a nature ramble," said Mr. Glenn with dignity, backing away with his hand on his shorts.

"Come along, Darren. We're going to look for fossils."

Darren was reluctant to leave the dogs.

"Who's a good boy then? Good dog! Aren't they nice dogs, sir?"

"Bitches," corrected his teacher loudly.

"We had a dog once," began Darren conversationally, "but he had to. . . ."

"Shut up, you little creep, and walk in front of me."

"This looks a likely place," he said stopping at the foot of a glossy glacier of chalk. "Let's have a nose around here." The chalk felt dry and silky under their feet. "Don't go too high."

"Found one!" shouted Darren at once.

"Let's have a look. No, I'm afraid not," he had to add, reluctant to disappoint.

"What about this one then?" holding up an equally undistinguished lump of chalk.

"I don't think so. Have another look."

Darren hurled his stone at the cliff face causing a small avalanche. Mr. Glenn grubbed silently. Black clouds smudged the sun.

"I say, Darren! I think I've—yes, it is—it's part of an ammonite!" He looked around. Some thirty feet above him, clinging to the stump of a scrubby bush, was Darren.

"Come down at once," he croaked.

Darren turned and waved, then gripped again the bending stem; a stream of stones trickled from each foot. He scrabbled up a little higher resting one foot against the bush.

"Darren! Come down. It's dangerous! If you don't come down at once I'm putting you in Detention!"

Darren inched upward.

"Right! You're in Detention!" His voice rose to a squeak. He felt his own feet tingle, his knees wobbled and he felt the ground sway as he looked upward. He shook his head hard and the landscape righted itself. Darren had not moved. There was nothing above him to grasp.

"Are you stuck?"

Darren, crouched on the chalk face, was paralyzed and dumb.

Glenn looked around wildly—the navy-blue ladies—anybody; only a useless black crow flapping wildly into a black bush high above.

"Hold on. I'm coming up—" he had to shout. Despite his stout socks and boots Mr. Glenn suffered acutely if he had to stand on a chair to change a light bulb. . . . He set off on all fours up the scree, keeping his eyes fixed on white stones, with plants too shallow-rooted to grasp, his shirt stuck to his back, slowly, slowly, toe-holds crumbling under his boots. A fine drizzle glazed the chalk, little lumps slipped under his fingers.

"It's all a question of momentum," he muttered. "Just keep going forward, don't stop, don't look down."

A little rock hit him on the forehead and then Darren hurtled past screaming. Glenn snatched at him and caught his sleeve; his fingers tightened on the bone in the skinny arm; he took his whole weight in one hand and pulled him up beside him, to hold him in so close an embrace that he saw a smudge of dried salad cream fringing his lip. Instinctively, he put up his hand to wipe his own mouth, lost his grip on the chalk and started to slide. Darren tried to pull him back but was dragged down himself. The radio fell from Darren's pocket and bounced down the stones. Teacher and pupil, a tangle of arms and legs, slithered, a grotesque terrified spider, after it. Glenn, catching a tuft of tough grass, dared look down; they were only ten feet from the ground. He guided Darren's fingers to a tiny ledge and placed his foot in a hollow. So they continued their unheroic descent.

At the foot Glenn sat down heavily on a heap of stones, his arms around his shuddering legs. Between his boots he saw the cracked blue case of Darren's radio; he picked it up; a battery rolled away.

"I'm afraid it's broken."

Darren snatched it, then threw it down and stamped on it, grinding the plastic and blue and orange wires into the chalk.

"Don't matter," he said. "It's only a cheap old thing. I've gotta Walkman at home."

"Like your digital watch," thought Mr. Glenn.

As they sat on the bus Mr. Glenn, his knees still shaking, gloomily composed tomorrow's essay: "A Ramble on the Downs," Darren Cheeseman, 2G.

"The best bit about the ramble was when I found a pair of old tights. Mr. Glenn got bit on the bum by a dog, then I got stuck up a cliff and my radio got smashed. Then we went home. Tired but happy at the end of a perfect day."

They stood on the drizzly pavement looking at each other, the two wets, chalk-stained, damp, grazed, bleeding in their ruined clothes.

"There's no point in going back to school now," said Mr. Glenn. "We can make our separate ways home from here."

Darren stared past him through his rainy glasses; Mr. Glenn followed his gaze to the hill far away, a white cake iced in vicious green; bland, treacherous, impossibly high, but conquered. Suddenly Darren shot out an awkward fist and punched Mr. Glenn lightly on the arm.

"See ya then, Glenda."

Mr. Glenn punched clumsily back.

"See ya, Cheesey."

FAMILY SERVICE

"I am going to remain very calm." Then a scream like a demon came out of her mouth.

"Is nobody in this house but me capable of putting away a cereal packet? Look at this tablecloth! There's milk and sugar all over it. And the floor! I don't know why I bother—if I come into this kitchen one more time and find the sink full of dishes, I'll—"

Helen Brigstock clamped her hand over her mouth.

"Shut up, shut up, shut up," she told herself. Her teeth fought against her fingers; she felt a painful bite as teeth met flesh. A cannonade of church bells exploded faintly beyond the steamed up window.

Now, as when a child, Helen saw Sunday written in gold. But today how bleared and smeared and tarnished the letters. Her bulgy self, her unsatisfactory family. The sun, in a cone of dancing dust, struck grease and crumb, her distorted face reflected in the spotted kettle, highlighting every failure.

The day that had started so well had begun to go wrong when she made the mistake of stepping onto the bathroom scales as she dressed after breakfast. She would have to lose at least five pounds before Christmas and it was already the second Sunday in Advent. Scrambled egg and buttered toast weighed heavily on her as she finished dressing. If she didn't have any lunch . . . or any roast potatoes at least. . . .

The potatoes had provoked her fury. She had come down to the kitchen to prepare them so that they, and the chicken, could cook while the family was at church and just because she had left the breakfast table first everybody had decamped, leaving the kitchen in a state of unbelievable squalor and the sink full of dishes that she would have to wash before she could peel the potatoes. She heaved a sodden saucepan from the washing-up bowl. Scummy scrambled egg wrecked her nail polish as she scrubbed. She would have no time to repair it. She almost told the church bells to shut up.

She turned the hot tap on hard to drown the image of her mother, her father and herself, arms linked, walking over a frosty field to church. Then there had been time to study the crystals on a leaf or frozen spider's web; once a fox had run past them, stopped, turned back and stared them full in the face.

At last, the faceted potatoes ranged whitely around the pink chicken in the oven, Helen ran upstairs to the bedroom.

"I don't believe it! I don't believe it!" A fat ladder had sprung up her new tights leaving her leg grinning through the rungs. She tore off the tights and started raking madly through a drawer, throwing things on the floor.

The piercing notes of a recorder transfixed her, stabbing tears from her eyes as she listened. Julian, her son, in his innocent way had reminded her of what Sunday was all about. Helen stood, with pastel underwear like sugared almonds round her feet. What did clothes matter?—as long as one had some on, of course. What did it matter if she was overweight? She had so much to be grateful for, her health and strength, one should just be glad that one had enough to eat. When one thought of the starving black millions. . . . Anyway, she could easily lose five pounds by Christmas.

Helen set off along the passage to Julian's room. She would sit on his bed and say, "Julian, I want to thank you. With your music you have just taught Mummy a valuable lesson. Oh yes, you have, darling. I know you think Mummy knows everything, but sometimes it takes a little boy to. . . ."

She tapped on, and opened, his bedroom door.

"Darling—What on earth do you think you're doing, lying on your bed, not even dressed, playing that stupid thing? Have you any idea of the time?"

Her eye caught a toy snake at the foot of the bed.

"You little reptile," she shouted. "You've got no consideration—get dressed at once! Have you forgotten that you're supposed to be reading a prayer in church or does it mean nothing to you?"

Julian had been named, secretly, after the eldest boy in the Famous Five books, a tall, well-spoken boy. This Julian, at eleven, was small for his age, and whatever they taught them at Pembury Court, and sometimes Helen wondered what it was, it certainly wasn't how to speak properly.

"Besides," she heard her own terrible voice go on, "that tune you were playing—if you were to read your Bible, I think you'd find that not only did Jesus never say that He was Lord of the Dance, but also that there is no record of Him ever having danced. . . ."

Mother and son, he lying on his back in pajama trousers, recorder dangling from his lip, stared at each other until Helen dropped her eyes and slammed out of the room to fling herself with a dry sob onto her own bed, biting the duvet.

"Pull yourself together, Brigstock!" she told herself sharply. "This won't do!"

She found a pair of intact tights and pulled them on. They came up as far as her bra.

"It doesn't matter." So what if they should roll down making an ugly ridge at the waistband of her skirt. "You're going to church to worship God. It doesn't matter what you look like." When the zip of her boot caught a mouthful of plump calf in its teeth, she didn't scream, so that she felt she had got the upper hand. Standing in the bedroom doorway, she shouted:

"Girls! Are you nearly ready? We've got to leave in eight minutes!"

"No answer came the stern reply," she said aloud, wryly. Where on earth was Roger?

"Roger?"

No answer from her husband. Oh, honestly!

"Roger!"

"I'm in the bathroom."

"Well, could you please hurry up! There are other people in this house besides you. Jane! Hannah! Are you two ready?"

She stumped along to Jane's room, stooping angrily from time to time to pick up pieces of fluff, thread, hair, that glared up from the red carpet. When she flung open Jane's door it was with a great gobbet, like some disgusting domestic owl's pellet, in her hand.

Jane lay face downward on her bed reading, presenting an extremely irritating pair of jeans to her mother.

"Jane, what on earth do you think you're doing?"

"I'm just having my Quiet Time."

"Your Quiet Time! I wish I had time to have a Quiet Time! If you really think you're virtuous lying there reading the Bible while your mother washes up and peels potatoes and picks up filth from the floor—you could at least read the proper version instead of that unpoignant rubbish with its silly drawings, do you want to reduce The Greatest Story Ever Told to a strip cartoon? Well, do you? And if, if. . . ."

Again Helen wished that someone would silence it, but the dreadful voice went on.

". . . if you've got any ideas about having 'chosen the better part,' forget them. I'd like to get hold of every single copy of that so-called 'Good-News Bible' and rip out the story of Martha and Mary. Talk about Unfair!"

Jane sat up, her fair hair falling back from her face.

"Sorry, Mom. Is there anything you'd like me to do?"

"Do? Do? Yes, you can get out the hoover and—oh, forget it—it's too late. Just get ready! And couldn't you put on a pretty dress for once instead of those awful jeans?"

Jane's voice was hurt.

"You said you liked them. . . ."

"I do—it's just—oh—"

Helen stood helplessly in the doorway, the wad of fluff greasy in her sweating hand, then crashed out of the room. She collided with Roger in the passage.

"Darling?"

She pulled past without answering. She locked herself in the bathroom and collapsed on the dirty-linen basket, head in hands, rocking backwards and forwards. "Oh God, I don't want to be like this. Please help me."

"Mommy?"

A loud knocking on the door.

"Go away. Just go away," she muttered.

"Mommy, are you in there?"

Helen flung open the door.

Little Hannah stood, a dramatic figure in vest and knickers.

"Mommy, it's not fair. Jane's allowed to go to church in jeans, so why can't I?"

"Not fair? Not fair?" screamed her mother. "Is it fair that there are splashes of toothpaste all over the bathroom floor and the dirty-linen basket is full of dirty clothes that no one but I will wash and that everyone else will expect to reappear miraculously clean and ironed? Is that fair?"

Hannah fled.

Helen heard Roger rattling the car keys.

"Oh, shut up!"

She stared at herself in the mirror—pale, red-eyed, her hair jumping at the comb in a mad electric mass. If only Father and Mother weren't watching. . . .

At last they were all in the car and Roger switched on the ignition. Helen turned around, deliberately calm.

"Got your prayer, Ju?"

"Yeah, it's here." He fluttered a gray piece of paper towards her.

"Good boy. Stop the car! Roger, stop!"

"What now? He's got his prayer."

"His nails! Get out of the car, Julian! His nails are disgusting! He's not standing up in church reading a prayer with nails like that!"

"There isn't time. We'll never get a parking space if we don't leave now." Roger pulled out.

"If anyone ever, except me, did anything, we wouldn't have this rush every Sunday."

"I did stack the dishes for you," came Roger's mild voice from his complacent baggy polo-neck sweater.

"For me? For me? You make it sound as if they were all my dishes—"

"Well, actually, darling, if you remember, your mother gave them to us on our—"

"Don't you drag my mother into this!"

"No one will see Julian's nails." Jane attempted to arbitrate.

"God will."

The church forecourt was jammed with the cars of the wise virgins The Brigstocks were forced to park in a side street and arrived panting on the long path through the gravestones.

Roger put his hand on Helen's arm; she shook it off.

"Couldn't you have put on a tie? I don't subscribe to this jeans and shirt-sleeves religion. Now we'll never get a decent pew—"

"Calm down, darling."

The peal of the bell had changed to a rapid commanding single note.

"It's the Hurry-Up Bell," said Hannah hanging heavily on her mother's arm, who wouldn't look at her, as if it had not been she who had invented the term in the children's earliest years.

"We'll be stuck behind the choirstalls again. Julian, get off that grave, there are dead people in them, you know! Of course, if some people didn't spend three hours in the bathroom—that reminds me, I must put air freshener on my shopping list."

"You know scrambled egg always upsets my stomach," said Roger.

She saw that she had managed to wound him, too, at last.

"That's the thanks I get for preparing a nice family breakfast."

"Hi."

Sylvia, her friend, loomed up behind a mausoleum.

Helen cracked her dry face into a smile.

"Beautiful morning," she said.

"Beautiful," agreed Sylvia, "if one happens to like paintings by Rowland Hilder," and laughed as she overtook them.

Trust her. Why did she always have to try to say something clever? Helen wondered why they were friends. Anyway, surely Sylvia must have seen that Rowland Hilder snowscape with sheep a hundred times on the lounge wall? Then, suddenly cheered by the sight of her friend's immense bum swaying in peasant skirt above cowboy boots, she felt her own excess pounds fall from her, although her tights threatened to sag or bag. The frosty grass glittered, the path shone blue, the names of the dead were picked out in rhinestones and fool's gold.

She put an arm through Roger's and Julian's and pulled them to a halt.

"I'm sorry I was so ratty, darlings. It's just that—"

Hannah screamed.

On the path in front of them lay a dead blue-tit. The family stood staring down at it. It lay, tiny, frozen; blue and saffron leaking into the melting path.

"Will you bury it, Daddy?"

"There isn't time, darling."

"We could put it in that tomb over there, look there's a hole in the side," suggested Julian.

"Don't be so ridiculous," snapped his mother.

Julian shrugged.

"But, Daddy." Hannah raised tearful eyes. "Someone might not see it and—and—walk on it!"

"Daddy told you, there isn't time! Maybe on the way out."

"Just because you don't care about a poor little dead bird.

Well, I think God's cruel to let a poor little bird die in His own graveyard!"

"It's all part of His plan, darling." Roger attempted to lift his rigid daughter, whose shoes were glued to the path. "We can't expect to understand. He sees the meanest sparrow. . . ."

"It's a blue-tit."

"Oh God." Julian strode on ahead.

"I've told you not to say 'God.' Especially on a Sunday."

Helen thumped her son between the shoulder blades of his school blazer, which had cost twenty-three pounds, although to look at the state of it you'd never guess. Behind her, she heard Roger's voice, infected by her, a hideous parody of her own.

"Will you stop sniveling, Hannah? Close your mouth! Did you clean your teeth this morning? They look like—like—mossy tombstones!"

"Well, I suppose everyone's forgotten that I'm supposed to be reading this bloody prayer," said Julian as the Brigstocks entered the church and almost snatched their books from the smiling sidesman. They found a vacant pew near the back.

"Mommy, can I go and sit with—"

"Of course you can't! We'll all sit together!"

Then she realized that Jane had sloped off to sit with her friends. . . .

She slumped heavily onto her seat.

"Of course, I'm parked behind a pillar!" thought Helen. She pretended not to notice that Roger was silently offering to change places and sank her knees on the cold stone floor, the clumsily broidered hassock swinging on its hook. She waited for the familiar peace to descend. Nothing happened. Her ruined hands writhed in her gloves. She became aware of Julian shoving up against her. She opened an eye to glare at him. An old lady was mopping and mowing, in a faint scent of lavender water and mothballs, her way into the pew. Why did old ladies insist on wearing musty velour jelly-molds on their heads? Helen sat up. The choir was coming in.

"Let us sit, or kneel, to pray."

Typical! Typical! She assumed that it was meant as a dispensation to the aged or handicapped; but half this casual congregation found sitting the best position in which to address its God. Well, she just jolly well hoped that God would prove as easygoing at the Judgement Day! Instead of closing her eyes, Helen stared at a window. The shadow of birds' wings flickered across the stained glass and fluttered on a pillar. A bowl of forced daffodils and honesty on the sill—the stained glass, the birds—sudden tears dissolved the lump in her heart making it warm and stringy like melted mozzarella.

"We have left undone those things which we ought to have done, and we have done those things which we ought not to have done—" said a voice in her head.

She had screamed at Julian's bare chest, which she so loved, with its pretty little bones, instead of offering him moral support when he was probably very nervous. She had shouted at him for not reading the Bible, and at Jane for reading the Bible, and at Hannah, and at Roger. . . .

Helen prayed that the prayers would go on until she was composed and had found a tissue.

"I'm sorry, Daddy," she prayed.

The congregation came to itself. Helen concealed a sniff in the shifting of knees. She hoped that she would have a chance to repair, secretly, her face before she had to greet the vicar at the church door in the brutal Sunday sunshine.

At a given signal, Julian left her side and walked nonchalantly up the aisle. He stood at the front of the church, on the chancel steps.

"Dear God," he began, as if reading a thank-you letter written to some obscure uncle. "We thank you for our Homes and Families, our Mothers and Fathers."

Helen heard no more; her eyes and ears were blocked with tears. Dimly she saw the sun streaming through stained glass tinting hair and ears ruby and emerald—Julian's ears, wonderful emerald transparent organs, his moist ruby mouth. Flesh; vulgar, beautiful—the choir sang an iridescent anthem.

The sermon came as an anticlimax. Advent. Helen tried to recapture her feelings, but they were gone, like the sun, which had disappeared, leaving the church dull and cold. Christmas—Helen heard only a panicky ripping of wrapping paper and the snickering Scotch tape.

"Stop sniffing," she whispered savagely at Hannah and thrust her own wet tissue in a sodden ball into her lap.

Outside the church Helen felt pincers on her arm. She looked. The old lady who had pushed into their pew had laid a black glove on her coat sleeve.

"Such a nice little family," she was saying. "I see you every Sunday."

Helen smiled. "I do think it's important for a family to worship together," she said.

The Brigstocks piled into the car and drove home to eat some pieces of a dead bird, which would have been browning nicely if Helen had switched on the oven.

SOFT VOLCANO

"There is nothing like the sound of children singing hymns for deceiving us into thinking that there is some hope for mankind."

So thought Rose Rossi as emanations of goodness came from the grey and green pullovers of the children on the virginia-creeper-wreathed, hop-entwined stage. Shrill recorders pierced the wooden rafters and played havoc with strained parents' voices and left them straying somewhere round the children's heads. The Harvest bread began to wobble and red apples were swelling and doubling their number.

Richard Garlick heard a raindrop fall on the mimeographed songsheet of the woman next to him. He looked at the window; it was closed. So far, aware of Janet on his left, he had sensed the woman on his right only as a brown velvet sleeve, a ringed hand, a shiny brown shoe, vague red clouds of hair. He turned his head slightly and saw the words on her paper all blurred and starting to run. She must have known what to expect, yet she had come unarmed with handkerchief or tissue. Women's tears usually irritated him, but these which rolled down steadily and motivelessly set up an answering pricking in his own eyes. Janet nudged him and thrust a couple of tissues into his hand. He placed them on the brown velvet knee.

"You know who that was?" Janet whispered in the playground as parents and children massed and blocked the narrow iron gate.

"Duncan Rossi's ex-wife, remember she bought the Mill House last year? You know, the racing driver!"

The divorcée passed them, pale and with pink-rimmed eyes, holding by the hand a red-haired boy. Then Gary and Mark hurled themselves on them and had to be zipped into anoraks and the family went home to the house beside the general store and sub-post office which Richard had inherited from his father.

There was the usual nine-fifteen rush in the shop the next morning, of mothers who had delivered their children to school. Mrs. Rossi drifted in on the tail-end, in a fur coat and muddy jeans, her dog, tied to the hook outside, howled loudly and tried to spring through the door every time a customer entered or left the shop. She asked Richard to cash a check and ordered a lot of groceries to be delivered to the Mill House. She gave no sign of recognition and Richard said nothing.

The sale of the Mill House had been negotiated the previous January, just before her divorce. The car had squelched up the path through the little wood. Duncan at the wheel with a hangover, herself sulking beside him and James in the back with a cold. She had looked at the grey house, the stone heron overlooking the millpond full of yellow leaves, hanks of dun grass, thin blackening nettles, rasping teazels, tangled English melancholy, and thought, "This will do very well."

Since then she and the boy had been abroad and it was just a few days since they had taken up residence there, and been surprised by the reddening leaves of the sumach trees in front of the house. All else that remained of cultivation were the Michaelmas daisies and papery disks of honesty. Half a mile up the river that fed their sluggish pond, among brambles' barbed arches and hollow hemlock stems and dried seed heads rattling in the wind, stood a hexagonal concrete pillbox, relic of the war, of which there were many on the North Downs. James had discovered it and intended to occupy it, taking with him matches and food. The entrance turned at a tangent into blackness. The smell drove him back. For a few minutes he stood outside, despising himself, then suddenly turned and fled home, as if a dead Nazi soldier had risen with a rusty bullet hole in his rotted uniform and was pursuing him stiffly and bloodlessly through the wood.

The scarlet sumachs were blazing like sunset at the top of the path. Richard had left the new Cortina Estate at the foot to save the tires from the sharp stones embedded in deep leaf-falls, and was carrying a heavy carton of groceries. As he walked two bottles clinked together and the gold and colorless liquid slopped in their necks. He thought he heard voices ahead of him and an animal tearing through the undergrowth; Mrs. Rossi's bloodhound bitch who left a lemon tang in the misty air. As he followed the citronella trail of antimate through the little wood he heard Mrs. Rossi's voice clearly,

"Yes, darling, they are beautiful, but poisonous." As he passed through their gate he saw a rope of red and green bryony berries looped over the hedge. The boy had disappeared when Richard arrived at the back door.

"Oh it's you, Mr. Garlick, stalking us through the woods. I was quite sure it was a murderer. It's so quiet here in the afternoons."

"I don't think you'll find many murderers in these parts, Mrs. Rossi," he said, putting down the carton on the kitchen table. There were a couple of chairs, several tea chests.

"Settling in now, are you?"

"Not really," she said, and made no mention of payment, and

Richard, wispy-haired with glasses, known in secret moments to his wife as Bunny, didn't like to.

"Thank you very much Mr. Garlick."

"Right then, I'll be off."

"By the way, I should thank you for the tissues yesterday. It was nice of you."

"It was nothing."

Neither seemed capable of dislodging him. At last the bloodhound came to their rescue, rushing in and propelling him with huge forepaws through the open door.

"Richard! That's the third time Gary's asked you to help him with his model!"

"What? Oh. Right, son, let's be having you!" He rubbed his hands together in simulated eagerness and advanced towards the little pieces of grey plastic.

Because he was in the shop most of the day, Richard was in the position, if he so wanted, of sociologist or chronicler of local mores. He had noticed, over the last year or so, that the topic of property values and house prices, the plight of young couples, discussed in unctuous tones by those who had achieved their mortgage, had given way to the subject of extensions. Janet, behind the little post office grille, among the stamps and leaflets, had been fired by all the talk, and now nothing would do but the loft must be converted into a den for the boys. Richard was sent up a ladder to clear it of junk in readiness for the men who were coming to give an estimate of cost. What Janet termed "junk" were the dear furnishings of his boyhood, among them glass jars powdered with sherbet crystals and sweet splinters, a cabinet of glass-fronted doors, and a long, bevelled mirror with dark green glass corners and Fry's Cocoa in chocolate colored letters across its face.

They were eased downstairs and placed, with a pang, outside the shop to await the dustmen. Richard saw his father's watery eye glinting in the mirror and longed for the evidence of his betrayal to be gone. He had hardly spoken to Janet during breakfast.

The dust-cart's dusty buzz was growing louder. Richard sat at the checkout and watched rain accessorize after the fact by blurring the glass and spotting the wood. The shop door crashed open and Mrs. Rossi stood there, soaked, bareheaded, accusing.

"You're not consigning those beautiful things to the dustmen!" she stated. "How much do you want for them?"

"You can have them," he said surprised.

"Don't be silly. Any antique dealer would snap them up."

Janet, who had emerged from behind her bars, was beaten back by a rush for Family Allowances and could manage only a twisting scornful finger at her temple over her customers' heads.

"They're yours if you take them away."

"Right," she said, "I will."

She went out into the rain and attempted to lift a corner of the cabinet but was forced to straighten up, red-faced and defeated. She pulled the mirror away from the wall it leant on and was almost knocked backwards by its weight.

"I'll hire a van," she said.

The dust-cart was drawing up.

"I'll bring them up this afternoon," he heard himself say. "I can borrow a van."

His reward was the first real smile he had had from her. They went inside.

"Can I talk to you?" she suddenly said quickly. "I've no

friends here. I sensed, I hope I'm right, that you are not badly disposed towards me."

The shop door jarred, a woman came in, took a wire basket, and after making some decisions, was caught agonizingly between the choice of tomato or fruity sauce. Mrs. Rossi hovered at the cheese display.

"Let me persuade you," said Richard at last, rising and plucking a bottle of ketchup from the shelf and depositing it in the woman's basket, her mouth open at his unwonted masterfulness.

"I'll have the other," she said, replacing his bottle. Two more people came in while she was at the checkout.

"I'll see you later," said Mrs. Rossi, giving up hope and leaving. The bell clanged behind her.

"That's him," said Mrs. Rossi. They were in the sitting room, where the Fry's Cocoa mirror had been propped against the wall. It was carpeted in green but otherwise was not much more settled than the kitchen, where the glass cabinet and glass sweet jars had been put, and James could be heard clashing a long spoon about in the jars scraping up the sweet sediment. She held out a framed photograph to Richard, of a black curly-haired man in oily overalls, grinning in a crooked laurel-wreath. Richard recognized the face from newspaper and television.

"He's always been a heavy drinker, but he could always get in shape in time for a big race. Lately he's been getting worse and worse. You know he hasn't won anything since the American Grand Prix. He has terrible rages. He's an ice cream Italian Scot," she added by way of explanation.

"If ever I told James off, he'd say 'Mommy doesn't love you, only Daddy does.' Can you imagine? Now I keep having the feeling that he's somewhere around. That he's watching us. He wanted James at the time you know. He's often threatened to kill me."

She was walking around the room, ran her finger along the windowsill, seemed defeated by dust, and sat down.

"I'm not dependent on him for money," she said, "I've got some of my own."

Richard tried to keep his mind on her problem while watching her mouth move and wondering how it would feel to kiss it.

"Perhaps if you were to take a job?" he ventured. "Something part time, so you wouldn't have so much time to brood."

"Are you offering me a job?" she laughed. "In the shop? Would you give me a pale blue nylon overall?"

"My wife doesn't object to wearing one." Even to him it sounded childish and huffy.

She didn't answer.

The dog started to scratch violently. They sat listening to the whirring of claws on skin. At last, when it seemed the air between them must crack, a clock took breath and struck four and released him. He stood up.

"I'd better get back. I shouldn't worry about your ex-husband. He couldn't possibly be here. If you're worried about anything, call the police." He started for the door with the difficulty he always had when disengaging himself from her presence.

"The phone's not fixed yet," she said.

"I'll look in tomorrow if you like."

"Thank you very much," she said humbly, and walked through the house with him, and the garden, to the front gate, and down to the riverbank above the millpond.

"I remember a few years ago we had a particularly wet winter and this pond flooded and—"

He realized she wasn't listening and turned to see her staring at the river with horror on her face.

"What is it? What's the matter?"

She pointed at a whisky bottle in the brown oily water.

"It's his brand," she whispered.

The bottle did indeed look a sinister emissary bobbing in the water, sucked under the massed leaves in the pond. Light had gone from the sky.

"Nonsense," Richard told her firmly, "nonsense, it could have floated down from anywhere." He realized she was clutching his arm.

"Go in now, it's getting cold. I'll look in tomorrow. Why don't you get someone, a friend, to come and stay?"

"I have."

As he left her Richard had the distinct feeling that Mrs. Rossi was slightly crazy, deranged; perhaps by her divorce.

"You haven't forgotten that it's the stoolball AGM have you?" said Janet. "I'll be back by about ten, I expect."

Richard had supervised the boys' bath and they were playing in the bedroom. He went up to tell them to go to bed. Mark was fooling about with a pair of plastic binoculars.

"Let's have a look," said Richard. He hung them around his neck and went to the window.

"These could be very useful," he said. "For observing wildlife or spying on the neighbors." He put them to his eyes and adjusted the focus. They were surprisingly powerful and picked out the lighted panes of the village hall windows, stars and clouds in the black sky, the church spire against the moon. He raked them through the woods, up to the Mill House. Light shone in the sitting room and two upstairs windows. He looked beyond the house up river. From the black mass of the river bank rose a thin twist of grey smoke. Realization kicked him in the stomach. Someone was in the pillbox, watching the Mill House, waiting. Rossi.

"Come on, Daddy, let's have a go!" Richard handed back the glasses, feeling sick and sat on the bed. His immediate impulse was to rush out, up to the Mill House. Janet was out, he would have to wait until the boys were asleep. He hustled them into bed and kissed each tenderly, with the fear that he might not see them again, and went downstairs, put on coat and gloves, and waited. The thought came to him that it would be wiser to call the police, but he dismissed it. He had never in his life been called on to do anything even slightly frightening or dangerous; he was an eater of meals on time, a sleeper in soft beds, wearer of slippers. His only brush with fear was when Janet went into hospital to have the boys. He crept upstairs and removed the book from Gary's sleeping hand and straightened the Action Man on Mark's pillow. He checked the central heating and closed the front door quietly behind him.

He walked quickly through the village, meeting no one, and ran across the wet field and into the wood. Sharp stones pierced the soles of his shoes as he ran. Pain in his lungs bent him double on the front doorstep as he lifted a finger to the bell. It drilled through the house, then silence blotted its soundwaves. He rang again and again, desperately. Then realizing why she wouldn't answer, sensing her terror in the locked house, poked open the letter box to call through it. Iron choked his voice, his head swelled like a black balloon. He tried to claw the fingers from his throat, then swung his foot back and kicked hard where he sensed his attacker's legs were. It struck home, and Richard fell back against the door as the fingers fell away. Rossi was rolling on the ground, a knife beside him. Richard grabbed it and threw it in a weak shoulder-wrenching underarm. A splash sounded. Rossi was rising. Richard pulled back his fist, shutting his eyes, and cracked it on to his jaw, and again. Pain jarred up his arm. He took off his glove to suck his knuckle, and realized that Rossi had been overcome not just by his blows but by the alcohol whose fumes were being pumped in reeking gusts from his panting body. He pulled himself up and stumbled through the front garden. Richard sat on the step, wiping his glasses which he hadn't thought to remove. Rossi belched as he disappeared. This crude eructation hanging in the night sky filled Richard with rage against him and his terrorizing of Rose. He set off after him. His footsteps spurred Rossi into a lurching run. He turned not right, into the wood, but left along the lane that led to the sand quarry. For a moment Richard saw him spreadeagled against the high wire fence like an escaping prisoner, then he was over. Richard found the gate and climbed to the top, jumped and fell into soft sand. A ghostly convoy of bulldozers stood. Rossi was running across the flat towards pale mountains of sand. A high wooden building on stilts bulked against the sky. The word "corrosive" glittered in the moonlight on a rusty tank. Richard lost Rossi in the white sandscape, his shoes were full and heavy, he stopped running and stood, air swirling around him like black ectoplasm, his heart banging, yet he was not afraid.

Suddenly he knew that it was Rossi's fear, not his own that he felt, and that Rossi was very near. He knew his enemy and Rossi did not. For all he knew Richard might be a fiend from hell. Rossi stumbled around the base of a sandhill. Richard started after him, his joints moved slickly, blood oiling his muscles. He was gaining on Rossi and could hear sawing breaths in his chest. Rossi took a despairing look over his shoulder and made for a giant crane or dinosaur whose neck stretched out some thirty feet over the highest mountain. Thick raindrops were pitting the sand. Richard reached the crane and saw Rossi climb over the cab and onto the monster's neck. The rungs must have been greasy with rain, but Rossi climbed on towards the top, where he must surely be trapped, and crawled dark and terrified against the sky.

Richard was suddenly sick of it all.

"I'm going home!" he shouted. "Come down."

The only words used between them. He turned to go, as if ground was falling away from his own tingling feet, arms tearing from their sockets, chest caving with the altitude. As, ground spinning under him, he turned to see if Rossi was descending, he saw him hanging, kicking wildly from the crane, kicking, struggling to hook his legs back up. His legs went still, he dangled, his fingers slowly opened out and he plummeted silently into the heart of the soft volcano. Rivers of sand ran down the sides, trickled and stopped.

Richard stood in the rain. He looked around at the sandscape undisturbed under the moon, the still machinery. There was nothing to be done. To reach Rossi he too must leap from the crane and suffocate in sand. Help would be too late.

He turned and ran.

While the bath was running he stood in the clouds of steam shaking every grain of sand from his socks and shoes, and all his clothes into the basin. Rain without and steam within; he lay back in the water and watched the black window pane liquify. The rims of his nails were greenish with packed sand. He took the nailbrush.

Janet's key twisted in the lock; he attempted a snatch of the St. Matthew Passion, but his throat choked up as if with sand.

"We've been asked to a party tomorrow," came Janet's voice.

Luckily, it was Wednesday. Rose Rossi didn't come in in the morning and the shop closed in the afternoon. Alone in the house, goldenrod beckoning like false blond women at the window, Richard saw how trees soughed and leaves fell, the church clock struck and cars passed, the world went on and the loss of one of its sons in a sandhill seemed to matter not at all. So this is all we are worth, he thought. None of us matters at all.

Married couples were jogging around the through-lounge of the party givers' house. The host claimed Janet, and Richard moved towards the lush buffet. He became aware of a strange noise below the music, a sort of drone. He looked around and saw that all the couples were singing the words of the songs of their youth, slightly behind the record, and Janet, eyes closed, was murmuring them too, and he only wanted to be with Rose Rossi. He went through to the kitchen.

"Do you remember," a woman was saying, "how, at parties when we were young, someone was always sick, and someone lost a shoe?"

"And when they put the lights out, all the girls had to sit on a boy's knee and 'snog,' whether they wanted to or not?" said another.

"Just getting a breath of fresh air," said Richard as he passed unnoticed through the back door.

He drove up to the Mill House, not caring any longer about his tires, and was shocked by a strange car parked outside the gate. He was furious; he kicked his tire. Her friend must have come. He walked around the house, wondering what excuse he could give for arriving. Outside the sitting room window he stopped.

There, caught in the Fry's Cocoa mirror were Rose and her friend. The friend's hair was pulled back in Rose Rossi's grasp as she kissed her mouth.

He wandered around the woods, sent stones crashing into the millpond and disturbed no one. Eventually, frozen, he drove back to the party. The smell of black coffee hit him as he walked in. Janet was in the kitchen seated on a stool with her head in her chest. He shook her shoulder, she looked up at him sideways and mumbled,

"I've lost my shoe."

THE
STAINED-GLASS DOOR

Jean MacAllister's rather large white face, which had hung soft and dreamy in the steam of her drinking chocolate, hardened as she turned from the kitchen window.

"She's out there again."

Nigel MacAllister yawned; scratching his chest, catching his finger in a gray curl.

"She's probably lonely. Bored. Anyway she'll be gone soon. You know how those people come and go. . . ."

"She doesn't. She's going in now, grinding out a cigarette with her foot. That lawn must be knee-deep in cigarette butts."

"If you can call it a lawn anymore."

"It was such a lovely garden. You'd think the Council. . . ."

Nigel yawned again; he had heard it all before—that beautiful house, the mirror image of their own, taken over by the Council; the blanket looped across the window instead of curtains, the rusting cars, the broken glass, the language. He gave his wife a slap, almost too hard, as she hung the washed mugs on their hooks.

"Come on then, or we won't get up in the morning."

They went upstairs.

"Nigel—is anything wrong?"

"I told you, I've got problems at work."

"Actually, you didn't."

As the sound of a plane ebbed in the darkness a rumbling came from Nigel's side of the bed and Jean's stomach gave a timid answering bleat. She could have felt sorry for those two stomachs had they lain side by side in white bloody trays in a butcher's window, which was how, for a moment, she saw them.

The following evening when Jean arrived home from her upholstery class with her little hammer, bristling with tacks, although nothing in that house needed re-upholstering—there were no children or animals to kick and claw, not even any visiting nieces and nephews—she stood for a moment looking at the sky. A jeweled insect was homing in on Gatwick through the stars. The house next door was in darkness, but the girl in the downstairs flat had neglected to pull down the blanket across the window and Jean saw her, in the light of a streetlamp, asleep on a divan, hair spread out, thumb in mouth.

As on almost every morning, Jean stood at the head of the stairs, restored and reassured by her house; the morning sunshine filtering through the stained-glass door, throwing pale pink and green and yellow bars and diamonds and lozenges of light onto the carpet, gilding the hall table, the flowers in the iridescent glass; the empty rooms unfolding quietly from the hall. Several brown envelopes lay on the mat; they were all that seemed to come nowadays. She hardly glanced at them as she threw them onto the sideboard.

Boring bills. She left all that side of things to Nigel.

Later, although it was not yet ten o'clock, in her cotton dress and sandals, she was beaded with sweat by the time she reached the High Street. Outside the baker's she bumped into a woman and looked into her powdered face, a red slick of lipstick or jam in icing sugar, and realized that this oozing doughnut had been driven, at this early hour, to pound the hot pavements to the off-licence; tell-tale bottles clashed glassily in her bag. Jean turned with relief to the wholesome shiny sticks of bread.

Later again that morning she saw, through a fine pink mist of Windowlene, the girl from next door with her baby on her hip, a plastic bag of washing on the seat of the pushchair, setting off for the launderette. Really, there would seem nothing to connect those two, the skinny blond girl and the unarguably coffee-colored baby; except that the tiny brown hand was tangled in the lank hair like a baby animal's clinging onto its mother's fur. As she rubbed the window clear it blurred unaccountably.

With a heavy hand she sliced slabs of French bread for the bread and cheese lunch she was holding, the proceeds from which were to go to Oxfam. Her friends pecked like starlings with greasy beaks; her bread hovered in the air as first Nigel, then the girl next door, superimposed themselves on the chatter about children's O—level options, a topic of very limited interest to Jean.

She sighed and smeared her bread with butter and pickle.

"I'm starving," she remarked through a mouthful of piercing crust. "Let's take our coffee onto the patio," she suggested, but the sunny stones were splintered by pop music from a radio next door.

"Will you turn that bloody thing down!" She suddenly erupted in a brown geyser of hot coffee. Her friends mopped and soothed, but all at once realized how time had flown and that so must they.

The MacAllisters had brought their friends, Peter and Mary, back to supper after a concert at the Fairfield Halls. Blue skeins of cigar smoke wound over the coffee cups, binding them, still softened by music and golden-bellied wood, together. The doorbell burst blue ropes, shattered golden wood. Jean returned from answering it.

"It was that girl from next door, Mandy. She wanted to use the telephone. I told her to use the callbox on the corner." Her voice rose.

"It was for her own good. These people have got to stand on their own two feet. That's the trouble with the Welfare State, it makes people lazy. Apathetic. Soft. I mean, Nigel's worked damned hard for everything we've got!"

She stalked into the kitchen, clashing bowls, leaving Nigel and Mary to rekindle a cigar and prod a candle with a dead match, dropping ugly black specks into the rosy wax. Peter followed with a couple of spoons.

"I wish she'd go!" Jean burst out. "I'm sick of her. Always looming. Intruding. Imposing her miserable life on mine. I mean . . ." above the thunderous tap, wrenching pink rubber gloves onto her fingers, "it's not my fault. . . ."

Peter sidestepped the spray as the water hit a fork and turned off the tap.

"Of course it's not your fault. Your trouble is, you care too much about other people. You're too sensitive."

The next morning Mary telephoned. "Have you been in the copse lately?"

"No. Why?"

"There are masses of blackberries there. Beauties. Come and have a bite of lunch after yoga and we'll go blackberrying."

"If you like."

The receiver gave a squawk, almost a hurt sound, as she put it down on her friend's voice.

She had not intended to bulge in her leotard and black tights that morning, her head achy with too much wine the night before, and Mary's wholemeal pizza would undo any benefit the exercise might give; but the half-empty freezer groaned like a threatening ice-floe for the soft fruit and she had made no jam yet. The afternoon found them in the copse armed with Tupperware containers. Jean felt the knots that Yoga had failed to untie dissolve in the sun and bird song as she gazed at a branch that bore bud, white flower, hard green berry, solid jelly brushed with red and the rich black culmination, all on a single stem. Mary grabbed her arm.

"What's that noise?"

A blackbird shrieked. Over their banging hearts a steady shuffling sound came nearer. The middle-aged women clutched each other among spilled berries. It came towards them.

A baby broke through the undergrowth. It crawled; laughing through lips juicy with squashed blackberries. Mandy strode up and scooped the baby, who kicked its legs in delight, under her arm and was gone, but not before they had seen her face, streaked with tears and dirt where an earthy hand had brushed them away.

Although they continued to pick greedily, the gloss was gone from the afternoon. As Jean hurried past the house next door, through the smell of a blocked drain, it seemed to lunge at her; her own house in a distorting mirror.

It seemed that she had lost the art of making jam. She boiled and boiled; the house was filled with the smell of apples and blackberries but the jam would not set.

Hot uneasy nights when she and Nigel sweated separately in bed followed hot days when Jean could do nothing but lie on the grass. The sprinkler on the lawn brought a cool damp hour on some evenings, then she did the ironing, alone in the house; through a glaze of gin. She ceased to notice the light falling through the stained-glass door; the stems of the flowers on the hall table swelled and stank; the pile of unopened brown envelopes on the dusty sideboard grew higher.

She woke one night, whimpering; her silky nightdress clinging like a rag. Unhappy noises came from the hot cages next door. Someone was shouting, the baby was crying, glass smashed.

"Nigel," she whispered in the darkness of her life grown rotten. "Nigel."

With a groan, he fell on her; she felt a tear fall onto her neck and burn the hollow of her collarbone.

Tomorrow she would clean the house, cook a wonderful meal, and over it get Nigel to tell her what was wrong. Together they would tackle and beat the foe, whatever it was. She nestled against the dear body that had been given into her care and moaned softly to think that he had not been able to trust himself to her.

It was afternoon by the time she was able to get onto the patio with the *Telegraph* crossword. In the gleaming house were flowers and such beautiful still lifes of fruit and vegetables that she would be reluctant to put them to the knife. She twirled the pen in her fingers; the sun struck its transparent plastic facets, threw revolving rainbows on the newsprint. Something dropped to the grass. A pear had fallen from the tree in next door's garden. The tree was heavy with golden fruit against the blue; ripe, heavy, going to waste. A bird even had its beak in one. She looked at the house. The family upstairs was out. The drug addicts in the middle flat were either asleep or dead. Mandy's radio was silent.

She was on the wall almost before she knew it. The pears fell into her hands and spread skirt. Scented flesh broke against her teeth. Suddenly, in a cracking of branches, Mandy's face thrust through the leaves. Jean jumped, breaking twigs, grazing the backs of her thighs on the wall and landed heavily on all fours. She looked up over her shoulder, like a dog. Mandy was standing on the wall, gigantic against the sky, hurling pears at her, shouting,

"You want it all, don't you? You want the lot! Well, go on then, take it! Have the bloody pears!"

Jean caught a pear as she fled inside. It lay in her hand, gilded, wormy.

By six o'clock the shameful incident, marinated all afternoon in her mind, was sufficiently tenderized and trimmed to be offered as an amusing anecdote to Nigel when he came home. But he did not come home.

Jean woke on the sofa to a smell of burning from the oven and to find that someone had drunk all the wine. She lifted the receiver to ring the police and let it fall. She knew that he had left her. Days and nights passed. Someone. There must be someone. Not her friends. There was only Mandy. Fellow sufferer. Betrayed. But golden pears blocked her path. Jean seized two withered apples from the fruit bowl, smiling in anticipation of Mandy's face as she understood the peace offering. There was a light behind the blanket, and music. Jean pressed and pressed the broken bell.

"There's gonna be a heartache tonight, heartache tonight. . . ." came thumping through the cracked stained glass.

Later she realized that she had been sitting for a long time in the skeleton of a chair. She had forgotten all about her upholstery class. She went to the telephone.

"Peter. How are you? It's Jean. Is Mary there?"

"Jean! Are you all right?"

"Of course, I'm all right. I merely wanted to ask Mary if she had any of that red Dralon left. Why shouldn't I be all right?"

"It's just that it's three o'clock in the morning. . . ."

Jean was woken by an unfamiliar noise from next door. Laughter. Feet were going up and down the path. She threw back the duvet and ran to the window.

Mandy was leaving in a taxi.

Jean struggled with the window and forced it open. She wanted to say something, make everything all right. She clawed through the wardrobe and pulled out a bag. "Mandy!" The car backfired a contemptuous burst of gray smoke at her. Mandy was gone. Escaped. Victorious. Jean hurled the bag through the window. It burst, spilling spurned, never-needed baby clothes over the road.

Mary might have telephoned her, but she would not have got through, because that morning the phone was cut off.

The man in the Social Security office gave Jean a funny look as she sat down in the peeling gray and yellow room. She knew she looked all right; she had checked in the Ladies in the pub.

"How was Brittany?" she asked brightly. He stared. "Don't you remember? I came in a year or so ago about my holiday insurance and we discovered that we were going to the same place." Evidently he did not remember.

The weather became colder. Jean lay shivering in the aftermath of a dream in which she and Nigel were putting up the tent on a campsite and Nigel had started to hammer the tent-peg into her head. She realized that it was more than a year since he had gone. She could still hear the hammering. A man was fixing a "For sale" sign to the fence. She remembered the face of a woman outside the baker's, whom she had despised as a doughnut. Now it was she who lay on the edge of a bed grown too vast; a white soggy meringue left on the side of someone's plate.

Surely she had had most need of blessing? Jean came down the church aisle more unsteadily than was possible from the mouthful of wine, although she had not risen from the altar rail after receiving the Sacrament. She had stretched out her hands again for the cup, but the blue glassy eyes of the vicar had cut them and passed over her.

If afterwards, in the porch, his white sleeve billowed for a moment like the sail of a rescue ship, it was at once drowned by a wave of eager young faces. A woman's voice called her name tentatively as she stumbled over the humpbacked gravestones, gray whales and basking sharks with granite teeth, that reared under her feet. She cursed herself for putting those two pound notes in the collection. Much good it had done her. Her heart was already thumping with the beginnings of shame. There was only one way, impossible now, to soothe it. Let soft seas of alcohol lap over the brain. She walked into the terrible yawning dry jaws of afternoon.

Something made her stop and look in her purse. She pulled out two pound notes. The miraculous green paper shook in her fingers. She must have put a pawn ticket in the collection bag.

"Thank you, God," she said as she went into the off-licence.

Tired, and buffeted by Christmas shoppers, Jean was thankful to get home. How pretty the holly wreath looked, festive against the stained glass. Nigel must have done it to surprise her. She knelt to kiss its berries; the cold prickles grazed her face. Her key wouldn't fit. She rattled and rattled. Tears burst from her eyes as she put her mouth to the letterbox, smearing the polished brass.

"Nigel," she called. "Nigel! I can't open the door!"

He opened it in a rush of spicy air. But it wasn't Nigel. A boy stood staring at her.

"Mom," he shouted. "Mo-om!"

She scrambled up. The holly had scratched her lip. With the metallic taste of blood she remembered. She turned back up the slushy path and into the house next door.

She kicked off her shoes and lit the fire and sat down to see what she had bought. A Bird's Trifle. How odd. Still, there was a little milk; it wouldn't matter if it had gone off slightly. Her coat fell open and she confronted a thigh; she must have forgotten to put her skirt on. She sat in her leotard stroking in pity the poor white flesh marbled with cold. The light went out. The gas fire went out.

In the light, from the streetlamp, falling through the blanket looped across the window she turned to the trifle. The Dream Topping. The hundreds and thousands melting in rainbow drizzle.

BABIES IN RHINESTONES

The Alfred Ellis School of Fine Art and the Araidne Elliot School of Dance and Drama stood semi-detached from one another behind a small tearful shrubbery of mahonia and hypericum, snowberries, bitter blue currants, spotted laurel and pink watery globes of berberis spiked on their own thorns. A crooked hedge of yellow-berried holly divided the two gardens. The artist's was distinguished by a rusting iron sculpture, while Miss Elliot's, or Madame as she was addressed by her pupils, held a gray polystyrene cupidon bearing a shell of muddy water.

In the green gloom of his hall Alfred Ellis held up a letter to the light to see if it contained any money. It was in fact addressed to Araidne Elliot and had come through the wrong door. As he crumpled it into his pocket he wondered again if she knew that her name should be Ariadne. He fancied, as he passed the half open door of his front room, or atelier, that something moved, but when he went in all the easels were posing woodenly in their places. In the kitchen he poured boiling water onto an old tea bag and was sitting down to read the paper when a round striped ginger face appeared at the window.

"Good morning, Ginger," he said as he let in the cat.

"I suppose you want your breakfast. I was about to read the Deaths, to see if I had died recently. Now I shall never know." He brushed at the bouquets of smudged paw marks on the black words and poured out a bowl of milk.

Dead or alive, half an hour later he set off for the shops. Ginger ran down the path before him. At the same time his neighbor emerged from her gate, struggling with a green umbrella. Araidne Elliot seemed more at the mercy of the elements than other people; the mild late autumn rain had, on her walk down the garden path, reduced her piled-up hair to a spangled ruin sliding from its combs. A scarlet mahonia leaf was slicked to the toe of her boot. A cluster of red glass berries dangled from each ear.

"Miss Elliot, you look the very spirit of autumn. . . ."

She did not reply, being unsure, as so often, if he was being unpleasant, and looked down at Ginger who was rolling on his back on the pavement at their feet, displaying his belly where the stripes dissolved into a pool of milky fur.

"Home, Rufus!" she said sharply. "You can't come to the library with me."

"Rufus?"

She blushed. "I call him that. I don't know his real name—he's not really mine, I'm afraid. He just walked in one day and made himself at home. He always comes for his breakfast and some-times he stays the night. He sleeps on my bed." She blushed again. "I wish I could keep him, but he's obviously got a home. . . ."

"His breakfast?" repeated Alfred Ellis. "That's impossible!"

"Oh yes, every day, but the funny thing is, he won't touch milk!"

"You little tart, Ginger," he said softly, inserting a not very gentle toe into the cat's wanton chest. Ginger gathered up his legs and departed, tail worn low, between two branches of a spiraea.

"What a very unpleasant shrub that is," said Alfred Ellis.

"How can you say that," she cried. "All flowers are lovely."

Her doubts about him as an artist tumbled through her head; a rat's skull on the windowsill, a drain blocked with dead leaves, his profile like a battered boxer's, the sculpture like a rusting vegetable rack in his garden. They walked on.

"This is yours," I think. He fished in the pocket of his stained corduroy trousers and handed her the letter.

"Not bad news, I trust?" he capered at her side, squinting over her shoulder.

"Not at all. Just a bill," she said coldly, putting it in her bag.

"Manage to spell your name right, did they?"

"I don't know, I didn't look. Why?"

He could hardly tell her that every time he saw the board outside her house he had to suppress an urge to seize a paintbrush and alter it.

"Those gray trousers with bald knees make him look like an old elephant who has been in the zoo too long," she was thinking as they crossed the railway tracks at the level crossing. Alfred Ellis suddenly stopped and waved an arm at a large bronze ballerina pirouetting in the wind.

"Ah, Dame Margot!" he cried. "An inspiration to us all, eh Miss Elliot? Born plain Alice Marks in this very borough and still dancing away in all weathers. . . ."

She strode away, her feet almost at right angles, a dancer in dudgeon. He laughed. He was often bored and it amused him to provoke his neighbor. He was often lonely too, and was disproportionately hurt by the news that his friend Ginger was so free with his favors.

He crossed the road and forced to return his greeting an ex-pupil who was obviously about to cut him.

"I thought of you on Saturday," she admitted. "Yes, I was helping with the school Autumn Fayre and one of your pictures turned up on the bric-à-brac stall. I almost bought it, but the frame was in such poor condition. . . ."

The artist turned away with what might have been a laugh.

He thought about her as he walked; one of too many ladies striding about the town with shopping trolleys, whose skin from years of smiling at the antics of dogs and children and husbands creased into fans of angst at the eyes, whose arms were muscled from turning over the pages of *Which* and cookery books borrowed from the library; they never had time to read fiction; whose faces were still faintly tanned from their camping holiday in France where they had sat in the passenger seat of the car with maps and Blue Guides and Red Guides on their laps, reflecting that if they had gone to Cornwall they would not be boiling along between endless fields of sweet corn and poplars; who had once suggested that they might stop and look at a cathedral, but had been hooted down by the rest of the family—and anyway the O–level results hung in a thundercloud on the horizon; who sometimes came to his art classes to draw dead grasses and bunches of dried honesty.

He was struck by a house garlanded with a green climbing plant and stood watching the wind lifting the leaves so that the house looked airy and insubstantial, as if it might take wing, and remembered a birthday cake that his grandmother had sent him when he was a boy, white icing and green maidenhair fern, and marveled that someone should once have thought him worthy of such a cake. A twist of smoke from his thin cigarette burned his eye. The pure white icing attacked his stained teeth as he went into the greengrocer's to buy the still life for his morning class. He was crossing the car park on his way home when he passed a stall selling fresh fish, cockles and mussels. He retraced his steps. So, banging his shin on the metal rim of a bucket of briny shells, he began his campaign of seduction.

"Oysters," he said, his teeth glistening in his beard.

"We haven't any."

He looked over white fluted shells holding tremulous raw eggs.

"Give me a mackerel. The bluest you have."

In his mind's eye he saw the mackerel with a lemon on a plate.

He was painting it that afternoon, the blue fish curved on the white oval plate, the lemon with the faintest blush of green, beside the darkening window when he saw a figure slinking through the dark grass under the holly hedge. He flung open the window and, wrecking his still life, waved the fist at the cat. Ginger stopped, sniffed, laid back his ears, lifted a loyal paw in the direction of Araidne's house, then leaped through the window.

"Gotcha!" Alfred slammed it shut. Soon heavy swirls of fishy steam mingled with the smell of linseed oil and paint and Ginger was arching his back, walking up and down the kitchen table, purring in anticipation. Half an hour later he lay replete and Alfred Ellis smirked and wiped his greasy fingers on his trousers as the sound of "Puss, Puss, Puss" came through the rain. Ginger raised an ear, shook his head and stuck out a hind leg to wash. A cloudy eye watched from the draining board.

In the morning Araidne Elliot had to plug in the electric fire to take the chill off the air before the Tinies' Tap Class.

"Bit chilly in here, isn't it?" said a mother, pulling her fur coat around herself.

"We'll soon warm up," replied Araidne listlessly. Rufus. She supposed he was the only person who loved her.

"Yes, well. Tara's only just got over a shocking cough, I was in two minds whether to bring her. She was barking all night."

Araidne's ears, on either side of her hairnet, strained to hear a meow. She looked in despair at her class. The cold was marbling the Tinies' thighs pink and blue to match their leotards and headbands. They seemed to troop incessantly to the toilet, returning with their leotards hiked up over their knickers. She feared that most of them had not washed their hands.

"I'm putting on my top hat. . . ."

If she was to fit a lock on the bathroom door, she thought as she danced, that took two-pence pieces . . . her cane flashed dangerously.

". . . polishing my nails."

In a dusty corner lay an unperformed revue: "Babies in Rhinestones," written and choreographed by Araidne Elliot, in which strings of sparkling babes, shimmering in precision, crisscrossed a vast stage under a spinning prismatic globe, scattered like broken jewelry, and grouped and regrouped in endless stars, rings, necklaces, bangles, tiaras of rainbow glass.

On the other side of the wall Alfred Ellis elicited some disapproval from his students as he executed a bit of inelegant hoofing through the easels to the tap, tap, tap of forty little shoes and one clacking big pair.

"Really, Mr. Ellis, that music is most distracting!"

"Lovely chiaroscuro on that teasel, Mrs. Wyndham Lewis," he attempted to placate her, "If I might suggest . . . the onions. . . ."

He added a few strokes of charcoal.

"I think I preferred it as it was," she said, recoiling from his fishy breath.

"What I object to," murmured one to another, "is the fact that one can never finish anything. One embarks on a *nature morte* one lesson, only to find that he's eaten it by the next . . . most unprofessional."

Araidne could hardly close the front door quickly enough; it clipped the heels of the last mummy, and forced herself to wait until the last car had pulled away before rushing out to check the gutters for a furry body.

She wondered if she would be able to pick it up. Her hair escaped like a catch of eels from its net as she stooped.

"Looking for something, Miss Elliot?"

The loathsome artist was grinning over his gate. She strode on, blushing. Rufus could be presumed alive so far, at least. She thought of his white-tipped paws, his meticulously striped tail, its white tip. She told herself that she was being absurd; he had simply been kept indoors; the people he lived, or condescended to lodge, with, showing some sense of responsibility at last. Nevertheless she scanned every garden that she passed and encountered some striped and tabby persons, but not the face of the beloved. She wandered for some time and at just after one o'clock arrived, or found herself, in a little road near the station. The few small shops were shut. There was nobody about; the little terraced houses looked empty. She heard her heels on the pavement and suddenly felt dispossessed, as if she was in a Tennessee Williams movie. *The Fugitive Kind.* She hesitated in front of a phone box; there was no one to call. It was a relief to arrive in the High Street. She purchased a bottle of pallid rosé and a stiff slice of Camembert to take to the end-of-term party of her French class, an event to which she looked forward with some gloom. Experience had taught her to avoid the Evening Institute on the first evening of the spring term, when, new aftershave failing to mask the scent of loneliness, people would be required to give details of their sad Christmases in French.

"On m'a donné beaucoup de cadeaux—er—le smoker's candle, le déodorant, le très petit pudding de Noel de Madame Peek. . . ."

It was as she came out of the delicatessen that she saw, slouching along with a baby buggy, cigarette in hand, her one-time star pupil, the one for whom she had had the highest hopes. Could it be three years ago that she had brought down the house with her rendition of "Send in the Clowns"?

"Karen!"

"Madame!" She dropped her cigarette.

"What's his name?" She peered into the buggy.

"Neil."

"I suppose we'll be seeing Neil in the Tinies' Class soon?" She chucked him awkwardly under the wet chin. "I could do with a nice boy. . . ."

"Couldn't we all?" replied her ex-pupil.

Araidne's eyes filled with tears. She couldn't resist calling after her in a slightly wavery voice.

"Shoulders back, Karen, and do tuck your tail in!"

While the riches of the sea, sardines painted in silver leaf, shrimps like pink corals, saucy pilchards, fins and tails, poured out in the artist's kitchen and Ginger waxed fat and indolent, his whiskers standing out from his round head in glossy quills, Araidne Elliot grew as boney and twitchy as a hooked hake. Alfred Ellis expected her daily to ask if he had seen the cat, but she did not come.

One morning, while picking a branch of snowberries from the front garden, he saw, further up the road, on the opposite side, a yellow removal van. He went to investigate and saw carried into the van a wicker basket whose lid was pushed open by a ginger face; it flapped shut, and then a striped tail flicked out in farewell.

"Mr. Ellis!" Araidne was at her open window with a letter in her hand. "I'm afraid the postman has muddled our mail again."

He took it, and seeing the postmark almost ran to his own house, without a word of thanks or a word about Ginger's departure. It was from a man who owned a small gallery in Gravesend, who had seen some of Ellis's paintings in the Salon de Refusés of the South Surrey Arts Society exhibition and proposed to visit him with a view to mounting a one-man show of his work. He gobbled gleefully at what would have been Ginger's supper as he read and reread the letter until it was creased and oily.

That evening he took down a large prepared canvas which had stood empty for months and would now receive his masterwork, the heart of his exhibition, the flowering of his genius; but his brush kept dancing to a faint beat coming through the wall—"From the top again, please Mrs. Taylor"—and the image of Araidne's old accompanist's resigned shoulders at the keyboard superimposed itself on the canvas, so eventually he had to admit defeat and switch on "Dallas." Later he went for a walk. It had rained, but now the air was frosty, the ivy all diamanté, the hedges cold and hard like marcasite.

"Rufus . . . Rufus," came palely through the starlight.

The Muse was still recalcitrant the next morning, so he thought that he might seduce her with a pint or two in convivial company. He saw Araidne in the High Street; she saw him too and turned, but too late; he was performing a grotesque dance at her on the pavement, and whistling.

"I'm sorry if my music disturbed you," she said stiffly. "I do have a living to make. . . ."

"Please don't apologize. The clog dance from "La Fille Mal Gardé" just happens to be my very, very, all-time favorite—especially when I'm trying to work."

"Excuse me."

He followed her at a distance and entered a shop behind her. She placed her basket on the counter and took out a packet.

"These tights aren't at all what I wanted."

"What do you want then?"

She burst into tears, grabbed her basket, and ran out of the shop.

Alfred Ellis winked at the astonished assistant, but he could have wept too. Before she had fled he had looked into her basket; a packet of Fishy Treats, two frozen cod steaks and a library book, *Some Tame Gazelle* by Barbara Pym.

In the pub he muttered into his beer, attracting a fishy glance from the landlord who knew him of old. The shop assistant had asked her what she wanted and the book had replied for her: "Something to love, oh, something to love."

"Some tame gazelle, or some gentle dove . . . give me a whisky, George. Better make it a double."

The seduction of Ginger seemed less amusing now.

"Something to love, oh, something to love," he murmured to the fruit machine as it turned up two lemons and a raspberry. He put a coin in the jukebox to drown the rusty voice of shame, but he had to go and look for her.

"Miss Elliot, please. Will you come and have a drink with me. Don't run away. I've got something to tell you. It's most important. It's about Rufus."

He saw her turn as white as the snowberries in his garden, as red as their twigs, and blanch again.

★   ★   ★

Two hours later two slightly tear-stained disheveled people with foolish smiles, clutching a cardboard cat carrier, a wicker basket, a sack of cat litter, a plastic tray and a carrier bag of tins, struggled down the High Street.

"I think Beulah for the little black one, what do you think?" Alfred Ellis was saying.

Araidne caught sight of their reflection in a shop window.

"Goodness, we almost look like a couple," she thought. She said, "We want to give them nice names, sensible names, that won't embarrass them when they go to school—grow up, I mean. Names are so important, don't you think?"

"I hated mine when I was a boy. Did you like yours?"

"I chose it." She admitted. "My real name's Gwen. I saw the name Araidne in a book and I thought it was so beautiful and romantic. So when I opened the dancing school I changed it to Araidne."

"Ah," he said.

"What about Tom for the boy? Can we put these down for a minute? My arms are breaking. Oh, I can hear a little voice! Oh, we'll soon be home, darlings."

Outside their houses he turned to go into his, she into hers. The cat carrier was almost torn in two. Instant sobriety, hangover, realization of what they had done. They stood on the pavement staring at one another. A cold wind blew up; the meows from the box grew wilder.

"Whose dumb idea was this anyway?"

"Yours, I think. But don't worry, I'm taking them."

"Oh no, you don't!"

"I refuse to stand here brawling in the street. Give me those kittens!"

She tried to snatch them, but he broke free and bolted down his path with them and she grabbed the rest of the stuff and hurried after him lest she be locked out and lose them altogether.

In his kitchen he set the box on the floor and opened it and they knelt on either side gazing at the two tiny faces, one black, one marked like a pansy, looking up, pink and black mouths opening on teeth as sharp as pins. Then, gently, with his big stained fingers, he lifted the kittens out, and on little rickety-looking legs they entered into their kingdom. Alfred Ellis capitalized on Araidne's softened look by opening a bottle of wine; she opened a tin of evaporated milk.

"Let's go into the other room, where it's more comfortable," he said, "and try and think of some solution. Perhaps they should stay here tonight, anyway, as they seem to be making themselves at home. . . ."

Some hours later two empty bottles and a pile of dirty plates stood on the table. Blue cigarette smoke lay flat across the air like branches of a cedar tree. Araidne lay heavy-eyed on the sofa with the kittens asleep in her lap. A gentle purring could be heard.

"Perhaps you should all stay the night," said Alfred Ellis, putting a balloon of brandy to his lips. "It would be upsetting for the kittens if you should go now. . . ."

Araidne slunk up her path in the morning, feeling very ill, just in time to preempt her morning class.

"From the top, Mrs. Taylor. But pianissimo, please."

She was obviously not in a good mood when she returned.

"Switch that thing off! I've got the most appalling headache in the history of the world. What on earth are you doing?" She shouted, wrenching the plug of his Black and Decker from the socket.

"It's the perfect solution," he said, his hair white with plaster dust. I'm drilling a passage from my house to yours so that the kittens can come and go as they please. There's half a Disprin left, if you want it," he added.

As he spoke a crack zigzagged through the plaster, then another.

"Oh dear. Perhaps we'd better take the whole wall down?"

The man from the gallery at Gravesend rang and rang the doorbell, and at last walked around the side of the house and looked through the window. The hindquarters of a man, covered in plaster and brick dust, were wriggling through a hole in the wall, while a woman, with a savage look on her face, stood in a lumpy sea of broken plaster, with two kittens running about her shoulders and biting her distracted hair, gulping a glass of water and grasping an electric drill as if she might plunge it into her companion's disappearing leg. He was a timid man, and he crept away.

The kittens proved to be bad wild infants who tore up canvasses and danced away with the ribbons of ballet shoes in their mouths. Araidne lost a pair of twins from her beginner's ballet class due to alleged cat-scratch fever; a major disaster as they had three younger sisters. She started to choreograph a ballet based on the kittens, but when Alfred opined that the adult human impersonating a cat was the most embarrassing sight in the universe, and the infant human doing so was only marginally better, she lost heart. Alfred received a deep scratch on his thumb while disentangling Tom from a curtain, infected it with paint, and had to wear a clumsy bandage, which made painting impossible. They hardly spoke, addressing most of their remarks to the kittens.

Then one gray day, while the taped carols of the Rotarians

pierced the woolly hat he had pulled down over his ears to muffle them, sidestepping a plastic-suited Santa shaking a tin, Alfred Ellis entered the Craft Market, a portfolio in his good hand, shamefacedly and without hope, and found himself appreciated as an artist at last.

He sold several rough studies, executed sinisterly, of the kittens; posing under an umbrella, gazing up expectantly from a pair of old boots, entangled in a ball of knitting wool and needles, Tom asleep with his arms flung out behind his head and Beulah curled into him with her paws crossed, and was commissioned by a local gift shop to supply it with more, and was approached by three golden retrievers who wanted portraits of their owners, or vice versa.

It was almost midnight. The kittens lay in one another's arms; their new jeweled collars sending reflections of firelight and the broken baubles they had torn from the tree, which stood in a huge jagged hole in the wall, sparkling around the room as the last bong of Big Ben rang in the future; babies in rhinestones. And the parents? They stayed together for the sake of the children.

ELECTRIC-BLUE DAMSELS

You see them in the Underground with their schoolbooks and across the counters of shops and waiting on tables in restaurants, slinging burgers and pushing brooms; girls and boys in whom an exotic cocktail of genes has been shaken into a startling and ephemeral beauty: birds of paradise nesting in garbage, or captive tropical fish shimmering in the gloomy backrooms of dank pet shops.

At almost sixteen Fayette Gordon was not weaving blossoms in her hair, or diving for pearls in a green translucent ocean; she was a pupil at a comprehensive school, and in these summer evenings, which should have been heavy with the scents of frangipani and mimosa instead of those of melting tarmac and diesel fumes, she worked in a chip shop with the traffic's surf pounding on the pavement's crumbling shore. Her ancestry and origins were mysterious to everybody, except perhaps her grandmother with whom she lived, whose clenched teeth behind purple lips suggested the loss of a short-stemmed pipe. Fayette was breathtaking; at least her year-tutor Maurice Barlow always caught his rather pipe-smelling breath on catching sight of her unexpectedly in the corridor or on the tennis court. At once his teeth felt scummy and he put away the pipe which convention, if increasingly begrudgingly, allowed him; a round red burn on his fuzzy thigh and a singed pocket testified to his haste on one occasion; her teeth, her blouse, her socks were so white.

It had been the worst sort of weather, as so often, for exams; the sort of weather which inspired unironic comments on "flaming June," when swotting sweating adolescents in rolled-up shirtsleeves dreamed of sea and sand and returned from Sundays at the coast with the bruised purple fruit of love-bites on their necks. Fayette's neck was unblemished and of course she did not sweat, except for a once-glimpsed row of tiny seed pearls beading her upper lip after a strenuous mixed doubles one lunch hour; her exam papers, although less than brilliant, would bear no unseemly smudges; she wore invisible white gloves. Maurice Barlow thought of white communion dresses, parasols and jalousies, iron lace balconies, guavas and jacaranda. Thin silver bangles rolled up and down her cinnamon-colored wrist as she wrote, and if he was invigilating he listened for the little clink of silver on wood and agonized if there was a long silence. Her hair, he had decided, was cinnamon too, the soft pale color of the most delicious Edinburgh rock, that he would never taste.

As he sat at his kitchen table with the back door open, writing reports on school-leavers, the radio throbbed out "Summer in the City." He took a sheet of paper and attempted to compose a reference. Fayette, he wrote, is Fayette Fayette Fayette Fayette. He crumpled it and threw it in the bin and went out into the backyard. He pulled up a few tufts of groundsel that grew beside the gate and found himself ambling down the pavement. As he was out, he thought, he might as well buy himself some supper. The pockets of his creased Terylene trousers were weighed down with loose change, the key to the stockroom cupboard, a confiscated knife, a dried-out Tipp-Ex and other schoolmasterly impedimenta. The stain of a felt-tipped pen on the breast pocket of his shirt gave his heart a wounded look. She stood in front of the vats of boiling oil, leaning on the counter, brooding into the summer evening.

"Ah, Fayette. Business slack, I see." Was in fact delighted to see.

"Be busy later when the pubs close."

He loved it when his pupils greeted him by name in the pub, except that most of them, he knew, were under age. They bought his silence in halves of lager. Good old Maurice. Pupils came and went but Maurice was always one of the lads. He watched Fayette dunk a basket of raw chips into the oil and wished that they would take forever to cook and suppressed a desire to lock the door so that he and she might stay pickled in time like those eggs in a jar on the counter. The oil sizzled and spat while the closing music of "EastEnders" was strained through the bead curtain behind which the proprietor and his family were watching television.

"Isn't that rather tactless?"

Maurice pointed to a tank of tropical fish, rosy and neon tetras brushing their fins against the plaster mermaid who reclined in the emerald green gravel combing her hair, in full view of their North Sea cousins dressed in overcoats of knobbly batter. Fayette did not answer.

"I wish you'd reconsider staying on for A levels."

Fayette disturbed a flock of butterflies of colored ribbon as she shook the last eleven years of her short life from her cinnamon-colored hair.

"No way. I've had enough of school. I can't wait to leave."

His eyes bulged cold and hard as the pickled eggs as she doused his chips in vinegar, smarting with salt at her dismissal of him and their years together.

"I think you're making a grave mistake, and one that, believe you me, you'll live to regret."

He tapped the fish tank in emphasis.

"Believe you me," mocked Fayette. "Don't do that, it frightens the fish."

"Fat lot you care."

True to her word Fayette left school without an expression of regret. Maurice could remember the days when tearful girls had queued outside the staffroom door clutching damp autograph books and farewell gifts, but that had been before everything was so uncertain, before teachers were fallible and world leaders exposed as murderous liars and frauds; when girls like Fayette could step out into a secure and radiant future of physiotherapy and nursing, and teaching and secretarial posts, and then babies in coach-built prams. Fayette had announced her own plans to the careers master: she had decided to be rich and famous. Her education had ended in four minutes of ecstasy for Maurice at the leavers' disco.

"I never realized this record was so long," she remarked as they danced.

He sat gloomily in the pub afterwards with a group of his colleagues, his Palm Beach party shirt exhibiting salty circles of drying sweat, nursing a tepid beer and dreaming of a Caribbean of the heart where he and Fayette could dance forever, of a room with a frilly iron balcony looking out over the wide Sargasso Sea. Or Fayetteville, Arkansas.

"Cheer up, Maurice. School's out for summer. Made any plans for going away yet?"

"I was thinking of the Caribbean. . . ."

"On your salary? A likely tale."

"Room for a little one? Budge up, you guys."

Sally Molloy swung her large tanned knees under the table, so that Maurice's and her thighs sighed against each other, nudging memories of grueling sessions of dry-skiing in East Grinstead. He had conducted a desultory affair with her over the years; he supposed he ought to ask her to marry him, she wasn't getting any younger, but something always happened to prevent him from popping the question; one of them got hiccups or cramp or the toast caught fire. He feared now that she was about to suggest a take-away, so while Patsy Armstrong, who taught social studies, engaged her in a discussion of the relative merits of the graffiti in the girls' and the boys' loos, and they laid contingency plans for the next term's half-day strikes, he stepped over Sally's designer trainers, and slipped into the night, hardly able to believe that the summer stretched before him without a prospect in sight of a cycling holiday in Holland, pot-holing in the Peak District, or following in the footsteps of St. Paul; three unappetizing carrots which had been dangled in front of him earlier in the year.

He had managed also to decline, by the inspired invention of a crop of verrucas, an invitation to stay with his married sister and her four small children and enjoy their new swimming pool. His refusal had been accepted with alacrity. Uncle Maurice was whistling, albeit a melancholy tune, as he set out early with his swimming trunks in a neat toweling Swiss roll under his arm for the local pool. The company of the school rat, who was with him for the holiday, was all that he desired or found congenial in his bereft state. Fayette had given up her job in the chippie on the day that she had left school. It was to buy food for this rat, whose name, coincidentally, was Maurice too, that he entered the pet shop with his hair still wet, cleaner and red-eyed from the chlorine. His heart stopped, and stumbled on its way again.

"So this is where the rich and famous hang out."

"Hello, Maurice."

"What are you doing here?"

"I work here, don't I?"

"Do you?"

She was all in white; a white T-shirt under white dungarees rolled to show the delicate bones of cinnamon ankles above white plimsolls, a smudge of sawdust delineating one cheekbone, and a small net sticking out of her chest pocket. Fish tanks glimmered like televisions with the sound turned down in the gloom of the back room. A man in a brown overall was serving a customer with biltong, or knotted strips of hide for dogs to chew. Maurice went into the back room; Fayette followed.

"Small cod and chips, open, salt and vinegar, please," he said, then stopped. It was like walking into a gallery and being stunned by wonderful paintings by an artist whose work he had never encountered before, or entering a cave of moving jewels, rubies, emeralds, topaz, diamonds and sapphires on black velvet; like looking into Chapman's *Homer*. He dismissed from his mind any comparisons between keeping birds in cages and fish in aquaria.

"What are those?"

"Electric-blue damsels."

In a flash of sapphire Maurice saw how he could get his heart's desire. They were the deepest, glowing, electric blue; slender and swift in the water.

"*Abudefduf uniocellata*," said Fayette.

"What?"

"Formerly known as *Pomacentrus caeruleus*."

Was this the girl who couldn't tell hake from huss?

He stood entranced in front of a tank of sea horses twining their prehensile tails around thin poles rising from coral fans; with their equine heads and long sensitive snouts they were as ancient and mysterious as fragments of sculpture found after centuries in the ocean among starfish and the waving fronds of anemones. The only sea-horses Maurice had seen hitherto had been dry and faded curiosities in the Shell Shop in Manette Street, across from Foyles. These were moist and living, magic and mythological, undulating and grazing the water.

"*Hippocampus kuda*. Did you know that they are unique in the animal kingdom in that the male becomes pregnant and bears the young?"

"No!" Maurice was enchanted at having become the pupil.

"He incubates the eggs placed there by the female for four to five weeks in a special pouch and hundreds of perfect tiny sea horses hatch out. Can you imagine? I can't wait to see that!"

Her eyes were shining at the thought; an enthusiastic hand fluttered a moment on his sleeve. He caught sight of his reflection in the side of a tank of black mollies in viridian weed, an albino rat displaying long teeth in an ecstatic smile, and remembered the purpose of his visit.

"Are you an arachniphobe, Maurice?"

"I don't think so. Why?"

She directed his gaze to a tarantula, but the sight that stayed with him was a pretty speckled eel curvetting upwards through the rocky water to nibble from Fayette's fingers.

His brain turned to coral: emperor and clown, harlequins, rainbows, unicorns, angels and devils, queens, jewels, damsels, glowlights, but-terflies, cardinals, swordfish, surgeons, anemones, starfish, sea horses, dancing shrimps, golden rams and silver sharks, flying foxes, albino tigers, lyretails, parrots and corals; freshwater and marine tropicals from the Indian Ocean and the Pacific swam through its branches. He took out a stack of library books. He joined the local Aquarist Society. He had to make frequent visits to the pet shop to be initiated into the mysteries of aeration and filtration, heating and lighting, salinity, and ultraviolet sterilization, ozonizing, feeding, bacteria and parasites. On one glorious evening Fayette allowed him to pick her up in his Morris Minor and drive her to an Aquarist meeting in the upper room of the library, but as there were no fish present she was bored and fidgeted and watched the clock, as in a dull lesson at school, eyed covertly by the flock of old goats who, until then, Maurice had considered a pleasant bunch of chaps.

The summer holiday was almost over. Maurice wondered how he would find the time to go back to school. He went into the pet shop intent on persuading Fayette to come with him to the aquarium at the zoo, and thereafter perhaps to Brighton, to all the aquariums in the country, in far-flung cities where they would have to spend the night.

"She's not here."

"When will she be back?"

"She won't. She's gone."

"Gone?"

He could have wrenched the tanks from the wall, screaming in splinters of glass and the gush of water and floundering fish, dying jewels drowning in air. But only for a second; he wouldn't hurt a fish.

"I only came in for some Daphnia."

"Of course."

He walked out of the shop, drowning in air.

One afternoon he encountered Fayette's grandmother in a tobacconist's but she did not remember him from the one parents' evening she had attended, in Fayette's first term, when she had been a shy and heartbreaking twelve-year-old, and he could not bring himself to enquire after his former pupil. He had had to tell his disappointed fellow-Aquarists that Fayette would not be joining them again. It was after one of their meetings as he was walking home through an evening made unbearable by night-scented stocks and nicotiana mingling with the smell of diesel and chips that he saw a poster attached to the wall of a cellar wine bar, advertising live music by the Electric-Blue Damsels. He descended the steps and swam through the rocky interior where young people clung like limpets to the recesses in the walls. Now he did not want to be hailed by any pupils or ex-pupils; good old Maurice no more, he shunned the company of all but the rat, his fish and his fellow-Aquarists.

The Electric-Blue Damsels were bad by any standards. The sound system was appalling. Dominating the all-female quintet was Fayette, now leaping to pound incompetently on a synthesizer, now screeching into a hand-held mike which splattered her voice on the damp cellar walls that threw it back in echoes through the cave. The audience loved them. Her cinnamon hair was a shock of electric blue and the long bare legs under the tiny vinyl skirt ended in blue shoes with spiked heels that could tear a man's heart out, sharp as the weapon of the surgeon-fish, that has a retractable scalpel at the base of its tail. As he stumbled out he remembered that electric-blue damsels are sometimes known as blue devils.

When he did not appear on the first day of term, Sally Molloy and Patsy Armstrong went to his house after school. There was no reply to their knocking so they went around to the back. A pond had been set into the yard, almost filling it; the tragic overbred face of a bubble-eyed goldfish mouthed at the surface as they picked their way past the edge, making them gasp. The back door was open. They couldn't believe what they saw: the kitchen had liquefied. At first they thought it had flooded, then they saw that an enormous tank had been sunk into the floor. A Japanese bridge spanned its length, rising over the floating weeds and waterlilies, and at its center stood Maurice scattering meal and watercress to a circle of the most enormous, most beautiful, metallic fish they had ever seen, phosphorescent gold and silver, monochromatic, pure white, black with reflections of scarlet or yellow, splashes of color like ideographs and sunsets, a blazing red triangle on a snow-white head.

"Hi," said Sally at last.

"Hi-utsuri," Maurice replied.

"What?"

He blinked, staring at them, and did not explain. He wondered for a moment who they were.

"Did you want something? I'm very busy."

"We just wondered if you were all right, as you didn't show up at school," said Patsy. The woman who had once been his lover was speechless with affront, then she noticed something helping himself to what looked like a nut rissole on the bridge. "That rat's school property, you know."

"I wouldn't play Emil Jannings to her Marlene Dietrich."

"What on earth are you on about?"

"*The Blue Angel.*"

They were none the wiser.

At the end of the bridge, in the front room, they could see the glitter of small fish in glass tanks.

"Did you get planning permission for this?"

He did not answer. The circle of koi fanned out and scattered like fragments in a giant kaleidoscope.

"Wouldn't they make wonderful dresses?" cried Sally. "For 'Come Dancing.' Did you sew on all the sequins yourself?"

He took a threatening step towards her as Patsy was adding, "Or curtain fabric. Gorgeous!"

"There's only one new girl in your form," said Sally as she retreated. "Scarlett MacNamara."

The combination of the exotic and the Celtic was suggestive of the name that caused him pain.

"What's she like?"

"Dark. Pretty. Very shy."

He turned to watch his koi.

"I think I should tell you," said Sally, "that Patsy and I are leaving at the end of term. We're setting up an aromatherapy center."

"Good."

They left Maurice standing on his Japanese bridge, staring out over the water like a man who was waiting for someone to come home.

CARDBOARD CITY

"We could always pick the dog hairs off each other's coats. . . ."

The thought of grooming each other like monkeys looking for fleas sent them into giggles—anything would have.

"I used half a roll of Scotch tape on mine," said Stella indignantly then, although she wasn't really offended.

"It better not have been my Scotch tape or I'll kill you," Vanessa responded, without threat.

"It was His."

"Good. *He'll* kill you then," she said matter-of-factly.

The sisters, having flung themselves onto the train with no time to buy a comic, were wondering how to pass the long minutes until it reached central London with nothing to read. They could hardly believe that at the last moment He had not contrived to spoil their plan to go Christmas shopping. For the moment it didn't matter that their coats were unfashionable and the cuffs of their acrylic sweaters protruded lumpishly from the outgrown sleeves or that their frozen feet were beginning to smart, in the anticipation of chilblains, in their scuffed shoes in reaction to the heater under the seat. They were alone in the compartment except for a youth with a personal stereo leaking a tinny rhythm through the headphones.

★   ★   ★

With their heavy greenish-blond hair cut straight across their foreheads and lying flat as lasagne over the hoods and shoulders of their
school duffels, and their green eyes set wide apart in the flat planes of
their pale faces, despite Stella's borrowed fishnet stockings which were
causing her much angst, they looked younger than their fourteen and
twelve years. It would not have occurred to either of them that
anybody staring at them might have been struck by anything other
than their horrible clothes. Their desire, thwarted by Him and by lack
of money of their own, was to look like everybody else. The dog hairs
that adhered so stubbornly to the navy-blue cloth and bristled starkly
in the harsh and electric light of the winter morning were from
Barney, the black and white border collie, grown fat and snappish in
his old age, who bared his teeth at his new master, the usurper, and
slunk into a corner at his homecoming, as the girls slunk into their
bedroom.

"It's cruel to keep that animal alive," He would say. "What's
it got to live for? Smelly old hearthrug."

And while He discoursed on the Quality of Life, running a
finger down Mommy's spine or throat, Barney's legs would splay out
worse than they usually did and his claws click louder on the floor, or
a malodorous cloud of stagnant pond water emanate from his coat. It
was a sign of His power that Barney was thus diminished.

"We'll know when the Time has come. And the Time has not
yet come," said Mommy with more energy than she summoned to
champion her elder daughters, while Barney rolled a filmy blue eye in
her direction. The dog, despite his shedding coat, was beyond reproach as far as the girls were concerned; his rough back and neck had
been salted with many tears, and he was their one link with their old

life, before their father had disappeared and before their mother had defected to the enemy.

"What are you going to buy Him?" Vanessa asked.

"Nothing. I'm making His present."

"What?" Vanessa was incredulous, fearing treachery afoot.

"I'm knitting Him a pair of socks. Out of stinging nettles."

"I wish I could knit."

After a wistful pause she started to say, "I wonder what He would. . . ."

"I'm placing a total embargo on His name today," Stella cut her off. "Don't speak of Him. Don't even think about Him. Right, Regan?"

"Right, Goneril. Why does He call us those names?"

"They're the Ugly Sisters in Cinderella of course."

"I thought they were called Anastasia and . . . and . . . ."

"Embargo," said Stella firmly.

"It's not Cordelia who needs a fairy godmother, it's us. Wouldn't it be lovely if one day. . . ."

"Grow up."

So that was how He saw them, bewigged and garishly rouged, two pantomime dames with grotesque beauty spots and fishnet tights stretched over their bandy men's calves, capering jealously around Cordelia's highchair. Cordelia herself, like Barney, was adored unreservedly, but after her birth, with one hand rocking the transparent hospital cot in which she lay, as a joke which they could not share, He had addressed her half sisters as Goneril and Regan. Their mother had protested then, but now sometimes she used the names. Under His rule, comfortable familiar objects vanished and routines were abolished. Exposed to His mockery, they became ludicrous. One example was the Bunnykins china they ate from sometimes, not in a wish to prolong their babyhood but because it was there. All the pretty mismatched bits and pieces of crockery were superseded by a stark white service from Habitat and there were new forks with vicious prongs and knives which cut. Besotted with Cordelia's dimples and black curls, He lost all patience with his step-daughters, with their tendency to melancholy and easily provoked tears which their pink eyelids and noses could not conceal, and like a vivisector with an electric prod tormenting two albino mice, he discovered all their most vulnerable places.

Gypsies had traveled up in the train earlier, making their buttonholes and nosegays, and had left the seats and floor strewn with a litter of twigs and petals and scraps of silver foil like confetti.

"We might see Princess Di or Fergie," Vanessa said, scuffing the debris with her foot. "They do their Christmas shopping in Harrods."

"The Duchess of York to you. Oh yes, we're sure to run into them. Anyway, Princess Diana does her shopping in Covent Garden."

"Well then!" concluded Vanessa triumphantly. She noticed the intimation of a cold sore on her sister's superior lip and was for a second glad. Harrods and Covent Garden were where they had decided, last night, after lengthy discussions, to go, their excited voices rising from guarded whispers to a normal pitch, until He had roared upstairs at them to shut up. Vanessa's desire to go to Hamleys had been overruled. She had cherished a secret craving for a tube of plastic stuff with which you blew bubbles and whose petroleum smell she found as addictive as the smell of a new Band-Aid. Now she took out her purse and checked her ticket and counted her money yet again. Even with the change she had filched fearfully from the trousers He had left sprawled across the bedroom chair, it didn't amount to much. Stella was rich, as the result of her paper round and the tips she had received in return for the cards she had put through her customers' doors wishing them a "Merry Christmas from your Newsboy/Newsgirl," with a space for her to sign her name. She would have been even wealthier had He not demanded the money for the repair of the iron whose flex had burst into flames in her hand while she was ironing His shirt. She could not see how it had been her fault but supposed it must have been. The compartment filled up at each stop and the girls stared out of the window rather than speak in public, or look at each other and see mirrored in her sister her own unsatisfactory self.

The concourse at Victoria was scented with sweet and sickening melted chocolate from a booth that sold fresh-baked cookies, and crowded with people criss-crossing each other with loaded trolleys, running to hurl themselves at the barriers, dragging luggage and children; queuing helplessly for tickets while the minutes to departure ticked away, swirling around the bright scarves outside the Tie Rack, panic-buying festive socks and glittery bow ties, slurping coffee and beer and champing croissants and pizzas and jacket potatoes and trying on earrings. It had changed so much from the last time they had seen it that only the late arrival of their train and the notice of cancellation and delay on the indicator board reassured them that they were at the right Victoria Station.

"I've got to go to the Ladies."

"OK."

Vanessa attempted to join the dismayingly long queue trailing down the stairs but Stella had other plans.

"Stell-a! Where are you going?" She dragged Vanessa into the side entrance of the Grosvenor Hotel.

"Stella, we can't! It's a HOTEL! We'll be ARRESTED . . ." She wailed as Stella's fingers pinched through her coat sleeves, propelling her up the steps and through the glass doors.

"Shut up. Look as though we're meeting somebody."

Vanessa could scarcely breathe as they crossed the foyer, expecting at any moment a heavy hand to descend on her shoulder, a liveried body to challenge them, a peaked cap to thrust into their faces. The thick carpet accused their feet. Safely inside the Ladies, she collapsed against a basin.

"Well? Isn't this better than queuing for hours? And it's free."

"Supposing someone comes?"

"Oh stop bleating. It's perfectly all right. Daddy brought me here once—no one takes any notice of you."

The door opened and the girls fled into cubicles and locked the doors. After what seemed like half an hour Vanessa slid back the bolt and peeped around the door. There was Stella, bold as brass, standing at the mirror between the sleek backs of two women in stolen fur coats applying a stub of lipstick to her mouth. She washed and dried her hands and joined Stella, meeting a changed face in the glass: Stella's eyelids were smudged with green and purple, her lashes longer and darker, her skin matt with powder.

"Where did you get it?" she whispered hoarsely as the two women moved away.

"Tracy"—the friend who had lent her the stockings, with whom Vanessa, until they were safely on the train, had feared Stella would choose to go Christmas shopping instead of with her.

Women came and went and Vanessa's fear was forgotten as she applied the cosmetics to her own face.

"Now we look a bit more human," said Stella as they surveyed themselves, Goneril and Regan, whom their own father had named Star and Butterfly. Vanessa Cardui, Painted Lady, sucked hollows into her cheeks and said, "We really need some blusher, but it can't be helped."

"Just a sec."

"But Stella, it's a BAR . . . we can't . . . !"

Her alarm flooded back as Stella marched towards Edward's Bar.

"We'll get DRUNK. What about our shopping?"

Ignoring the animated temperance tract clutching her sleeve, Stella scanned the drinkers.

"Looking for someone, Miss?" the barman asked pleasantly.

"He's not here yet," said Stella. "Come on, Vanessa."

She checked the coffee lounge on the way out, and as they recrossed the fearful foyer it dawned on Vanessa that Stella had planned this all along; all the way up in the train she had been expecting to find Daddy in Edward's Bar. That had been the whole point of the expedition.

She was afraid that Stella would turn like an injured dog and snap at her. She swallowed hard, her heart racing, as if there were words that would make everything all right, if only she could find them.

"What?" Stella did turn on her.

"He might be in Harrods."

"Oh yes. Doing his Christmas shopping with Fergie and Di. Buying our presents."

Vanessa might have retorted, "The Duchess of York to you," but she knew better than to risk the cold salt wave of misery between them engulfing the whole day: A gypsy woman barred their way with a sprig of foliage wrapped in silver.

"Lucky white heather. Bring you luck."

"Doesn't seem to have brought you much," snarled Stella pushing past her.

"You shouldn't have been so rude. Now she'll put a curse on us," wailed Vanessa.

"It wasn't even real heather, dumbbell."

"Now there's no chance we'll meet Daddy."

Stella strode blindly past the gauntlet of people rattling tins for The Blind. Vanessa dropped in a coin and hurried after her down the steps. As they went to consult the map of the Underground they almost stumbled over a man curled up asleep on the floor, a bundle of gray rags and hair and beard tied up with string. His feet, black with dirt and disease, protruded shockingly bare into the path of the Christmas shoppers. The sisters stared, their faces chalky under their makeup.

Then a burst of laughter and singing broke out. A group of men and women waving bottles and cans were holding a private crazed party, dancing in their disfigured clothes and plastic accoutrements; a woman with long gray hair swirling out in horizontal streamers from a circlet of tinsel was clasping a young man in a close embrace as they shuffled around singing "All I want for Christmas is my two front teeth," and he threw back his head to pour the last drops from a bottle into a toothless black hole, while their companions beat out a percussion accompaniment on bottles and cans with a braying brass of hiccups. They were the only people in that desperate and shoving crowded place who looked happy.

Stella and Vanessa were unhappy as they traveled down the escalator. The old man's feet clawed at them with broken and corroded nails; the revelers, although quite oblivious to the citizens of the other world, had frightened them; the gypsy's curse hung over them.

*   *   *

Harrods was horrendous. They moved bemused through the silken scented air, buffeted by headscarves, furs and green shopping bags. Fur and feathers in the Food Hall left them stupefied in the splendor of death and beauty and money.

"This is crazy," said Stella. "We probably couldn't afford even one quail's egg."

Mirrors flung their scruffy reflections back at them and they half-expected to be shown the door by one of the green and gold guards and after an hour of fingering and coveting and temptation they were out in the arctic wind of Knightsbridge with two packs of Christmas cards and a round gold box of chocolate Napoleons.

In Covent Garden they caught the tail end of a piece of street theater as a green spotted pantomime cow curvetted at them with embarrassing udders, swiping the awkward smiles off their faces with its tail. A woman dressed as a clown bopped them on the head with a balloon and thrust a bashed-in hat at them. Close to she looked fierce rather than funny. The girls paid up. It seemed that everybody in the city was engaged in a conspiracy to make them hand over their money. Two hot chocolates made another serious inroad in their finances, the size of the bill souring the floating islands of cream as they sat on white wrought-iron chairs sipping from long spoons to the accompaniment of a young man busking on a violin backed by a stereo system.

"You should've brought your cello," said Vanessa and choked on her chocolate as she realized she could hardly have said anything more tactless. It was He who had caused Stella's impromptu resignation from the school orchestra, leaving them in the lurch. His repetition, in front of two of His friends, of an attributed reprimand by Sir Thomas Beecham to a lady cellist had made it impossible for her to practice at home and unthinkable that she should perform on a public platform to an audience sniggering like Him, debasing her and the music.

"It's—it's not my kind of music," she had lied miserably to Miss Philips, the music teacher.

"Well, Stella, I must say I had never thought of *you* as a disco queen," Miss Philips had said bitterly.

Her hurt eyes strobed Stella's pale selfish face and falling-down socks as she wilted against the wall. Accusations of letting down her fellow musicians followed, and reminders of Miss Philips's struggle to obtain the cello from another school, her own budget and resources being so limited. She ignored Stella in the corridor thereafter and the pain of this was still with her, like the ominous ache in her lower abdomen. She wished she was at home curled up with a hot-water bottle.

"Bastard," she said. "Of all the gin joints in all the suburbs of south-east London, why did He have to walk into ours?" Mommy had brought Him home from a rehearsal of the amateur production of *Oklahoma* for which she was doing the costumes, ostensibly for an emergency fitting of His Judd Fry outfit, the trousers and boots of which were presenting difficulties. The girls had almost clapped the palms off their hands after the mournful rendition of "Poor Judd is Dead." It would always be a show-stopper for them.

Stella wished she had had one of the cards from Harrods to put in the school postbox for Miss Philips, but she hadn't, and now it was too late. Vanessa bought a silver heart-shaped balloon for Cordelia, or, as Stella suspected, for herself. They wandered around the stalls and shops over the slippery cobblestones glazed with drizzle.

"How come, whichever way we go, we always end up in Central Avenue?" Vanessa wondered.

Stella gave up the pretense that she knew exactly where she was going. "It'll be getting dark soon. We must buy *something*."

They battled their way into the Covent Garden General Store and joined the wet and unhappy throng desperate to spend money they couldn't afford on presents for people who would not want what they received, to the relentless musical threat that Santa Claus was coming to town. "If this is more fun than just shopping," said Stella as they queued to pay for their doubtful purchases, quoting from the notice, displayed over the festive and jokey goods, "I think I prefer just shopping. Sainsbury's on Saturday morning is paradise compared to this."

Stella was seduced by a gold mesh star and some baubles as fragile and iridescent as soap bubbles, to hang on the conifer in the corner of the bare front room, decked in scrawny tinsel too sparse for its sprawling branches and topped with the fairy with a scorch mark in her graying crêpe-paper skirt where it had once caught in a candle. The candles, with most of their old decorations, had been vetoed by Him and had been replaced by a set of fairy lights with more twisted emerald green flex than bulbs in evidence.

"I wish we hadn't got a tree," Vanessa said.

"I know. Cordelia likes it, though."

"I suppose so. That's all that matters really. I mean, Christmas *is* for kids, isn't it?"

Vanessa showed her the bubble bath disguised as a bottle of gin which she was buying for Him.

"Perhaps He'll drink it."

"Early on Christmas morning, nursing a savage hangover, He rips open His presents and desperate for a hair-of-the-dog He puts the bottle to his lips. Bubbles come out of His nose and mouth, He falls to the floor—"

"Screaming in agony."

"—screaming in agony, foaming at the mouth. The heroic efforts of his distraught stepdaughters fail to revive him. An ambulance is called but it gets stuck in traffic. When they finally reach the hospital all the nurses are singing carols in the wards and no one can find the stomach pump. A doctor in a paper hat tells the sorrowing sisters—or are they laughing, who can tell?—that it's too late. He has fallen victim to His own greed. How much does it cost?"

"Two pounds seventy-nine."

"Cheap at twice the price."

After leaving the shop they collided with a superstructure formed by two supermarket trolleys lashed together and heaped with a perilous pyramid of old clothes and plastic bags and utensils and bits of hardware like taps and broken car exhausts and hubcaps, the handlebars of a bicycle fronting it like antlers and three plumes of pampas grass waving in dirty Prince of Wales feathers. The owner was dragging a large cardboard box from beneath a stall of skirts and blouses.

"What do you think he wants that box for?" Vanessa wondered.

"To sleep in, of course. He probably lives in Cardboard City."

"Cardboard City?"

"It's where the homeless people live. They all sleep in cardboard boxes underneath the Arches."

"What arches?"

"*The* Arches, of course. Shall we go home now?"

Vanessa nodded. They were wet and cold, and the rain had removed most of their makeup, saving them the trouble of doing it themselves before they encountered Him. The feet of Stella's stockings felt like muddy string in her leaking shoes.

They were huddled on the packed escalator, two drowned rats going up to Victoria, when Vanessa screamed shrilly.

"Daddy!"

She pointed to a man on the opposing escalator.

"It's Daddy, quick Stella, we've got to get off." She would have climbed over the rail if Stella hadn't held her.

"It's not him."

"It is. It is. *Daddy!*"

Faces turned to stare. The man turned and their eyes met as they were carried upwards and he was borne inexorably down. Vanessa tried to turn to run down against the flow of the escalator but she was wedged. The man was gone forever.

"It wasn't him, I tell you." Stella fought the sobbing Vanessa at the top of the stair, they were yelling at each other in the mêlée of commuters and shoppers. She succeeded in dragging her through the barrier, still crying, "It was him. Now we'll never see him again."

"Daddy hasn't got a beard, you know that. And he'd never wear a balaclava. Come *on*, Vanessa, we'll miss our train."

"It was him. Let's go back, please, please."

"Look, stupid, that guy was a down and out. A vagrant. A wino. A meths drinker. It couldn't possibly have been Daddy."

On the homebound train Stella carefully opened the box of chocolate Napoleons. There were so many that nobody would notice if a couple were missing. She took out two gold coins and sealed the box again. For the rest of their lives Vanessa would be convinced that she had seen her father, and Stella would never be sure. The chocolate dissolved in their mouths as they crossed the Thames.

"Where is Cardboard City?" whispered Vanessa. "How do you get there?"

" 'Follow the Yellow Brick Road. . . .' "

The silver heart-shaped balloon floated on its vertical string above the heads and newspapers of the passengers.

" 'Now I know I've got a heart, because it's breaking.' "

"It's just a slow puncture," Stella said. She stuck a gift label on to the balloon's puckering silver skin. It ruined the look of it, but it was kindly meant. Vanessa looked out of the window at the moon melting like a lemon drop in the freezing sky above the chimney tops of Clapham and pictured it shining on the cold frail walls and pinnacles of Cardboard City.

"I don't want Daddy to sleep in a cardboard box," she said.

"It's a great life," Stella said savagely. "Didn't you see those people singing and dancing?"

DREAMS OF DEAD
WOMEN'S HANDBAGS

It was a black evening bag sequined with salt, open-mouthed under a rusted marcasite clasp, revealing a black moiré silk lining stained by seawater; a relic stranded in the wrack of tarry pebbles and tufts of blue and orange nylon string like garish sea anemones, crab shells and lobster legs, plastic detritus, oily feathers, condoms and rubbery weed and clouded glass, the dry white sponges of whelk egg cases, and a brittle black-horned mermaid's purse. This image, the wreckage of a dream beached on the morning, would not float away; as empty as an open shell, the black bivalve emitted a silent howl of despair; clouds passed through its mirror.

Susan Vigo was much possessed by death. Sitting on a slow train to the coast, at a table in the compartment adjacent to the buffet car, she thought about her recurring dream and about a means of murder. A book and a newspaper lay in front of her, and as she inserted the word "limpid" in the crossword, completing the puzzle, she saw aquamarine water in a rock pool wavering limpidly over a conical white limpet shell. Her own id was rather limp that morning, she felt; the gold top of her pen tasted briny in her mouth. The color of the water was the precise clear almost-green of spring evening skies when the city trembled with the possibility of love. She wondered dispassionately if she would ever encounter such a sky again, and as she wondered, she saw a handbag half-submerged on the bottom of the pool among the wavering weeds, green and encrusted with limpets, as though it had lain there for a long time, releasing gentle strings of bubbles like dreams and memories. A mermaid's purse, she remembered her father teaching her, as she made her way to the buffet, was the horny egg case of a skate, or ray or shark, but to whom the desolate handbag in her dreams had belonged, she had no idea, only that its owner was dead.

The buffet car steward seemed familiar, but perhaps the painful red eyes were uniform issue, along with the shiny jacket spattered by toasted sandwiches; his hair had been combed back with bacon grease and fell in curly rashers on his collar, his red tie was as slick as a dying poppy's petal. As Susan waited in the queue she told herself that he could have no possible significance in her life, and reminded herself that she made many journeys and had probably encountered him before, leering over the formica counter of another train. Nevertheless she watched him, it was her habit to stare at people, with an uneasy notion that he was Charon ferrying her across the Styx—but Charon would not be the barman, but the driver of this Inter-City train, sitting at the controls in his cab, racing them down the rails to the Elysian fields, and she was almost certain that she and her fellow passengers were still alive and their coins were for the purchase of refreshments and not the fees of the dead. The barman's years of bracing himself on the swaying floors of articulated metal snakes had given him the measure of his customers. The woman in the simulated beige mink, in front of Susan in the queue, asked for two gin and tonics, one for an imaginary friend down the corridor, and was given two little green bottles, two cans of tonic, and one plastic cup with a contemptuous fistful of ice cubes. Her eyes met the barman's and she did not demur. One of his eyes closed like a snake's in a wink at Susan as the woman fumbled her purchases from the counter. "It takes one to know one," thought Susan refusing to be drawn into complicity by the reptilian lid of his red eye as she ordered her coffee. Her face in the mirror behind the bar, her shirt, her scarf, her brooch, the cut of her jacket spoke as quietly of success as the fur-coated woman's screeched failure.

Failure. That was a word Susan Vigo hated. She saw it as a sickly plant with etiolated leaves, flourishing in dank unpleasant places, a parasite on a rotting trunk, or a pot plant on the windowsills of houses of people she despised. If she had cared to, she could have supplied a net curtain on a string as a backcloth and a plaster Alsatian, but she had a horror of rotting window frames and rented rooms, and banished the image. Susan Vigo was not the sort of woman who would order two gins for herself on a train. She was not, like some she could name, the sort of writer who would arrive to give a reading with a wine-splashed book and grains of cat litter in her trouser turnups, having fortified herself with spirits on the journey for the ordeal, who would enter in disarray and stumble into disrepute. The books in her overnight bag were glossy and immaculate with clean white strips of paper placed between the pages, to mark the passages which she would read. She did not regard it as an ordeal; she had memorized her introductory speech, and was looking forward to the evening. She had done her homework, and would have been able to relax with a book by another author had consciousness of the delivery date of her own next crime novel not threatened like a migraine at the edge of her brain. The irony was that the title of her book was *Deadline* and for the first time in her life, she feared that she would not meet hers. Notice of it had appeared already in her publisher's catalogue and she had not even got the plot. It was set on the coast, she knew that; it involved a writer—yes, and horned poppy and sea holly and viper's bugloss, stranded sea-mice leaking rainbows into the sand, and of course her Detective Inspector Christopher Hartshorn, an investigator of the intellectual, laconic school; a body—naturally; a handbag washed up on the beach—the sort of handbag that had foxtrotted to Harry Roy, or a flaunting scarlet patent number blatant as a stiletto heel, a steel-faceted purse, a gondola basket holding a copy of *Mirabelle* or *Roxy*—she didn't even know in which period to set her murder—a drawstring leather bag which smelled of raw camel hide, a satchel with a wooden pencil box, a strap purse, containing a threepenny bit, worn across the front of a gymslip—old handbags like discarded lovers. She sifted desperately through the heap of silk and plastic, leather and wicker—it had to be black, like the handbag in her dream. . . .

Susan lived in Hampstead, on a staple diet of vodka and asparagus, fresh in season, or tinned. It made life simple; she never had to think about what food to buy except when she had guests, which was not very often; she was more entertained than entertaining. She loved her flat and lived there alone. She had once been given two lovebirds but had grown jealous of their absorption in each other and had given them away. Trailing plants now entwined the bars of the cage where the pink and yellow birds had preened, kissing each other with waxy bills; she preferred their green indifference. There was not a trace of a plaster Alsatian. The man who had seduced her had introduced her to asparagus, its tender green heads swimming in butter, with baked beans—her choice. Professor Bruno Rosenblum, lecturer in poetry who although his juxtaposed names conjured up withered roses on their stems, had once strewn the bed with roses while she slept. Waking in the scent and petals, she had wept. "'Ah, as the heart grows older, it will come to such sights colder,'" she thought now, in the train, remembering, as the past, like the dried petals of potpourri exhaled a slight sad scent, and "Perhaps G.M. Hopkins got it right—it is always ourselves for whom we are grieving—enough of this" she turned from the dirty window slashed with rain that obscured the flat landscape and the dun animals in the shabby February fields, to her book. She wondered if she could, perhaps, take its central situation or *donnée*, and by changing it subtly, and substituting her own characters, manufacture a convincingly original work. . . .

"'If you want to know about a woman, look in her purse.'" The detective dumped the clues to the dead dame's life into a plastic bag and consigned it to Forensic. Susan's own handbag, if studied, would have told of an orderly life and mind, or of an owner who had dumped all her old makeup in the bin and dashed into an expensive chemist's on the way to the station: no sleazy clutter there, no circle of foam rubber tinged with grimy powder, no sweating stubs of lipstick and broken biros leaking into the lining, or tobacco shreds or dog-eared appointment cards for special clinics or combs with dirty teeth or minicab cards acquired on flights through dawn streets from unspeakable crises. Susan could see as clearly in her mind the contents of the handbag of the woman who had bought the two gins as she could see her black stilettos resting on the next seat, and the fall of fake fur caressing her calf. She saw her lean forward and open a compact the dark blue of a mussel shell, and peer into a mirror, and her imagination supplied a crack zigzagging across the glass, presaging doom. The man directly opposite Susan was reading a report and was of as little interest as he had been at the start of the journey; on the other side of the aisle a family, parents and two children, finished their enormous lunch and settled down to a game of three-dimensional noughts and crosses, which involved plastic tubes and marbles, clack clack clack. The marbles bounced off Susan's brain like bullets. "Why can't they just use pencil and paper?" she thought irritably: the extra dimensions added nothing but cost and noise to the game. She put her hands over her ears, and, resting her book on the table, tried to read, but her concentration was shot to pieces. She closed her eyes, and the handbag in her dream returned like a black shell, which if held to the ear would whisper her own mortality.

There was this handbag washed up on the beach—what next? She waited for a whole narrative to unwind and a cast of characters to come trooping out, but nothing happened. There was this crime writer traveling on a train, panicking about a deadline when suddenly . . . a single shot passed through the head of the buffet car attendant's head, shattering the glass behind him . . . Susan's fascination with firearms dated from a white double holster studded with glass jewels and two fancy guns with bluish shining barrels and decorated stocks; she had loved them more than any of her dolls, taking them to bed with her at night, loving the neat round boxes of pink caps. She could smell them now, and the scent of new sandals with crêpe soles like cheese.

Dreams of dead women's handbags: the click of a false tortoiseshell clasp, the musty smell of old perfume from the torn black moiré lining, and powder in a shell, lipstick that would look as ghastly on a skull as it did on the mouths of the little white flat fish on the seaside stall, skate smoking cigarettes through painted mouths, the glitter of saliva on a pin impaling whelks. She saw a man and a woman walking on a cliff top starred with pink thrift, a sea gull's white scalloped tail feathers; the woman wore a dress patterned in poppies and corn and the man had his shirt-collar open over his jacket, in holiday style. A child skipped between them on that salty afternoon when the world was their oyster.

Amberley Hall, where Susan was heading, was a small private literary foundation where students of all ages attended courses and summer schools in music, painting and writing. She had been invited to be the guest reader at one of their creative writing courses, and was looking forward to seeing again the two tutors, both friends, and renewing her acquaintance with Amberley's directors whom she had liked very much when she met them the previous year when she herself had been a co-tutor. The house was white and stood on a cliff; reflections of the sea and sky met in its windows. Susan hoped that she would be given the room in which she had slept before, with its faded blue bedspread and shell-framed looking glass and vase of dried flowers beside the white shells on the windowsill, sea lavender faded by time, like a dead woman's passions and regrets. The clatter of marbles became intoler-able. Susan strode towards the buffet car. The train seemed to be going very slowly. She began to worry about the time and wish that she had accepted her hosts's offer to meet her at the station.

"Going all the way?" the barman asked as he sliced a lemon with a thin-bladed knife. The other woman had not been offered lemon.

"I beg your pardon?"

"Going all the way?"

"No. Not quite."

"Business or pleasure?"

Susan had never seen why she should answer that question, so often asked by strangers on a train.

"A bit of both," she replied.

Again his eyelid flickered in a wink.

"Ice?"

"Please." She hoped her tone matched the cubes he was
dropping into her glass with his fingers, one of which was girdled with
a frayed Band-Aid. Stubble was trying to break through the red nodules of a rash on his neck; he looked as though he had shaved in cold
water in the basin in the blocked toilet, with his knife. The arrival of
two other customers brought their conversation to an end.

As she approached her seat with her vodka and tonic she stopped in her
tracks. That woman in the fur coat had Susan's overnight bag down on
the seat and was going through her things.

"What do you think you're doing?" She grabbed her furry
arm; her hand was shaken from it.

"I'm just looking for a tissue."

"But that's my bag. Those are my things!"

The woman was pulling out clothes and underclothes and
dumping them on the seat while the noughts and crosses clicked and
clacked, tic tac toe. She scrabbled under the books at the bottom of the
bag.

"Stop it, do you hear?"

"She's only looking for a tissue," said the man opposite mildly,
looking up from his report.

"I'm going to get the guard. I'm going to pull the emergency
cord."

The other woman's full lips trembled and she started to cry.

The man took a handkerchief from his breast pocket, shook it
out and handed it to her.

"Have a good blow."

She did.

"I'll give you a good blow!" said Susan punching her hard in the chest, at the top of a creased *décolletage* where a gilt pendant nestled in the shape of the letter M. The lights went out. The train almost concertinaed to a stop.

"Now look what you've done, pulling the communication cord."

"I didn't touch it," Susan shouted. "What's going on? What's the matter with everybody? I didn't go near it."

She felt the woman move away, and sat down heavily on her disarranged bag, panting with affront and rage, the unfairness of it all and the fact that nobody had stood up for her. Tears were rolling down her face as she groped for her clothes and crammed them back into the bag. Marbles rolled across the table and ricocheted off the floor. The tips of cigarettes glowed like tiny volcanoes in the gloom and someone giggled, a high nervous whinny. Susan began to sweat. Rain was drumming on the windows like her heartbeats, and she knew that she had died and was to be locked for eternity in this train in the dark with people who hated her. This was her sentence: what was her crime? Battalions of minor sins thronged her memory. Her hand hurt where she had punched the woman; she sucked her knuckle and tasted blood. The lights came on. Susan screamed.

The barman stood in the doorway, his knife in his hand.

"Nearly a nasty accident," he said. "Car stalled on the level crossing."

People started to laugh and talk.

"Could've been curtains for us all," he said as the train brayed and the orange curtains at the black windows swayed as it started to move.

The woman in the fur coat came sashaying down the aisle, reeled on a marble, and plonked herself down beside Susan.

"Sorry about that little mistake, only I mistook it for my bag. They're quite similar. Here, let me help you put it up."

They swung it clumsily onto the rack, next to a dirty tapestry bag edged in cracked vinyl. Susan looked into her eyes, opaque as marbles, and perceived that she was mad. She picked up her book.

"Like reading, do you?"

"When I get the chance."

"I know what you mean. There's always something needs doing, isn't there? I expect you're like me, can't sit idle. What with my little dog, and my crochering and the telly there's always something, isn't there?"

"Crochering?" Susan heard herself ask.

"Yes, I've always got some on the go. I made this."

She pulled open her lapels to show a deep-throated pink filigree garment.

"It was a bolero in the pattern, only I added the sleeves."

Susan smiled and tried desperately to read, but it was too late: she saw in vivid detail the woman's sitting room, feet in pink fluffy slippers stretched out to the electric fire that was mottling her legs, the wheezy Yorkshire terrier with a growth on its neck, the crochet hook plying in a billowy sea of pink and violet squares; a bedspread for a wedding present to a niece, who would bundle it into a cupboard.

She almost said, "I'm sorry about your little dog," but stopped herself in time, and before she was tempted to advise her to abandon her bedspread, the guard announced that the train was approaching her station. She gathered her things together with relief and went to find an exit. As she passed the bar the steward, who had taken off his jacket and was reading a newspaper, did not raise his head. She saw how foolish she had been to fear him.

⋆   ⋆   ⋆

"Thank God that's over," she said aloud on the platform as she took deep breaths of wet dark air which although the station was miles inland, tasted salty, and the appalling train pulled away, carrying the barman and the deranged woman to their mad destinations. She came out into the forecourt in time to see the rear lights of a taxi flashing in the rain. She knew at once that it was the only one and that it would not return for a long time. She saw a telephone box across the road, and shielding with her bag her hair that the rain would reduce to a nest of snakes hurried through the puddles. At least, being in the country, the phone would not have been vandalized. A wet chip paper wrapped itself around her ankles; the receiver dangled from a mess of wires, black with emptiness roaring through its broken mouth, like a washed-up handbag.

A pub. There must be a pub somewhere near the station that would have a telephone. Susan stepped out of the smell of rural urine and started to walk. She would not let herself panic, or let the lit and curtained windows sheltering domesticity make her feel lonely. Perhaps she could hire a car, from the pub. She imagined the sudden silence falling on the jocular company of the inn and a fearful peasant declaring, "None of us villagers dare go up to Amberley Hall. Not after dark," and a dark figure in a bat-winged cloak flying screeching past the moon.

Mine host was a gloomy fellow who pointed her to a pay phone. The number was engaged. Temporarily defeated, Susan ordered a drink and sat down. It was then that she realized that her overnight bag had been transformed into a grubby tapestry hold-all with splitting vinyl trim. A cold deluge of disbelief engulfed her and then hot pricking needles of anger. She drowned the words that rose to her lips; this wasn't Hampstead. How could it have happened—that madwoman—Susan was furious with herself; she would have scorned to use the device of the switched luggage in one of her own books, and here she was, lumbered, in this dire pub, with this disgusting bag, and worse, worse, all her own things, her books—the reading. . . . She was tempted to call it a day then, and order another drink, and consign herself to fate, propping up the bar until her money ran out and they dumped her in the street, but she made another attempt at the telephone, and this time got through. Someone would be there to pick her up in twenty minutes. She thought of ordering a sandwich but the knowledge of the meal, the refectory table heaped with bowls of food awaiting her, restrained her, and she sat there half listening to the jukebox, making her drink last, wishing she was at home doing something cheerful like drinking vodka and listening to Bessie Smith, or Billie Holiday singing "Good Morning Heartache."

She thought she had found her murder victim, a blond woman with a soft white face and body and a pendant in the shape of the letter M and a stolen bag; she lolled in death, her black shoes stabbing skywards, on a cliff top lying in the thrift that starred the grass and was embossed on a threepenny bit, tarnished at the bottom of an old handbag. Threepence, that was the amount of pocket money she had received; a golden hexagonal coin each Saturday morning. The early 1950s: a dazzle of red, white and blue; father, mother and child silhouetted against a golden sunburst in a red sky like figures on a poster, marching into Utopia.

   The dead woman's dress was splashed with poppies and corn—no, that was wrong—it must be black. Her mother had had a dress of poppies and corn, scarlet flowers and golden ears and sky-blue cornflowers on a white field; Ceres in white peep-toe shoes, the sun sparkling off a Kirbigrip in her dark gold hair. Her father's hair was bright with brilliantine and he wore his shirt-collar, white as vanilla ice cream, open over his jacket. Susan's hair was in two thin plaits of corn and gripped on either side with a white hair-slide in the shape of Brumas the famous polar bear cub. Susan sat in the pub, becoming aware that it was actually a small hotel and staring at a red-carpeted staircase that disappeared at an angle, leading to the upper guest rooms. In a flash she realized why the barman in the train looked familiar, and blind and deaf to the music and flashing lights she sat in a waking dream.

The child woke in the hotel bedroom and found herself alone. Moonlight lay on the pillows of the double bed her parents shared. The bed was undisturbed. They had come up from the bar to tuck her in. "You be a good girl now and go to sleep. We're just popping out for a stroll, we won't be gone more than a few minutes." Her father's eyes were red—she turned her face away from his beery kiss. Her mother's best black taffeta dress rustled as she closed the door behind them. She pulled a sweater over her nightdress and buckled on her holster and her new white sandals and tiptoed to the door. A gust of piano playing and singing and beer and cigarette smoke bellied into the bedroom. She closed the door quietly behind her and slid slowly down the banister, so as not to make any noise. She was angry with them for leaving her alone. She bet they were eating ice creams and chips without her. She crept to the back door and let herself out into the street. Although she had never been out so late alone, she found that it was almost light—girls and boys come out to play, the moon doth shine as bright as day—she would burst into the café and shoot them dead—Susan saw her in the moonlight, a small figure in a white nightdress in the empty street with a gun in each hand. The café was closed.

She turned onto the path that led to the cliffs. Rough grass spiked her bare legs and sand filled her new sandals and rubbed on her heels. She holstered her guns because she had to use her hands to scramble up the steep slope, uttering little sobs of fear and rage. She reached the top and flung herself panting onto the turf. At the edge of the cliff sat two figures, from this distance as black as two cormorants on a rock against the sky. The sea was roaring in her ears as she wriggled on her belly towards them. As she drew nearer she could see the woman's arms, white as vanilla in her black taffeta dress and the man's shirt-collar. She stood up and drew her guns and took aim but suddenly she was frightened at herself standing there against the sky and just wanted them to hold her, and shoved the guns back in the holster and as she did the man put his arm around the woman's shoulder and kissed her. The child was running towards them, to thrust herself between their bodies shouting joyfully "Boo!" as she thumped them on their backs and the woman lost her balance and clutched the man and they went tumbling over and over and over and the woman's handbag fell from her wrist and went spiraling after them screaming and screaming from its open black mouth.

When the landlady, impatient at the congealing breakfast, came to rouse the family in the morning she found the child asleep, cuddling up to a holster instead of a teddy. The parents' bed was undisturbed. It seemed a shame to wake the little girl. She looked so peaceful with her fair hair spread out on the pillow. She shook her gently.

"Where are your mummy and daddy, lovey?"

The child sat up, seeing the buckle of her new sandal hanging by a thread. Mummy would have to sew it on.

"I don't know," she answered truthfully.

"Susan. Hi." Tom from Amberley Hall was shaking her arm. "You look awful. Have you had a terrible journey? You must have."

"Perfectly bloody," said Susan.

"I'm afraid you've missed supper," said Tom, in the car, "but we'll rustle up something for you after the reading. I think we'd better get straight on with it if you don't mind. Everybody's keen to meet you. Quite an interesting bunch of students this time. . . ."

His voice went on. Susan wanted to bury her face in the thick cables of his sweater. As they entered the house she explained about the loss of her bag.

"Just like Professor Pnin, eh, on the wrong train with the wrong lecture?" he laughed. Susan wished then profoundly to be Professor Pnin, Russian and ideally bald; to be anybody but herself in her creased clothes with her hair snaking wildly around her head and a tapestry bag in her hand containing the crocheted tangle of that woman's mad life.

"It was the right train," she said, "but I haven't got anything to read."

"I did get in touch with your publishers to send some books to sell, but I'm afraid they haven't arrived. Never mind though, some of the students have brought their own copies for you to sign so you could borrow one. Five minutes to freshen up, OK? We've put you in the same room as last time."

"No bloody food. No bloody wine. Not even any bloody books," said Susan behind the closed door of her room. She aimed a kick at the bookcase: each of those spines faded by sea air representing somebody's futile bid to hold back eternal night. Precisely five minutes later she stepped, pale, poised and professional, into the firelit room to enchant her audience.

When she had finished reading, a chill hung over the room for a moment and then someone started the clapping. As the appreciative applause flickered out, bottles of wine and glasses were brought, and the evening was given over to informal questions and discussion. A gallant in corduroys bowed as he handed her a glass.

"You're obviously very successful, Miss Vigo, or may I call you Susan? Could you tell us what made you decide on writing as a career in the first place? I mean I myself have been attempting to—"

"I wanted to be rich," interrupted Susan quickly before he could launch on his autobiography. The firelight striking red glints on her hair, and her charming smile persuaded her listeners that she was joking. "You see, I was always determined to succeed in whatever career I chose. I came from a very deprived background. My parents died tragically when I was young and I was brought up by relatives." Her lip trembled slightly; a plaster Alsatian barked in corroboration.

"What was your first big breakthrough?"

"I was very lucky in that I met a professor at university, a dear old soul, who took an interest in my youthful efforts and who was very helpful to me professionally. He's dead now, alas." She became for a moment a pretty young student paying grateful tribute to her crusty old mentor. Most of the audience were half in love with her now.

"What made you turn to crime, as it were, Susan, instead of to any other fictional form?"

Susan's slender body rippled as she giggled, "I don't know

really—I developed a taste for murder at an early age, and I've never looked back, I suppose."

"Can I ask where you get your ideas from?"

The frail orphan sipped her wine before replying.

"From 'the foul rag-and-bone shop of the heart.'"

PERPETUAL SPINACH

Old Cartwright belonged to the snow-shoveling generation. The dread sound of metal scraping the pavement woke his young neighbors and even before they were aware of the strange feathery light in the bedroom they knew it was snowing, and pictured him holding out his spade to catch the first sparse flakes falling from the sky. They groaned at the thought of that old man shoveling their shared path, as he surely would, and pulled the duvet over their heads, burying themselves in goose feathers.

Despite his London ancestry there was something bucolic about Old Cartwright; a sense of warm rabbits dangling from his belt, or a brace of wood-pigeons with rubies of blood on their breasts. He rode a stiff old black woman's bicycle to his urban allotment, pedaling slowly with one corduroy trouser leg, the color of ploughed fields, caught up in a cycle clip and the other tied up with string. The bicycle, like its owner Miss Defreitas, his subtenant, who lived above Mr. Cartwright, was old and stiff and black, and was furnished with wicker baskets front and rear in which he brought back bouquets of carrots, potatoes and beans, frilly dark savoy cabbages, rhubarb and, endlessly, spinach. "I can see why it's called perpetual spinach," Olivia had said despairingly, plunging her hands into yet another washing-up bowl full of wet leaves. He set traps of jam jars filled with beer for the slugs and snails and they floundered and drowned, swelling to grotesque bleached alcoholic fungi before he threw them in a jellied heap on the compost. His crops were nourished on blood and bonemeal; the veins of his beetroots ran red above their swollen globes, his tomatoes were solid balls of hemoglobin and under their toxic green umbrellas the sanguineous sticks of his rhubarb were as thick as vultures' legs. Until his retirement he had been a driver on the Southern Region of British Rail, and Miss Defreitas had cleaned trains. She had been one of those women whose dustpan and brush were as much a reproach to commuters, swinging their feet out of the path of the cartons and cups and cigarette butts left by their predecessors, in the guilty knowledge that they would be replacing the rubbish as soon as she had gone, as Old Cartwright's spade was to Nick and Olivia. Miss Defreitas received his vegetables with politeness, although she continued to buy sweet potatoes and other strange tubers and roots which he could not identify, and refused to try. At first, Nick and Olivia had indulged in lewd speculation about the relationship of their elderly neighbors, but apart from Sunday lunch, which they took turns to cook, when Old Cartwright returned from the pub and Miss Defreitas from church, and the occasional sultry evenings when she brought out a kitchen chair and sat fanning herself while he slopped water over the begonias in the bed at the side of the yard, they led separate lives.

"This is ridiculous," Nick said, hobbling to the window wrapped in the duvet, leaving Olivia exposed on the bed. "Doesn't he know that if you clear the snow from outside your house you are responsible if anybody slips and breaks a leg?" He banged on the window and shouted at Cartwright to put back their snow. The double glazing muffled his voice and Old Cartwright, looking up with dimmed eyes, perceived him to be wearing an off-the-shoulder ball gown and raised his spade in an old-soldierly salute.

"If this keeps on, we can build a snowman later," said Olivia.

"Dress it up in one of Old Cartwright's caps and pelt it with snowballs," agreed Nick coming back to bed. The radio came on and he pressed the snooze button.

"Why do those old fogeys have to get up so early?"

"Because they haven't anything better to do," Olivia snuggled into him.

Why, despite the earthy bundles of produce left on their doorstep, Nick and Olivia sometimes wondered, did they regard him as a horrible old man? True, they had once heard him braying through the fence in mockery of the laughter at one of their parties where the guests spilled into the yard on summer nights, and one of their friends had asked if there was a donkey next door. She was pissed, of course; they all were. "Only a silly ass," Nick had replied quick as a flash; it was hilarious, but generally Cartwright was no trouble. They did not know about the slugs and snails, having resisted his invitations to visit the allotment, but taking the grisly tidbits suspended from his washing line for the birds as an indication, fantasized a gamekeeper's gibbet of crucified fur and feathers on his toolshed wall. Before they had learned that he had been a train driver they had decided that he was a ratcatcher. There was an empty rabbit hutch by his back door, mossy-roofed, with wire netting rusted to brittleness. At their firework party, Miss Defreitas had appeared at her window as a floating white nightdress against the blackness. Olivia held out a sparkler to her but a rocket whizzing toward the house made her disappear in a burst of golden stars, leaving the midnight sky and her window darker than before.

"Stupid old cockroach," Nick had said, but Olivia had been pleased that their youthful pyrotechnics had lighted up her drab life for a minute or two.

"You ought to get yourself an allotment," Old Cartwright had told Nick, leaning over the wooden fence that separated their backyards. It was broken, pulled down or held in the arms of an old Russian vine, and was, as he was fond of pointing out, their responsibility. "Keep the missis in fruit and veg. I'll have a word with my committee. There's a waiting list, but a word in the right ear. . . ."

He rubbed his own right lobe between an earthy finger and thumb while the thin burned-out cigarette stuck to his lip waggled in complicity.

"I wouldn't have time to look after an allotment," Nick responded in weak alarm from the lounger where he lay with a book and a pitcher of Pimms, swiping at a wasp as if warding off a barrage of onions and tomatoes. He swung his legs, still golden from a Turkish holiday, in cut off denim shorts, to the ground and took refuge in the kitchen, leaving the Pimms, like one of Cartwright's traps, to entice a variety of winged insects to a sweet and sticky death among the mint and melting ice floes.

"Oh, you've just broken my dream," Olivia said, when he told her. "I had a really funny dream last night. Henry was on a bicycle going to the allotments. When I say funny, it wasn't really funny, it was scary for some reason; I can't remember. . . ." Henry cycled across her consciousness, his tabby trousers encircled with a bicycle clip and a piece of string, and the image faded.

"Look—he's got earth in his pads! That proves. . . ."

"Been scratching in the begonias next door."

"I suppose so."

As she put down the food for Henry and his black companion Ruby, she thought for a second that a thin burned-out cigarette stuck from his mouth, but it turned out, to her relief, to be a tiny white feather.

It had been in a summer smelling of basil and tomatoes that they had moved into one of the rows of pretty artisan's dwellings, some still hung like the cottage next door with net curtains and others with the colored rattan and bamboo blinds of *arrivistes*, such as themselves. Old Cartwright had occupied his house for sixty years; Nick and Olivia, who intended to remain in theirs for not more than two or three, were shocked by the way he had let his property deteriorate. It looked doubly disreputable beside their repointed brickwork and fresh paint; Miss Defreitas had geraniums in white plastic pots on her front windowsill and there was even a gnome and a stone tortoise in the tiny front garden. One night Nick and Olivia had attached a piece of battered cod from the chip shop to the end of the gnome's fishing rod, but one of their cats had eaten it before morning and spoiled the joke; and their plan to replace the stone reptile with a live one had been thwarted so far by the import ban on tortoises. They had a special loathing of the curtain of colored plastic strips that hung across the open back door in summer.

"Makes it look like a betting shop," grumbled Nick to their closest friends Annabel and Mark, as they set up the barbecue.

"If there's a chance of it ever coming on the market," Mark said, "we want to be the first to know."

"That would be brilliant," sighed Olivia.

"Do they use that old tin bath?" asked Annabel pointing to the thing hanging from a nail on the outside wall.

"Not anymore," said Nick.

"We shall use it," Mark said, "in front of the kitchen fire. Annabel can scrub my back when I come off shift at t'pit."

"Brilliant. Very D.H. Lawrence." They laughed as sparks flew like fireflies and the smell of grilled flesh made their mouths water and the cats came crashing over the fence. It was such a lovely evening that it was three o'clock before the last meaty and winey kisses were exchanged and the last goodbyes shouted into the sleeping street and the last car door banged.

In the morning Old Cartwright complained to Olivia that the cats had broken one of his begonias. She reported it to Nick, adding, "I'm never sure whether I like begonias or not. I can't decide if they are beautiful or obscene."

"Need one preclude the other?"

"They're like roses but too fleshy—if he didn't plant them so regularly, so far apart, with all that bald earth in between, they might look better . . . anyway, he accused the cats of breaking one."

"Did they?"

"Mmm. I denied it of course. How pathetic, one measly flower. . . ."

"You'd think Miss Defreitas might run to something more exotic. I mean, begonias and geraniums in plastic pots—some bougainvillaea or mimosa—a bit of tropical splendor—"

"I don't think Martinique is in the tropics."

"—the brilliant hues of hummingbirds darting through the frangipani, the flash of a hyacinthine macaw's wing reflecting the waters of a blue lagoon. . . ."

"You'd like a hummingbird, wouldn't you?" Olivia seized the black cat, Ruby, and kissed her nose. "Or a hyacinthine wing . . . that's funny, Nick, Ruby smells of perfume . . . it's not mine, sort of sickly, and cheap . . . I wonder what she's been up to?"

"All cats lead secret lives their owners know nothing about. Have you any idea where Henry goes at night?"

"No, but I wish he'd stay in."

"She's not very good value, is she, our Miss Defreitas? I mean, remember when we peeked into her church and she was just standing there, in her pink hat, singing a hymn, not flinging herself around, rolling her eyes and waving her hands in the air and shouting, 'Hallelujah, yes Lord, I'se a comin'!' and speaking in tongues. She really ought to make more effort."

Ruby leaped from Olivia's arms, scratching her shoulder.

Summer seemed far away as Monday morning's cold-chisel broke the lover's embrace and they, having decided to leave their cars at home, set out to walk to the station. "Here comes the Green Wellie Brigade," said Old Cartwright as they passed.

"Boring old f—," Nick started saying and ended in a bellow as Olivia rubbed a cold handful of snow down his neck. The snow exhilarated her; she felt as frisky as a young husky in harness.

"Do you think we'll have a white Christmas, Mr. Cartwright?" she called, knowing how he loved to expound weather lore. He looked up at the sky.

"Plenty more where that came from," he pronounced, "but it'll all be gone in a couple of days."

"Why bother to shovel it up then?" asked Nick, rubbing the back of his neck with his scarf. "Hope you fall and break your leg," he muttered, as Miss Defreitas came out of the front door with a mug of something steaming. "What a pair."

★ ★ ★

That evening there was a ring at the front door. Annabel answered it, as Nick and Olivia were busy in the kitchen.

"There's a funny old man at the door," she called, coming into the kitchen. "I think it might be your next-door neighbor. Something about calor gas . . ."

Old Cartwright stood, stamping his feet on the step, in overcoat and gloves letting a current of icy air into the hall. Nick noticed his nose was crosshatched with red veins with a dewdrop threatening to fall. He was asking Nick to drive him and an empty gas cylinder to the hardware store in the morning.

"They was supposed to deliver Wednesday, only they never came," he explained. "I wouldn't ask, only . . . nice and warm in here, innit? Normally I wouldn't ask, only. . . ."

"Oh, all right," Nick cut him off. "It'll have to be early. I've got a meeting at ten. It's very inconvenient."

"Bloody liberty," he said, when he had got rid of Cartwright. "I hope he doesn't think I'm going to make a habit of chauffeuring him all over the place." He had to send Cartwright back into the house in the morning to get an old blanket to wrap the cylinder in so that it would not damage the car; the thing weighed a ton even when empty. The house was as cold as it was outside, he noticed when he rolled the new cylinder over the doorstep. Miss Defreitas leaned over the banister in her black coat.

"This place is like an icebox," he told them. "You ought to get in touch with the council, or somebody, get some double glazing and draught proofing." Soggy newspaper was wedged around the windows.

Nick and Olivia spent Christmas with Olivia's parents near Godalming. True to Old Cartwright's prediction it was not white, but simulated snow drifted in the leaded windowpanes and the porch was picked out in frosted fairy lights and the old cedar tree in the front garden was hung with colored bulbs. The only fly in the ointment, or mulled wine, for Olivia and Nick, was that they had had to ask Old Cartwright and Miss Defreitas to feed the cats, and from time to time, scratching the heads of Olivia's parents' Jack Russell and hyperactive Red Setter, they wondered how they were getting on.

They let themselves into their own house to find a brown skeleton of a Christmas tree, like an ancient murdered princess still wearing her jewels, surrounded by a circle of needles. There was no thud of flying feet to greet them, no loud welcoming purring, not even the swish of a resentful tail.

"Ruby, Henry," called Olivia from the back door. Miss Defreitas appeared silhouetted against an upstairs window, and Old Cartwright poked his head out of the back door. Olivia shut her door quickly. Nick was inspecting the cupboard. He brought out several tins of cat food.

"They haven't been feeding them," Olivia shrieked. "They must have starved to death! Oh Nick, where are they?"

"Don't panic. Don't cry, they'll be around somewhere, hang on, the pilchards have gone, and the salmon for their Christmas dinner—and the cod in cheese and butter sauce have gone from the fridge . . . they can't have starved. They're punishing us for going away—you know what cats are like, they'll turn up at suppertime, large as life. You sit down, I'll make a cup of tea."

"Don't you think it's odd," Olivia asked as they sat in the kitchen, relieved to have their hands around their familiar mugs of tea, "that those particular items should have gone?"

"If you're thinking what I think you are, I'm sure cat food

would be more to our neighbor's taste—Whiskas and two veg, followed by rhubarb and custard."

When Olivia had cooked rhubarb according to Old Cartwright's instructions, with no water and a spoonful of strawberry jam, she had had to throw away the pan, one of a set, a wedding present. She, as the rhubarb had done, still seethed at the memory. The cat-flap banged and Henry and Ruby stalked in, tails in the air.

"They're enormous! They must have put on a stone! What on earth have they been feeding them on?"

"Curried goat? Yams? Perpetual spinach?"

"Whatever, they look marvelous. Come on then pussies, have you missed your mommy then?"

The two cats walked straight past them and into the bedroom. Nick and Olivia had to laugh, they looked so disdainful.

"Shouldn't we go next door and thank them?"

"Tomorrow will do—let's go to bed. I find Godalming somewhat inhibiting."

"I noticed. Do you think we should have brought them something?"

"I thought you put some bits of turkey in a bag?"

"Old Cartwright and Miss Defreitas, silly, not the cats."

"They loved looking after them. Gave them something to do, poor old things. Give them the turkey if you like, of course. . . ."

"No, it's for the cats."

They went to bed. The cats leaped on and walked, purring, all over them.

"Ouch. Ruby, delighted as I am to see you, do you mind not sitting on my face?"

"Yuk, Henry absolutely stinks of cigarette smoke. Mind your claws!"

"I suppose they're just pleased to see us—ouch, get off. This is ridiculous. Go and eat your nice turkey." He pushed the cats off the bed. "That's better. Oh God, I didn't mean bring it in here to eat—they're dragging it all over the bed, it's disgusting. Get off! What's the matter with them?"

The cats tore the meat with teeth and claws, purring and chewing simultaneously; their eyes were huge and yellow. Olivia and Nick lay there, under their weight, almost afraid to shoo them off, waiting for them to finish. Then they started to wash; the bed throbbed with their snouting and licking; it seemed they would never finish; they must have swelled to the size of tigers as their tongues rasped vast tracts of fur, licking their own and each other's enormous limbs and backs and faces, slicking paws across great ears, with whiskers rattling like embattled porcupines' quills. At last they decided to sleep, one on either side of Nick and Olivia, pulling the duvet taut across them, weighing it down so that the two humans lay side by side, swaddled like mummies, slick with sweat, unable to turn or move their restless legs, pinioned in misery all the intolerable night.

In the morning the cats resumed their normal size and seemed to be their old selves, except for the fact that Ruby never quite lost the smell of perfume and Henry's coat still reeked of tobacco smoke. Olivia and Nick got out of the way of encouraging them to jump onto their knees, although they would have said they were as fond of them as ever. They kept meaning to go around and thank their neighbors for feeding them, but they kept putting it off, and then it seemed too late. Life went on as before. Old Cartwright cycled to the allotment when the weather wasn't too bad to tend his winter and early spring greens; the wing mirror was ripped off one of the cars, and the radio stolen. Olivia and Nick entertained friends and went to the cinema and restaurants, the fence sagged and bits broke off as the cats came and went, aconites appeared in the front garden; Miss Defreitas gave them a reproachful good morning as she stepped aside in the sound of church bells to let them pass her on the path with their heavy cartons from the Wine Warehouse.

One Saturday morning in April Annabel and Mark came over. Mark and Nick were in the front room fortifying themselves before attempting to mend the fence, standing at the window with glasses in their hands. The cats were sprawled on the path luxuriating in the dust and sun on their fur. Down the road Nick saw Old Cartwright pedaling homewards, encounter Miss Defreitas coming out of the shop, and dismount. He took her shopping bag and hung it from his handlebars. She was carrying a fan of unripe bananas, bright green against her black coat. They approached the zebra-crossing.

"Don't you worry about them, with that dangerous road?" Mark said, meaning the cats. Nick was watching Old Cartwright and Miss Defreitas and misunderstood.

"Oh, they're indestructible. Besides, they always use the crossing."

As he spoke a lorry slewed across the zebra, hurling Miss Defreitas and Old Cartwright in an arc of bodies, bicycle and bananas that was suspended in the air, then came crashing in a blitz of vegetables into the protective grill on the off-licence window, bounced, and fell in a twisted heap to the pavement.

Witnessing the accident knocked Nick for six. Both he and Olivia were surprised at how the accident affected them. Nobody could eat lunch. The policemen who came to interview Nick and Mark found the four of them holding a wake, sitting stunned and tear-stained around the kitchen table heaped with the empty bottles and full ashtrays of the bereaved. It took the officers some time to convince the mourners that Old Cartwright and Miss Defreitas had not been killed, but were in hospital, mangled like the bicycle, critically ill but still alive. The bicycle itself was a write-off. Olivia and Annabel rushed off to the newsagent's to buy Get Well cards; they found the perfect one for Old Cartwright, a still life of fruit and vegetables, and a lovely one for Miss Defreitas, with white lilies, that said "With Deepest Sympathy," that they were sure would be to her taste.

Then they realized that they didn't know where to send the cards. Nick said he would ring the local hospital to enquire but was informed that there was no casualty department there and before he could ask where the nearest one was the phone was put down.

"Yellow Pages," said Mark.

"Local Thomson's Directory," suggested Annabel.

"That's the one sponsored by that ghastly cat in a T-shirt, with no trousers, isn't it?" said Olivia, but in the event they couldn't find the directories, which Olivia had forgotten she had pushed under the bed when they were repapering the bedroom. The quartet spent the rest of the day in a subdued game of Trivial Pursuit, and later the girls made some toast and pâté. Nick was sick.

The local paper gave a graphic account of the accident to the two pensioners and said that a court case was pending but did not name the hospital to which the victims had been taken. The cards grew dusty on the mantelpiece. Olivia realized that "With Deepest Sympathy" was perhaps not suitable after all. They came home from work one day to find a downstairs window in the house next door had been broken. Miss Defreitas's geraniums grew leggy and yellow. The gnome and tortoise were stolen. Olivia kept meaning to ask in the shops if there was any news of their neighbors but as the weeks passed it became too embarrassing to expose her own unneighborliness in not having visited them. Then one Sunday morning when Nick was buying hot bread for their breakfast the man who served him remarked, "Shame about old Harry Cartwright."

"Yes, a great shame. Wonderful old character, old Harry."

"And her, of course, Miss Whatsername. Pity it wasn't instantaneous really."

"Yes, it would have saved a great deal of trouble, I suppose—I mean suffering."

He left with his bread to the pronouncement that something—faulty brakes or drunk drivers—made the shopkeeper's blood boil.

The boards of several rival estate agents were nailed up in the front garden of the house next door. Nick was on the phone to Mark and Annabel at once. They put in a bid, and with a bit of judicious gazumping, their offer was accepted. Olivia and Nick were ecstatic. Summer would be one long spritzer.

Annabel and Mark came over for a celebratory breakfast, a foretaste of the Sundays when they would be neighbors.

"Cheers," said Mark, raising his glass of Buck's Fizz. "You'll have to do something about that fence, old man. I believe it's your responsibility."

A carillon of church bells broke on the summer air like brass confetti, as if in joyful collaboration with the clinking glasses, pealing a benison over the future. At that moment Ruby jumped out of the open window and stalked up the road towards the church, thin and black with her tail at a resolute but pious angle. The cat-flap crashed and Henry strode into the room with something in his jaws. He dropped it in the center of the circle of friends. Olivia screamed. It was gray and furry and very dead. It could have been a rat or a decaying vegetable. Nobody could bear to touch it.

VIOLETS AND
STRAWBERRIES
IN THE SNOW

As he lay reflecting on the procession of sad souls who had occupied this bed before him, the door burst open with an accusing crack.

"You know smoking is forbidden in the dormitories!"

"I'm terribly sorry, nurse. I must have misread the notice. I thought it said, 'Patients are requested to smoke at all times, and whenever possible to set fire to the bedclothes.'"

In the leaking conservatory which adjoined the lounge, puddles marooned the pots of dead Busy Lizzies and the brown fronds of withered Tradescantias, and threatened with flood the big empty doll's house that stood incongruously, and desolate, with dead leaves blown against its open door; a too-easy metaphor for lost childhoods and broken homes and lives. At seven o'clock in the morning in the lounge itself, the new day's cigarette smoke refreshed the smell of last night's butts, whose burnt-out heads clustered in the tall aluminum ashtrays. A cup, uncontrollable by a shaking hand, clattered in a saucer. The Christmas-tree lights were winking red and green and yellow and blue, and on the television, creatures from another sphere were sampling mince pies and sipping sherry in an animated consumer guide to the delights of the worst day of the year. There was port and wine and whiskey and whisky too, and Douglas Macdougal sat among the casualties of alcohol and watched what once would have been his breakfast vanish down the throats of those to whom nature, or something, had granted a mandate or dispensation, those who were paid in money and fame as well as in the satisfaction, which had brought a virtuous glow to their cheeks, that they were imbibing in the national interest. There were no saucer-like erosions under their eyes, no pouchy sacs of unshed tears; and in subways and doorways, on station forecourts and in phoneboxes, in suburban kitchens a thousand bottles clinked in counterpoint. Cheers.

"You were as high as a kite last night when they brought you in." The man seated on his left pushed a pack of cigarettes toward Douglas.

"Well I've been brought down now. Somebody cut my string. Or the wind dropped."

A colorful kite crashed to earth; a grotesquely broken bird among the ashtrays and dirty cups, trailing clouds of ignominy.

Although a poster in the hall showed a little girl, her face all bleared with tears and snot, the victim of a parent's drunkenness, it became apparent that not everybody was here for the same reason. A woman with wild, dilated bright eyes glided back and forward across the room, as if on castors, with a strange stateliness, passing and repassing the television screen, and from time to time stopping to ask someone for a cigarette, from which she took one elegant puff before stubbing it out in the ashtray and continuing her somnambulistic progress. No one refused her a cigarette; Douglas had noticed already a kindness toward one another among the patients, and no one objected when she blocked the television screen where peaches bloomed in brandy and white grapes were frosted to alabaster. No one was watching it. The inmates sat, bloated and desiccated, rotten fruit dumped on vinyl chairs, viewing private videos; reruns of the ruins they had made of their lives, soap operas of pain and shame, of the acts which had brought them to be sitting between these walls bedecked with institutional gaiety, or fastforwarding to scenes of Christmases at home without them; waiting for breakfast time, waiting for the shuffling queue for medication.

To his right a woman was crying, comforted by a young male member of staff.

"Just because a person hears voices in her head, it doesn't give anyone the right to stop them being with their kids on Christmas Day."

"But I'm sure they'll come up to see you Mary."

"But I won't be there when they open their presents . . ."

"But they'll come to see you, I'm sure . . ."

Her voice rose to a wail, "But they don't like coming here!"

The tissue was a dripping ball in her hand. He patted her fist.

"They'll be coming to see you, Mary—it's Christmas."

Douglas felt like screaming, "She knows it's fucking Christmas, that's the point, you creep!" but who was he to say anything?

"You don't understand," she said, and male, childless, half her age, an adolescent spot still nestling in the fair down on his chin, how could he have understood?

Douglas was shaking. He didn't want any breakfast. Although the routine had been explained by two people he hadn't been able to take it in. He was afraid to go into the kitchen where the smell of dishcloths mingled with the steam from huge aluminum kettles simmering on an old gas cooker. He hovered in the doorway for a minute, taking in the plastic tub of cutlery on the draining board, the smeary plastic box of margarine, the cups and plates, inevitably pale green, that belonged to nobody. *Timor mortis conturbat me.* He had been saying that in the ambulance, but mercifully could remember little else. A faint sickly smell clung to his shirt. He had refused to let them undress him, clinging to a spurious shred of vomity dignity that was all he felt he had left, aware of his bloated stomach, and had slept in his clothes. Up and down staircases, down windowless corridors whose perspectives tapered to madness, past toothless old men who mimed at him asking for cigarettes, repassing the women with heavy-duty vacuum cleaners, past the closed but festive occupational therapy unit with a plate of cold and clayey mince pies on its windowsill, past the locked library, he ranged on his aching legs, until at last he found a bathroom. As he washed himself, and the front of his shirt and his stubby face, avoiding the mirror, the words of a song doubled him up with pain. "Oh Mandy, will you kiss me and stop me from shaking. . . ." He used to sing "Oh Mandy, will you kiss me and stop me from shaving . . ." when his daughter ran into the bathroom and he picked her up and swung her around and dabbed a blob of foam on her nose. If he had had a razor now he would have drawn it across his aching throat, across the intolerable ache of remembered happiness.

Downstairs again he was given some colored capsules in a transparent cup, and then it seemed that his time was his own. It was apparent that, a long time ago, a severely disturbed patient had started to paint the walls with shit and the management had been so pleased with the result that they had asked him to finish the job, and then had been reluctant to break up the expanse of ocherous gloss with the distraction of a lopsided still life painted in occupational therapy and framed in dusty plywood or even one of the sunny postcards which are pinned to most hospital walls, exhorting the reader to smile. The television, with the sound turned down, was showing open-heart surgery; the naked dark red organ fluttered, pulsated and throbbed in its harness of membranes. Douglas turned to the man sitting next to him.

"What do we do now?"

"We could hang ourselves in the tinsel."

Like several of the residents, he was wearing a gray tracksuit, the color of the rain, the color of despair. He held out his hand.

"I'm Peter."

"Douglas."

"I was going to walk down to the garage to get some cigarettes, if you feel like a walk."

Douglas shook his head. His pockets were empty. If he had had any money at the start of this débâcle, he had none now.

"Do you want anything from the shop, then?"

"Just get me a couple of bottles of vodka, a carton of tomato juice, and a hundred Marlboro."

"No Worcester?"

"Hold the Worcester. A couple of lemons, maybe, and some black pepper."

"You're on, mate."

Peter was taking orders for chocolate and cigarettes from the others, then he set out into the sheet of rain. Douglas was summoned to see the doctor, a severe lady in a sari: afterward he remembered nothing of the interview.

Back in the lounge a ghostly boy watched him with terrified eyes, and gibbered in fear when Douglas attempted to smile; whatever the reason for his being here was, it had been something that life had done to him, and not he to himself; some gross despoliation of innocence had brought him to this state. Douglas watched a nurse crouch beside him for half an hour or more, coaxing him to take one sip of milk from a straw held against his clamped bloodless lips; the milk ran down his white chin and she wiped it with a tissue. This sight of one human being caring for another moved him in part of his mind, but he felt so estranged from them, as if he had been watching on television a herd of elephants circling a sick companion. He might have wept then; he might have wept when Peter returned battered by the rain and dropped a packet of cigarettes in his lap; he might have wept when he held Mary's hand while she cried for her imprisonment and for her children, thinking also of his own, but he couldn't cry.

"Perhaps all my tears were alcohol," he thought. He picked up a magazine. *Don't let Christmas Drive you Crackers,* he read. *Countdown to Christmas.* He thought about his own countdown to Christmas, which had started in good time some two weeks ago, in the early and savage freeze which had now been washed away by the gray rain.

"Slip slidin' away, slip slidin' away . . ." the Paul Simon song was running through his head as he skidded and slid down the icy drives of the big houses where he delivered free newspapers. His route was Nob Hill and the houses were large and set back from the road. "This is no job for a man" he thought, but it was the only job that this man could find. He had seen women out leafleting, using shopping trolleys to carry their loads, and he had considered getting one himself as the strap of his heavy PVC bag bit into his shoulder, but that would have been the final admission of failure; and the suspicion that nobody wanted the newspapers anyway crystallized his embarrassment to despair.

What struck him most about the houses was the feeling that no life took place behind those windows; standing in front of some of them, he could see right through; it was like looking at an empty film set where no dramas were played out. Beyond the double-glazed and mullioned windows his eye was drawn over the deep immaculate lawn of carpet, the polished frozen lake of dining table with its wintry branched silver foliage of candelabra, past the clumps of Dralon velvet furniture and the chilly porcelain flowers and birds, through the locked

French windows to the plumes of pampas grass, the stark prickly sticks of pruned roses in beds of earth like discarded Christmas cake with broken lumps of icing, the bird table thatched and floored with snow and the brown rushes keening around the invisible pond. Latterly, ghostly hands had installed, by night, Christmas trees festooned with electric stars that sparkled as coldly and remotely as the Northern Lights. Douglas conceived the idea that the inhabitants of these houses were as cold and metallic as the heavy cutlery on their tables, as hollow as the waiting glasses.

It was late one morning, on a day that would never pass beyond a twilight of reflected snowlight, that he got his first glimpse of life beyond the glass; there had been tire marks and sledge marks in the silent drives before, but never a sight of one of the inhabitants in this loop of time. Her hair was metallic, falling like foil, heavy on the thin shoulders of her cashmere sweater, he knew that it was cashmere, just as he knew that the ornate knives and forks that she set on the white tablecloth were pewter. Pewter flatware. He had found the designation for these scrolled and fluted implements in an American magazine filched from one of the cornucopias, or dustbins, concealed at the tradesmen's entrance to one of these houses. He stood and watched her as she folded napkins and cajoled hothouse flowers into an acceptable centerpiece. What was her life, he wondered, that so early in the day she had the time, or perhaps the desperation, to set the table so far in advance of dinner. She looked up, startled like a bird, or like one whose path has been powdered with snow from the feathery skirt of a bird, and Douglas retreated. He retrieved a real newspaper, not one of the local handouts which he delivered, from next door's bin and stood in the wide empty road, glancing at the headlines, with a torn paper garland, consigned to the wind, leaking its dyes into the snow at his feet.

Glasgow— World's Cancer Capital, he read. Nicotine and alcohol had given to his native city this distinction.

"Christ. Thank God I left Glasgow when I did."

He poured the last drop down his throat and threw the little bottle into the snow, taking a deep drag on the untipped cigarette, which was the only sort which gave him any satisfaction now. He coughed, a heavy painful cough, like squashed mistletoe berries in his lungs, and returned to the room he had rented since he had left his wife, and children. The next time that he saw the woman she was unloading some small boys in peaked prep school caps from a Volvo Estate. She was wearing a hard tweed hat with a narrow brim, a quilted waistcoat and tight riding breeches, like a second skin, so that at a distance it looked as if she wasn't wearing any trousers above her glossy boots. Douglas was tormented by her. He looked for her everywhere, seeing her metallic hair reflected in shop windows, in the unlikely mirrors of pubs which she would never patronize. He stood in the front garden staring at her sideboard which had grown rich with crystallized fruits, dates and figs, a pyramid of nuts and satsumas, some still wrapped in blue and silver paper, Karlsbad plums in a painted box, a bowl of Christmas roses; his feet were crunched painfully in his freezing, wet shoes, his shoulders clenched against the wind; he wanted to crack open the sugary shell of one of those crystallized fruits and taste the syrupy dewdrop at its heart. Once he met her, turning from locking the garage, and handed her the paper. He couldn't speak; his heart was sending electric jolts of pain through his chest and down his arms. He stretched his stubbly muzzle, stippled with black, into what should have been a smile, but which became a leer. She snatched the paper and hurried to the house. If a man hates his room, his possessions, his clothes, his face, his body, whom can he expect not to turn from him in hatred and fear? There was nothing to be done, except to wrap himself in an overcoat of alcohol.

Whisky warmed the snow, melted the crystals of ice in his heart; he skidded, slip slidin' away, home to the dance of the sugar-plum fairy tingling on a glassy glockenspiel of icicles, to find the woman who organized the delivery round of the free newspapers on his doorstep. She was demanding his bag. He perceived that she was wearing acid yellow moonboots of wet acrylic fur. She blocked the door like a Yeti.

"There have been complaints," she was saying. "We do have a system of spot-checks, you know, and it transpires that half the houses on your round simply haven't been getting their copies. We rely on advertising, and it simply isn't good enough if the papers aren't getting through to potential customers, not to mention the betrayal of trust on your part. There has also been a more serious allegation, of harassment, but I don't want to go into that now. I had my doubts about taking you on in the first place. I blame myself, I shouldn't have fallen for your sob story . . . so if you'll just give me that bag, please . . . and calling me an abominable snowman is hardly going to make me change my mind. . . ."

She hoisted the bag, heavy with undelivered papers, effortlessly onto her shoulders and stomped on furry feet out of his life.

So Pewter Flatware had betrayed him. He turned back from the door and went out to reproof his overcoat of alcohol, to muffle himself against that knowledge, and the interview with the Yeti on the doorstep, and its implications.

A year ago, when he had had a short stay in hospital for some minor surgery, his voice had been the most vehement in the ward expressing a desire to get out of the place. He remembered standing in his dressing gown at the window of the dayroom, staring across the asphalt specked with frost, at the smoke from the incinerators and the row of dustbins, and saying, "what a dump." The truth was that he had loved it. When he had been told that he could go home, they had to pull the curtains around his bed, but the flowery drapes had not been able to conceal the shameful secret that he sobbed into his pillow. The best part had been at night, after the last hot drinks and medication had been dispensed from the trolley, and the nurse came to adjust the metal headboard and arrange the pillows and make him comfortable for the night. Tucked up by this routine professional tenderness into a memory of hitherto forgotten peace and acceptance, he felt himself grow childishly drowsy, and turned his face into the white pillow and slept. He restrained the impulse to put his thumb in his mouth.

Now he was lying in a bank of snow under the copper beech hedge of the woman with tinfoil hair, a lost dissolute baby, guzzling a bottle. The kind white pillow was soft and pure and accepting; he turned his face into it, into the nurse's white bosom, and slept, deaf to the siren that brought the Silver and Pewter people to their leaded windows at last, and blind to the blue lights spinning over the snow. He was now on the other side of sleep, on a clifftop, wrestling with a huge red demon which towered out of the sea, unconquerable and entirely evil. He woke in the ambulance, gibbering of the fear of death, and was taken to the interrogation room of the mental hospital, in whose lounge he sat now, reading a magazine article on how to prevent Christmas from driving you crackers.

At some stage in the interminable morning, one of the nurses brought into the lounge her own set of Trivial Pursuit, and divided the hungover, the tearful, the deranged, the silent and the illiterate into two teams, but the game never really got off the ground. The red demon of his dream came into Douglas's mind, and at once he realized that it had been the Demon Drink; a diabolical manifestation, a crude and hideous personification of the liquid to which he lost every battle. But the demon assumed other disguises by day; liquefying into seductive and opalescent and tawny amber temptresses who whispered of happiness, that it would be all right this time, they promised; they would make everything all right and each time that he succumbed he couldn't have enough of them, and their promises were broken like glass, and at night as Douglas lay neither asleep nor awake, the demon took his true shape and led him to glimpses of Hell, or at least of the most grotesque excesses of the human mind. He had not dared to go to sleep in his dormitory bed; all night thin ribbons of excelsior had glittered around the doorframe and the barred windows; it sparkled pink and phosphorescent and crackled in nosegays on the snores of the sleeping men, and danced in haloes of false fire above their restless heads.

"I hate going to bed," he heard Peter say to a man called Bob, "it's like stepping into an open grave." And then, "I'm so terrified of drinking myself to death that I have to drink to stop myself from thinking about it." Bob was a big gentle man with broken teeth, and his bare forearms were garlanded with tattooed hearts and flowers. Peter asked him what had happened to his teeth, and about a scar on his hand.

"They sent me up to D ward and the nurses broke my teeth. They broke two of my ribs as well."

He said it quite without rancor: this is what happens when you are sent up to D ward. Unable to bear the implications of Bob's statement, Douglas concentrated on a somewhat haphazard game of Give Us a Clue that was in progress across the room. Charades had been proposed, and abandoned in favor of this idiosyncratic version of the television game, and Douglas was invited to join in. As he rose from his chair, he saw that Peter was crying, and he saw Bob reach out his scarred and flowery hand and place it on Peter's knee and say gently through his broken teeth, "I wish I could help you with your troubles, Peter."

In his shamed and demoralized state Douglas felt that he had come as near as he ever would to a saint, or even to Jesus Christ. The sight of the big broken man giving a benediction on the other's self-inflicted wounds moved him so that he sat silent and clueless in the game, unable to weep for anyone else, or for his own worthlessness. Then an old man stood up, his trousers hoisted high over his stomach to his sagging breasts. He extended his arm, closed thumb and forefinger together, and undulated his arm.

"What's that then?" he demanded.

"Snake," said Douglas.

"Yep. Your go."

Douglas sat; the embodiment of the cliché: he didn't know whether to laugh or to cry.

> "For When the One Great Scorer comes
> To write against your name,
> He marks—not that you won or lost—
> But how you played the game."

The debauched Scottish pedant swayed to his feet, grinning uncertainly through stained teeth, and played the game.

In the afternoon his daughters came to visit. He would have done anything to prevent them, if he had known of their intention. He wanted to hide, but they came in, smelling of fresh air and rain, with unseasonal daffodils and chocolates, like children, he thought, in a fairytale, sent by their cruel stepmother up the mountainside to find violets and strawberries in the snow. He took them to the games room which was empty. Here, too, the ashtrays overflowed; those deprived of drink had dedicated themselves to smoking themselves to death instead. The girls had been to his room, and had brought him clean clothes in a carrier bag, and cigarettes. He was so proud of them, and they, who had so much cause to be ashamed of him, made him feel nothing but loved and missed. They laughed and joked, and played a desultory game of table tennis on the dusty table with peeling bats, and mucked about on the exercise bicycle and rowing machine which no one used, and picked out tunes on the scratched and stained and tinseled piano. There was an open book of carols on its music stand: that will be the worst, he thought, when we gather around on Christmas Day to emit whatever sounds come from breaking hearts. Two of the girls lit cigarettes, which made him feel better about the ash-strewn floor, and Mandy, who did not smoke, let no flicker of disapproval cross her face; all in all they acted as if visiting their father in a loony bin was the most normal and pleasurable activity that three young girls could indulge in on a Saturday afternoon. It was only when the youngest said that she was starving, and he said that there were satsumas, which another patient had given him, in his locker, and she made a face and replied "Satsumas are horrible this year" that they all looked at each other in acknowledgement that her words summed up the whole rotten mess that he had made of Christmas. The fathers have eaten sour grapes, and the children's teeth are set on edge. Douglas broke the silence that afflicted them by saying, "Good title for a story, eh?" A reminder that in another life he had been a writer. Someone was waiting for the girls in a car, and as he led them to the front door, he hurried them past a little side room where Bob was hunched in a chair, his great head in his hands, his body rocking in grief. Douglas heard the laughter of staff, a world away, behind the door that separates the drunks from the sober. In his carrier bag he found a razor, electric. Now I can shave myself to death, he thought, as opposed to cutting my throat. There were also some envelopes and stamps, a writing pad and pen. There were no letters that he wished to write, but he took the paper and pen, and wrote "Satsumas Are Horrible This Year," as if by writing it down he could neutralize the pain; turn the disgrace to art. It would not be very good, he knew, but at least it would come from that pulpy, sodden satsuma that was all that remained of his heart.

Later, he went into the kitchen to make a cup of tea for himself and for several of the others: like ten-pence pieces for the phone, and cigarettes, coffee was at a premium here. He was hungry, not having eaten for days, and thought of making a piece of toast, but he did not know if he was allowed to take any bread, and the grill pan bore the greasy impressions of someone else's sausages. He realized then what all prisoners, evil or innocent, learn; that what seems such a little thing, and which he had forfeited, the act of making yourself a piece of toast under your own lopsided grill, is in fact one of life's greatest privileges. He stood in the alien kitchen that smelled of industrial detergent and fat and old washing-up cloths, seeing in memory his children smiling and waving at the door, their resolute backs as they walked to the car concealing their wounds under their coats, forgiving and brave, and carrying his own weak and dissolute genes in their young and beautiful bodies. Violets and strawberries in the snow.

OTHER
PEOPLE'S BATHROBES

Her underwear slipped through his fingers in silky shoals of salmon and grayling; stockings slithered like a catch of rainbow eels. He moved about the bedroom like an assassin, although he was alone in the flat, as if he was watched by eyes other than his own which glanced off the mirror's surface like fish scales reflecting the rainy morning light. Several times when he and Barbara had been together, he had felt that they were not alone; over his shoulder an invisible circle of her friends was whispering, condemning him, warning her. He imagined their nights laid out on lunchtime restaurant tables shrouded in white linen, and dissected with heavy silver knives and forks. He did not know what he was looking for as he went through her things—some evidence as dangerous as a gun lying in the silken nest, that he could possess and use to destroy her when it suited him.

Last night they had come out of the cinema knock-kneed with grief, holding onto each other against the pain of someone else's tragedy. The restaurant smelled of fish and lemon, and clouds of steam banked the lower halves of the windows and evaporated in rivulets down the black glass. He was hungry throughout, and after, the meal. She had eaten almost nothing and her refusal of wine had inhibited his own intake, as the springwater bubbling glumly in its mossy green glass dampened his desire, although her stockinged foot, slipped from its shoe and stroking his leg under the table, suggested that it had refreshed hers.

"I'm sick of mangetout peas," he had grumbled. "I want proper peas, without pods, from a tin."

She had smiled at him indulgently, as at a child, although his petulant mouth was in danger of becoming merely peevish. Meanwhile he salivated discontentedly in memory of the food of his brief happy childhood. A low-slung moon hung in the north London sky as she drove them home; the golden crescent of a pendulum slicing the blackness; it would taste of melon if sucked, a wedge of honeydew. He sat beside her in silence, aware that he was, as always, in the passenger seat.

There was nothing in the bedroom to incriminate her: dresses gave evidence of nothing that he did not know, shoes were mute and jewelry jangled to no purpose, scent left false trails and no glove pointed the finger. Books that might have betrayed her were not called to witness.

"There are some robes you can use," she had told him on the first night he had spent with her. That had been three weeks ago and he was still there, still wearing borrowed bathrobes and dressing gowns. This morning he was dressed in a blue kimono with a red and gold dragon writhing up its back and tongues of flame licking his shoulders. He went to the window and lifted the corner of the blind. The trees in the street were hung with leaves the color of cooked swede, and mashed swede lay in heaps in the gutters; pyracantha flung 'bright sprays of baked beans against the houses opposite. In his twenty years he had worn too many dressing gowns belonging to other people. He sighed and pulled the sash tighter around his diminishing waist and padded into the kitchen.

He opened the fridge and the freezer compartment and then slammed them shut, sending shivers through the bottles of mineral water shuddering in the door. There wasn't even any real coffee, just that stuff that you had to muck about with filter papers, and a small jar of decaffeinated powder, and a tiny tin of sweeteners instead of sugar. He shook four or five white pellets into a cup and added coffee and a dash of skimmed milk as he waited for the kettle to boil.

"No bleeding bread of course. . . ."

He microwaved the lone croissant into a blackened shell and smeared it with low-fat spread. He could have murdered a fried egg sandwich washed down with a mug of hot sweet tea. She, of course, had breakfasted on her usual fare of a tisane and half a dozen vitamin and mineral tablets. He lit a cigarette and took it and the newspaper into the main room of the flat—he never knew what to call it: front room, although it was, or lounge, were wrong—and pushed aside the white vase of black porcelain roses and white plastic tulips and put his feet up. Smoking was frowned on almost to the point of total ban, but since the early morning when she had sensed his absence in the bed and come into the kitchen and screamed at the sight of his legs sprawled on the kitchen floor, his head wedged firmly in the obsolete cat-flap, a forbidden cigarette clamped in his lips spiraling smoke helplessly into the dawn chorus, she had relaxed slightly the interdiction. She had thought he was dead. It had taken an hour, a lot of soap, and finally a screwdriver to release him.

When he had bathed he would run the Hoover over the carpets; there was little for it to vacuum up except a light frosting of the low-fat crisp crumbs which he had consumed while she got ready for bed. It was the

Hoover which had brought them together: he had arrived in response to her inquiry to a cleaning agency and had stayed on to help her prepare for a dinner party, as she moved about the kitchen with a brittle energy that teetered over into panic, her pale hair crackling with electricity in the stormy light pouring through the window. When the first guest arrived it was he who opened the door, a glass of wine in his hand, and entertained them until she emerged from the bathroom where she had fled. She could hardly have arrested in mid-arc the bowl of salted pumpkin seeds he was proffering to her friends and explain that he was the cleaner, and so he had stayed. It was not until they all sat down to eat that she realized that an extra place had been set already at the table.

After the Hoovering he would take her italic list and a plastic carrier bag, as well preserved and neatly folded as if it had been ironed, and wander down to the shops. He took the radio and another cup of coffee and his cigarettes into the bathroom and as he idled in the scented oil watching mingled smoke and steam being sucked through the extractor fan on the window he could not avoid remembering the previous night.

She had wanted both of them to go to bed early because she had had a hard day before they met in the evening, and she was nervous about a sales conference the following morning. The publishing company for which she worked had been taken over recently, and anxiety about losing her job and treachery within the firm had smudged blue shadows under her eyes, and bitten nails, spoiling her gloss, betrayed her fears. By the time Adam had joined her in the bedroom she had fallen asleep; her hair frazzled out like excelsior on the pillow, the tag of a sachet of camomile tea drooping over the rim of the mug on the bedside table. He slid into bed, smelling the sweet-sour odor of the infusion on her breath as he leaned over her face and took her, all flowers and mineral water, in his arms and slowly and cynically began to make love to her. Their hip bones clashed; the morning would see his faint bruises mirrored in milky opals on her skin. He thought that her ambition was to be the thinnest woman in London this side of anorexia, and he remembered reading of a young girl who had almost achieved sainthood by dint of never eating; people had flocked to witness this miracle and marvel at the beautiful and holy maiden pink and white as roses and angel cake, sustained on spiritual food, until one night a nun had been caught sneaking into her room with a basket of goodies. He wondered sometimes if Barbara, too, was a secret snacker but there was never any evidence. He licked the whorls of her ear, as cold as one of her porcelain roses, with the tip of his tongue, while in imagination he piled a plate with processed peas swimming in their bluish liquor, pickled beetroot staining the fluffy edges of a white instant-mashed potato cloud, a crispy cluster of acid yellow piccalilli; he added a daub of ketchup to his garish still life, and then he had to stifle a laugh in her shoulder as she responded because only he knew that the rhythm they moved to was that of a song that had been running through his head since they had got home. Food, glorious food . . . dah da da da dah dah. He had forgotten some of the words he had sung as a ruby-lipped treble taking the lead in *Oliver;* backstage, after the last performance, before the last tremulous tear had been flicked from the lashes of the departing audience, Adam had been expelled for extortion. Food, fabulous. Food, beautiful. Food, glor-i-ous food!!! Pease pudding and saveloy, what next is the question? While we're in the mood—Glen Miller took up the baton with a flash of brass and buttons, or Joe Loss, sleek as an otter in a dapper dinner jacket or tuxedo. "Tuxedo Junction." And then Adam and Barbara expired together in an ecstasy of cold jelly and custard and he let her drop back onto a steaming heap of hot sausage and mustard. She traced with her finger his lips which were parted in a grin.

"Darling."

"Best ever?" he asked.

She nodded, smiling and showering the pillow with pease pudding from her hair as he licked the dollop of mustard from her nose.

He had slept badly in an indigestion of shame. Bits of bad dreams lay on his mind, as unappetizing as congealing food left overnight on a plate. He watched beneath half-closed lids as she gathered up the clothes she would assume as silken armor against her threatening day, moving quietly so as not to wake him, but each door, each opened and closed drawer hissed her panic. He felt her hover over him for a moment after she had placed a mug of coffee on the coaster on the floor beside him, then with a jangle of keys, a revving of the car, she was gone and he was left floundering in the billows of the duvet trying to sleep away part of the long morning. He wished to spend a little time as possible in the company of someone he disliked as much as himself.

People who had encountered Adam as an angelic-looking child had assumed that he was a good little boy. He shared their estimation of himself until at the age of six years he had been surprised by impulses that were far from good. A girl in his class at the infants' school brought in, one morning, to show the teacher, a dolls' chest of drawers that she had made by gluing four matchboxes together and covering the top, back and sides with glossy red paper, the sort of paper that they made lanterns from at Christmastime. The handles of the drawers were yellow glass beads. Adam coveted and coveted this object all morning.

She had allowed him to hold it at dinner play, as long as he didn't open the drawers, and had made him give it back. It was beyond the price of the matchbox tractor which he had offered in exchange. He could not have said why he wanted the chest of drawers so much: he had no use for it beyond the pleasure of opening and closing the drawers. He could keep matches in it, he had decided, if he had had any . . . perhaps it was because it was so tiny and perfect and because he could not have contrived so neat an artifact with his own clumsy fingers, which behaved in craft lessons like a bunch of flies on flypaper—his Christmas lantern had been a disaster, with the slits cut the wrong way, and had ended up, shamefully, in the wastepaper basket. He brooded through the afternoon story and squinted at it through the steeple of his fingers as they sang, "Hands together, softly so, little eyes shut tight," plotting. He had hidden behind a hedge after school and jumped out on her from behind, pulling her knitted hat over her eyes, and snatched the chest of drawers and run off. The school was a very short distance from home, with no roads to cross. He was out of sight, although not out of earshot of her wails, by the time she had freed herself from her hat.

"What's this?" His mother was waiting for him at the entrance to the flats.

"I made it at school."

"Isn't that lovely. Just like something they make on 'Blue Peter,' " she had said as they went up in the lift.

"It's for you," he had heard himself say. There was even a pink ring from a cracker in one of the drawers, which fitted her little finger, just above the second joint.

So, eating tinned spaghetti on toast in the afterglow of his mother's kiss that afternoon, he had realized that he could assault and rob and lie; arts which he had polished over the years, after his mother's death when he was ten years old, during his six years in care and throughout his sojourns in squats all over London.

"That's that," he said to himself as he rewound the Hoover's flex. "Now for the next item on my thrilling agenda." As he stowed it away in what she called the "glory hole," although a neater glory hole than this one with no cobwebs and everything stacked on shelves could not be imagined, his eye fell on a cardboard carton. He pulled it out, not knowing what he expected to find. His heart beat faster as he opened the flaps—a baby's shoe perhaps, a bottle of gin or the heads of her former lovers, as in Bluebeard's Castle, their beards dripping blood. What it contained was books: children's books, schoolgirl annuals, an illustrated *Bible Stories* whose red and blue and gold illuminated sticker stated that it had been presented for regular attendance at St. Andrew's Sunday School in a year before Adam had been born, a stamp album with a map of the world on its cover, that released a shower of shiny and brittle stamp hinges like the wings of long-dead insects when Adam set it aside with the thought that it might be worth selling; the books that heap trestle tables at every jumble sale, even to the copy of *The Faraway Tree* by Enid Blyton, with the statutory request in faded and wobbly pencil that if this book should chance to roam, box its ears and send it home, to: Barbara Watson, 59 Oxford Road, Canterbury, Kent, England, Great Britain, the Northern Hemisphere, the World, etc., etc., *ad tedium*. Barbara had been crossed out and Brenda substituted; then Barbara had deleted Brenda, but in vain. The names fought each other in sisterly rivalry all down the page and it was not clear at the end who had triumphed; Adam heard slaps and tears, and the pulling of hair. *Britain's Wonderland of Nature*: a large green volume with a butterfly embossed on its cover and glossy color plates which must have been her best book, Adam thought. It had been given to her by Uncle Wilf in 1960.

At the bottom of the box was a photograph album. He lifted it out and took it into the black and white room. Perhaps this was what he had been looking for. He lit a cigarette to heighten the experience.

The album had a faded blue cover and crumpled spider's web paper separated the leaves; the small photographs affixed to the storm-gray pages had crimped edges, like crinkle-cut chips, and there, flies in amber and butterflies in glass, was Barbara's past. It seemed that she had spent all her childhood on a beach against an unfailingly gray sky. The photographs were captioned in a loopy adult hand. Here were the infant Barbara and Brenda, the tangled strings of their sunbonnets blowing toward a sullen sea; a comical snap of Barbara in giant grown-up sunglasses, mouth open in dismay, holding an empty cornet whose unstable scoop of ice cream had evidently just fallen to the beach. Here was Uncle Wilf, with Aunty Dolly at Tankerton—he must have been a widower then, when he purchased *Britain's Wonderland of Nature*, Christmas 1960. Adam pictured him entering the glass doors of W.H. Smith, sleet, like a dandruff of sorrow on the stooping shoulders of his black coat, to buy books for his nieces, the icy wind, or memories of the time he had rolled his trousers and Dolly tucked her skirt up around her knees and stood with the sea gushing between their toes smiling into the camera before she had vanished off the edge of photographs, bringing a tear to his eyes. At Whitestable, Dad, whose name was Ron, Adam discerned, had for some reason come without his trunks and, presumably unable to resist the call of the sea, was wearing what looked suspiciously like his wife's bathing suit rolled to his waist. All the sad south coast resorts were represented in shades of black and white and gray; Adam sat in the room whose color scheme echoed the childhood tints, his cigarette burning unnoticed in a cube of black onyx striated with white, turning the pages. He had the family sorted out now, grandparents, uncles, aunts and cousins, Mum or Mavis in white shoes, Dad; Brenda and Barbara so close in age as to be almost twins, and no longer bothered to read the captions.

By the age of four or so Brenda had become noticeably plump; beside her Barbara was as frail as an elf. Brenda swelled with the years like a raisin soaked in water; she grew into a quite unfortunate-looking kid. There was one shot of her that arrested him: she stood scowling, with her bare feet planted apart on the shifting pebbles, thighs braced, her solid little body eggcup-shaped, straining the rosettes of her ruched cotton bathing suit, her candy-floss hair parted at the side, and caught in an ungainly bow blowing in the wind that blurred the sails of the toy windmill in her hand, every line of her face and body expressing such defiance and discontent that Adam found himself smiling. Behind her the horse of a merry-go-round galloped in a frieze refrigerated by time. Someone had added a comment in pencil to her mother's writing. Adam took the album to the window the better to see.

"Barbara is a fat pig," it said, and a penciled arrow pointed undeniably to the photograph and was corroborated by the words, "singed Brenda." It was impossible. "Barbara is a fat pig, singed Brenda." So Barbara had been the fat plain one all along. Adam sat down heavily and lit another cigarette. He felt cheated, as if Barbara had deceived him deliberately. Under that designer exterior there was a common little fat girl. It was all a sham. She was no better than he was. He snapped the album shut. Instead of feeling triumphant at finding the weapon he had sought, he felt sad, almost like crying. Then he began to feel angry with Brenda. He flicked through the pages again and noticed that Brenda in each photograph had pushed slightly in front of Barbara, and she was often dressed in organdy and flounces of artificial silk while Barbara was in cotton. Why was Brenda always wearing party dresses to the beach, and an angora bolero, while Barbara was in print with a school cardigan?

"It seems to me, Brenda, that it was you who were the pig. And you couldn't spell," he said to the Christmas-tree fairy with her bucket and spade. He wondered how many times Barbara had been singed by Brenda. What were Mum and Dad, Mavis and Ron, doing to have such a discrepancy between their daughters? He hoped Uncle Wilf had loved Barbara the best.

He closed the album and put it away in the carton with the other books and closed the cupboard door. He found Barbara's shopping list and shopping bag and set out for the shops. He could not rid himself of the picture of Barbara in the bathing suit with Brenda's cruel caption, and the quotation—he had played Viola in *Twelfth Night*—"thus the whirligig of time brings in his revenges," spun around in his mind like the windmill in her hand and the merry-go-round in the distance, and above the jangle of fairground music he heard the teasing voice of Mum and Dad and all the aunts and cousins, and Brenda's taunting laughter. He had been wrong in thinking that Barbara was no better than he was: she was much better. Everything she had she had earned for herself, while he was driven through life in the passenger seats of other people's cars and lounged in other people's bathrobes. More, she had created herself. He stopped dead in his tracks on the pavement, colliding with a woman with matted hair, draped in a shawl of black refuse sacks.

"I'm in love," he told her.

"Piss off."

"Yes, yes I will," he said and gave her a five pound note from Barbara's purse, which was clawed into her shawl as she spat at his feet.

Something amazing had happened. He had fallen in love, for the first time, with a cross little girl holding a windmill at the end of her goosefleshed arm. If she had been singed by Brenda he would erase the burns, like scorch marks from a table. If she wanted revenge he would oblige, on the whole pack of them. If she wanted a white wedding with all the family there, including Brenda whose childhood had been entwined with hers like the strings of two sunbonnets on a windy day, that was all right with him too. He went into the shop; for him the best part of the movie had always been when the guy arrived at the girl's apartment with a paper sack of groceries with a fifth of bourbon sticking its neck out: to him that was New York: romance. Unbeknownst to herself, Barbara bought herself a bottle of champagne. As he walked home with his love feast in a plastic carrier bag he saw that the pavement was strewn with Lychee shells, broken to show their sunset pink interiors, like shells on a beach in the rain. Outlined against the hectic light everything assumed a poignancy: a bag of refuse and a broken branch of blue eucalyptus made a haiku on the wet curb. He felt healed, as if someone had poured a precious jar of alabaster over him.

He was in the kitchen when he heard her key in the lock. She stepped inside, all unawares, in her black raincoat rolling with ersatz pearls, coming home to a steaming bowl of Heinz vegetable soup, just like mother used to make.

THE THIRTY-
FIRST OF OCTOBER

It was the time of year when people stole down garden paths to lay huge woody marrows and boxes of wormy windfalls, and jars of sloppy chutney with stained paper mobcaps on each other's doorsteps, but not on hers. There would be no sparklers on November the Fifth either, although, not five hundred yards away the young men and boys of the village had been building for weeks an enormous bonfire, a superstructure of wood, branches, mattresses, tires and junk and garden refuse, on the village green; now it was almost complete; a sign ordered that there should be brought NO MORE RUBISH, and members of the bonfire committee were taking turns to sleep out in a little wooden shelter in its shadow to guard it from premature pyromaniacs. A spit had been erected and stood in readiness for the pig that was to be roasted; the early morning air of that day would be tainted with the smell of oozing tissues until a bruised cloud of cooked meat drizzled droplets of fat into the evening air, which would linger for days while the bonfire smoldered, mingling with the gray ash that would coat her front garden and invade the house through the ill-fitting windows. Once she had joined in the procession, but now the prospect of the burning torches of pitch, the faces in the lurid light, the Guy dragged on a rail filled her with dread, evoking other primitive rituals, witch hunts and sacrificial blood spilled on the fields. She leaned against the window, staring into the darkening afternoon, waiting for absolutely nothing at all.

After an Indian summer, the first frost had wrecked the gardens, leaving the hydrangeas in blackened ruins that hulked on either side of the gate that led onto a rutted lane. On the other side of the lane stretched fields. The house next door, one of a pair of cottages, had double-glazed aluminum-framed picture windows, and a snouty little porch of bottle glass, and sliding patio doors at the back. A slice of varnished oak beside the front door bore the name Trevenidor. When she and Paul had moved in he had fantasized that the house had been named in sentimental tribute to a Cornish resort where their neighbors had honeymooned, but when they met Trevor and Enid it became apparent that they had intertwined their own names in a true-lover's knot. Trevor and Enid had two daughters, Kimberley and Carly; now seven and five years old.

She had been pleased by the fact that there were children next door; she had thought that they might alleviate the loss of her own two daughters who were both living abroad, but she blushed now to recollect her fantasies of little figures draped in floury aprons, their pudgy fingers dimpling as they pressed the raisin buttons into ginger-bread men, their faces rosy in the warmth of her spicy kitchen; of collecting wildflowers and blackberries and nuts with two little yellow-haired companions. There *were* hazelnuts, and blackberries in the hedges, but they were small and bitter and splashed with gray mud and sprayed with pesticides; and once a year Trevor drove down the lane with a mechanical ripper that tore the tops off the bushes, leaving the branches stripped bare; broken and bleeding. In the first flush of neighborliness she had offered to baby-sit, but she had been rebuffed. On Enid's darts night Trevor stayed at home, and on the rare occasions that they went out together, Enid's mother, an even larger version of her daughter, was ensconced in Trevenidor. Carly and Kimberley had met her overtures of friendship with silent, bright blue-eyed scorn, clinging to their mother in a parody of shyness, burying their faces her short skirt, pulling it around her columnar thighs until they were slapped off like mosquitoes, and when their new neighbor had extended a biscuit to her, Carly had burst into tears, as if it had been a stone or a serpent; and then later she had heard her name tossed mockingly over the hedge—"Claw-dee-ya, Claw-dee-ya."

In the winter frost formed patterns on the insides of Claudia's windows and snow drifted in, dredging the sills like icing sugar. Last year she had steeled herself to confront Trevor over the hedge and ask him to look at the central heating; the bottom halves of the radiators remained cold, while the tops gave out such feeble heat that she could see the clouds of her breath. Trevor, risking Enid's displeasure, for she had referred pointedly to him as My Husband ever since Paul's departure, squatting on his haunches, exposing more of his lower back than Claudia would have wished to see, gave the radiator a shake, causing a tiny avalanche of plaster behind the damp wallpaper and pronounced, "Not much I can do. I know the cowboy who installed it—your whole system's corroded."

"I'll just have to turn it up, then . . ."

"You can turn it up as high as you like, lady; you'll always be cold."

His words left her with the chill of the grave.

She went to the dining table which she used as a desk, picked up a book, and let it drop. It was one that she should have been reviewing, but the deadline was slipping away. "What was your book called again, only I couldn't see it in the van?" Enid had asked early in their acquaintance. Claudia had not explained that the mobile library was unlikely to carry two books that had been out of print for years, and thereafter she had avoided the van lest she encounter Enid in its crowded interior. She had been highly praised as a miniaturist once, and in vain did she remind herself of little bits of ivory; her talent had diminished until it had disappeared. She depressed a key of the disused piano; damp felt struck rusty wire, and the note hung in the air. A silvery blight was stealing over the veneer, clouding the flowers that wreathed the candleholders. It was Paul's piano, and Enid had asked him not to play it in the evenings because it disturbed the children.

Soon Kimberley and Carly would be home from school, and when darkness had fallen they would come pushing and giggling up her path, pinching each other's arms in their simulated terror, for all the world as if they were Hansel and Gretel, and she was the wicked witch. Trick or treat. What could possibly be a treat to them? The hedges and ditch testified to the chocolate bars and lollies they consumed daily on the way home from school, and although it was only late October they had anticipated Christmas already by devouring the contents of two mesh stockings, filled with sweets, one of which had blown into Claudia's garden. As she had shaken a slug from its interstices and put the torn stocking in her dustbin, she had felt a pang of pity for the children for whom there was no magic. What they would like most from her was money. She had seen their money boxes; pink ceramic pigs with lipsticked snouts and flirtatious painted eyelashes and grotesque rumps, bearing little resemblance to the inmates of the asbestos and corrugated iron stalag whose stench drifted across the fields when the wind was in the wrong direction, where Trevor worked.

Two weeks previously, by a blunder on the part of a secretary, Claudia had been sent an invitation to a party given by her erstwhile publisher. Turning it over and over in her hands, she had searched it for a sign that it was a practical joke, but there was no one who would think her worth playing a joke on. Except Kimberley and Carly, who, last Hallowe'en, had emptied her dustbin on her doorstep; it hadn't been funny but she had heard Enid and Trevor laughing. She had stood the invitation on the mantelpiece, beside the jar of shriveled rosehips, for all, that is herself, to see. She had taken the bus to the town, where she had found at last, in despair, a diaphanous dress in the Help the Aged shop, but it had been so cold on the night of the party that she had had to wear her kingfisher blue chunky cardigan, bought from Enid's catalogue in more halcyon days, bulkily uncomfortable and protruding its cuffs from the sleeves of her coat.

In the confusion of her arrival in the loud room, where the heat, after her cold walk from the tube, had turned her face to fire, she had forgotten to deposit her cardigan with her coat. Finding herself ignored and jammed up against the drinks table, there had been nothing to do but help herself to red wine. Once, she turned and met the shock of her face; eyes bloodshot with drink and smoke, and a red clownish patch on each cheek, brilliant under the electrified chandelier, above the wrongly-buttoned cardy; but by then she had been too far gone to çare. She had realized at once that she would have done better to have come in her jeans, as others had, to have pretended a casualness that she hadn't felt; her attempt at finery was so far from the chic of those women who had dressed up. For them, she supposed, this was just another evening, somewhere to stop off before going out to dinner, or home, but she, shamefully, had invested all her hopes in it, and they died among the cigarette butts and broken pretzels and rejected gherkins on the table behind her. When, as she was burrowing for her coat, a woman spoke to her, and, recognizing her name, said that she admired her work, Claudia had been so grateful that she had latched onto her, and found herself one of a party billowing down the road to a restaurant. She was happy; she was back where she ought to be; she felt a sudden conviction that her talent, after all, had not deserted her.

Only the next morning, sitting on the first train home, traveling with a gang of railway workers, apart in a corner, the picture of debauchery in her laddered tights, aware of their gentle mockery, had she realized that she had not been invited to the restaurant. Her pinched cold face flooded with blood as snatches of the evening floated among the black specks in front of her eyes; she had babbled of the pig farm and conjured up Enid and Trevor and Kimberley and Carly to sit among the guests partaking of whitebait and avocado, plonking bluish knuckles and bloodied, half severed trotters on their plates. Now she felt as alienated from her fellow-diners as she did from her neighbors, and from the men with their sandwiches and newspapers, their camaraderie, their sense of being in the right place at the right time. It was then that she looked down and saw the tidemark of mud on her shoes, that must have been there all the time, adding the finishing touch to her garish rig; and putting her head in her hands, discovered that somewhere in the debris of the evening, lost perhaps on her gallop to the station for the last, missed, train, lay an earring, one of her only valuable pair, given to her by her grandmother.

The irrecoverable loss of the earring burned in an opalescent pain in her throat, as if she had swallowed it, long after the inflammation of the self-inflicted social wounds had abated. The earrings had been promised to her daughter, and at some time the loss must be discovered, or confessed. The end of the evening was a merciful blur, and she would never see those people again, but the earring bereaved of its twin would be an everlasting token of her disgrace.

Her anger at herself turned on Trevor and Enid. She had moved her bedroom to avoid the grunts that she imagined came through the wall, but she lay sleepless in her cold bed, in the musty smell of mildew whose spores she sometimes thought pervaded her own skin, warming herself with a scenario in which Trevor had somehow mistaken his wife for a sow, and Enid lay helpless on the slatted floor, unable to speak or to turn, squeezed between the metal sides of the farrowing pen, subjected to the torments that he inflicted unthinkingly daily on his charges; and then Trevor himself, pale, bristly boar, was driven with sticks up the ramp of his own lorry, squealing with fear, en route for the abattoir.

Changing her room to escape the pork and crackling of Enid and Trevor's intimacies meant that she was woken by the dawn chorus from Kimberley and Carly, each of whom seemed to rise each morning with a renewed ambition to earn her sister a smack; she had to put her pillow over her head to blot out the sounds of their play which came through so clearly that Claudia, sick with insomnia, almost felt the hair yanked out of her own head and teeth puncturing her own skin. They had plastic kitchens and castles and typewriters and sewing machines and cassette players, vanity sets galore; Sindy dolls and Barbie dolls and Cabbage Patch dolls and Care Bears, Rainbow Brites, Emus, and My Little Ponies complete with grooming parlors for their silky pink and turquoise manes and tails; but the girls' real favorites were two life-sized baby dolls who shared a twin buggy. These two babies vied with each other in naughtiness, but being the progeny of such mothers, they weren't very good at it and their mischief was uninventive and repetitive; nevertheless, it was always severely punished. Had they had any sense they would have unbuckled themselves from their buggy and legged it over the fields in their Babygros to the NSPCC, but being mercifully senseless, they smiled their vinyl smiles and took whatever was coming to them; unlike Tiny

Tears, who wept throughout the proceedings and refused to be toilet trained despite the penalties incurred.

But one day the children's grandmother had brought them someone whose arrival left all the other toys in a neglected heap. Orville was an apricot poodle puppy, with overflowing eyes that left the tracks of tears down the sides of his face, giving the impression that he was always crying, which was perhaps a true one. Kimberley and Carly were beside themselves; here was a real live baby who did spectacularly rude and naughty things. He was squeezed and cuddled and was expected to obey their every command and whipped with his little lead until even Enid protested; he was yanked by the neck until he whimpered for mercy; and plastic earrings were clipped to his ears and ribbons tied to his tail. When he had soiled Enid and Trevor's duvet, Claudia could only applaud silently his magnificent *coup de théâtre*, but she could not tell if it had been by intention, or simply because his stomach had been squashed too hard; and of course the consequences for him had been dire.

Claudia had thought that Orville was an uncharacteristically inventive name, until she had discovered that he had been called after an ingratiating, lime-green, fluffy duckling, a ventriloquist's dummy with a plastic beak, who wore a nappy; she had seen the puppy Orville in a makeshift nappy one day, strapped into the buggy, with one of the naughty twin's bonnets on his head; when she had remonstrated with the children, Enid had shouted at her through the open window to leave the kids alone. A few days later she had met them coming home from school.

"Where's Orville?" she said.

"He had to go to the vet's because he chewed up the wallpaper," replied Carly.

"Will he be all right?" she had asked, stupidly, and then she had realized that she had quite misunderstood.

"And it cost £5.99 a roll," said Kimberley.

"Come on you two!" shouted their mother, seeing them fraternizing. "You'll miss your program!"

"We're getting two gerbils instead," Carly shot back over her green quilted shoulder as they ran off heavily, in their white latticed knee socks.

"God help them, in their cage . . ." Claudia thought.

"I don't think that's a very good idea," she called after them.

"None of your business, you old ratbag," came faintly down the lane.

Old ratbag. Old. Ratbag. Their words hurt far more than they should have; after all, they were only children. She reminded herself that she had always got on with children. She hurried on; the thought of her own children made her feel as desolate as a scarecrow, with the freezing wind whipping the rags of her self-esteem. They had taken her name and made it ugly—Claw-dee-ya, Claw-dee-ya; they had made her ugly. What was a ratbag? She knew what it meant, but what was it? She could go and knock on their door and say, "Sorry to bother you, Enid, but could you tell me what a ratbag is? Perhaps you could look it up in your *Pears' Cyclopedia?*" Slam.

She was trapped as surely as the gerbils in their cage. There was no work available locally and she could not afford to move. Next month she must default on the mortgage. Buying a house in the country had been, she saw now, one of the death throes of a desperate marriage. When Paul had left, by mutual consent, and the first heady inflorescence of being alone had evaporated like cow-parsley in July, she had found the freedom to gaze uninterrupted for hours over the flat fields of rape, inhaling the odors of the pig farm; she had fields of time, acres of time, stretching as far as the eye could see, to an uncertain horizon.

A headache zigzagged at her temple like a little firecracker as she stood at the window. She had no aspirin to alleviate it, and could not borrow any from Enid, who anyway was out, collecting the girls. Each morning, after walking them to school, Enid heaved her hams on to the minibus which transported workers to the pharmaceutical research laboratories, where she was employed in the canteen, serving lunches to the animal technicians, and one of the perks of the job was that she never ran short of painkillers and cold cures and vitamin drinks.

That Hallowe'en morning Claudia had walked to the village to pick up the magazine that she had ordered. Foolishly, she had told the woman in the shop the reason that she wanted it. The woman had already checked it out. The story wasn't there.

"I was wondering if you wrote under another name . . . ?" she said.

"No. No I don't."

The fiction editor in her glitzy office, of course, could neither have known or cared that, miles away, beyond the rim of her consciousness, stood a small woman in wellingtons in a sub-post office in her public shame, concealing under an Army surplus jacket something that resembled a breaking heart.

"Hope deferred. Hope deferred. Hope deferred maketh the heart sick," her boots beat out on the rutted lane; her fingers numb around the rolled-up magazine, the glossy cylinder that contained someone else's story. The lost earring came into her mind.

"Swings and roundabouts," she said to herself as she passed the deserted recreation ground. It was absurd to care so much, but that story, in a magazine too prestigious to be among the shop's regular stock, had been going to vindicate her, to prove to Enid, and thence to everybody, that Claudia had some status in the outside world, and to earn her, if not friendship, at least some grudging respect; and also to reassure herself that she still existed. Next month's would be the Christmas issue, and it was unlikely that her muted autumnal tale would take its place among the glossy gift-wraps, the shimmering scarlets and greens and golds of a feast that she would not be celebrating.

It was almost dark, and as Claudia pulled the curtains for the night, at four o'clock, Kimberley and Carly passed her window, their yellow silky hair streaming under black pointed paper witches' hats, their pointed noses, red from the cold air, pecking towards each other in conspiracy, wagging their hats towards her house and laughing, before they ran indoors.

Claudia went into the kitchen and took her sharpest knife and sharpened it. As she worked, she expanded her fantasy to include Kimberley and Carly, naked, trussed and basted, glistening with fat, their crispy skin crisscrossed and stuck with cloves, oranges stuffed in their mouths. She was very hungry; she had not eaten all day. When she had finished her preparations, she sat down in the dark to wait for the children.

They were a long time coming. She sat on the edge of her chair, straining her ears for their steps, hearing only a car door slam, down the lane, the dull explosion of a far-off firework, the blood beating in her head. She put a log on the fire and lit the candles. Everything was ready; so why didn't they come? The table floated on the darkness like an altar and on its surface glittered a long knife.

The gate moaned on its hinge. There was the sound of

footsteps, a shuffling on the doorstep; then the knock. Claudia flung open the door, with a low triumphant cry of "Trick!"

The hiss died on her lips. There was a confusion of a woman's face above a paper sack from which protruded the neck of a bottle of wine and the white jagged heads of chrysanthemums. It was the woman from the party.

"Oh dear, I can see you weren't expecting me. Have I got the wrong day? That would be typical of me—I thought you said—I brought these . . ."

"Come in."

Claudia held back the door, and her visitor stepped in, still prattling in her nervousness, into the flickering light and smell of melting wax. "I do apologize—I was sure—I'll just put these down—I left the car down the lane . . . oh, a real fire, how lovely. And a turnip lantern!"

"Oh that—" said Claudia, glancing at the wicked face, lit from within by a guttering candle, "it was just a little surprise for the children . . . Here they are now. Would you give it to them?"

Her shadow swooped over the ceiling as she picked up the lantern and held it out to her *dea ex machina*, with nails that gleamed in its light like blood.

"I'll just get rid of this."

She carried the knife into the kitchen and dumped it in a pile of peelings in the sink.

ALL THE PUBS IN SOHO

The pansies were in a blue glazed bowl on the kitchen table, purple and yellow, blue and copper velvety kitten's faces freaked with black, and also in a bed by the back door where they straggled on leggy stems around the drain and the leaking water butt. There was not a trace of blood. Joe's father's words had conjured up a wreckage of broken flowers streaked and spattered with red; the scene of a gory murder. An innocent bee investigated the absence of a crime.

Joe could not understand why they had provoked his father to such rage at breakfast making him choke on bitter marmalade, spitting a jellified gout of rind onto the newspaper. It had reminded Joe of the time a girl with a bad cold had sneezed onto her sum book, and Miss Hunt had ripped out the page and carried it at arm's length to the wastepaper basket, and he had felt sick at breakfast as he had then, when he had also burned with sympathetic shame. Beside the blue bowl of pansies a blue bottle grazed in spilled sugar and negotiated a white papery onion, which was actually garlic, but Joe, like most of the population of Filston, Kent in 1956, was unacquainted with this pungent bulb. A bunch of brushes stubbled with paint stood in a jar; there was a smell of turpentine and paint and linseed oil, the nicest smell that Joe had ever known.

That summer the Sharps, that is Joe, his two little brothers and their parents Peter and Wendy, he of the camel-hair coat and thin moustache and crimped waves of rusting hair, she of the Peter Pan collars and velvet hair bands, had moved into their tall white house set back from the main village street behind a black railing hung with rest-harrow, and had furnished it with blows and tears and cold cocoa and unemptied potties.

Not long afterwards two strangers had descended from the London train and had been observed taking turns to haul a heavy suitcase along the High Street and up the hill towards Old Hollow Cottage. They wore American plaid shirts and jeans, which men did not wear in Filston unless they were of the bib-and-brace working overall variety. The small dark one had slung over his shoulder a dark green corduroy jacket and the taller fair one carried a jacket of muted claret. They were reported to have been drunk on arrival, but this may have been apocryphal information, supplied by hindsight. It was a long walk, uphill on the narrow road between dry banks bulbous with the grotesque roots of the overhanging trees while clouds of midges nibbled the heavy air and sweat ran into their eyes, as far as the crossroads where a broken signpost rusted in a little island of grass and ox-eye daisies, then downhill between fields of cows in pasture and ripening corn to the hollow that gave the cottage its name. That night they cruised into the car park of the Duke's Head with a shrieking of dry brakes, on an old black bicycle they had found chained with cobwebs among the nettles in the shed; one working the brakes and the other perilously side-saddle on the crossbar. Their hands were stippled with nettle stings. They had not had to do anything more scandalous to become notorious.

It was his father's vituperation about "those bloody pansies at Old Hollow" that had brought Joe to the cottage on this empty summer holiday afternoon. He had had nothing else to do. Under the table, on the wine-colored jacket, a wild-looking black and white cat, with burrs and green knobs of goose grass in her fur, was stretched out, nuzzled by a heap of squeaking multicolored kittens. Joe stepped over the threshold and crept towards them.

In the bedroom at the back of the one-storyed cottage the fair-haired young man lay on his side on the bed smoking, reading and from time to time looking at the dark one who was sitting in a creaking wicker chair, wearing only a pair of jeans, drawing him; sunshine leaked around the sides of the yellow curtain pulled crookedly across the window, brushing his skin with bloom, turning his hips into a peach, blue smoke from the cigarette in his trailing hand swirling in the lemony light. There was a faint mushroomy odor of mildew in the room. Suddenly a tenderly drooping line became a gash in the paper as the artist dropped his pencil and ran from the room.

"What——?"

The fair man felt too lazy to follow. The other returned with a struggling figure clasped to him, its legs kicking at his shins. Its T-shirt, stained with elderberry juice, was pulled askew, scratched legs kicked from the khaki shorts.

"Look what I found in the kitchen." He let go with one hand and flung a pair of jeans at the bed.

"Cover yourself up."

The fair man pulled the bedspread cover over himself. The child was struggling and snarling in the captive arms.

"Good afternoon," said the man on the bed as he struggled into his jeans. "Who are you?"

The child was trying to bite now, making futile lunges with its teeth, snapping the air.

"I think it's a wild boy of the woods," said the fair man. "Abandoned as a baby and brought up by the wolves."

"They aren't any wolves in England," snarled the wild boy with distinctly middle-class scorn.

"What excuse have you, then, for breaking and entering? Have you come to spy on us? Or to steal?"

"I only came to see the bloody pansies!"

The dark man released him. He stood panting and rubbing his arms where they had been held. The two men looked at each other, then the fair one said in a silly voice, "Well, here we are, duckie. Allow us to introduce ourselves. I'm Arthur and this is my friend Guido."

The child gave an uncertain giggle, looking from one to the other.

"Don't be silly."

He was beginning to think that they might not murder him, even the fierce dark one, Guido.

"I knew we shouldn't have come here," said Arthur.

"Who are you then?" Guido asked the child.

"Joe."

Arthur raised himself on an elbow and studied him.

"Are you sure it isn't Josephine?"

A blush ran down Joe's freckled face and neck and out of his sleeves and down his arms.

"If he says it's Joe, it's Joe," said Guido sharply.

"Well Joe, what do you say to a cup of tea?"

Joe nodded, too mortified to speak. There was the air of a stray dog following the stranger who patted his head in the street about him as he followed Guido into the kitchen without looking at Arthur.

"How old are you, Joe?"

"Nearly nine."

Guido filled the kettle and put it on the stove. The smell of gas mingled with the turps and linseed oil filled Joe's head, and mixed with his excitement at being there and having tea with two grown-ups was the odd feeling that he was completely at home.

"Are you an artist?"

"A painter. Do you like painting?"

"Well—I can draw an elephant from the back, and a star without taking the pencil off the paper. Shall I show you?"

"That's OK. I believe you. Can you carry the tray into the garden? I'll go and get Arthur."

Joe carried the round tin tray carefully and set it in the grass. He lay on his back and watched the sky. The sound of raised voices came from the kitchen. Joe sat up at once, tensed to run. He felt sick. He came from a house where a veneer of anxiety lay on every surface like dust, where at any moment a bark might rip up comics and scatter toys, where a fist thumping the table might make cups leap in fear vomiting their contents onto the tablecloth, just as Joe had once been sick when his father caught the side of his head with his knuckles, and where Mommy's forehead wrinkled like the skin on cocoa and her chin puckered in fear and placation. He expected every domestic discourse between two adults to degenerate into a battle in which by being co-opted to one side, he was considered the enemy by the other, and so always ended as the loser whoever else was in power when a truce was called. But then Guido and Arthur came out together to join him. Arthur was holding a whisky bottle.

"I thought we'd have a wee celebration, as Joe's our first visitor." He poured whisky into two cups.

"To Joe."

"Joe."

Gradually Joe stopped shaking enough not to slop the strong

red tea from the cup which Arthur handed to him; it was the most beautiful cup he had ever seen, a pearly white shell that stood on tiny china periwinkles on a flat fluted saucer—Beleek, a legacy from Arthur's Irish grandmother.

He realized that no one would have told him off if he had slopped it. The cake was dry and crumbled like sand on a plate painted with a blue fish. They were sitting under an old apple tree hung with small red apples. Joe looked up into its branches and then at Guido, for permission.

"They're very sweet," said Guido.

Joe reached up and an apple fell into his hand. The skin was warm and the white flesh did taste sweet. They sprawled in the grass and talked; Guido and Arthur smoked, Joe ate apples and cake. They accepted what he said without once telling him not to be silly, or to stop showing off or not to interrupt or not to dip his cake in his tea and scoop out the residue of crumbs and sugar with his finger. It all went to his head like whisky. Suddenly something in the light told him it was late. He sat up abruptly, his old panicky self. "I've got to go. I've just remembered someone's coming to tea. What shall I do?"

"Take the bike," suggested Arthur.

"But—"

"You can bring it back tomorrow."

Joe, swooping and curvetting down the hill, straddling the crossbar, standing on the pedals, clenching the screaming brakes, the heavy black handlebars bucking in his hands, heard over and over again the words, "You can bring it back tomorrow," and made them into a tuneless song that was snatched by the wind whistling past his ears.

He came into the room on the awful words from his mother's visitor.

"So it's to be St. Faith's then?"

She disposed of Joe with sponge cake in her mandibles.

"No!" he shouted. "I won't."

The glory of the afternoon fell from him as he confronted the wavering tableau of his mother's shocked face above a new pale blue necklace, the best teapot garlanded with roses floating in her hand above the tablecloth, his brothers' smeared faces above the trays of their high chairs, the yellow and red wedges of cake.

"Josephine, where on earth have you been? I specially asked you not to be late for tea. I don't know what Mrs. Williams will think of your hands and face, and put on a clean frock at once."

"I'm not going to St. Faith's."

As Joe backed from the doorway, it was what Mrs. Williams would think that was uppermost in his mother's mind: that she was a poor mother who could not control her plain and disobedient daughter, that the little boys were noisy and not toilet trained, that the blue outlines of the transfer still showed at the edges of the satin-stitched flowers on the tablecloth that she had just finished embroidering that morning and had not had time to wash or iron, and that already a stain was seeping through the linen onto the table beneath the cloth. A bad mother and a bad housekeeper.

"Well, it seems the best of a rather poor bunch," she whined, referring to St. Faith's as if her disparagement of the local educational establishments might attach some credit to her disappointing daughter.

Joe was not a pretty child. Now her freckles stood out on her blanched skin against the red and white gingham dress that was quite wrong for her coloring, as her mother and Mrs. Williams realized simultaneously. "You might have brushed your hair," her mother despaired. "She insists on having it short although it doesn't suit her," she apologized, regretting the ringlets that might have been.

"Nice and cool for the summer, eh?"

Mrs. Williams gave a conspiratorial pat to the sweaty reddish feathers glued to the mutinous forehead. Joe tossed her hand away.

"I'm not going to St. Faith's, I'm going to the village school and I'm not going to wear a stupid hat, and I'm not . . ."

"Just drink your milk. She likes to play at being a boy, I'm afraid . . . I can't think why."

"I don't."

"Please don't keep interrupting. The grown-ups are talking. Help yourself to bread and butter."

"I've had tea. With my friends."

Wendy sighed and turned away.

"Another cup of tea, Mrs. Williams? Oh dear, I'm afraid the pot's gone cold."

Joe sat silent, a milk moustache framing her savage mouth, her stomach turning to scrambled egg at the thought of walking through the village in the uniform of St. Faith's. Even if she crumpled the hat and hid it in her satchel, there could be no concealment. It was hopeless. If she could do something heroic, rescue one of the other children from the river or a fire, maybe they would forget the way Daddy had shouted at them and chased them from the garden. If only she could wake up tomorrow morning and be a boy and have a suit of gray shorts and a jacket with a zip and elasticated waist and cuffs—Roy Noble had a dark blue corduroy suit, that was the best, but she would settle for a threadbare gray, worn with gumboots—and he had a television. She had heard his mother call, "Roy, it's telly time," and he had run in leaving her alone in the rec holding onto Timothy's pushchair.

". . . Nancy, boys. . . ."

The words clattered onto her empty plate.

Mrs. Williams went on, ". . . so she went up to him in the

shop and said, 'Mr. Morelli, I'm the President of our local Artists'
Circle, and I wondered if you'd like to come for coffee one morning
and meet some of our members,' and do you know what he replied?"

"No. What?"

Mrs. Williams leaned towards her and lowered her voice.

"He said, 'You know what you can do with your blankety-
blank coffee!'"

"No!" Wendy gasped.

"Can you imagine? In Carter's!"

"My husband says that people like that ought to be shot. I
mean to say, it makes my flesh crawl, just to think—ugh." She
shuddered, holding out an arm so that they might see the pale hairs
express their horror.

"There are men who love other men, just as there are women
who love other women," said Joe.

"Leave the table at once!"

"There's nothing wrong with it. Just because someone loves
somebody they get put in prison and people call them all—"

"That's enough! I don't know what's got into you this
afternoon."

An unmistakable smell that could not be ignored was staining
the disastrous tea party.

"Josephine, take Timmy to the bathroom and wipe his hands
and face, and bring him back and then go to your room."

Her eyes signaled desperately that Joe should change Timothy's nappy, as if there were a chance that Mrs. Williams had not
noticed.

"What can a little girl like you know about such things?" Mrs.
Williams's voice held reproach for the whole family.

"I just know."

"I can't think where she—neither Peter nor I would dream of discussing such matters in front of a child. . . ."

Joe did just know, she thought, as she yanked Timothy from his chair. When Guido and Arthur had talked to her, it was as if she had always known, but had just been waiting for someone to say it. She had known too, without being told, that she should say nothing of her visit at home.

"Love between men. Love between women," Wendy thought, as with increasing embarrassment she realized that she had told Josephine to remove the wrong child. Away from the magazines she read, in the real world inhabited by Peter and herself, in the marital bed lumpy as semolina, there wasn't even much love between men and women.

"Would you like to look at the garden?" she asked, and called, "Oh, Joe, look after Giles, would you?"

A big old black bicycle, a heap of junk, was sprawling on the lawn.

Carter's, where Guido had ground the Artist's Circle under his heel like a cardboard disc whose triangles graduate through the shades of the spectrum, was the biggest shop in the village. There was Dawson's, which was handy for sweets, for a packet of fags on a Sunday, and a branch of the South Suburban Co-operative Society, but people like Wendy did not shop there. Carter's had a wooden floor that sloped down to the glass-fronted biscuit containers that fronted the mahogany counter, a wire for cutting cheese, a red bacon slicer, bins of dried fruit and glass jars of sweets, and a wines and spirits licence. The back of the shop smelled of paraffin and Witch firelighters and neat bundles of chopped firewood bound with wire and aluminum buckets and coal scuttles and clothes pegs and new rope. Fruit and vegetables were displayed at the side entrance. The emporium was owned by Mr. Carter, who presided over the bacon and cheese and cold meats and wines and spirits, and was staffed by seven part-time assistants known collectively as the Carter girls. Each was mysterious in her own way, but it was Dulcie, the youngest, who conceived a passion for Arthur.

Dulcie had been engaged, and her fiancé, called up for National Service, had been killed. Her future was hacked to pieces on the mud floor of a hut in Kenya. Her fiancé's dismembered remains lay under a white marble gravestone in Filston churchyard and her dreams were split by savage painted faces and flashing knives. She had been cheated of her rights, and had had to sell her ring back to the shop at a loss to help to pay for his funeral, and had been condemned to remain with her miserly widowed father on a squalid smallholding called Phoenix Farm. It became a joke among the other Carter girls that Dulcie blushed when Arthur came into the shop. Her usually bitter mouth simpered, her offhand manner became solicitous as she packed his shopping bag.

"Mind them eggs," she would say as she placed them carefully on top of his purchase, or, "You ought to take somethink for that cough." Other customers could arrive home with dripping bags of a dozen broken eggs, or cough themselves to death for all she cared, but she worried about Arthur. She picked her way past the steaming heaps of sodden straw through the mud in her high heels, carrying over her arm an overall washed every night and starched as white as chalk in the hope that he might come in. She was disappointed if Guido was with him but it was better than nothing. She could not understand why Mr. Carter was so against them and she thought it slightly peculiar that neither of them was married, but that was her good luck. Mr. Carter had installed a new refrigerator, and stocked its shelves with new exciting ice creams. As usual, when they entered the shop, fine ice crystals of disapproval frosted the air around Guido and Arthur as they hovered at the throbbing fridge, unable to agree which flavor would most please Joe.

"The Neapolitan's very nice," suggested Dulcie, her face burning in the chill.

"Eat Neapolitan and die," said the funny foreign one.

"No, honestly, it's ever so nice," insisted Dulcie, offended.

Anyway it would have melted by the time they got it home.

On the afternoon of her half-day Dulcie was slouched at the bus stop contemplating the prospect of plodding around the shops of the nearest town, then catching the bus home again to get her father's tea. Boredom twittered in the hedges, crawled among the flints of the wall on which she leant and grazed the green slope of the opposite hill. She threw her half-smoked cigarette into the road, just for something to do. She was twenty; she should have been coming up to her second wedding anniversary in a new house on the new estate. It wasn't fair.

Incredibly, she saw Arthur walking down the empty road towards her. She prayed that the bus would not come.

"Fancy meeting you here!" she stuck out her thin hip and put her head on one side. It did not seem a very surprising or unlikely meeting to Arthur.

"Hello."

He didn't alter his pace.

"Coming to the dance?" she called after him. He stopped.

"What dance?"

"That one. A week Saturday." She pointed to a poster that announced a Grand Dance, to be held in the Village Hall.

"I don't dance."

"Oh go on, it's a good laugh. I'm going," she added as an incentive.

Arthur hesitated, not knowing what to say, watching a string of black and white cows crossing the hill, beyond the brittle rainbows of the split ends of her hair. He had quarreled with Guido and stalked out of the house, propelled by his anger until stopped by this girl.

"What's your name?" she was saying.

"Arthur."

"Arthur." She sounded disappointed. "That's nice. You're not foreign are you, like your friend?"

"Scottish."

"Oh. Your friend though, he's foreign, isn't he?"

"An Eye-tie. A wop. Second generation."

"I thought he was foreign. Aren't you going to ask what my name is then?"

"No," said Arthur, exhausted by this interchange.

"Oh, you are awful." she slapped familiarly at him. "It's Dulcie. Silly isn't it? I hate it." She heard with alarm the rumble of the bus around the corner. "You coming to the dance, then?"

"I told you, I can't dance."

"I'll teach you. Go on, it's a laugh. Eight o'clock Saturday, I'll see you there," she called over her shoulder as she swung onto the bus, and then she slumped into a seat enervated by her own daring. By the time the bus had reached the town she was convinced that not only had she and Arthur a firm date for Saturday week, but that *he* had asked *her* to the dance. She bought a pair of shoes and matching handbag, and a bag of sweets which she popped rapidly and mechanically into her mouth, crunching without tasting so that when she got off the homeward bus she was surprised to find an empty bag in her hand. She stood for a moment in the field stroking the shiny patent leather of the shoes and handbag before going upstairs to hide them from her father under the floorboard, with her mother's empty blue shell of Evening in Paris, and her bottle of California Poppy.

Meanwhile Arthur had sat on a swing in the deserted rec behind the Village Hall where the Grand Dance was to be held, smoking and scuffing his feet in the dusty trough worn by the generations of children's feet. When the packet was empty and he had tossed it over his shoulder, he suddenly laughed and left the swing performing a wild parabola on its rusty chains, and was whistling when he dropped into Carter's for more cigarettes. If, like Dulcie, Mr. Carter thought that Arthur looked like a movie star, it was of no film that he would care to see; his manner was within a moustache breadth of offensive as he handed over a bottle of bad red wine and rang up the inflated price on the till. Arthur, for his part, gave not a thought to the absent Dulcie, who might have served him. He wished that he had the bike so that he could get home faster. Guido was lying asleep on the bed, open mouthed, smelling faintly and sweetly of stale white wine.

He was always Joe at the cottage. Once Guido had got on the bus and had seen him and Wendy sitting there in Mother and Daughter polka-dot frocks, made by Wendy from a Simplicity pattern, which had proved not so simple, and Joe's polka-dot hair band had slipped around to show the elastic. He never knew if Guido had seen them or not and neither of them had referred afterwards to the encounter. Wendy would have been surprised to discover that she had become a smoker; her account at Carter's showed evidence of cigarettes and of chocolate and other delicacies which she had not consumed. Carter's was so handy, she just gave Josephine the list and she did most of the shopping. Arthur and Guido were doubtful when Joe gave them presents and hesitant about accepting them, but he was so hurt if they refused that they took the gifts.

"You don't have to bring us presents, Joe. We enjoy your company. Just bring yourself." Joe did, as often as he could. The kittens were growing adventurous and Poppy, the mother, was quite friendly now, her coat almost glossy; Arthur had found her in a field with her neck in a snare and had brought her home and nursed her and she had rewarded him with a litter of kittens two days later. Joe played with them or talked to Guido while he painted, receiving grunts in reply, or bashed about on Arthur's typewriter or gathered mushrooms which they fried in butter until they were black. Nobody told him not to touch the matches, or not to lick his knife or not to pick the blisters of hot paint from the back door. The corn in the field next to the house was almost ready to be cut, the blackberries in the garden were flushed with red, the heavy red tomatoes splitting their sides and breaking their stems. Guido had cleared a patch and had planted squash and zucchini, and they fried their yellow flowers, fluted like the horn of the gramophone that poured music onto the garden, in batter. In the front room there was a broken sofa and piles of books which had come from London in a van with Guido's easel. Joe looked at the pictures, turning over the thick and glossy pages heavy with damp in the mushroomy air and read poetry which excited him even though he did not understand it; he loved the feel of the foreign books printed on thick paper with rough edges, he felt that if he could read them they would tell him everything that he wanted to know, although he did not know yet what that was. At home at night he lay in bed listening to the rise and fall of voices below, his body tensed for the modulation that was the signal for him to put his pillow over his head.

★   ★   ★

One afternoon, having escaped at last from amusing Timothy and

Giles, Joe was so startled to hear a loud woman's voice over the hedge that he swerved violently on the bike, bruising himself agonizingly on the crossbar. He rolled in silent screams on the grass, buffeted by the woman's laughter and alien men's voices. He stood outraged on the edge of the gardens pierced with jealousy. Several other men and Arthur and Guido were lounging about in the grass and, on a kitchen chair, like a queen among her courtiers, was a black-haired woman. The worst thing, the thing so shocking to the child who flicked unperturbed through books of painted nudes, was that she had taken off her blouse and sat in her brassière. Joe stared in horror as a kitten crawled between those shocking white circle-stitched cones. His freckles fused in a dull red stain, but the woman was not embarrassed, and neither, it seemed, were any of the men. He had never seen Mommy in anything less than her petticoat, four thin straps slipping down her sloping shoulders as she brushed her hair, and this lady was much older than Mommy.

"Come away, Joe, and have a drink." Arthur's voice was more Scottish than usual. "This is Joe, everybody, the wee friend we was telling you about."

Joe came forward, avoiding looking at the woman, but she grabbed his arm and pulled him towards her. She thrust her face into his with a clacking of earrings.

"Guido, where did you find this enchanting little redhead?"

She ruffled his hair. He wriggled away. The kitten leaped from her chest, puncturing a breast with a hind claw. She screamed. A tiny bead of blood rolled onto the white brassière.

"I'm bleeding, Arthur, do something—"

"It's only a little scratch," said Joe, his voice thick with scorn. He picked up the kitten and stroked it, comforting it.

"Anyone would think that it was that creature who was wounded, not me. Doesn't anybody care that I'm bleeding to death?"

"Oh shut up, Cathleen, and have another drink."

She squeezed the last drop of blood from the tiny wound. Arthur splashed wine into her glass. Incredibly to Joe, he did not seem to hate or despise her. Joe turned to Guido but he was talking to a horrible man with a stained moustache that curled wetly into the corners of his mouth. Joe could not believe that Arthur and Guido liked these people, but they were laughing and joking with them as if they had really missed them.

"Whatsa matter, Joe?" called Arthur, and gulped as an unripe blackberry thrown by Cathleen landed in his mouth.

"Nothing," said Joe.

Everybody looked ugly. Arthur's eyes were bloodshot, his lips too red. "He looks like a wolf," thought Joe. Pieces of wolves' dinner, chicken bones webbed with sticky skin lay in the grass, rejected by the kittens, the air was heavy with smoke and wasps attacked the carcass of a cream cake. A squashed wasp lay on the open book beside Cathleen's chair. They were all talking loudly about people Joe had never heard of. He went into the kitchen. Guido followed him.

"Look at this mess!" said Joe in his mother's voice, waving an arm at the table piled with greasy plates and smeared cutlery and glasses and crusts and dirty paper napkins. The lovely smell of paint and linseed oil was glazed with stale cooking.

"Poor Poppy, you hate them too, don't you?" said Joe picking up the cat who was cowering under the table and receiving a scratch from a flashing paw, which he scorned to notice.

"Why so sulky, Joe? Come into the garden and amuse us. Tell us all the gossip."

"Don't know any," said Joe.

Wendy, had she been otherwise, would have found a rich source of gossip in Mrs. Cheeseman who came in to clean two mornings a week, but her nervousness manifested itself in a shrill bossiness, and Joe could see that Mrs. Cheeseman despised them. She was the widowed mother of two teenage daughters, Ruby and Garnet, and had four cleaning jobs as well as keeping her own house immaculate and winning most of the prizes at the Horticultural Show. Her stoicism on her widow's pension put the Sharps to shame. Joe had once seen her throw a piece of his Meccano from the bedroom window.

"Don't be jealous, Joe. It's very dull for Arthur here with only me to talk to."

"And me."

"And you too, of course."

"And the cats."

"And the pussycats."

Joe went back outside to hide the tears in his eyes just as Cathleen pulled Arthur onto her lap, pressing him against the squashy white cones and nuzzling his ear.

"Aw, get off, Cathleen, will you."

"Not until you give me a kiss."

Arthur pecked at her cheek.

"Not like that. A proper kiss. What are you staring at?" She turned on Joe who stepped back from the savagery of her eyes.

"Nothing."

"Like hell you are. I do believe it's jealous. Arthur, has our little freckled friend got a crush on you by any chance?"

"Leave him alone Cathleen."

Guido had come out into the garden, his face snouty and

mean with alcohol. It wasn't clear whom he meant Cathleen to leave alone.

"Such a waste," Cathleen said to Arthur. "You're much too pretty."

"I said, lay off. Arthur, you look like a clown, but you're not funny."

Cathleen had smeared a red cupid's bow on his forehead, and another on his cheek.

"What's wrong, Guido? You're not jealous, are you? Of me, a mere woman? Stop being such a tedious old queen. Here, Freckles, stop gawping and get me another drink."

She thrust out her clownish tumbler.

"Don't stick your fingers in the glass. Where are your manners?"

"I was trying to rescue a fly," said the erstwhile enchanting little redhead.

"Oh for God's sake."

Arthur had struggled free but she kept hold of his hand. He squatted beside the leg of her chair, whose feet were embedded in the grass by her weight, with her rings digging into his hand. He did not look unhappy. The man with the stained moustache began to sing; the petals of the last rose of summer blew about on a beery wind while tears ran down his cheeks.

"Guido. Guido." Joe pulled at his arm. Guido shook him off.

"Look, why don't you go and pick some mushrooms?"

"I did."

Joe flung the paper bag of mushrooms to the grass and burst into tears. Everything was spoiled. He blundered towards the bicycle to escape from the party of badly behaved adults. Home seemed almost a haven. Then he felt an arm around him and he was pulled to Arthur's chest.

"What's all this about? Hey, come on. . . ."

He took a handkerchief and dabbed ineffectually at Joe's eyes and tweaked his nose until he had to laugh.

"That's better. Come away into the kitchen and have a cup of tea with me."

"You still look like a clown," said Joe.

"Well, at least I made *you* laugh."

When they returned to the party everybody was in a good mood. Guido said that it was his birthday next week and that he and Arthur were coming up to London to celebrate and that everybody must join them.

"We'll bring Joe," he said. "We'll take him to all the pubs in Soho."

"Look at his face," said Cathleen. "Look at that wicked grin. Such decadence in one so young," but she said it nicely. And she had put on her blouse. Joe forgave her. He was prepared to love her. He accepted a sip from her glass and then another and let himself be pulled on to her knee. The gramophone poured Euridice, Euridice in its scratched voice over the garden.

The trees reared up crazily at him as he zigzagged down the hill, a little drunk. "All the pubs in Soho. All the pubs in Soho," sang in his ears. Soho shone over the horizon, a golden city of shimmering spires where he would go with Guido and Arthur and be happy.

"I picked you some mushrooms."

Joe stood in the doorway of the bathroom holding out the

crushed paper bag which he had retrieved from the grass and forgotten to leave in the cottage kitchen.

"They're probably toadstools. Put them in the bin at once and wash your hands."

"No, they're definitely mushrooms. We've had them lots of times."

"Who's had them?" she asked sharply.

"Me and my friends."

She hauled Giles out of the bath.

"You haven't been playing with those rough children again, have you? You know what Daddy said. I don't know what he'd say if he knew you'd been picking toadstools. It's absolutely forbidden, do you understand?"

She stared in exasperation at her unnatural child in the stained khaki shorts, her lips stained with what must be blackberry juice, clutching a bag of poisonous fungi, and turned to Giles who was lying across her lap. Despite her ministrations his bottom was sprinkled with the sore stars of nappy rash.

"Mommy?"

"Yes."

"What's Soho?"

"It's a place in London. A not very nice place."

"Why not?"

"Well—pass me the baby powder please."

"Why not very nice?"

"Will you keep still, Giles. Timothy, if you get off that pot once more, Mommy's going to be very cross." The baby squirmed in her lap.

"Why isn't it very nice?"

"Because not very nice people go there. Now will you stop

asking silly questions and make sure Timothy stays on his pottie? It's not the sort of place people like us go to."

"Hah," said Joe.

It was obvious that Mommy knew nothing about Soho. He saw its name in letters of gold shining through the powder and steam. It was exactly the sort of place people like himself went to.

The floor of the village hall was dusted with talc for the feet of the dancers and dusty silver twigs were stuck into green-painted tree stumps for decoration. Crates of beer, and more ladylike drinks, were carried across from the pub and stacked on the trestle-table that formed the makeshift licenced bar and colored light bulbs looped the stage where the band stood; the bare bulbs that hung from the ceiling were dressed in crêpe paper skirts, and bunches of balloons attracted ribald remarks. The Grand Dance, after a sticky start, was in full swing. Dulcie danced with the first man who asked her, Geoff Taylor, who had always fancied her, although she did not fancy him, tossing her head vivaciously, studiously not looking at the back of the hall where the summer night streamed through the double doors, so that Arthur might arrive and see her in another man's arms, dancing with the lights sparkling in her hair. She had not seen him alone since their meeting by the bus stop and interpreted his every word as secret confirmation of their date and had read all sorts of romantic implications into his most mundane request. She pictured him lounging in a dark suit and white shirt with a red carnation in his buttonhole, a cigarette between his lips, watching her. She was a good dancer but her new shoes hurt. After four or five dances with different partners she stood by the bar sipping orangeade through a straw watching a wrinkled balloon deflate. The band played on. Incipient blisters throbbed on her heels. She giggled hectically with a group of girls, then danced again, desperate that he should not arrive to find her wilting like a wallflower; her smile was fixed in fresh lipstick on her face, her eyes were now unable to keep off the door. Only the knowledge that she had told no one that Arthur was coming to the dance—she had been saving that triumph—saved her from bursting into tears but in the penultimate dance, the Carter girls hokey-cokeying wildly, her face dissolved and she rushed from the hall, tearing off her shoes and running blindly barefoot across the recreation ground.

Feet pounded after her and Geoff Taylor caught her arm, swinging her around to face him as the last waltz smooched out among the stars. She sobbed against his chest the story of how Arthur had asked her to the dance and stood her up.

"Him? That queer bloke?"

She nodded, not understanding the adjective.

"I'll bloody kill him."

She blew her nose, too miserable to be ladylike.

"I've got the bike. Do you want a lift home?"

Soon she was on the back of the motorbike, her arms clasped around his waist, holding her shoes with the heels sticking into his stomach as they blasted up the village street, towards Phoenix Farm, her skirt billowing out behind her like a parachute.

As Arthur passed the Duke's Head on his way to the post office he was seduced by the smell of warm beer in the sunshine through the open cellar door. The landlord slopped down his pint on the counter with no more than the usual contempt. A tractor stopped and a young man jumped down and followed him into the bar which was empty except for two old men in caps playing dominoes and a dog-faced woman in tweeds morosely sucking a Mackeson while a little dog died quietly at her feet. Pipe smoke was caught in the golden cones fluting through the bottle glass and turned them blue. In the morning air the polished glasses and horse-brasses among the low beams had the clarity of a hangover; a strong smell of hops came from the dusty dry garlands on the ceiling and from the clear brown beer in Arthur's glass. He felt a frothy head of well-being wash over his boredom. He looked at the young man who had followed him, taking in the faint and not unpleasant scent of old manure around the patched dungarees, the brown arms under the rolled sleeves of the faded workshirt, the scowling face under a cow's lick of Brylcreem. Incongruously, he was drinking whisky. Arthur raised his own glass and nodded to him but the young man obviously drowning his sorrows at 11:30 on a summer morning spat a flake of tobacco from his lip and shoved his empty glass across the bar for another shot.

"Going it a bit, aren't you Geoff?"

One of the old men called out. Geoff uttered something incomprehensible to Arthur and they all laughed, one of them choking wetly on his pipe stem, and Arthur found himself smiling too. He ordered another beer; he had no desire to leave this pleasant place. The onslaught of the second drink prompted him to conviviality. He almost ordered drinks all around, but he had only enough money left for stamps. In his inside pocket was an envelope containing poems which he was posting to a magazine in London.

Reluctantly he went out into a morning gold and blurred at the edges, the road ran like a river at his feet. Suddenly he was on his back on the asphalt with grit and blood in his hair and Geoff Taylor's fist smashing into his mouth and an iron-capped boot chipping at his legs while its owner exhorted him to stand up and fight. He tried to get up grasping handfuls of road and was kicked back with a boot in the chest. His head caught the curb. Bone bounced off stone. A wild blow glanced off Taylor's stomach and Arthur grabbed his shirt and pulled himself up and and landed a punch on his jaw which sent him reeling back on his feet and followed it through but missed as Taylor stepped aside. Arthur's head was a broken ball of pain; he could taste blood in his mouth. He tried to grab Taylor around the waist to throw him but his legs buckled and he collapsed on his knees. Taylor's fist crunched again into his face and withdrew bloody, then he kicked him systematically all over his body and finally stamped on his outstretched hand.

The tractor's engine sputtered away into silence. Arthur could hear a blackbird singing in the watery tones that herald rain. His whole body was in pain. He knew that his hand lay, an injured creature, in the road beside him. "It's a good thing it wasn't Guido. I can write with my left hand," he thought, then red and black swirled, dissolved as he lost consciousness.

The president of the local Artist's Circle saw him lying in the gutter, and crossed the road. It was only what she would have expected of him.

Clinging onto hedges and walls Arthur managed to stagger as far as Carter's where he leaned on the door and fell into the shop with a jingling of its bell.

"Help me."

"Get out of my shop," said Mr. Carter who was cutting cheese with a wire. The Carter girls in their white overalls stood like monoliths behind the counter. Dulcie gave a little scream and started forward.

"Get back to your work, Dulcie."

Dulcie looked at the bloody misshapen bruised swede that had been her idol trying to speak through lips glued to its teeth with blood.

"Yes, Mr. Carter," she said and started weighing broken biscuits.

"We don't want your sort here," said Mr. Carter. "Get out, and mind my clean floor. Go back where you came from."

Arthur crawled out. He made it across the road to the surgery and swayed in the little porch hung with Virginia creeper, leaning on the bell. The doctor's wife answered.

"Yes?" she asked.

"Doctor."

"The doctor's having his lunch. I suppose you'd better come into the surgery and wait."

She left him slumped on a fumed oak chair whose chintz cushion was tied on with tapes. He had to brace himself to stop from sliding to the floor.

"You have got yourself in a mess, haven't you?" she said as she closed the door behind her.

Eventually the doctor came, clouded in evidence that he had enjoyed a small cigar after his lunch.

"This is going to hurt," he said with satisfaction, expecting Arthur to wince and mince, and Arthur screamed silently with the effort not to play the role expected of him as the doctor swabbed and strapped his ribs with distaste.

"You ought to have that hand X-rayed. And your head," he concluded without telling Arthur how to go about it. "You'll live," he said.

Arthur tried to thank him.

"Don't thank me. You're not one of my patients, thank God, so I'll be sending you my bill. Know where you live, but what do you call yourself?"

Arthur looked at the red cloudy water in the basin and sodden lumps of cotton wool like obscene red snowballs, and fainted.

"Pull yourself together, man. How are you going to get home? Can you pay for a car if I get you one?"

Arthur nodded. He just wanted to be with Guido. He didn't know if Guido would be able to pay but he was past caring.

The local taxi service was operated by the landlord of the Duke's Head, and so it was he who dumped Arthur on the cottage doorstep and stood jiggling coins in his blazer pocket while Guido ran to find the money for his exorbitant fare.

"You should have seen his face," he told his customers in the bar that evening, "when he saw the state of little Miss Nancy. I thought he was going to burst into tears."

Wendy, who was there with Peter, almost felt sorry for Guido for a minute, but the thought of two men kissing made her feel sick: she could not conceive that they might do anything but that.

"Perverts," said Peter.

"If there weren't ladies present . . ." said the landlord.

Two ginger cats, named Gin and Lime, one smooth, one fluffy, smirked on the bar. Wendy didn't really like leaving the children alone in the house but Peter got so cross if she made a fuss, and Joe was quite capable . . . .

"You're looking very pretty tonight," said Peter. "That sherry's brought quite a sparkle to your eyes."

"Thank you kind sir," she said, with dread.

All the cats, Poppy and her kittens, ran at Joe when he pushed open the kitchen door.

"Guido? Arthur?"

He went into the garden. They weren't there. His heart started to race; a sick feeling came into his stomach. The silence had a quality of finality, as if the air had closed forever on the spaces left by bodies, and voices were gone without echoes. He ran back into the kitchen ignoring the importunate cats. There were two notes on the table. One was addressed to the woman from whom they had rented the cottage, and one to him.

> Dearest Joe,
>
> I expect you've heard what happened. We are going back to London and then to the south of France where Cathleen has a house.
>
> Please look after the pussy cats.
>
> —Will write. In haste,
>
> Guido. Arthur.

Arthur's name was shaky, as if written with his left hand.

"No," cried Joe, "you can't , you can't," in desperate belated entreaty. He ran out into the road and gazed at its achingly empty blue curve, the edges fretted with birds' songs and skirmishes. "Come back! I want to come with you. What about me?" he shouted. "What about all the pubs in Soho?" He sank sobbing onto the grass verge. "Come back! Come back!"

A rough furry head thrust into his wet face purring loudly.

He opened a tin of pilchards and while the cats ate he read again Guido's note. What had happened? He had no idea. Why couldn't they have taken him with them? Wild thoughts of burning the letter to the landlady and living in the cottage himself rushed through his brain and were swamped by reality the color of cold cocoa. Guido and Arthur were the only bright color and affection he had known and they were gone leaving him entirely alone. The thought of St. Faith's inspired more tears.

He went into the bedroom. A torn and stained shirt had been thrown into a corner. Joe picked it up, screamed, and dropped it. It was stiff with dried blood. He thought Arthur had been shot.

"Please don't be dead. Please don't be dead. Please don't be shot."

But Arthur had signed the letter so he couldn't be dead.

Joe took the shirt and lay on the bed with it in his arms rocking from side to side as he wept.

From time to time a sob still shuddered in his chest as he gathered up Poppy and the kittens and struggled to get them all into a large cardboard box which he tied around and around with string. It took him almost an hour; as soon as he had pushed down one wild head or paw another sprang out. At last he carried the squeaking wailing box outside and left it by the bicycle at the front hedge. He went into the field and dragged a bale of straw through the hedge and into the kitchen. He took the bottles of turpentine and linseed oil and methylated spirit from the draining board and splashed them over the straw and around the kitchen, and went into the bedroom. Tacked to the wall was a little sketch of Arthur lying on the bed. He tore it out and put it in his pocket, and splashed methylated spirit over the bed. He took a box of matches from the kitchen table and set fire to a corner of the sheet and to the corner of the bale of straw.

The journey home wheeling the bike with the cats bumping awkwardly on the saddle was agonizing. His back hurt with the effort of balancing the box and although he had draped it with the bloody shirt he had to stop every few steps to push back a terrified head. He knew that if one got out he would never get it back again. The spinning pedal hit him sharply on the ankle many times until his leg was a mess of oil and blood. The chain came off and dragged rustily in the road. His grief was overtaken by his dread of what would happen when he got them home.

He came into the kitchen. Daddy was home early.

"Look what's come for you. Isn't that a lovely surprise? It came from Peter Jones this afternoon," said Mommy. There was an enormous box on the table. It must be a present from Guido and Arthur. His heart leaped.

"Well open it then," said Daddy impatiently.

Joe lifted the lid and parted the tissue paper. Inside lay the brown velour hat with a yellow striped band and the brown serge wraparound skirt and yellow blouses of St. Faith's School.

"Well, you might at least try to look pleased," said Daddy. "This little lot cost me a small fortune. What on earth have you been doing? Your face is disgustingly filthy. Let's hope St. Faith's will—"

Mommy, who had been twisting nervously at her blue poppet beads, broke them and they went pop pop pop over the kitchen floor.

"I only hope you realize how lucky you are." Daddy's voice went on.

But at that moment Joe realized like a blow to the stomach that Guido could not write. He didn't know the address. He picked up the hat and threw it on the floor and stamped on it. His father's hand caught him across his tear-stained face. Joe seized the hand and bit it.

"I hate you, Daddy, you tedious old queen," he screamed, kicking his father in the shins.

Behind him in Old Hollow, the cottage blazed like the fires of hell; the cats burst out of their box in the shed, and the nude study of Arthur fell to the floor in his rage.

WHERE THE CARPET ENDS

The Blair Atholl Hotel was berthed like a great decaying liner on the coast at Eastbourne; if it had flown a standard from one of its stained turrets it would have been some raffish flag of convenience hoisted by its absentee owner, flapping the disreputable colors of the Republic of Malpractice and Illegality.

The front windows had a view of the Carpet Gardens and the pier, but the back of the hotel, where Miss Agnew lived, gave on to the drain pipes and portholes of another hotel and a row of dustbins where sea gulls and starlings squabbled over the kitchen refuse. Miss Agnew, impelled by the vicissitudes of life to book a cabin on this voyage to nowhere, was one of the off-season tenants who occupied a room at a reduced rate at the top of the hotel, where the carpet had ended. These people of reduced circumstances were required to vacate their rooms just before Easter when the season started, or pay the inflated price required of summer holiday-makers. After the third floor, the mismatched red and black and orange carpets gave way to cracked linoleum and, in places, bare boards. A terrifying lift, a sealed cage behind a temperamental iron zigzag door, carried them up to their lodgings, separated from each other by false plywood walls that divided what had once been one room into two compartments. One floor above them, huddled precariously like gulls, perched a colony of homeless families, placed there by the council in bed and breakfast accommodation, whose misery filled the pockets of the landlord and his manager.

If, as Le Corbusier had said, a house was a machine for living in, the Blair Atholl, thought Miss Agnew, was a machine for dying in; but at least there, unlike the residents of the many old people's rest homes in the town, they were doing it on their own terms. The residents of the fourth floor formed a little community in exile, rescuing each other when the lift stuck, knocking on a door if someone had not been seen about, purchasing small sliced loaves for the sick and Cup-A-Soup and tins of beans to be heated on the lukewarm electric rings, and braving doctors' receptionists, in the smelly telephone booth, to beg for a home visit but dreading above all an admission to hospital, from which one so seldom returned. They met in the conservatory at the back of the hotel in the evenings for a rubber of bridge or to watch a program on television, which was a reject from the lounge, whose horizontal hold had gone, and formed a little human bulwark against the sound of the sea and the approaching night. It did not do to think too much, Miss Agnew had decided; to dwell on people and cats and dogs and houses in the past was to inspire one to board the next bus to Beachy Head, but sometimes she could not resist stopping to speak to a cat or a dog in the street, and the hard furry head and soft ears under her hand evoked lost happiness so painfully that she strode away berating herself for laying herself open to such pangs, her red mackintosh flapping like the wings of a scarlet ibis startled into flight.

She did not know why antagonism had flared up between herself and the manager, Mr. Metalious. She paid the rent on time and she was surely no more bizarre than any of her fellow residents: the Crosbie twins, seventy-year-old identical schoolboys who dressed on alternate days in beige and blue pullovers they knitted themselves, and gray flannel trousers and blazers. She felt sure they would have affected caps with badges if they had dared; they did wear khaki shorts in the summer and long socks firmly gartered under their wrinkled knees. Or than the transvestite known as the Albanian, a smooth-haired shoe salesman who by night flitted from the hotel, a gauzy exotic moth, to sip the secret nectar of the Eastbourne night. Or than Miss Fitzgerald who left a trail of mothballs and worse in her wake and cruised the litterbins of the town and rifled the black plastic sacks her fellow tenants left outside their doors on dustbin day. Or than Mr. Johnson and Mr. Macfarlane who spent their days philosophizing in the station buffet. Or than the Colonel whose patriotism embraced British sherry. Or than silent Mr. Cable. Or Mrs. MacConochie. Miss Agnew thought that perhaps she reminded Mr. Metalious of some teacher who had humiliated him in front of the class, or a librarian who had berated him for defacing a book. She had followed both these professions in her time, but she was not interested very much in his psyche, and anyway videos were more in his line than books. Perhaps she had alienated him when, on moving into the hotel, she had asked him to carry her box of books to her room. He had acquiesced with a very bad grace, telling her that his duties did not include those of a hall porter: perhaps her decision that he would have been offended by a tip had been the wrong one. Whatever the cause, and even before she had overheard him refer to her as a stuck-up old cow, she knew he did not like her.

"Nothing today, Miss Agnew," he would call out as she passed her empty pigeonhole beside his desk.

"I wasn't expecting anything," she told him truthfully, but he was determined to regard the lack of post as a confirmation of her low status and as a triumph for himself.

Anyone less bovine than Miss Agnew would have been hard to imagine; she was more ovine, as befitted her name which she believed to derive from the French, with her long mournful face framed by a fleece of off-white curls. Now that it didn't matter any more, she was thinner than she had ever hoped to be. The most she had hoped for in this town, which she had more than once heard referred to as "God's Waiting Room," was anonymity. She was desirous to be known only as Miss Agnew and she expected nothing more of her pigeonhole than dust or a catalogue for thermal under-wear, and why he picked on her for this particular humiliation she did not know. None of the residents got much post, except the Albanian who received thin cobwebbed envelopes addressed in a spidery hand, and the Crosbie twins who corresponded copiously with each other in the course of each of their infrequent quarrels.

It was lunchtime and Miss Agnew was seated at a table in the window of Betty Boop's, a small vegetarian restaurant that suited her herbivo-rous taste, ruminating over a piece of leek flan. She had managed, by taking very small mouthfuls and laying down her knife and fork between each bite, to prolong her meal for twenty minutes or so, when she saw Miss Fitzgerald pass, head bowed against the wind to avoid a spume of salty vinegar being blown back into her face by the northeaster from what was undoubtedly someone else's discarded bag of chips.

Since a recent survey had condemned Eastbourne as a town of guzzlers, Miss Agnew had become aware of the habit of the populace of snacking out of paper bags; the precinct was sugary with half-eaten doughnuts, meaty with burgers and strewn with the polystyrene shells that had held pizza and baked potatoes, the toddlers under the transparent hoods of their striped buggies clutched buns and crisps and tubes of sweets; and now there went Miss Fitzgerald conforming, for once, to a local custom.

Miss Agnew was thinking about Beachy Head; it was comforting to know that it was there. When she had walked there in the summer she had been dazzled by the color of the sea, opal and sapphire as in Hardy's poem "Beeny Cliff," and she had felt a melancholy empathy for the writer because for her, as for him, "the woman was elsewhere . . ." and nor knew nor cared for Beeny or Beachy Head and would go there nevermore. Miss Agnew had felt a powerful force pulling her to the cliff's edge, and only the thought that she would probably plummet messily onto the boiling rocks rather than curve like a shining bird through the sky into the iridescent sea had propelled her backwards on the turf. The Crosbie twins had told her that many more bodies were recovered than were reported; the local police and press had a policy of suppressing such information, *pour décourager les autres*. She wondered how largely Beachy Head loomed in the minds of her fellow residents.

Now she gulped down her elderberry wine, paid the bill, and succumbed to an impulse to follow Miss Fitzgerald, feeling amused at herself and more than slightly ridiculous as she turned up the collar of her mac like that of the trench coat of one of the private eyes in the detective stories she used as a drug against insomnia when she lay awake in the night and felt the hotel slip from its stone moorings and nose towards oblivion. She tracked her quarry past the pier that strode on shivery legs into a sea of gunmetal silk-edged with flounces of creamy lace, like the expensive lingerie she had loved once. Now she was glad of her thermal vest and her hair blew about her head as brittle and dry as the wind-bitten tamarisk and southernwood bushes.

Hotel gossip had it that Miss Fitzgerald, despite her rags and carrier bags, was very rich. Any discussion of her eccentricities would include, at some point, the refrain, "She comes of a very good family, you know." The black sheep driven from some half-ruined Anglo-Irish castle, Miss Agnew surmised, as she hurried along, merging into the wall when Miss Fitzgerald stopped to investigate a litterbin, muttering furiously as discarded newspapers and polystyrene foam cups and boxes showered the pavement. The few people she encountered made wide curves around her, swerving into the road as she marched on with the tail and paws of a long-deceased animal around her neck lashing the wind. Were there sheep in Ireland, Miss Agnew wondered? Pigs and chickens certainly, and gray geese in Kilnevin: perhaps St. Patrick had rid the Emerald Isle of sheep with the snakes. She reflected that she was getting sillier and sillier every day that she spent at the Blair Atholl; it was because she had nothing to think about. Perhaps she was manifesting early symptoms of Alzheimer's disease, brought on by the gallons of tea she had poured over the years from the aluminum teapot; aluminum found in quantities in tea, she had read recently, was a contributory factor to the disease, and that friendly familiar teapot, like a battered silver ball reflecting the firelight in the facets of its dented sides, must have made her an almost inevitable candidate for premature senility. Why else would she be following Miss Fitzgerald's erratic and litter-strewn progress, playing detective in the icy wind? The teapot had belonged to Pat, the friend she had lived with for thirty-three years. The lease of the flat had been in Pat's name too, and when it had expired Miss Agnew had neither the means nor the desire to renew it. She hoped that Pat was not watching now, and feeling that her friend's purposeless life negated the years they had spent together, but the brightness and laughter and strength that had been Pat was a heap of ash in a plastic urn, so of course she couldn't see her.

Miss Fitzgerald struck up a side road and Miss Agnew followed her past the guest houses with hanging baskets and gnomes and cards in the windows advertising vacancies, whose names, the Glens and the Blairs and the Lochs and the Braes, suggested that they were passing through a settlement of Scots in exile. They emerged into the long road called Seaside and Miss Agnew found herself studying a green plaster rabbit and a set of ruby-red plastic tumblers on the deck of a broken radiogram in the window of a junk shop, while Miss Fitzgerald contracted some business with its proprietor. A sign stuck to the glass said: "Lloyd Loom Chairs Wanted Any Condition. Good Prices Paid." How odd, thought Miss Agnew, that those prosaic wicker chairs should have become collector's items; if you waited long enough everything came back into fashion, but she knew that she would not. Not yet antique, and certainly unfashionable, she stepped into an adjacent shop doorway as Miss Fitzgerald emerged still talking volubly and stuffing something into one of her plastic carriers. Miss Agnew remembered that there was a creaking circle of green wicker chairs in the Blair Atholl conservatory, which she felt suddenly sure were genuine Lloyd Looms. Miss Fitzgerald crossed the road and stood at the bus stop, but Miss Agnew decided to walk on a little before retreating to the Blair Atholl, although a heavy shower had started to fall.

This part of town seemed to be called Roselands; there was a men's club of that name, and a café; the name shimmered softly in tremulous green leaves and pink blowzy petals, the name of a ballroom or dance hall in a film, where the lost and lonely waltzed away their afternoons, reflected in mirrors full of echoes and regret.

Miss Agnew opted for the Rosie Lee Café, which seemed cheerful and steamy, where memory would not draw up a chair at her table and sit down, but as she pushed open the door she saw a fellow resident of the Blair Atholl, Mr. Cable, a redundant bachelor late of the now-defunct Bird's Eye factory, seated there smoothing out the creases from a very black-looking newspaper prior to applying himself to the Quizword. She retreated. The shower had spent itself now. All the bright and garish gardens she passed, the tubs and window boxes of the terraced houses, and the flowers in the interstices of the paving stones, the shining windows and letter boxes had a desperate air, as if neatness could stave off desolation; a cold salt wind was blowing off the sea and a palm tree rattled behind a closed gate. Tall pampas grass was lashing the houses with canes, softening the blows with hanks of dirty candy-floss, and punishing again. There was too much sky in East-bourne, Miss Agnew thought, she found its pearly vastness terrifying; gold light poured from the Downs gilding bleakly the cold glass panes of a Victorian red-brick church and blazing in puddles on the road and pavement. Mothers with prams and pushchairs on their way to collect older children from school seemed unaware of, or immune to, all this gold that rolled from the spokes of their wheels, drenched them and turned their baby carriages to chariots of gold.

Miss Agnew had to pause to snatch her breath back from the wind outside a low building set back from the pavement; it was a newly refurbished home for the terminally old. A large yellow van with "Sleepeezee" on its side was parked in the drive and a mattress was being carried in. Behind a window Miss Agnew saw a girl in a white uniform bounce up towards the ceiling and as she came down a young man bounced up. Up and down they went, trampolining, bounce up, bounce down, laughing, until for a second they were in mid-air in each other's arms before tumbling down in an embrace on the new mattress; the living were larking about on the deathbeds.

Miss Agnew was at once elated and distressed. An image came into her mind of her parents, long ago tucked up in their marble double bed with a quilt of green marble chippings to keep them warm. She caught a bus back to the town center, and as she sat on its upper deck, she decided that it was right that the young should embrace in the face of death, and closed her ears to the profanities of a bunch of smoking school-children sprawling about the back of the bus; their harsh cries sounded as sad as the voices of sea birds on a deserted beach at dusk.

As she stepped out of the lift on the fourth floor she noticed a pram, belonging to one of the bed-and-breakfast families, wedged across the narrow stair that led to their quarters, and saw the disappearing draggled hem of a sari above a pair of men's socks. She shook the raindrops from her mac and hung it up and made herself a cup of soup and a piece of toast. Later that evening she went down to the conservatory to watch the nine o'clock news.

"Pull the door to, would you?" said Mrs. MacConochie. "There's a draught." The wind was buffeting the glass panes, the television picture shivered.

"I don't want to be part of this," Miss Agnew said to herself, looking around, at the Crosbie twins counting stitches, the defeated fan of playing cards in Mrs. MacConochie's hand, Mr. Cable clawing his winnings, a pile of one-pence pieces, across the baize table whose legs were crisscrossed with black insulating tape. Wicker creaked under old bones, the horizontal hold slipped and Miss Fitzgerald mumbled under a cashmere shawl. "I don't want to be a drinker of Cup-A-Soup in a decaying hotel room, whose only post is a catalogue for thermal underwear," thought Miss Agnew, "just as I do not want to join the respectable army of pensioners in their regimental issue beige and aqua raincoats, whose hair is teased, at a reduced rate on Wednesdays, into white sausages that reveal the vulnerable pink scalps beneath, and who are driven to luncheon clubs in church halls by cheerful volunteers. I am not nearly ready to sleep easy on a Sleepeezee mattress. Something's got to happen."

The weather forecast ended.

"Have you put on your stove?" Mrs. MacConochie asked Mr. Cable. He had. It was Mrs. MacConochie's colonial past that made her thus refer to the dangerous little electric circles with flayed flexes that failed to heat the residents' rooms; her own room was almost filled by a Benares brass table with folding beaded legs, and burnished peacocks with colored inlaid tails, and a parade of black elephants with broken tusks; herds of such elephants trumpeted silently in the junk shops and jumble sales of Eastbourne.

The Albanian paused outside the conservatory, then stuck her head around the door.

"Good evening everybody."

There was a murmur at this diversion; they glimpsed tangerine chiffon and a dusting of glitter on the blue-black plumes of her hair. She smiled, like a dutiful daughter, round the circle of her surrogate family, but there was nobody there to tell her to take care and not to be home late, and she melted away into the mysterious night.

"Pull the door to, would you?" called Mrs. MacConochie, wrapping her tartan rug tighter around her knees. "There's a draught."

"Something must happen," said Miss Agnew to herself again as she prepared herself for bed. "Something will change."

In the morning nothing had changed. A sea gull laughed long and bitterly outside her window. Mr. Metalious still disliked her; there was nothing in her pigeonhole. A gray rain was slashing the street. As she crossed the foyer she passed the Albanian, a poor broken moth caught by the morning, dragging dripping wings of tangerine gauze across the dusty carpet, blue-jawed and sooty-eyed in the fluorescent light.

The only thing that was different, she noticed as she entered the conservatory, was that all the Lloyd Loom chairs had gone, and Miss Fitzgerald was standing under a paper parasol in the rain, watching a van pull away from the back entrance of the hotel.

A PAIR OF SPOONS

Villagers passing the Old Post Office were stopped in their tracks by a naked woman dancing in the window. Not quite naked, for she wore a black straw hat dripping cherries and a string of red glass beads which made her white nudity more shocking. When they perceived that the figure behind the dusty glass was a dummy, a mannequin or shop-front model, they quickened their steps, clucking, peevish and alarmed like the pheasants that scurried down the lane and disappeared through the hedge. After a while only visitors to the village hidden in a fold of the Herefordshire hills, those who had parked their cars outside Minimarket and, seduced by the stream with its yellow irises and dragonflies, had wandered along the grassy bank that ran down one side of the lane, were struck by the nude with cherry hat and beads, frozen in mid-dance by their scandalized stares.

The Old Post Office, which used to do business from the double-fronted room jutting out into the lane, had stood empty for several years following the death of the retired postmaster. Posters advertising National Savings, warning against the invasion of the Colorado Beetle, and depicting heroic postmen struggling to the outposts of Empire still hung on the walls, curled and faded to the disappointing pinks, yellows, greens and blues of a magic painting book, while stamps and pensions were dispensed and bureaucratic rituals were enacted now through a grille of reinforced plastic at the back of Minimarket. In that shop window was a notice board and prominent among the advertisements for puppies, firewood, machine-knitted garments and sponsored fun-runs, walks, swims and bake-ins, was a card which read in antiqued scrolly script: We buy Old Gold, Silver, Pewter, Brass and Broken Jewelry, any condition. China, Clocks, Furniture, Books, Comics, Tin Toys, Dinkies, Matchbox, etc., Lead Farm Animals, Clothes, Victoriana, Edwardiana, Bijouterie. Houses Cleared. Best Prices. Friendly Old-Established Firm. Ring us on 634 and we will call with No Obligation.

Parts of the Old Post Office house predated the fourteenth-century church whose clock and mossy graves could be seen from the kitchen window through a tangle of leggy basil plants on the sill above the stone sink. Anybody peeping in on a summer evening would have seen the Old-Established Firm, Vivien and Bonnie, sharp-featured and straight backed, tearing bread, keeping an eye on each other's plates, taking quick mouthfuls with a predatory air as if they had poached the pasta under the gamekeeper's eye; two stoats sitting up to table. Their neat hindquarters, in narrow jeans, rested on grubby embroidered cushions set with bits of broken mirror and sequins which overlapped the seats of the Sheraton-style fruitwood chairs; they rested their elbows on a wormy Jacobean table whose wonky leg was stabilized by a copy of Miller's Antiques Prices Guide. It was Vivien, with her art-school training, who had calligraphed the notice in the village shop: after meeting Bonnie, she had taken a crash course in English porcelain and glass. Bonnie relied on the instinct which had guided her when she started out as an assistant on a stall in the Portobello Road, where she had become expert in rubbing dust into the rough little flowers and fleeces and faked crazed-glaze of reproduction sheperd-esses, goatherds, cupidons, lambs and spaniels, and which had taken her to co-owner of this ever-appreciating pile of bricks and beams. Vivien and Bonnie moved through Antiques Fayres like weasels in a hen house. To their fellow dealers they were known, inevitably, as Bonnie and Clyde, or the Terrible Twins.

At night they slept curved into each other in their blue sheets like a pair of spoons in a box lined with dusty blue velvet, or with stained pink silk in summer: two spoons, silver-gilt a little tarnished by time, stems a little bent, which would realize less than half of their value if sold singly rather than as a pair.

They had grown more alike through the years since they had been married in a simple ceremony at the now-defunct and much-lamented Gateways club. How to tell them apart? Vivien bore a tiny scar like a spider-crack on glass on her left cheekbone, the almost invisible legacy of the party that followed their nuptials, where Bonnie's former lover had thrown a glass of wine in her face. Or had it been Vivien's rejected girlfriend? Nobody could remember now, least of all the person who had flung the wine.

"Vivien is more vivid, and Bonnie's bonnier," suggested a friend when the topic of their similarity was raised.

"No, it's the other way round," another objected.

"A bit like dog owners turning into their dogs. . . ."

"But who is the dog, and who the owner?"

"Now you're being bitchy."

That conversation, which took place in London, would have struck an uneasy chord of recognition in Vivien had it been transmitted over the miles. She had become aware of an invisible lead attached to her collar and held kindly but firmly in Bonnie's hand. There were days when she seemed as insubstantial as Bonnie's shadow; she became aware that she mirrored Bonnie's every action. Bonnie took off her sweater, Vivien took off hers; Bonnie reached for her green and gold tobacco tin; Vivien took out her own cigarette papers; Bonnie felt like a coffee, so did Vivien and they sipped in unison; Bonnie ground pepper onto her food and Vivien held out her hand for the mill; when Bonnie, at the wheel of the van, pulled down her sun visor, Vivien's automatic hand reached up and she confronted her worried face in the vanity mirror. At night when they read in bed the pages of their books rasped in synchronicity until Bonnie's light clicked off and then Vivien's pillow was blacked out as suddenly as a tropical sky at sunset.

"You go on reading, love, if you want to. It won't disturb me."

"No, I'm shattered," replied Vivien catching Bonnie's yawn, and swallowing it as the choke-chain tightened around her throat. The next morning, noticing that her Marmite soldiers had lined up in the precise formation of Bonnie's troop, she pushed her plate away.

"Do you think you could manage on your own today? I don't feel so good."

"You do look a bit green around the gills. I hope you're not coming down with something."

Bonnie laid one hand on Vivien's brow and with the other appropriated her toast.

"You haven't got a temperature."

"Well I feel funny."

"We're supposed to be going to pick up that grandmother clock from that old boy, and there's the car boot sale—oh well, I suppose I *can* go on my own . . . hope to Christ he hasn't done anything stupid like having it valued, you can't trust those old buzzards, dead crafty, some of them. . . ."

Their two egg shells lay on her polished plate, hardly damaged, sucked clean by a nifty rodent.

Vivien guided the van out into the lane; Bonnie had taken off one of the gates on the rearside wing once when she was cross. Vivien waved her off and watched the dust settle. She felt an immediate surge of energy and fueled it with a doorstep of toast spread with honey found in the cupboard of a house they had cleared, crunching on the cells of a comb rifled from the hive by the fingers of a dead woman. The bees had all buzzed off by the time Bonnie and Vivien had hacked their way through the tangled garden, and the empty wooden hives, weathered to gray silk stood now in their cobbled yard.

Vivien left her sticky plate and knife in the sink and, sucking sweetness from her teeth, locked the door and set off down the lane with a wave to the woman dancing in the window. The vicar, passing by on the other side, ducked his head in the cold nod that was the most, in charity, that he need vouchsafe the Londoners since Bonnie had made him an offer for the paten and chalice.

"Morning, vicar. Lovely morning, isn't it? Makes you feel good to be alive," Vivien called out uncharacteristically, surprising them both.

The incumbent was forced to look at her across the lane, a skinny lumberjack cramming into her mouth a spray of the red currants which hung like cheap glass beads among the fuchsias in her red and purple raggedy hedge, and caught a glitter of glass flashing crimson fire on plastic flesh, and a dangle of cherries.

"Hedge could do with a trim," he said.

"Oh, we like it like that," reminding him that she was half of the dubious duo. She was sucking the end of a honeysuckle trumpet. At this rate she wouldn't need the hedge trimmer he had been about to offer. She would soon have eaten the whole hedge.

"Ah well," he concluded.

His skirt departed to the east and Vivien's jeans loped westward. She was trying to suppress the little maggot of anxiety whose mealy mouth warned that Bonnie might telephone to find out how she was. As she passed the callbox she had such a vivid image of Bonnie impotently misting up the glass panes of an identical construction standing among moon daisies on a grassy verge, while the phone rang and rang in their empty kitchen, that she could only assume that telepathy was at work. She thought, and walked on, stopping outside a garden at a box of worm-eaten windfalls with "Please help yourselves" scrawled on a piece of cardboard. Vivien filled her pockets. She came to a gate, placed one hand on the topmost bar and vaulted into a field of corn, and followed a natural track through the furrows, now spitting husks and crunching sweet kernels, now negotiating an apple, until she was faced with barbed wire and a ditch of nettles. She stood wavering wildly on the wire and hurled herself forward, landing, with only the softest malevolent graze of leaves on her bare ankles, in a field whose hay had been harvested, leaving its scent in the air. The field was bordered on three sides by massive trees, oak, sycamore, ash, chestnut, and although it was only July, recent rain had brought down a scattering of tiny green conkers. "Like medieval fairies' weapons," thought Vivien, whose fancy, when not stamped on by Bonnie, flew on such flights, "those spiked balls on chains." Aluminum animal troughs rusted in a heap. At the far end of the field was a gate set in a high hedge and Vivien walked towards it dreamily with the sun freckling her face and her arms beneath her rolled-up sleeves.

The latch lifted but she had to force the gate against hanks of long grass, and squeezed herself through the gap. She was at the edge of a garden and now she saw a house which was not visible from the field. Old glass in the windows glittered like insects' wings. No dog barked. The house exuded emptiness, shimmering in the heat haze while housemartins flew in and out of their shells of honeycombed mud under the eaves. As she walked over the lawn she realized that the grass here had been cut not very long ago: it was springy beneath her feet, studded with purple milkwort and daisies and buttercups that seemed to acknowledge the futility of growing too tall. Somebody, therefore, cared for the garden. The roses needed to be deadheaded, the petals were falling from the irises and peonies revealing shiny seed cases, but apart from the soggy roses and a faint mist here and there of lesser willowherb and an occasional intrusive cow parsley and weedy seedling brought up by the rain, the flowerbeds were orderly. She meant only to peep through the windows.

It was strange, she thought, as she walked on rose petals around the back ground-floor windows, pressing her face against the old dark glass, how she did not feel like a trespasser, but as though she had inadvertently locked herself out of those rooms hung with faded velvet curtains and had the right to walk on the pale carpets and curl up in that yellow velvet chair with a blond dog at her feet. She stared at old wooden kitchen cupboards holding china and utensils behind their half-open sliding doors, the mottled enamel gas cooker, the pyramidal iron saucepan stand, the fossilized pink soap and rusty brillo pad on the draining board, the clean tea towels, bleached and brittle as ancient flags. A movement by her foot made her look down. A toad regarded her with amber eyes. She crouched and reached out to pick it up. The toad leaped for the dank shadow under a flat scratchy plant. Vivien thrust her fingers after it and scrabbled in dead leaves and needles. Instead of pulsating skin, she struck metal. She drew out a key. It came as no surprise that the key fitted the lock of the scullery door, and turned, through cobwebs and flakes of rust, to admit her to the stone-flagged floor. The mangle, the stone sink, the disconnected twin-tub, had been waiting for her.

Vivien moved through the rooms, acknowledging the pile of enamel dogs' dishes in the kitchen, the Chinese umbrella stand holding walking sticks, knobkerries and a brace of Union Jacks, the wellies sealed with cobwebs, the waterproof coats and jackets on the pegs, the polished tallboys, chests of drawers, the empty vases, the glass-fronted cabinets holding miniatures and enameled boxes, scent bottles and figurines, the groves of books, the quiet beds, the framed photographs, the high dry baths, the box spilling shoes. Everywhere she saw herself reflected, framed in elaborate gilt on the walls, elongated in tilted cheval glasses, in triplicate and thence to infinity above dressing tables, dimly in the glass of pictures. She touched nothing. At last she let herself out again, locked the scullery door, and put the key in her pocket.

"The state of you!" Bonnie scolded. "Where've you *been*? I've been back for an hour. I rang to see how you were but there was no reply. . . ."

"Just for a walk. I needed some air."

"You could have got that in the garden." Bonnie waved an arm at the sofa spewing horsehair onto the cobbles.

"It's damp and smelly," Vivien protested. "Did you get the clock?"

"No, I didn't." Bonnie brushed grimly at grass seeds and burrs clinging to Vivien's clothes. "You look as if you've been rolling in the hay. Have you?"

"Chance would be a fine thing. Ouch."

The village maidens had a tendency to obesity and anoraks and, this summer, fluorescent shorts. Bonnie slapped at Vivien's jeans, reactivating the nettle stings. Stung into memory of her first sights of the house, and walking again in its peaceful rooms, Vivien half-heard Bonnie's voice.

". . . decided not to part with it for sentimental reasons, lying old toad, then he let slip that he'd heard the Antiques Roadshow might be coming around next year . . . thought I'd really cracked it . . . who did he think he was kidding, you could practically see him rehearsing the greedy smile of wonderment that would light up his toothless old chops when they told him his crappy clock was worth a small fortune . . . I'd like to tear up his bus pass, he practically promised me . . . sell their own grandmothers, these people. . . ."

"I thought that was precisely what he wouldn't do?" Vivien returned to the present.

"What?"

"Sell his grandmother. Clock."

"*Don't* try to be clever, it doesn't suit you."

I am clever, thought Vivien, and it might suit me very well.

"Shall we go to the pub later?" she said.

"No. What do you want to go there for? I thought we agreed that the ambiente was nonsimpatico?"

"Well, yes. I just thought you might fancy going out for a change."

Vivien ripped the ring-pulls from two cold beers from the fridge and handed one to Bonnie. It was true that the pub was uncongenial. The locals were a cliquey lot. Bonnie could take off their accent brilliantly. "Oooh-arr" she had riposted to those guys' offer to buy them a drink, and suddenly she and Vivien were on the outside of a circle of broad backs. No sense of humor. And boring—most of their conversation was limited to the agricultural; there were so many overheard references to filling in dykes that the girls could not but feel uneasy, especially as those ditches were not a feature of the local landscape. Aggression flared in wet patches in the armpits and on the bulging bellies scarcely contained in T-shirts that bobbed like balloons along the bar. The landlord, who was in the early stages of vegetabliasis—so far his nose had turned into an aubergine—snarled at them, as if he thought they would turn the beer.

"Let's go and sit in the garden," said Vivien, leading the way. "How was the car boot sale?"

"Like a car boot sale."

They ate outside, sucking little bones and tossing them against the rising moon, straining their eyes in the dusk to pick out their autumn wardrobe from the L.L. Bean catalogue, and going into the house only when it grew too dark to read even by moonlight and starlight, and it was time to luxuriate with a nightcap in the pleasures of *Prisoner: Cell Block-H*, propped up in bed by pillows, in front of the television. Long after Bonnie had fallen asleep, whimpering slightly as if dreaming of chasing rabbits, Vivien lay awake with a glass-fronted cabinet glowing in the dark before her eyes. A slight flaw or bend in the glass gave a mocking, flirtatious twist to the rosy lips of the procelain boy in a yellow jacket and pink breeches, ruffled in a gentle breeze the green feather in his red hat, lifted the wings of the bird in his hands, and raised an eyebrow at the little girl clutching a wriggling piglet against her low-cut laced bodice over a skirt striped with flowers. A black and gold spotted leopard with a pretty face and gold-tipped paws lounged benignly between them, and putti, half-decorously wreathed, offered baskets of flowers.

Vivien, falling into sleep, put her hand out in the moonlight and found that the cabinet had no key. The moon hung between the open curtains like a huge battered gold coin almost within her grasp.

A week passed before Vivien could return to her house. At the wheel of the van, at the kitchen cooker, in dusty halls where people haggled over trinkets and dead people's clothes and crazed enamel hairbrushes and three-tiered cake stands, she cherished her secret. Had she asked herself why, she might have replied that it was because it was the only secret she had ever had from Bonnie; or she might have said that for the first time she wanted to look at and touch beautiful objects without putting a price on them, or even that there was something in the air of the house that stayed her hand from desecration, but she was careful not to ask herself any questions. Once or twice she caught Bonnie giving her a look. They slept uneasily, with bad dreams of one another.

It happened that Bonnie had to attend a surprise family party for her parents' Golden Wedding. The anticipation of the celebration, where she would stand as a barren fig tree among the Laura Ashley floribunda and fecundity, put her in such a black mood that Vivien expired a long sigh of relief, as if anxiety had been expelled from her by the despairing farewell toot, as the van lurched like a tumbrel into the lane. The golden present, exquisitely encased in gold foil, with gold ribbon twirled to curlicues around a pencil to disguise its essential tackiness, had been wrapped by Vivien but her name did not appear on the gold gift tag. Bonnie's Russian wedding ring and the true lover's knot, the twin of that which circled Vivien's little finger, would dissolve into invisibility when she crossed the family threshold. An uncle would prod her stomach and tell her she ought to get some meat on her bones, a man likes something he can get hold of; a sister-in-law, made bold by Malibu and cake, might enquire after Bonnie's flatmate while rearranging by a fraction of an inch her own present of a pair of gilded ovals framing studio portraits of gap-toothed grandchildren. Later the same sister-in-law would offer on a stained paper plate the stale and indigestible news that she had once been disconcerted by a desire to kiss a schoolfriend, and on the homeward journey the memory of her confession would jolt into her stomach and the motorway verge would receive a shower of shame and disgust for the unnatural recipient of her secret. Meanwhile, however, Bonnie was being introduced to the fiancé of a niece, who was omitting her name from his mental list of wedding guests even as they shook hands.

"You might have made the effort to put on a skirt for once," her mother told her. In fact, Bonnie and Vivien did occasionally outrage their friends by wearing skirts. The last time had been when they turned up at the Treacle Pudding Club in a heat wave in their batiks and had been refused entry, but she didn't tell her mother this. Bonnie went into the garden and made herself a roll-up.

"You'll die if you smoke," said a small boy in a red waistcoat with matching bow tie on elastic.

"Want a drag?" Bonnie held out the cigarette."

He shook his head so hard that his eyes rolled like blue doll's eyes, as if they would fall out, and ran in to report the death threat, and shot her with a plastic machine gun from an upstairs window. Bonnie looked at her watch, reflecting with relief that the late-night, half-hearted discussions with Vivien about adoption, early in their marriage, had fizzled away with the morning Alka-Seltzer. If they *had* been allowed to adopt one, they would have to have had it adopted. She went in to the telephone on the public shelf above the hall radiator and dialed home, clamping the receiver to her ear to keep out the sounds of merry making, the mouth piece poised to muffle her low desperate "Hi babe, it's me. Just needed to hear your voice;" words that she was to be deprived of muttering. No comfort came from the shrilling 1940s handset in the Old Post Office kitchen and, blinded by a paper hat which someone had slipped over her head, she went back to join the party.

★   ★   ★

"I rang. You weren't there," she said as she slammed the van door and strode past Vivien who had run to meet her, into the house.

"Is that my doggie bag?" Vivien pulled at the purple Liberty carrier in Bonnie's hand. "What have you brought me?"

"Nothing. You didn't deserve anything. I ate it in the van. Where were you, when I needed you?"

Vivien might have replied, "I was in my house, perfectly happy. I was reading, grazing among the books, and walking in the garden, and suddenly I thought of the hard little face, the mean mouth that I fell in love with, and I came running home."

She said, "I went for a walk, babe. I was very lonesome all by my little self, without you."

Bonnie, half-placated, dropped the bag onto the table.

"There's a bit of cake left."

Vivien drew it out.

"You've eaten off the icing. You pig."

"Yes," said Bonnie sternly.

"What's this?" Vivien scrabbled in Bonnie's bag and pulled out by the leg a mothy-looking toy.

"My old teddy. It's so threadbare I thought we could pass it off as Victorian. They're fetching a good price now."

"Oh Bonnie, you can't sell that, he's cute. Look at his little beady eyes."

"Give it here. I'll pull one off, make it even cuter—nothing more poignant than a sad teddy, is there?"

"No! I won't let you. How could you be so cruel? I'm going to keep him. He's probably your oldest friend . . ."

. . . A tiny Bonnie, rosy from her bath, toddled up the wooden hill to Bedfordshire, holding a sleepy teddy by the paw . . .

"Actually she's a girl. Tedina. I used to smack her with my hairbrush."

Vivien thought a flicker of fear passed over Tedina's tiny black eyes. She rooted in a box and found a Victorian christening robe.

"Perfect," said Bonnie. "Fifty quid at least."

"There's a fatal flaw in your plan," Vivien told her. "Teddy bears weren't invented in Victorian times."

"Don't be stupid. Of course they were. Albert brought one back from Germany or something one Christmas. They're called after him." Sensing a flaw in her argument, if not in her plan, Bonnie let the subject drop. Tedina, in her white pin-tucked robe was carried upstairs to their bed by Vivien and the hairbrush, a section of the carapace of a dead tortoise set in silver, was put tactfully in a drawer.

It was when she picked up the local paper that she saw an unmistakable photograph, the notice that read "House for Sale By Auction with contents." She stuffed the paper under a pile of back numbers of *Forum* and *Men Only* that, with a plastic Thomas the Tank Engine, had been purchased as a job lot, with a Clarice Cliff bowl thrown in, for a tenner. "They're not quite the sort of old comics and toys we had in mind," she had explained backing towards the door, when her eye fell on the bowl, holding a dead busy lizzie.

Its owner, a desperate-looking woman hung about with small children, had intercepted her quick appraisal.

"What about the bowl, then? That's antique, it belonged to my grandma."

"There's no call for that sort of Budgie-Ware," said Bonnie, her tongue flicking over dry lips, her nose quivering. "We've got two or three we can't shift, taking up space, gathering dust," as she flicked the bright feathers of the two birds on a branch of ivy that curved around the pale gray bowl patterned with dark gray leaves.

"They used to give them as prizes at fairgrounds," Vivien

added, lifting the bowl to read the signature on its base. "They were known as fairings."

"I thought those were biscuits," said the woman dully. "Cornish Fairings?"

"Of course, *some* of them *were* biscuits," Vivien conceded. "In Cornwall."

The deal having been struck, the woman was so grateful she made them a cup of pale tea by dunking the same tea bag in two mugs. There were no biscuits. She stroked the birds surreptitiously as she wrapped them in a piece of newspaper. One of the children started to wail "I don't want those ladies to take our budgies."

There was the sound of a slap as the door closed. Vivien and Bonnie went whistling to the van.

Six wooden chairs stood in a row in the backyard. Bonnie and Vivien were hard at work in the morning sun, removing the chipped white gloss paint from two of them.

"We'll need some more stripper" Bonnie said, straightening her back painfully. "God, how I hate this job."

"You go and get some and I'll carry on with what's left," Vivien suggested and Bonnie was only too willing to agree. Fifteen minutes later, satisfied that Bonnie was too far on the road to turn back for anything she might have forgotten, Vivien stripped off the Cornish fisherman's smock she wore for working, pulled on a sweatshirt and walking as quickly as possible without attracting attention, made for the house.

"This may be the last time I shall come here," she told it as she stood inside the scullery door, which she left unlocked in case she had to make a quick getaway. The rooks she had startled into raucous proclamation of her guilt lapsed into spasms of complaint in the copper beech. Nobody had rallied to their alarm. Vivien went from room to room, resisting the desire to stroke the dust from satiny fruitwood, walnut, maple, mahogany, to lift the plates from the dresser to read the maker's name, and the marks on the dulling silver in the kitchen, to dust the dead flies from the window ledges and to light the candles in their porcelain sticks. There, on the shelves and in the faded, painted bookcases were all the books she would never read. She longed to take one and curl up in her yellow velvet chair and read the morning away until the yellow dog prevailed upon her to follow him into the garden where a straw hat with lattices broken by time, and a trug awaited her. She admired for the last time the spilled jewels of the crystal doorknob, and stood in front of the glass cabinet committing to memory the figures therein: the man and woman riding on mild goats to meet each other, he with kids' heads peeping from his panniers, and she with hers filled with flowers and a basket of babies on her back, riding home-wards in the evening in the cawing of rooks, the . . .

"Is this a private party, or can anybody join in?"

Vivien screamed, whirling around. There, filling the door-way, just like Bea Smith in the latest episode of *Prisoner: Cell Block-H,* stood Bonnie, with a knobkerrie in her hand.

"So this is your little game. I've known you were up to something for days."

"Bea-Bonnie, I can explain."

"You'd better. You've got a lot of explaining to do—my God, are those what I think they are?"

She advanced on the cabinet.

"Don't touch!"

"Why not? You must've left your dabs all over everything. So this is what you were up to. Planned to sell the stuff behind my back and make yourself a juicy little profit, didn't you?"

Bonnie slumped into the yellow chair. "You were going to leave me, weren't you? Run off and set up on your own."

Her words were thick and bitter like the tears which rolled from her eyes.

"I'll kill you first." She leaped up, brandishing the knobkerrie.

"How can you think, I don't believe I'm hearing this—"

Vivien caught her raised arm, they fought for the weapon, Bonnie trying frantically to bring it down on Vivien's head, Vivien struggling to hold the murderous arm aloft. A kick in the shins brought howling Bonnie to her knees and Vivien dragged the knobkerrie from her hand. Vivien twisted one of her arms behind her back and pushed her face downwards to the carpet.

"Babe, I love you," she explained, punctuating her words with light blows from the knobkerrie. "I swear I wasn't planning to run out on you. I haven't touched anything here, and I'm not going to. Understand?"

"Ouch, you bitch, get off me." Bonnie spat out carpet fibers.

"If I let you get up, do you promise to sit quietly and listen?"

"Ouch. Thuk." She spat.

"Very well. Go and sit over there."

Bonnie slunk, snarling like a dog, to the sofa at which her master pointed the club. A resurgence of rage brought her half to her feet.

"Sit!"

Vivien could see, even after ten minutes of explanation, that Bonnie would never quite believe her. "It was like being under a spell. As if I was meant to be here. It's so beautiful. So peaceful. I just wanted to be here. It was like being in another world for a little while."

"Another world from which you excluded me."

"I was going to tell you. I was going to bring you here later today. I swear."

"A likely story. Are you sure there's no one else involved? You've been meeting someone here haven't you? Where is she, hiding under the bed? Or is it a he?"

"Don't be so bloody stupid! Look, I'll show you all over the house, you can look under every bed if you like. Can't you get it into your thick skull that I just liked being alone here?"

"No I can't. I never want to be alone without you. I just don't believe you."

Vivien led Bonnie from room to room. They found no brawny limbs in fluorescent shorts under the beds—nothing but dust, a pair of silver shoes, and hanks of horsehair from a torn mattress. Dresses and suits hung empty in the cupboards, linen lay innocently in chests and clean towels were in the airing cupboard, if the spiders in the baths should want them. They pulled their sleeves over their hands to touch knobs and handles. In a chest of drawers they found dozens of kid gloves with pearl buttons never unfastened, in a mille-feuille of virginal tissue.

"Satisfied?" They were back in the drawing room.

"Bonnie?"

Bonnie was standing in the center of the room with a rapt expression on her face.

"Bonnie? It's getting to you, isn't it? The magic of the place. You understand now?"

"What I simply cannot understand, or believe, is how someone who had been in the business as long as you have could be so incredibly stupid as to let such an opportunity pass."

"You don't understand at all. . . . I hoped. Oh forget it. Let's go."

"How could you be so *selfish?* Not telling me. Those wonderful pieces. Just sitting there. Shows how much you value our relationship."

"It's not like that. . . ."

"Isn't it?"

"No it isn't."

Vivien knew she could not defend herself against the charge of wanting to keep the house a secret, or wanting to be alone there. She did not know if that, or her lack of professional loyalty or acumen, was the more hurtful.

"Anyway," she said, "this is the last time I'll be coming here. The house goes up for auction next week."

"Does it? That doesn't give us much time then."

"No, Bonnie. We're not taking anything."

Vivien looked from the miniatures and figurines to Bonnie, tear-stained and tense as a whippet, poised on the edge of their marriage.

"Come on then," she said.

They raced for the stairs. They plundered the glove drawer, forcing their fingers into the unstretched kid; a pearl button hit the floor and rolled away.

"There's a pile of plastic carriers in the kitchen. Where's the van?"

"At home. I watched you leave the house, parked the van and followed you on foot."

"Good. Thank goodness you didn't bring it here. I should have realized someone was there when the rooks started squawking." Vivien panted as they worked, each knowing instinctively what to take. A team. Although Bonnie would need kid-glove treatment for a while.

"How did you find the key?"

"A toad showed me the way."

"A toad? Sure you don't mean a robin, like in *The Secret Garden*? I know how you love poring over those mildewed kids' books."

As Bonnie spoke she jiggled a hairpin, found in a dressing-tale tray, in the lock of a china cabinet.

"Brilliant," Vivien said but she walked over to the window and looked out into the garden as Bonnie lifted out the first cupid and the pretty spotted leopard with gold-tipped paws. They left no mess, no trace of their presence. Vivien locked the door and replaced the wiped key under the plant. As they passed the drawing-room windows she saw the person she might have been, watching them go from the velvet yellow chair in the room defiled by their fight.

They met nobody on the way home but if they had it would have been apparent that those two weirdos from the Old Post Office had been doing their shopping, and not stinting themselves from the look of their bulging bags.

At home Vivien said, "We must be mad. We'll be the obvious suspects when the stuff's missed. The only dealers for miles around. . . . We could put it back. . . ."

"And risk getting caught in the act, apart from the fact that this is the biggest coup of our career? No way, José. By the way, how did you know the house is going up for auction?"

"It was in the local paper."

"Oh. Well, the plan is, we'll drive up to London first thing tomorrow. We can stay with Frankie and Flossie for a few days while we unload the stuff. And I think I know somebody who will be *very* interested. . . ."

"But. . . ."

"Those frigging freeloaders owe us. Think of the times they've pitched up here without so much as a bottle of Sainsbury's plonk. Besides, they're our best friends!"

The kid gloves shriveled and blackened on the barbie, giving a peculiar taste to the burgers and green peppers that sweated and spat on the grid above them. The tiny pearl buttons glimmered among the discs of bone, horn, glass and plastic in the tall jar of assorted buttons.

"Shampoo?"

"Shampoo!"

Bonnie and Vivien had returned in high spirits from their successful stay in London. They had taken in a sale of the stock of a bankrupt theatrical costumiers on the way back. It was nine o'clock in the evening. The man on the doorstep heard music and caught a glimpse of two figures, beyond the nude in her hat and necklace, locked together in a slow dance once known as the Gateways grind, out of sync with the jaunty song.

"Good evening, ladies. Filth," he smiled, flashing his ID at the wolf in a lime-green beaded dress who answered the door.

"Who is it?" came the bark of the fox just behind her.

"It's the Filth—I mean the police," came the slightly muffled reply. For a moment they stood, the wolf in green and the fox in a scarlet sheath fringed with black, staring at him with glassy eyes, then simultaneously pulled off their heads, and he felt that they had removed their sharp, sly masks to reveal features identical to the heads they held in their hands, so that he still faced a fox and wolf, but with fear in their eyes.

He touched delicately one of the tubular beads on Bonnie's dress, standing in his linen suit crumpled from a day's policing. "Nice," he said. "Bugle beads, aren't they? That's Blossom Dearie, isn't it?" He sang "*There ought to be a moonlight saving time, so I could love that man of mine . . .*" glancing towards the uniformed constable at the wheel of the police car.

"You'd better come in," said Vivien the Fox. The animals, on high heels, led him into the front room. He saw a bottle of champagne and two glasses.

"I don't suppose you'd like a drink? You can't when you're on duty, can you?"

"You've been watching too much television," he replied, picking up a dusty green glass from a sideboard. "Regular Aladdin's cave you've got here, haven't you? Cheers." He raised his glass to the model and looked around at the piles and rails of clothes, the jumble of china and glass, silver, brass and pewter, the old books, the trivia, the ephemera that refused to die, the worthless and the valuable bits of furniture, the glass jar that held the tiny pearl buttons snipped from two pairs of burned skin gloves.

"I caught one of her shows at the Pizza on the Park," he said. "Blossom Dearie."

"Oh, so did we!" Vivien exclaimed, "Perhaps—"

"How can we help you?" Bonnie broke in.

"There's been a break-in. At an empty house down the road, the old Emerson place. Some valuable pieces taken. I've got the list here. We thought you might come across some of them in your travels, or someone might try to pass them off on you, you being the most local and obvious outlet—if our perpetrators are the bunch of amateurs we suspect they are. If that should happen, we'd be very grateful if you would let us know."

"Of course." Vivien took the photocopied list he held out. It shook in her hand although there was no draught that humid evening.

"Let's see." Bonnie read aloud over Vivien's shoulder. "Meissen Shepherdess with birdcage. Harlequin and Columbine, cupids representing four seasons. Leopard. Man and woman, riding goats, Staffordshire. Chelsea, Derby, Bow . . . pair of berry spoons, circa 1820. . . ."

She whistled. "There's some nice stuff here. Priceless. Any idea who could have done the job?"

"We're working on it. Whoever it was did a pretty good demolition job on the drawing room and kindly left us a few genetic fingerprints. Shouldn't be too difficult."

The fox went as red as the cherries on the dummy's hat, as if she had been responsible for the violation.

"But those lovely things—the shepherdess, the leopard, the porcelain—what were they doing in an empty house? Wasn't there a burglar alarm at least to protect them?"

"The house and contents were due to be auctioned the following day. It was just bad luck. Old Mrs. Emerson's godson, she left it to him, has no interest in the place apart from the proceedings from the sale—serves him right, really. Nasty piece of work—greedy and careless—a dangerous combination. More money than sense already. There's an old local couple who kept an eye on the place—he did a bit in the garden, kept the grass down, and she kept the dust down. It seems likely that one of them forgot to reset the alarm the last time they were there, but that's academic really. They're both in deep shock. Aged ten years overnight. Heartbroken. Keep saying they've betrayed old Mrs. Emerson's trust. From the look of them they'll be apologizing to her in person soon. . . . Well, thank you for your co-operation. Sorry to intrude on your evening."

"We were just pricing some new stock," Bonnie felt obliged to explain, waving a hand at the fox and wolf heads staring at them from the floor, as he rose to leave.

* * *

"Phew!! What an incredible stroke of luck! That someone should actually break in while we were away! I can't believe it! Somebody up there must like us. . . ." Bonnie sank into a chair kicking off her high-heeled shoes.

"And us prancing around like a couple of drag queens in animals heads," she went on, "I thought I would die. I could hear those prison gates clanging, couldn't you! Cell Block H, here we come! Let's have a look at that list again. 'Silver salt spoon, convolvulus design handle'? How come we missed that?"

"I don't know."

Vivien crossed her fingers behind her back and hoped that Tedina, who had watched her unscrew the brass knob of the bedpost and drop in a silver spoon, would keep her mouth shut. Then the spoon with its convolvulus wreathed stem would lie safely and inaccessibly locked in the bedpost, a tiny silver secret salvaged from her house, as long as the marriage lasted. She pulled the chenille bedspread that served as a curtain across the window, refilled their glasses and turned over the record.

"Where were we, before we were so rudely interrupted?"

She held out both her hands and they resumed the dance; the Friendly Old-Established Firm, back in business.

ANGELO

The long brown beans of the catalpa rattled in the wind, brittle pods dangling in bunches among the last flapping yellow leaves of the tree, so ancient and gnarled that it rested on a crutch, in the courtyard of St. James's, Piccadilly. Splintered pods and big damp leaves littering the stones were slippery under the feet of the friends, enemies and those who wished to be seen at Felix Mazzotti's Memorial Service. Drizzle gave a pearly luster to black umbrellas and brought up the velvet pelts of collars, and cashmere and cloth, moistened hats and vivified patterned shawls and scarves.

Violet Greene settled herself and her umbrella in a pew beside a stranger. The umbrella's handle was an ivory elephant's head, yellow and polished by time like a long old tooth, the grooves in its trunk smoothed by generations of gloves. The heavy white paper of the Order of Service in her black velvet fingers, thick gold-leaf braid trimming white stone, glittering brass; Violet concentrated on these, and caught the little black eye of the elephant's head, which *was* an old tooth, taken from some Victorian tusker too long ago to worry about, and carved into little replicas of its original owner. Around her neck Violet wore a string of jet beads, mourning jewelry which Felix had given her forty years before. Felix's mother had been English, his father Italian, and although he was officially a Catholic he had never felt the slightest twitch on the thread. Hence this church rather than the Brompton Oratory of Farm Street. The lapse of time between the news of his death, and the funeral which had been a private affair in Italy, and the memorial service had accustomed people to his absence from the world, and time in any case rushes in as the sea fills holes in the sand.

When someone is shot, Violet had read, they often feel no pain at first; she had waited, after the bullet's impact of the news, for the wound of loss to bleed and burn, but she had not seen Felix for five years—which was good because she had no picture of him as the really old man he had suddenly become—although they had spoken occasionally on the telephone, and it was hard to remember that he was dead. One day she had decided to believe that he was still in her terraced garden among the olive trees that gave the beautiful green oil of which he was so proud, and felt a release. It was so simple she wondered why she had not thought of it sooner. He had once told her that his olive oil gave him more pleasure and sense of achievement than all the books he had written. It had seemed such an arrogant remark, one that could have been made only by somebody as successful in the world's eye as he was, that she had felt irritated for days. Even though she refused to recognize his death, questions would persist: What were we like? What were we like together? Who was I then? She had been sixteen when they met, he a much older man of thirty. A mere boy. And was that girl herself, Violet Clements, in a silky dress printed with pansies under a cheap, black cloth coat shivering in the March wind on the steps of a house in Gordon Square? On her way to the church in a taxi this morning she had passed a bed of blue and yellow pansies, and watched the colors quivering, trembling with the taxi's motor, the dyes running together in the rivulets of the wet glass.

Her black velvet beret with its soft pleats like the gills of a large field mushroom was skewered with a black pearl clasped in two tiny silver hands, and she wore an emerald scarf of fine wool in a loose triangle across the shoulders of her black coat. Violet Greene she was now, and supposed that Greene, her fourth surname would be her last, although she would not quite have put money on it. She rather liked it; the pre-Raphaelite purple and viridian of her name, the hectic hues of Arthur Hughes, or of bright green Devon Violets scent in a round bottle with painted flowers. Or Cornish, Welsh, Scottish or Parma violets—the cachou odor was the same, and a sniff of it would recall seaside holidays with the boys, salt-caked plimsolls and rough sandy towels bleaching on the rail of a wooden veranda. A present for the best mother in the world bought with pennies saved out of their ice-cream money. Today a delicate waft of toilet water was all but indiscernible as she moved.

The organ was playing a medley, a melancholy fruit cocktail in heavy syrup, as the pews filled. Violet was clasping her hands, not in prayer but to restrain them from plucking a silver hair from the coat in front of her, when a finger prodded her own back. She turned.

"Hello, I like your hat. Is it what's called a Van Dyck beret?"

Violet had made a decision long ago not to dislike a girl simply because she was young and beautiful, so she smiled at the whisperer under her hooded eyes, still violet but faded, like the flowers. Someone's daughter or granddaughter, some child in publishing or from a gallery, in PR met at some party—she was still invited to more than she bothered with; a fixture on some guestlists after so many years on the sidelines of the arts. [She couldn't . . .] She couldn't remember. All black lycra and red lipstick, with long fair hair that required to be raked back from her face every few seconds; the sort of girl seen at the cinema with a giant bucket of popcorn, climbing over people's legs, drawing attention to herself.

"It's my first time at one of these," the girl confided in her loud whisper. "I s'pose you must've been to hundreds. . . ."

"Thousands," Violet confirmed drily.

The girl's hat lying on the pew was the kind of crushed velvet thing you would see on a stall at Camden Market between racks of discarded dresses that might have belonged to Violet long ago and she had evidently lost confidence in her ability to wear it. Violet never went out without a hat, linen and straw with a rose or cherries or a floating scarf; canvas, wool or feline print; she was known for her amusing and assured headgear in a time when so few women knew how. Her ear picked up a few bars of "What'll I do" interwoven plaintively through strands of "Sheep May Safely Graze," "Voi Che Sapete," "Memories" and "For All We Know" . . . *For all we know, this may only be a dream. We come and go like ripples on a stream. Time like an ever rolling stream bears all its sons away. They fly forgotten as a dream. . . . Imagine there's no heaven* . . . she was aware of the girl behind her slewing around in her pew, and the velvet hat was proving useful, she saw as she turned her head a fraction, waving frantically at some young people hesitating noisily at the back of the church, flapping them into the seats bagged for them. They should have been holding enormous paper cups of Coca-Cola rattling with ice-cubes, and straws to hoover it up, rather than those unfamiliar prayer books with which they had been issued.

Here we are, out of cigarettes . . . *two sleepy people by dawn's early light and too much in love to say good-night.* . . . Who had chosen this music? Felix's third wife, the charmless Camilla, over there in the Liberty hair band? Camilla was, in the first flush of middle-age but still young enough to be his granddaughter, with children from her first marriage, who took none of his references, responded to his jokes with serious replies, mirthless barks or groans, didn't smoke, and bridled at the mention of Violet's name. There were bits of bridle or snaffles or some piece of harness across her shoes; vestiges of the nurse she had become to Felix clung to her as if demanding respect for an invisible uniform of self-sacrifice. It was hideous to imagine her snouting through naive old letters, selecting the worst photographs of Violet for the authorized biography. The only redress would be to write her own memories, but Violet lacked the energy or inclination to do it, and although she had given up poetry many years ago, she remembered the torture of trying to recreate the truth in words, even when only trying to describe a landscape or a lampshade.

Her uncharitable thoughts about Camilla were prompted by Camilla's hostility to her, concealed today for appearance's sake. She resented being cast as a witch, an *old* witch because Felix had loved her best. Violet Clements had been orphaned at fourteen and a year later had left her aunt's crowded house to make her own way in the world. She had got a job at a small printing press whose decorative hand-blocked volumes were collectors' items now, and at night she had filled notebooks with her own verses by the gaslight of her attic room. She had met Felix at a tea party given by one of their poets, where absinthe was offered in rose-painted cups. The poet, killed in the war and his work forgotten, had called for a toast to "the green fairy" as he poured the romantic liquid. Violet took only a sip or two of infamous anise but she was under the green fairy's spell, in love with and in awe of the shabby glamour of the bad fairy's court.

Felix's invitation to coffee to show him her poems filled her with joy and terror for he was an established novelist and man of letters and so she was trembling with awe as much as from the March wind when she rang his bell. Shocked, for Felix wore a spotted dressing gown, she backed down the steps blushing and starting to apologize, not looking at his bare legs, thinking she had got the wrong day. He laughed. He led her into a room with an unmade bed.

"But it's the morning!"

He had laughed again.

The poems in her bag, so carefully selected, wilted like wallflowers at a party. It was cold, painful, and above all excruciatingly embarrassing. Violet's face had blazed for hours like the gas-fire he lit afterwards, and drinking the black bitter coffee which he had made at last, she could neither look at him nor speak.

"Violet Greene has a string of lovers," she overheard some-body say years later, and she saw herself on Primrose Hill, against a yellow sky, pulled across the horizon by the pack of dogs whose leashes cut into her hand. Four of her former lovers were in the church today, she counted, and Felix, if she were to admit to it, was scattered over the grass at Kenwood where leafless autumn crocuses shivered on their white stalks like girls gone mauve with the cold. Camilla had brought his ashes to England in a casket.

"Who would true valor see
Let him come hither;
One here will constant be,
Come wind, come weather;

"There's no discouragement
Shall make him once relent
His first avowed intent
To be a pilgrim."

Violet's eyes blurred, and she had to control her mouth which was unable to do more than mime the words. From Kensington nursing home and Oxford, Sutton Scotney, Bloomsbury, Maida Vale, Hampstead and points south the pilgrims had come this wild morning, old playmates summoned by the cracked bell of Fitzrovia.

"Bloody Brighton train!"

Maurice Wolverson edged into the pew beside her, knocking her umbrella to the floor, in a fury about leaves on the line.

"Not a bad house," he commented, looking around.

Mingled smells of damp wool and linseed oil came off the camel-hair coat whose velvet lapels were stippled with flake-white, and then an amber peaty aroma rose as he unscrewed the silver top of his cane. He drew out a long glass tube and offered it to Violet, who shook her head. His last part, four years ago, had been a walk-on in a television sit-com set in a seaside home for retired thespians. He had taken to daubing views of Brighton's piers to block out the sound of the swishing tide while waiting for the telephone to ring. A cluster of tarry shingle was stuck to the sole of his shoe and a red and white spotted handkerchief in his pocket made a crumpled attempt at jauntiness.

"They'll have to paper the house when my turn comes," Maurice muttered. Violet patted his knee.

"Choirboys. On a scale of one to ten . . . ?"

Violet slapped his knee.

Looking back she was incredulous, and indignant on the behalf of all foolish young women who took themselves at a man's valuation, that her fear and distaste had been compounded by worry that her body might not meet Felix's high standards, for he and his circle were harsh arbiters of female pulchritude. She had been half afraid that the jaded gourmet might send back the roast spring lamb.

"Well, what did you expect?" he had asked, "turning up on my doorstep looking like that?"

Apologies had come years later. Even now, Violet knew that she brightened in men's company, became prettier, wittier, revived like a thirsty flower, with a silver charge through her veins. She had never succumbed to sensible underwear or footwear and no giveaway little pickled-onion bulge distorted her shoes.

Her eyes closed as she listened to the anthem, and she felt a pang of affection for Felix's olive oil, and let the viscous yellow-green drip slowly from the bottle with the label he had designed, until it brimmed on the spoon, sharing his pleasure in it, not arguing. She had hated him often as he pursued her down the years like Dracula in an opera cloak or a degenerate Hound of Heaven, and she had carried a bagful of grievances against him about with her, but now the drawstrings of the bag loosened and all the old withered hurts, wrongs and frustrations flew out and upwards to the rafters, unraveled and dissolved in the gold and amber voices of the choir. As they knelt to pray, she ran the jet beads through her hand like a rosary, feeling the facets through the fingers of her gloves.

A nudge in the ribs jolted her. "Was it Beverly Nichols or Godfrey Winn who had a dog called Mr. Sponge?" came in a stage whisper.

Violet squeezed her eyes shut tight: "Oh God, please bless Felix and let him be happy and reunited [. . .] with his family and, — " If there were a heaven, it was a good thing for her and most of this congregation that there was no marriage or giving in marriage there. Imagine the complications.

"Which of them—got Willie Maugham's desk in the end?"

"Oh God, *I* don't know." She didn't know, didn't know if her prayer would get through the myriad, innumerable as plankton, prayers eternally sluicing the teeth of heaven's gate. A snowball's chance in hell perhaps. "Ask them yourself—later! Her words hissed like the sizzling snow.

A teenage boy, perhaps one of Camillas's, was standing at the front of the church, clearing his throat. He read badly, as if he had never read any poetry until this public occasion; it was Francis Thompson's "At Lord's" that the boy was murdering but could not quite kill. Violet's eyes filled again, and her unshed tears were brackish with bitterness. The poem had brought her back to Felix once when she had been on the point of leaving him. They were in a taxi, his coat was speckled with ash and she had recoiled from his tobacco-stained kiss. They must have been passing Lord's for she had mentioned the poem, that she thought was her own discovery, a manly poem that had touched her girl's heart, and Felix had at once recited it, word perfect, and she had felt an overwhelming tenderness for him. How dared Camilla know about it? He had spread himself thin like rich pâté eked out over too many slices of toast. Desolate, small and old, she would have given almost anything to be riding in that taxi through the blue London twilight now. But Felix was in Italy, she braced up, pontificating over a bottle of young wine or extra virgin oil, holding it up to the light.

She forbade the tears to spill, it would not do for people to see her—unmanned. A man's woman—yes, she had always been that. Her women friends had always taken second place to the man in her life. "Flies around a honeypot," Felix would snort with jealous pride after every party. Had the essence of herself been dissipated, though, and nearly all her choices made for her, by some man's or boy's need which outweighed her own?

At a splash to her right, she glanced at Maurice. Tears were rolling down his cheeks and dripping on to his Order of Service. She gave a sharp nod at the handkerchief in his top pocket. Upstaged. She swallowed an untimely giggle that threatened to turn into a sob.

As Denzil, Sir Denzil Allen, ancient ousted publisher, began his address, Violet thought, this is odd. Very odd, if you come to think of it, as she did. She referred to her Order of Service to confirm her suspicions: all the speakers and readers were men. Felix had been such a lover of women, many of his closest friends had been women and yet those women he had loved and who had known him best, herself chief among them, were to sit in their pews and have him expounded to them by these men. Well, that was the way of the world which she had made no attempt to change, and she could have been Violet Mazzotti and have organized this service herself, and made a better job of it. Women had not always been nice to her. She remembered the resentment, the thinly veiled spite of some of Felix's old friends when they were living together. Men too. Had she really expected them to say, "Welcome, Violet Clements, lovely and gifted youthful poet. We embrace you as one of us?" She could understand them now, but she had often been hurt and she stuck to her resolve never to snub a young girl, however pretty or silly, in whom shyness might be mistaken for arrogance.

Across the church she could see Sibyl Warner, the novelist, making a rare appearance. Heavily veiled, once a great beauty, she had long been a recluse from a world which assumed the right to comment on time's alterations. "My God, I didn't recognize you! You've changed!" That wound inflicted twenty years ago by Jill Blakiston, in an affronted tone which hinted at betrayal and that the photographs on the jackets of Sibyl's books must have been forgeries. Jill sat behind Violet today, a retired editorial director, rummaging in a £1000 worth of crocodile bag, quite unaware of what she had done, but Violet had been there and seen Sibyl flinch and gulp her drink in her eagerness to leave.

Something had shocked Violet almost as much as the revelation that people could go to bed in the morning. "Mind if I pee in your sink?" Felix had asked. It was a year after they had met and she was living in a respectable boarding house in Mornington Crescent. She most certainly had minded. There was her cake of carnation soap on the rim of the basin and her sponge and toothbrush in a glass. "This is intolerable," Felix had said. "The sooner you move in with me the better."

Her landlady, catching Felix tiptoeing down the stairs at one in the morning, told her to pack her bags at once and so, in a cloud of disgrace and defiance, she departed to Gordon Square. Living in sin entailed, she found out, a great deal of scrubbing shirt collars and darning socks and hours of copying out manuscripts and typing. But it had been fun too. Fun—what a funny, bizarre, orange paper-hat word. After a while afternoon drinking clubs and hangovers and cooking for Felix's drunken friends wasn't fun any more. Felix sailed to America in 1938, for which some still condemned him. Violet had refused to accompany him and when he returned she was Violet Morton, a widow with two children, the younger boy born posthumously after the Battle of Britain. Violet had married George Maxwell–Smith to give the boys a father, and divorced him after he had gambled away his father's furniture factory and fled with the girl in accounts. Her third husband, Bobby Greene, a painter, had succumbed to cancer after just eighteen months of happy marriage. His pictures hung on her walls and there had been intimations recently of a small renaissance of interest in his work.

"Hold Thou Thy Cross
Before my closing eyes.
Shine through the gloom
And point me to the skies. . . ."

An amethyst cross, grown huge, loomed gleaming through swirling mist, suspended above Felix's bed; Felix rising vertically ceilingward with his feet pointing down. An amethyst cross on a silver chain that had belonged to her mother, pawned and never redeemed.

As always after one of these occasions Violet was left with the thought that all that really matters in this life is that we should be kind to one another.

"Imogen, there's no heaven!" she heard a boy say outside, under the Indian bean tree leaning on its crutch.

"Ha ha, very funny," said Imogen, the girl who had been behind Violet, and blew her nose, saying, "Has my mascara run all over the place? You know, I really quite enjoyed that."

A group of black-coated youngish Turks was lighting cigarettes, and one of them cast a satirical eye at the knot of Violet's friends moving towards her, and made a remark at which the others laughed. Violet wondered when the power had passed to those young men with sliding smiles and snidey eyes; when had they staged their coup? She glanced around and thought: you—girl in a black dress squirming away from the poet you had thought to flatter with your charm—you have read none of his work but someone told you he is a poppet, and now he's threatening your cleavage with the dottle from his pipe. Who are all these rouged dotards, you wonder, boys and girls, these deposed old Turks who sidle up to you with swimming eyes like macerated cocktail cherries pleading for a reissue of their mildewed masterworks, a mention on the wireless, or a book to review that you will never send? Who are they, these mothballed revenants that you thought dead for years, these relics of whom you have never heard. Who? Well, my dears—they are you.

Violet was weary: wake up, Denton Welch, Djuna Barnes, Mark Gertler, Gaudier-Brzeska, Gjurdieff, et al—it's time for your next brief disinterment. Angels were warming up to dance on the heads of pins. A bored meow from Schroeder's Cat. Stale buns, duckies. It was reassuring to be kissed by old kid and chamois leather, badger bristle shaving-brushes and paintbrush beards, comfortable if elegaic to be surrounded by elegant decaying warehouses that had stored fine wines and cheeses and garlic for most of the century, and some who were as stout as their sodden purple-seeping vats and others as frail as towers of round plywood boxes that might topple and be bowled along by the wind.

"Are you coming along for drinkies?"

"No, Maurice dear, my grandson's taking me out to lunch."

He was, but on the following day. Violet had had enough. It had been gracious of Camilla to invite her today, perhaps, but enough was enough. She disengaged herself and started to walk towards Fortnum's, rather worried about Maurice. Who would pour him into the Brighton train in the frightful gloaming when the lights of shops and taxis blaze bleakly on wan faces and all souls seem lost? Would some sixth sense carry him along, a buffeted buffoonish bygone, with the cruel and censorious commuters, or might he find himself alone on the concourse but for a few vagrants, Lily Law bearing down on him, the last train gone and all bars closed, or would he wake without a passport at Gatwick Airport, or in a black siding at Hassocks or Haywards Heath? She consoled herself with the knowledge that it was the drinks afterwards which had persuaded him to make the journey, to the service, and that after a certain hour everybody on the Brighton train was drunk. Deciding against Fortnum's, she turned down Duke Street into Jermyn Street, making for St. James's Square. The shop windows were lovely, still dressed for autumn with colored leaves and berries, nuts and gilded rosy pomegranates, but behind the glass of one display an aerosol forecast snow.

Violet loved the symmetry of the gardens, that square within a circle within a square within a square. She sat on a bench with a sense of being alone with the equestrian statue of Guilelmus-III at its center and the birds that fluttered in the foliage and pecked about in the fallen leaves on the paving stones. An obelisk marked each corner of the inner square, a tiny leaved rambling rose had captured one of them and held it in its thorns, and a wren emerged from a bush, saw her and disappeared. Her eyes were still sharp enough to identify a bird; she was fortunate in that. She was fortunate in having a tall, fair-haired grandson. Had there been a touch of smugness in her tone when she had spoken of him to poor lonely Maurice? Well, she *was* proud of Tim and delighted that he should want to take her to lunch; too bad, why should she temper her feelings to Maurice's sensibilities? She did try not to condescend to those who were not the mother of sons and had only granddaughters, instead of big handsome boys who made one feel cherished and feminine and even a little deliciously dotty and roguish at times, and it was pleasant to bring out carefully selected stories from her past as if from a drawer lined with rose and violet potpourri spiced with faint intriguing muskier fruitier notes. Maurice had been involved in some unpleasantness in the bad old days, she recalled, but he must have put aside all such foolishness now, as she had. The long windows of the London Library glittered, reminding her how once she would have hoped love lurked there, playing peek-a-boo around the book stacks. She toyed with the idea of a cup of coffee in the Wren, the wholesome café attached to the church, or something worthy to eat, but putting that aside in favor of her own little kitchen and bathroom, along with the unpleasant image, like a gray illustration in a book, of Maurice in a suit of broad arrows breaking stones in Reading Gaol, she decided to take the Piccadilly line to Gloucester Road.

There wasn't a seat and Violet had to stand, but just for a moment or two until a rough-looking lad heaved himself up and nodded her into his place. Violet thanked him courteously, giving a lesson in manners to any who should be watching, and a rueful, apologetic little smile to the dowdy woman left standing. It doesn't do to judge by appearances, she thought, of the boy, while acknowledging that he, naturally, had done just that. It didn't surprise her because it had always been so; men had never stopped holding doors open for her, and even when she and the boys had been marooned in that rotting thatched cottage in Suffolk after George's defection, there had been some gum-booted Galahad to dig her out of a ditch or rescue a bird from the chimney.

A startlingly beautiful boy was sitting opposite her. She couldn't take her eyes off his face. About sixteen, with loose blue-black curls, olive skin and a full, tragic mouth. He must be South American. Venezuelan, she decided, in a city far from home. He had the face of an angel. She named him Angelo. There was a panache, a muted stylishness, about his black leather jacket, dark charcoal sweater over a white T-shirt, black jeans, silver ring and earring, the black-booted ankle resting casually across the knee. Fearing that he might imagine there was something predatory in the way she drank in his beauty, she averted her attention to the ill-featured youth on Angelo's right, but she was drawn back to Angelo's almond-shaped, lustrous, long-lashed eyes. Hyde Park Corner came and went. Violet shut her eyes, abruptly suffused by a sadness she didn't know what to do with, and a statue came into her mind, a little stone saint in a wayside shrine whose lips had crumbled, kissed away by thousands of supplicants' desires. She wanted to warn the boy: Angelo, beware. People will prey on you, want to possess you, corrupt you, exploit you for your beauty until there is nothing left of you and you are destroyed; but there was a wariness about Angelo's face which said that he had learned that long ago.

She opened her eyes. A sudden instinct told her that Angelo and the youth who had given up his seat and the lout on his right were connected, and pretending not to be. A lunge of silver, her bag ripped from her hands, fingers tearing at her rings, and as he grabbed the necklace, black against a blazing yellow and grape-purple flash of anguished desire to snatch back and relive her years, she was aware of a knife at her throat and that Angelo was a girl.

THE CURTAIN
WITH THE KNOT IN IT

"You can see my window from here. It's the one with the curtain with the knot in it."

Alice shivered, although the April late afternoon sun was turning the dayroom of Daffodil Ward into a greenhouse.

"Goose walked over your grave." Pauline gave her abrupt laugh.

Alice looked out reluctantly across to the staff residential block, a three-storeyed cube of mottled brick, and located a dull curtain tied in a knot at a top floor window.

Why, she wondered, had she shuddered like that? Was it the knot. Or the intimation that Pauline the Domestic had a life beyond Daffodil?

Pauline laughed again, at the antics of Jack, one of the patients, who had almost managed to slide under the tray that confined him to his chair.

"Come on Jack Be Nimble, Jack Be Quick," she said as she pulled him back. "You'll be having your soup in a minute."

If a coypu were to laugh, Alice thought, or did she mean a capybara? Something with unattractive teeth and lank fur, unpopular with visitors at the zoo. The two women were of an age and dressed similarly, but with a world of difference between Alice's visitor's tracksuit and trainers and what was visible of Pauline's; pinkish-white and grayish-white peeking from under her nylon gingham overall. Pauline's hair hung limply from a rufflette of brown and yellow gingham, while Alice's was in a longish shiny bob.

Ada had been shouting from her chair for the curtains to be pulled since the rain had stopped and the sun had appeared two hours earlier, and now Sister was exasperated into swiping out spring with a swish of the orange curtains.

Alice's father had been wheeled into the ward so that something could be done to him, so she sat on a massive vinyl chair attempting to read a Large Print book whose pages had been glued together with Complan. Pauline went about her work, tearing sheets of pale blue paper from a large roll and slapping them down at each place on the long table, and on the trays of the chairs where the immobile were propped up on lolling and slipping pillows. Supper would not be served for an hour, but those who could Zimmer themselves there or who could be yanked and hoisted were seated at the table. Children's BBC blared on the television.

Anybody familiar with the tragedies, the dramas, the macabre comedies played out daily in places such as Daffodil, and the aching, aching boredom, the cross-purpose nature of every exchange, will need no description of suppertime in this nursery of second childhood. Suffice it to say that it was a Wednesday and the big wooden calendar read *SUNDAY*, that the two budgies, presented by a well-wisher after the goldfish's suicide, twittered unregarded, that a voice called incessantly "help me, help me, somebody please help me;" the never-opened piano and record player were there, and the floral displays in beribboned baskets, faded to the color and texture of Rice Krispies, and in the side ward people who had died long ago were cocooned in cots and tended as if they might, some day, hatch into something marvelous, or exude skeins of wonderful silk.

When it became apparent that Dad had been put to bed, Alice went to say good night to him.

"Don't know why you bother coming every day," said Pauline. "He doesn't know you from a bar of soap, nemmind though, I've got a soft spot for your Dad myself."

She was pouring powdered soup into the orange plastic breakers from an aluminum jug. George was spooning out his reconstituted bits of mushroom and laying them neatly on his blue paper. Mrs. Rosenbaum didn't want any soup because she was dead.

"Aren't you staying for your tea tonight?" Pauline asked Alice.

"No, I'd better be going. Got a lot to do at home."

She felt unequal to the nice milky one, two sugars, tonight. A misunderstanding early in their relationship made it impossible now for her to explain that she liked her tea black and unsweetened. "I look after my *friends*." Pauline would say darkly, with a pointed glance at Dolly's daughter who had unwittingly offended and was therefore not allowed tea. Alice's worst fear was that Dad would not die before Pauline's, as yet unspoken but looming, invitation to an off-duty cuppa in her flat.

Croxted Memorial, originally a cottage hospital, was built to a strange hexagonal design, with a small Outpatients and Casualty tacked onto one side, and even after a year of visiting, Alice could get lost, take a wrong turning and end up where she started or at the dead end of the permanently locked Occupational Therapy, or the kitchens with their aluminum vats and trolleys. The gray floor gleamed with little bubbles of disinfectant, a sign that read *Cleaning in Progress* half blocked her path, as it did every day although there were so few visitors or staff around that the place was like a morgue in the evenings, and there was Kevin the cleaner, leering over the handle of his heavy-duty polisher, pallid as a leek with a tangle of pale dirty roots for hair. She knew she should have taken the other exit.

"Off out somewhere nice, are we?"

She gave a smile which tried to be enigmatic, distancing and hinting at a world beyond his overalls and disinfectant.

"When you coming out with me then?"

Alice pulled out her diary and flicked through the pages, aware of him squirming with incredulous lubricity.

"Let me see, I think I'm free on the twelfth."

"You what. . . ."

"Yes. The Twelfth of Never." She snapped the diary shut triumphantly.

That was cruel, **Alice**, she admonished herself as she inhaled healing nicotine and evening air after the dead atmosphere which was Pauline's and Kevin's element, standing on the asphalt marled with white blossom while a blackbird sang in a cherry tree. Still, Kevin's idea of a venue for a good night out was probably that dark place behind the boiler room, where the wheelie bins lived.

Alice had lied to Pauline about having things to do, and deceived Kevin. The pages of her diary were almost all blank. Since she had been made redundant her world had shrunk until Daffodil and the long journeys by foot and tube and bus were her whole life. She no longer thought of herself as Alice at the Mad Hatter's tea party nearly so often as she had in the beginning. Her father, a Detective Inspector struck down and withered by illness over the years, was all the family she had and she loved him and grieved for his plight. She did not cry tonight; she had cried in so many hospital car-parks over the years.

Kevin watched her from the doorway, drawing deeply on a pinched roll-up. His glance went up to a window with a knotted curtain, billowing, deflated, in the wind that had sprung up, ruffling his hair.

Inside, in Daffodil, Pauline ruffled George's white hair as she collected his dishes.

"All right, Georgie Porgie?"

Writhing in agony from the pressure sore that was devouring him like an insatiable rodent, he drew back his lips in what Pauline took to be a smile.

"Pudding and Pie," she added.

"You haven't eaten your sandwiches," she accused Mrs. Rosenbaum, whipping away the three triangles of bread and ham. When she had been brought in, Mrs. Rosenbaum had tried to explain about eating kosher, but none of the staff or agency nurses had been able to take it on board, and she had shrunk into silence under her multi-colored crochet blanket, while her feet swelled in the foam rubber boots fastened with velcro that Physio had provided, as slow starvation took its course.

The commodes that doubled as transport up the wooden hill to Bedfordshire were rolling into the dayroom.

"Come on Mary, Mary Quite Contrary," said Sister Connelly as two of the Filipinos, they all looked the same to Pauline, and they never spoke to her anyway, started loading Mary on board. Quacking away in Foreign like a load of mandarin ducks. Thank God it was nearly time to knock off. She was really cheesed off today. Ada was singing, if you could call it that, "Ere we are again, appy as can be. All good pals and JOLLY . . ." She always got struck there.

"Change the record, Ada!" Pauline shouted as Ada started it up again.

"Pack it in, Joey. I've got a headache." She told the budgies. "Noisy buggers!"

"What are their names?" Alice had asked her once.

"I call them Joey. Can't tell them apart." Pauline had replied.

"One's more emerald and the other's more turquoise."

"You don't have to clear up after them!"

It was all right for some people with nothing better to do to go all soppy over a pair of budgies.

"I know why the caged bird sings," Alice had said, but before she could go on Jack had tipped his chair over. Alice had had to sign a form as a witness, to show that there had been no negligence, after the doctor had been called, but that was the last they had heard of the matter.

Outside at last, Pauline had an impulse to take off her sneakers and walk barefoot over the daisies in the grass, but Kevin was lurking around so she didn't. A blackbird was singing in the cherry tree, black against the white blossom. Pauline stood still for a moment, then, "I've got a lot to do at home," she said to herself and headed for the concrete stairs that led up to her flat. It was her thirty-seventh spring. Later that evening she went down to the payphone and dialed a number. She knew it by heart; it had stuck in her brain as soon as she had looked it up, and she had rung it many times. On the third ring Alice answered. Pauline hung up.

"Just having a chat with my mate," she said as the dietician and his girlfriend came through the door in white tennis clothes with grass stains and a faint smell of sweat. They didn't look at her as they took the stairs two at a time, laughing at something. Pauline went slowly after them and finished off the last of the ham sandwiches from supper at Daffodil.

"She's gone, that little lady." Pauline jerked a thumb toward the place where Mrs. Rosenbaum had sat. It was the following afternoon. Alice made her heart blank, and looked down at her book.

"Having a nice read?"

Pauline tipped the book forward. "Janette Turner Hospital. She must be the same as me."

"She's Australian, I think." Alice didn't want to be too much of a know-it-all.

"No, I mean, she must've been found in a hospital, like me. I was left in the toilets at Barts, that's why they give me the name. Pauline after the nurse who found me, and Bartholomew after Barts. Ee-ah, nice milky one, two sugars."

"Thanks, Pauline, you're a pal."

As she drank her tea, Alice realized that she had been given the central fact about Pauline. That beginning had determined her progression to this institutional job, that overall, the trolley, the table for one in Spud-U-Like, the holidays spent in shopping precincts.

"I had my picture in all the papers," said Pauline, and Alice saw a crimson, new-born baby waving feeble arms from swaddling clothes of newsprint, on a stone floor under a porcelain pedestal.

"Your mother—did they—did she?"

Pauline's eyes filled as she shook her head, strands of hair whipping her clamped mouth. "I've never told anybody that before. Nobody here, I mean. Not that they'd be interested anyway, toffee-nosed lot."

Alice had noticed that the staff hardly gave Pauline a glance or a word. Poor, despised capybara, whose cage everybody walked past.

That revelation led to Alice's following Pauline up the concrete stairs after visiting time, with a sense of danger, feeling she had taken an irrevocable step. She hadn't known how to refuse the long-threatened invitation after Pauline's tears. To her horror Pauline at once took an unopened bottle of Tia Maria from a cupboard in the tiny kitchen, which was a scaled-down replica of the kitchenette at Daffodil.

"Ah, the curtain with the knot in it! At last!" Alice cried, a bit too gaily, as they carried their glasses through.

"Tell me, Pauline, why does it have a knot in it?"

"I'm a fresh-air fiend. All the cooking smells from foreign cooking get trapped in here so I leave my window open and I have to tie the curtain back or it knocks my ornaments off in the wind."

"I'd imagined a much more sinister—I mean exotic—explanation, but I see your balloon-seller's head has been glued back on at some stage."

Pauline topped them up.

"Mind if I smoke?" Alice asked.

"That's all right. I'll get the ashtray."

It had been washed but Alice detected a smear of gray under its rim which indicated that Pauline had at least one other visitor, who smoked.

"It's a lovely flat, Pauline. A little palace. You've made it really homely."

"It is home"

"Well yes, of course."

"You haven't seen the bedroom yet, have you?"

Alice gasped. Fifty pairs of eyes stared at her from the bed; the big eyes of pink and yellow and white and turquoise fluffy toys, and squinting eyes of trolls with long fluorescent hair.

"Meet the Cuddlies," said Pauline. "Sometimes I think they're more trouble than all my patients put together."

Alice felt sudden fear, of all the goggle-eyes, the garish nylon fibers, strong enough to strangle. Pauline had lured her here to kill her. Get her drunk on Tia Maria and do away with her. In cahoots with Kevin.

"What a wonderful collection. Well, I suppose I'll have to think about going, Pauline. Long journey and all that." Oh God. That was the mistake people always made in films; saying they were going instead of just making a run for it when the murderer was off-guard.

"Oh, I was going to do us a pizza. Won't take a minute in the microwave." Pauline was bitterly disappointed. That was what friends did, ate pizza on the sofa in front of the telly. Then her face broke into a smile when Alice said, "OK, great. Thanks, that would be lovely. Mind if I use your loo?"

"Help yourself."

As Alice left the room she paused. "Pauline, mind if I ask you something? Kevin, are you and he . . . I mean does he come here sometimes?"

"Not often." Pauline was upset at the intrusion of Kevin into the evening. "I let him come up once in a while. Only when I'm really browned-off."

Cheesed-off. Browned-off. Alice had an image of Pauline's brown and yellow overall bubbling in a microwaved Welsh Rarebit.

Pauline put Kevin out of her mind and went into the kitchen as Alice closed the bathroom door behind her. She selected two pizzas from the tiny freezer and got a sharp knife from the drawer to score along the marked quarters. The doorbell rang.

Alice, in the bathroom with her ear to the wall, heard the freezer door slam, and the metallic scrape of cutlery. The doorbell. In total panic she wrenched open the bathroom door. Kevin stood inside the front door, blocking the way. And Pauline had a long knife in her hand.

Alice made a rush for the door, shoving Kevin out of the way but Pauline was right behind her, grabbing the back of her sweatshirt, saying, "Alice, wait! What about the pizzas?" Alice was pulled around, and for black moments all three were struggling together in the narrow hallway in a tangle of bodies and knife. Then the knife got shoved in. Five inches of stainless steel straight to the heart.

They looked at her lying there. There was no question that she was dead.

"Bloody hell," said Kevin. "I only come up for a cup of sugar."

It occurred to neither of them to call the police.

"I'll have to get her bagged up," said Kevin then.

The Domestic was red-eyed and shaky in the morning as she handed out the breakfasts. She looked as if she'd been awake all night. She had; the accusing whispers of the Cuddlies had not let up. She could hear them still through her open window as she crossed the grass, the window with the curtain with the knot in it. Her hair was lank and uncombed under her scrunched rufflette of gingham, but nobody gave her a glance anyway.

"Come on Dolly Daydream, let's be having you," she said with her abrupt mirthless laugh. "Tea up. Nice milky one, two sugars."

Once, not so long ago, Alice's father, the former Detective Inspector, who was trained to observe, would have looked up with a pleased, though puzzled, smile sensing something amiss as she handed him his tea. She had always had a soft spot for him too, but now he didn't know her from a bar of soap.

CLOUD-CUCKOO-LAND

The Rowleys glowed in the dark. On wet winter mornings Muriel was fluorescent, streaming in the rain like a lifeboatperson with a lollipop guiding children over the big crossroads where the lights, when they were working, controlled twelve streams of traffic. As often as not there was an adhesive lifeboat somewhere about her person for her coat and cap were studded with stickers, bright and new, peeling and indecipherable, of any good cause you could mention, and gray smudges were the ghosts of charities which had achieved their aims, given up or been disbanded in disgrace. Her husband Roy had reflective strips on his bicycle pedals, and his orange cape and phosphorescent armbands, his rattling collection tins of all denominations were a familiar sight outside supermarkets, at car boot sales and in the station forecourt. There were neighbors who doused the lights and television and dropped to the floor if they had warning of his approach, but most people preferred to give, if only a few pesetas or drachmas, because everyone knew the Rowleys would do anything for anybody. A landslide victory in the local radio station poll had earned them its Hearts of Gold Award, and they had been presented with a box of Terry's All Gold Chocolates, a catering-size jar of Gold Blend coffee and a bouquet of yellow lilies with pollen like curry powder. In a different household the permanence of the stamens' dye, staining the wall behind the vase, a heap of books, a clutch of raffle tickets and a pile of laundry might have been a minor disaster.

Visitors to number 35 Hollydale Road, having cleared the assault course of the little hall, Roy and Muriel's still PVC and nylon coats, the bicycles which still wore the red noses of that charitable bonanza, Red Nose Day of a few years back, boxes of books, dented tins of catfood and jumble and birdseed, stacks of newspaper tied with string, turned left into the front room, where Roy was, this early afternoon, occupied in sorting through a pile of National Geographics. Since his retirement from the buses he had been so busy that now he joked about going back to work for a holiday, although he did put in two mornings a week at the Sue Ryder shop. One of his regular passengers had written a letter once to the *Evening Standard* praising his cheerfulness and he had enjoyed a brief fame as "the whistling conductor;" people had queued up to ride on his bus. "The Lily of Laguna" had been his favorite, and "I Believe," and "What a Wonderful World," until a polyp on his throat had put paid to that. Roy was an autodidact who had left school at fourteen and was now a gaunt man whose hair stuck up in black and gray tufts; his teeth protruded and his bare ankles, between the cuffs of his navy blue jogging pants and his brogues, were bony. There were traces in him still of the little boy in the balaclava waiting for the library to open, and the skinny eager student at the WEA. He was squinting at the close print of the magazines through a pair of glasses picked from a pile awaiting dispatch to the Third World and now and then a brown breast zonked him in the eye. There was not a surface in the room uncovered by papers, propaganda and paraphernalia. He was distracted by a movement past the window and glanced up to see old Mr. and Mrs. Wood from 43 creeping along to the shops with their bags inflated by the late October nor'easter. He noted how frail they had become with the end of summer. The clocks went back that weekend.

"'The Woods decay, the Woods decay and'—Muriel!" He shouted her name. "Muriel! The Woods have had a fall!"

Muriel rushed through from the kitchen, was tripped up by a bale of newspapers and kicked on the ankle by a bicycle, and saw Roy kneeling beside the Woods who were stretched out on the pavement, as two white plastic bags drifting along were snatched by a gust of wind and tossed like balloons into the branches of an ornamental maple. Punching the familiar digits on her mobile phone, Muriel summoned an ambulance, and hurried, her blue acrylic thighs striking sparks off each other, to wrench open Walter Wood's beige jacket with a sound of ripping velcro, and pinch his purple nose and clamp her mouth to his blue lips. Roy was attending to Evelyn Wood.

"Don't try to struggle," he soothed her, "the ambulance is on its way."

When it arrived, the Woods were covered with a grubby double duvet and a scattering of yellow leaves.

"Got the Babes in the Wood for you, Keith," Muriel called out to the ambulance crew, who were old friends and soon had the Woods strapped comfortably on board.

"He slipped on—something slippery," Roy explained, "and took her down with him. They came a fearful cropper. I saw it happen." As Keith closed the doors a voice came from within:

"Monstrous . . . two world wars . . . Passchendaele, Givenchy, Vimy Ridge . . ." and was cut off by the siren.

The onlookers went indoors, three subdued young mothers with pushchairs ambled on and curtains fell back into place as the blue light turned the corner. Muriel gave the duvet a shake and headed home to replace it in the bedroom as Roy surreptitiously scuffed a few more leaves over the condom he kicked into the gutter, the slimy cause of Walter's downfall. He felt sick. It was not the sort of thing you expected in Hollydale Road, a pallid invader from a diseased and alien culture.

"Don't suppose we'll be seeing them back in Hollydale," Roy predicted in the kitchen.

"No. Here—I've made us some nice hot Bovril—I expect they'll be sent to Selsdon House eventually. Hopefully. Still, perhaps it's a blessing it happened when it did, before the bad weather. I do worry about the old folk in the winter, when the pavements are icy."

Roy dunked a flapjack into his Bovril and sucked it. The Rowleys were such good sports that if anyone found a half-baked raffle ticket or a paper rose or a lifeboat in one of Muriel's cakes they took it in good part, although among the cognoscenti it was a case of "once bitten. . . ."

"No word, I suppose, Mommy?"

Roy nodded towards the breadbin where they stuffed the daily post. "I would have said. Still, she may have tried to ring—you know how busy the phone is."

A subdued hooting came from the bathroom.

"Drat that barn owl!" exclaimed Muriel. "Doesn't seem to know it's supposed to be nocturnal! Where does it think I'm going to get fresh vermin from at this time of day? That's something they don't tell you in those wildlife documentaries. Its beak's well-mended now, thanks to that superglue, but it obviously has no intention of taking itself off, thank you very much! Knows which side *its* bread's buttered—well, I suppose I'd better fetch him down." She concluded with maternal resignation.

As Muriel went upstairs the portable phone rang from the draining board.

"Helpline. Helpline. My name's Roy. Is there a problem you'd like to talk about? Something you want to share?"

A gruff throat was cleared.

"Take your time," Roy encouraged. "I'm here to listen when you're ready to talk. . . ."

Helpline Helpline had been established to counsel people addicted to ringing, or setting up, Helplines. Roy and Muriel had been roped in to manning the local branch.

"When did you first begin to think you might have a problem?" As Muriel came in with Barney on her shoulder, and Roy motioned her to be quiet, a hoarse monotone was saying truculently,

"The Bisexual Helpline was busy, so I dialed this number."

"I'm glad you did—um—could you tell me your name, any name will do, this is all in the strictest confidence of course—it just makes it easier for us to communicate. I said I'm Roy, didn't I?"

Barney was swooping towards him, sinking talons into his shoulder. Roy winced.

"Leslie."

"So, Leslie—is that with an 'ie' or a 'y' by the way? Not important—you're having a bit of trouble with your bicycle are you? What's the problem, gears, lights, mudguards? Well, we can get that sorted, and then, if you feel up to it, we can address the subtext of your cry for help, i.e., why are you hooked on helplines, and how we at Helpline Helpline can—excuse me a moment, Leslie don't go away—I've got a barn owl on my shoulder—"

"And I've got a monkey on my back," said the caller and hung up.

"Damn! I was just making the Breakthrough. We'll really have to make a determined effort to return Barney to his own environment. At the weekend, maybe. After the Mini Fun Run."

He picked up the sandwich Muriel put down on the table and was opening his mouth when Muriel said, "Don't eat that, it's Barney's. Worm and Dairylea." A silence fell and each knew the other was thinking of their own chick who had flown the nest. Who would have imagined, least of all themselves, that the Rowleys would have a daughter who would be decanted onto the doorstep by disgruntled cab drivers at all hours, and who had now taken up with a Jehovah's Witness? They had fallen out with Petula over the issue of blood transfusion; as operations and transfusions were, so to speak, Roy and Muriel's lifeblood, it was a vexed question. Giving blood was part of their credo. They had medals for it. There were gallons of Roy and Muriel's blood walking around in other folk.

Roy put his arms around Muriel, feeling pleasant stirrings of desire as man, wife and owl formed an affectionate tableau, until Muriel felt sharp claws rake her trouser-leg.

"Look who's feeling left-out, then. Come on, Stumpy. Come on, darling."

She sat down with the cat on her knee. Roy adjusted the drawstring of his jogging pants.

"We're not allowed to call him Stumpy anymore, according to the Politically Correct lobby. No, we must henceforth refer to our truncated companion as 'horizontally challenged. . . .'"

"What *is* your daddy on about now?" Muriel asked the cat.

"Like calling him Nigger."

"Why on earth would we? He's a tabby tomtom, aren't you pet? Nigger was *black*, you daft thing. Well, this won't get the baby a new frock . . . I promised to pick up Mrs. B's prescription and pension before Lollipop time."

As Muriel popped on her mac the phone went and she heard Roy answer "Helpline Helpline."

Petula Rowley had once told her father that whenever she heard him explain to a new acquaintance or a reporter from the local media how he had been "bitten by the Charity Bug," she saw a large striped glossy beetle rattling a collecting tin at her. She had added that she felt like stamping on that antlered stag and Colorado hybrid; but she herself had been the unwitting cause of her parents' metamorphosis from an unremarkable, well-disposed but uncommitted youngish couple into the baggy-trousered philanthropists of the present day. When Petula was five the Educational Psychologist, called in by her worried headmistress, had diagnosed a boredom threshold at danger level, and it was as therapy that Muriel and Roy had enrolled their little daughter, all the more precious now for her handicap, in a dancing class which put on shows in old people's homes and hospitals. Not very long after the family had been barred from Anello & Davide where they bought Petula's ballet shoes, those expensive pale pink pumps like two halves of a seashell, Petula had refused to attend the class. Muriel took her to the Tate to see Degas' *Little Dancer* in her immortal zinc tulle to no avail and they were requested to leave the gallery. Muriel had Petula's ballet shoes cast in bronze anyway. They posed on top of the television for years until somehow, without anybody really noticing, they became an ashtray, and later a repository for paperclips and elastic bands. Petula had defected, but her parents were well and truly hooked on Charity. Was it the smell of hospitals or of tea steaming from battered urns that got them; the smiles on old people's faces or the laughter of sad children, or the cut-and-thrust of the committee meeting where Roy could be relied on to come up with "Any Other Business" or one more Point of Order, just when folk were putting on their coats with thoughts of the adjacent hostelry? He was proud to share his initials with Ralph Reader of Gang Show fame; the Rowleys had ridden along on the crest of a wave, and Petula was dragged behind in the undertow, her boredom threshold quite forgotten.

As Roy returned to the task of sorting the magazines, contributions to the next car boot at Stella Maris, the school whose pupils Muriel escorted across the road, he was conscious of the discomfort in his chest; the pain of estrangement from his daughter, that Milk of Magnesia couldn't shift. The Third World spectacles slid down his nose and fell to the floor, and as he picked them up a tiny screw rolled out and the tortoiseshell leg came away in his hand. Roy groped another pair with heavy black frames from the pile and put them on. The room lurched at him, furniture, window glass and frame and the trees outside zooming into his face as he turned his head. He sat down, seasick, in a huge armchair.

As the nausea passed Roy became aware of a thick gray cobweb slowly spiraling from the lightshade in the center of the ceiling, saw that the shade itself, which he remembered as maroon, was furred by dust and trimmed with dead woolly bear caterpillars, and that loops and swags of cobweb garlanded the picture rails, tags of Scotch tape marked Christmases past and a balloon had perished and melted long ago, and soot and dust had drifted undisturbed into every cornice and embossment of the anaglypta wallpaper. Curled, yellowing leaflets and pamphlets and press-cuttings ringed with coffee stains were all about him, a pile of grubby laundry on the stained sofa, something nasty on the sleeve of the Live Aid record, unplayed because they had nothing on which to play it; his knees were blue mountains with a growth of Stumpy's fur, and downy featherlets caught in a dried-up stream of Bovril. Then his ankles! Roy could not believe the knobs and nodules below the fringe of black gray foliage, the wormcasts and bits of dead elastic, the anatomical red and blue threads and purple starbursts.

"These aren't my feet," he said. "Some old man has made off with Roy Rowley's feet while he wasn't looking and dumped these on me."

Other people's babies—that's my life.
Mother to do-ozens but nobody's wife!

Roy heard a voice singing at the front door and then a key in the lock, and then a yoo-hoo and then some old girl was in the room shrugging off a sulphurous yellow coat banded with silver, and waving a virulent green lollipop, like a traffic light on a stick, under his nose.

"Yum yum, piggy's bum, you can't have none," she taunted in imitation of a child's voice, popping the green glassy ball into her mouth, with the stick protruding. She crunched glass and glooped the ball out with a pop.

"One of my little boyfwends gave it to me," she lisped, and started to sing "We are the lollipop kids" like an overgrown Munchkin, then stopped. Roy was staring at the great, bobbly pink and gray diamonds on her jumper, the greasy gray elf-locks on her shoulders. It was he who had made her promise never to cut her hair short—how long ago had that been?

"Why are you staring at me like that? You look as if you've seen a ghost—or have I got something on my face?"

"No—not really. I've seen it advertised in the paper, you can get some shampoo-stuff for grey—I mean a gadget for shaving sweaters. It removed all the pills and bobbles—it brings them up like new. . . ."

"What pills and bobbles? What are you talking about now? What does?" He had made her feel silly about the lollipop.

"This gizmo I was telling you about."

All her pleasure in the sweet was gone.

"I reckon it's you who could do with a shave," she said and waddled—no, this was his beloved Muriel—walked out of the room.

"Mommy," he called after her.

"I'm going to see about Barney's tea."

Roy walked over to the mirror which hung on a chain on the wall above the cluttered mantelpiece and breathed on it and rubbed a clear patch on its clouded glass. Gray quills were breaking the surface of his skin and there was an untidy tuft halfway down his neck; he was scrawny and granular, his nose was pitted like a pumice stone; and hadn't he seen an ad for another gadget too, for trimming the ears and nose?

"I look a disgrace," he observed wonderingly. "A tramp. A scarecrow in a pigsty—that I thought was a palace." It was like some fairy tale featuring a swineherd or a simpleton who, ungrateful for his sudden riches, found himself back in his squalid hut; but was the world he saw through the black glasses a distortion, or reality to which he had been blind?

"Getting vain in our old age, are we?" Muriel, good humor evidently restored, had returned.

"When you've finished titivating yourself, I've brought you a cup of tea."

A hand like a cracked gardening glove seamed with earth was thrusting a pink mug at him; he saw the stained chip on its lip and the tea oozing through the crack that ran down its side.

"Ta muchly, love," he said weakly, lowering himself carefully on to the chair.

"You look different," commented Muriel.

"So do you," he thought.

"I can't put my finger on it."

She studied him, her great face in cruel close-up going from side to side. Roy was beginning to get a headache. Muriel had slipped her feet into a pair of pom-pommed mules and the rosehip scarlet dabs of varnish which time had pushed to the tips of her big toenails marked the end of summer.

"When I've had this, I'd better get the rest of those Save Our Hospital leaflets through some more doors," he said. "Shouldn't take too long. What are we having for supper?"

Muriel's mouth concertinaed in hurt wrinkles. Friday night was Dial-A-Pizza and early-to-bed night; a bottle of Black Tower was chilling in the fridge above the owl food.

"Is there any aspirin, love? I think I'm getting one of my heads."

Muriel dipped into her pockets and tore off a strip of Aspro. He swallowed two tablets the size of extra-strong peppermints. By the time Roy was walking back up Hollydale, his leaflets distributed by lamplight without the aid of spectacles, his head was clear.

"I've got a bone to pick with you!"

It was Mr. Wood shouting from the doorway of 43. Roy hurried across, surprised and pleased to see the old boy home and on his feet but guilty that he hadn't telephoned the hospital to enquire. Walter Wood's face was purple in the porchlight and he was gesticulating at a padded neck brace that held his head erect.

"I hold you responsible for this!" he was shouting.

"Me?"

The French letter slithered into Roy's mind.

"Me?" Roy repeated. Not guilty, surely?

"Yes you! If you and your do-gooding wife hadn't been so keen to bundle us off to the knacker's yard—we were just a bit shaken, getting our breaths back—and you might advise your better half to lay off the vindaloo if she's going to make a habit of giving the so-called kiss of life! They kept us lying on trolleys in the corridor for hours, like a pair of salt cod—couldn't even go to the toilet. I got such a crick in my neck they had to issue me with this!" he thumped his surgical collar. "The wife's got one too. She's worse off than I am because they had to commandeer a trolley from the kitchen for her. She's up in the bathroom now, trying to wash the smell of soup and custard out of her hair. I doubt she'll ever look a cooked dinner in the face again."

He pointed to the frosted bathroom window and Roy became aware of the sound of water gurgling down the drainpipe.

"You and your everlasting charity! You want to come down to earth and do something about that front garden of yours, it's a disgrace to the street! You're living in Cloud-Cuckoo-Land, my friend!" A Save Our Hospital leaflet was flung as Roy retreated, and was sucked back into the purple vortex of Walter Wood's rage, plastering itself across his face.

Indoors, having slunk through the fluffy Michaelmas daisy seed-heads of his shamed garden, Roy resolved to try a different pair of spectacles, but the multi-eyed heap of insects was gone.

"The Brownies came for them while you were out," Muriel told him.

A fey image of little folk batting at the window with tiny hands and fleeing with their haul through the falling leaves startled him. I'd better watch my denture in case the Tooth Fairy gets any ideas, he thought, but said that he was going to have a quick bath before the pizzas came. If the Rowleys had been less charitable, a visit to the optician would have been taken for granted; as finances stood, Roy decided to buy a pair off the peg at the chemist as soon as he had time. He put on the black-framed glasses to go upstairs and felt at once the strain as his eyes were pulled towards the huge lenses, and the giant staircase reared in front of him.

He surveyed the bathroom—a locker room after the worst rugby team in the league had departed to relegation, he thought, as he picked at the guano of owl droppings and toothpaste on the mirror. Once immersed with antiseptic Radox emeralds dissolving around him, he felt better, lifted the dripping sponge, squeezed it over his head and began to sing, gruffly.

> " 'I believe for every drop of rain that falls,
> A flower grows.
> I believe that somewhere in the darkest night
> A candle glows . . .
> Every time I see a newborn baby die . . .' "

Good God! He started again.

> " 'Every time I hear a newborn baby cry,
> Or touch a leaf, or see the sky—
> Then I know why
> I believe.' "

Roy Rowley with a packet of seeds and a bundle of gardening tools versus desert sands unfertilized by innumerable millions of bones.

> "I believe that every time I take a bath,
> A river dries.
> I believe . . . NO!
> *I* believe that Someone in that Great Somewhere hears—how absurd!"

Terrified, he stuffed the sponge into his mouth.

★   ★   ★

"Never mind, lovey, there's always next Friday," Muriel consoled him in bed. "It happens, or doesn't if you get my meaning, to the best of men at times."

"How would she know?" Roy wondered bitterly. Barney's great glassy yellow eyes winked lewdly from the top of the wardrobe. Stumpy was sniffing a circle of pepperoni stuck to the lid of the box beside the bed.

"He likes it but it doesn't like him!" Muriel informed Roy.

"I know."

Roy woke late with a headache and the fleeing remnants of a dream in which he and Muriel were being turned down as foster parents. The smell of frying bacon curled around his nose and he could hear Muriel and Barney's muted voices.

"Tu-whit, tu-whoo—a merry note, while greasy Joan doth keel the pot." He thought.

When he barged into the kitchen wearing the glasses the phone rang. Sidestepping Muriel's morning kiss, Roy picked it up.

"Yes?"

"Oh. Um, I must've got the wrong number. I thought this was the Helpline . . ."

"It is. Got a problem ringing helplines have you, pal? Well, try a bit of aversion therapy—piss off! There that should put you off wasting your own time and everybody else's!"

Muriel was open-mouthed with a rasher sliding from the fork suspended in her hand. Roy removed the spectacles; he had seen that the kitchen, the heart of the home, was splattered with the grease of thousands of marital breakfasts, and shoals of salmonella swam upstream to mate and lay their eggs. Anxiety from his oneiric ordeal crackled in static electricity from the viscose stripes of his dressing gown, caused horripilation of the pajama-ed limbs, itching of the feet in furry socks and irritation of the scalp. He and Muriel had been unpleasantly accused, judged, condemned in his dream, he remembered with shock that he had been sentenced to some kind of heavy-laboring Community Service for which he had been late, miles away, attempting to read the time on somebody's large upside-down watch. He had been trying to conceal his disgrace from Petula, desperate not to lose her respect, so that she might still turn to him as a daughter to a father. Owl's beak chomped an unspeakable morsel; Muriel departed in yellow to take a partially-sighted friend shopping, Saturday got underway. He had to put the glasses on to examine the pile of post. The fowls of the air, the fish and mammals of the sea, the North Sea itself besought Roy Rowley of Hollydale Road to save them. An ancient Eastern European face under a headscarf howled in grief and told Roy that winter was coming and there was no end to the killing and no food and no shelter from the snow. Roy thrust all their pleadings into the breadbin. Nothing of course from Petula. Stumpy was importuning for a second breakfast. As Roy spooned a lump of catfood into his bowl, some slithered over his hand. It felt curiously warm to the touch although the tin was almost at its sell-by date. The red buttocks of a tomato squatting on a saucer caught his eye. Roy sliced and ate it quickly, for if his new vision were to encompass lascivious thoughts towards fruit and veg, he was lost. He could see Petula in a pink dress standing by the piano in a church hall piping, "Jesus bids us shine with a pure clear light, like a little candle burning in the night. In this world of darkness, we must shine. You in your small corner, and I in mine."

There was a ten bob note in her heart-shaped pocket, but it

had been worth it to hear the collective "Aaah" when she skipped on to the stage.

There was no possibility of a visit to the chemist that day. The Mini Fun Run took over entirely. "Why do they do it?" Roy questioned in the autumnal park, stopwatch in hand, as agonized red and purple thighs juddered past him, and breasts were thrown about in colored vests. "The world need never have known. Whatever happened to feminine mystique?"

To his left an aerobics class in very silly costumes was performing a display. How sad to think of them entering sports shops to purchase those garments and then, in the privacy of their own homes, dressing up in the clinging silver suits under magenta bathing costumes and matching headbands and wristlets to step on and off jogging machines and hone their muscles on mail-order Abdomenizers and Thighmasters. A police dog was trying to rip the padded arm off an officer disguised as a criminal in a rival attraction; sales of curried goat and rice, burgers, kebabs and Muriel's Rice Krispie cakes were steady; the event was a success even though the mini hot-air balloon Roy had booked let him down. Muriel, in the gray livery of the St. John Ambulance Brigade was tending to a bungee jumper who had come to grief. Soon be Guy Fawkes, and she'd be on the Front Line again. Roy was booked for the Scouts Sausage Sizzle. Suddenly he had no taste for it. He'd rather just stay indoors, worrying about other people's pets.

At the last moment, that evening, Muriel felt that she could not face the rehabilitation of Barney, and Roy set out alone on his bicycle with the owl in a duffel bag and an ersatz Tupperware box of bits and pieces that were to be scattered around the new habitat.

"I'll just stay here and have a good 'owl'" Muriel had told him, "I just hope he gets acclimatized before bonfire night," and bravely waved a scrunched Kleenex as he pedaled away. She had sent her annual letter to the local paper reminding people to check their bonfires for slumbering hedgehogs.

"He was out of that duffel bag like a cork from a bottle, Mommy, was our boy. I caught hold of him for a moment and he looked me right in the eye as if to say 'Thank you, Uncle Roy and Aunty Muriel for having me, but I'm an endangered species and it's up to me now to do my bit in the conservation and breeding stakes.' I tossed him gently into the air and he took to it like—a duck to water! I don't mind admitting, Mommy, I was quite moved—that poem, you know. 'Everyone suddenly burst out singing,' came into my mind when I saw him rise above the treetops, silhouetted against the crescent moon."

"What's that tapping sound? That tap tap tap on the window?" Muriel said sharply.

It was a strand of jasmine, come loose from its pin.

Then he saw that she had all Petula's old photos out, the baby pictures and school portraits and holiday snaps.

That night Roy couldn't sleep. "Do-Gooders" Walter Wood had called them, tarnishing the Hearts of Gold Award. I do try to do good, he thought, is that so wrong? Then he was in the dayroom of the Sunshine Ward at the threatened hospital, tickling the yellowed ivories of the old joanna: "The way you wear your hat, the way you sip your tea . . . the memory of all that . . . no, no, they can't take that away from me . . ." and he looked around his captive audience, hatless and uncomprehending and at the spouted feeding cup from which an old boy sucked his tea and knew that, yes, they could take everything away.

If they took away his charity work, if he were to stop running from errand of mercy to good deed and stand still, what would Roy

Rowley be? An empty tracksuit filled with air? He snuggled up to Muriel's back and his bony fingers rested on gently rising and falling pneumatic flesh, aware of her dedicated, donated organs working a quiet night-shift. But what if that pump which drove them should suddenly stop and he feel no movement under his terrified hand?

Sunday, and an urban cockerel, gardens away, dissolved brick and asphalt in the morning mist as Roy lay in bed reluctant to leave its safety, and took him back to the muddy green rural outskirts of Orpington of his boyhood. Sometimes in late autumn the birds sing as if they are on the verge of spring rather than winter, and Roy listened dully to their songs thinking about the city built in the air by the birds, where Walter Wood had accused him of living. If only. He could see, on the chair, an empty blue-gray nylon harness and a deflated pair of Y-fronts. O black lace and shiny ribboned rayon and white cotton, when that Lloyd Loom linen basket with the glazed lid was new! The sheets in which he lay, once yellow, had come, like the fiberglass curtains, from Brentford Nylons in the days when he and Muriel had thought it posh, when they had paused for a moment each time they entered the bedroom to admire that flounced valance and the kidney-shaped dressing table's matching skirt. He itched, and longed for the touch and scent of sun and wind-dried cotton. Soon he must face the day through those dystopic lenses. He was not going to church this morning, although Muriel was, having a standing arrangement to push one of the old girls from Selsdon Court, the sheltered accommodation to which she had prematurely consigned the Woods. Roy would be on parade in a couple of weeks, on Remembrance Sunday, in his Rover Scouts uniform, and Walter Wood would be there in his medals. Roy had been demobbed undecorated from his National Service. His memories were of boils on the neck and skin chafed to a raw rash by khaki, and blisters. Walter Wood's protest as he was carried away to the ambulance came back to Roy as he shaved—the roll call of Great War battles. Roy dreaded the service at the war memorial now; feared that the fallen might look down on those they had died to defend and reckon their sacrifice futile: Fall in, you rusty tins of Andrews with your lids jammed half-open in an eternal grin; Present Arms, you broken-handled verdigrised half-spoons and clogged-up combs; To the left, wheel!, Optrex eyebaths and tubigrips and old blue unopened rolls of bandage. Atten-shun Germolene and Brolene and hemorrhoid cream and Dentu-creme, the packet of razor blades rotted to the shelf, the nest of Kirbigrips, the melted square of Ex-lax, the cloudy dregs of Aqua-Velva.

He went to breakfast to find that some small girls had brought Muriel an injured woodpigeon in a box. She handed Roy a plate of bacon, eggs and beans. She was dressed for church in a turquoise leisure suit. A deckle-edged snapshot of his parents was flashed past his eyes: Mother in a gray costume with white gloves, Father in pinstripes, both wearing hats. He acknowledged his own Sunday attire, a clownish suit that would have baffled them and cost them about a month's wages.

"I'll pop Woody in the old rabbit hutch when I go out," she said.

"We should call him Herman or Guthrie," said Roy, fighting his vision of humankind as worth no more than the contents of its collective bathroom cabinet, the gray underwear hiding under its bright uniforms. Muriel smiled.

"Or Allen," he added.

"Ooh no! You won't forget the boot sale, will you lovey?" Roy could feel the dull pain of Petula's loss as he ate, and stifled a burp in his kitchen-roll serviette.

"Pardon me for being rude, it was not me, it was my food," he said mechanically.

The bare twiggy branches of the trees stuck up in witches' brooms as Roy walked down the road, the fallen leaves of a magnolia grandiflora lay like bits of brown leather; old shoes. A van was parking in the forecourt of the council estate and two masked men in yellow protective clothing got out carrying fumigating equipment. There was a mattress lying on top of a heap of rags and Roy saw, and recoiled from, had to look again in hopeful disbelief then horror, the sodden outline of what had once been a human being rotted to the stained ticking. Those men in yellow; they and their kind were the ones who really knew how the world worked, and kept it going. He stood, what else could he do, a well-intentioned bloke in an anorak; a drone. And of course they, those yellow ones, were the most respected and rewarded members of the community for what they did, weren't they? Like hell they were.

At the car-boot he delivered his magazines and sundry other goods and strolled around the playground with a notion of picking up a better pair of glasses, and stopped in front of a blanket on the ground. It was a thin tartan car rug and the goods displayed were a baby's dummy, two feeding bottles with perished teats, a splayed-out wire and nylon bottle brush, some Anne French cleansing milk, two pairs of pop-sox in unopened packs, a pair of jeans and a tube of colored bath pearls. Roy paid for the bath pearls with a five pound note, guessing the young woman would be unable to change it. Three children with purple smudges under their eyes and the necks of baby birds watched silently.

"Don't worry about it. Some other time," he said and hurried away blushing to the roots of his tufty hair, with the bath pearls in his hand. Petula used to like the red ones; when she was little she would burst one and squash it against her arm or leg in the bath, and then scream, "Help! Help! I've cut myself really badly!" and bring Mommy and Daddy rushing in panic. They fell for it every time.

"Royston!" the matey misnomer caught him as he made for the exit, past a selection of plastic balls for dispensing liquid detergent, a battered Cluedo, a doll in a dingy knitted dress, and a blur of similar merchandise. Roy went over to the stall where an old acquaintance, Arnie, was doing a brisk trade in Christmas wrapping paper, counterfeit French perfume and watches.

"Like the bins," said Arnie, indicating Roy's glasses. "Very high-profile executive whizz-kid."

"You wouldn't if you could see the magnification of your face," Roy thought. "A temporary expedient," he said. "I don't think they're quite me."

"Pathetic, isn't it, what some people have the nerve to try to flog. It's an insult really." Arnie nodded at the plastic balls, which the vendor was piling into a pyramid, to increase their allure. Roy could only agree.

At home, after telephoning its founder to regret that he must remove his commitment to Helpline Helpline and hearing that the service had been discontinued, Roy wandered into the back garden. He was sitting hunched on the old swing, kicking a half-buried tambourine sunk under a wodge of once-sprouted birdseed. A relic of Petula's brief post-punk stint as a Salvation Army Songster.

"You look like a garden gnome sitting there."

"Petula!"

"Hello, Dad. I like the face furniture."

Roy wrenched off the glasses. He did not want to see Petula through them, and they had misted up besides.

"Pet. My little Pet. Is it really you? Let me look at you."

He was hugging her so tightly that he could see nothing but smelled the fruit tang of her shiny hair.

"What's in the hutch this time?" she asked. "Oh, it's a woodpigeon. Hello, Woody. Remember that time we made the Blue Peter bird pudding, Dad? Yuk, it was 'orrible, wasn't it? I was really sick. Still, I suppose we shouldn't have eaten it all ourselves. Mom went spare. Where is she, by the way, church? Shouldn't you be getting the dinner ready? I'll give you a hand. It's freezing out here. Can we go in and have some coffee? And I must put these flowers in water."

"I can't wait to see your mother's face when she walks in!" said Roy, in the kitchen, groping at the coffee.

"Put your specs on," advised Petula.

"No, I'm better without them. They're the wrong prescription. They're giving me gyp."

"Try these."

Petula took a rhinestone butterfly-winged pair from her bag. "I don't need them—they're from my fifties period. Found them at a car-boot," she said. Her father's daughter.

They took their coffee into the front room.

"What a tip," said Petula affectionately. She hooked the glasses over Roy's ears before sweeping aside a box of recycled envelopes and Christmas gift catalogs and sitting down. "They suit you. How are they?"

"Perfect. They're brilliant—might have been made for me. Everything's right in focus. Marvelous! Just the ticket. Let me look at you properly."

He saw a striking young woman in her thirties, with dark

feathered hair and big silver earrings, a bright patterned chunky sweater above black leggings and red boots.

"A sight for sore eyes," he said.

He studied himself in the mirror through the sparkling unswept frames, and wondered if he might introduce a little tasteful drag into his next entertainment. Then he saw that Petula had arranged a bunch of red carnations in a vase, and forbore to remind her that women in Colombia gave their fingers, even their lives, to the cultivation of those scentless blooms that deck our garage forecourts and corner shops.

Walter Wood passed the window, and shook a fist.

"We had a bit of a misunderstanding—" Roy started to explain in unhappy embarrassment as the plastic carriers fluttered in the tree outside.

"Miserable old scrote. The thing is, Dad, I want to come home. I've left Barrington. And I've had it up to here with the Witnesses—all that dragging around doorsteps flogging *AWAKE!* and other boring literature, honestly I might just as well have stayed at home with your interminable Flag Days! I was bored to sobs after a fortnight." She began to sing, to the tune of "Born to Lose"—"Bored to sobs, I've lived all my life in vain. Every dream has only brought me pain. All my life, I've always been so blue. Bored to sobs, and now I'm bo-ored with you! Not you, Daddy. I know I've disappointed you in the past—I couldn't be cute like Petula Clark or develop an adult larynx like Julie Andrews, but I'll make you proud of me one day."

"Darling, I've always been so proud—when we went out with you in your little coat, and your doll's pram, and people used to say 'she's just like a little doll,' and I was as proud as a peacock when your mother brought you down to the bus garage to meet me and I used to show you off to all my mates—and later—"

He had been going to say that he loved her in all her reincarnations and admired her independence of spirit but she cut in defensively with, "It wasn't easy for me either, you know, you and Mom always being so involved in other people's problems. Sometimes I used to think that you could only relate to someone if they were disabled in some way—sorry, Stumpy, no offense. I had fantasies about wheelchairs and kidney machines. I was in therapy for a while—well it was a group I went to—but I had to leave when it transpired that I was the only person there who hadn't been abused by her father. Amazing how it came back to them one by one. God, it was embarrassing—I felt so inferior. I must have been a singularly unattractive kid . . . sorry, Dad, only kidding—I never fancied you either. Joke. Anyway, we'd better rattle those pots and pans, Mom'll be home any minute, even allowing for coffee in the crypt. 'What's the recipe today, Jim?' Pigeon pie? Only kidding."

Tears, laughter and lunch coming to an end, Woody who had joined the party perking up in his box, Friday night's white wine quaffed, Muriel posed the question that Roy had not liked to put.

"Have you had any thoughts of what you might do next, Pet? Careerwise, I mean?"

"Well, I had thought of becoming a therapist. I read somewhere that any screwed-up, pathetic inadequate with no qualifications can set themselves up, so I thought—that's for me! I could use the front room—it would be money for jam. Then again, I thought I might have a baby. Sometime around next March the first seems like as good a time as any. . . ."

"Oh . . . Pet!"

Petula looked her mother straight in the eye.

"I'm afraid I must warn you, Mommy, that there's a fifty percent chance that the baby will be dyslexic—it runs in Barrington's family."

"Oh, the poor little mite! We must do everything—hang on, I've got a leaflet somewhere. . . ."

Petula settled back comfortably against the cushion Roy had just placed at her back and held out her cup for more coffee.

Late that afternoon as Roy set out on his bike to fetch some things that Petula had forgotten to bring, he saw that as the light faded the western sky was white above layers of cloud, pale gray and dark gray, barred like cuckoos' wings, and he rode on towards them, the reflective strips on his pedals spinning starry arcs from his feet in the gathering dusk.

SHINTY

In the autumn the little girls of the Vineyard school would build fragile mansions from the fallen leaves in the shrubbery. The houses had no roofs except the laurels, rhododendrons and firs above but the grandest of them boasted walls three or four feet high and many rooms. The ground plans were scratched with sticks on the sandy soil and marked out with foundations gathered from the deciduous drifts of oak, sweet chestnut leaves, acorns, beech mast and pine needles. Wind, rain or spiteful shoes could demolish in seconds the work of many playtimes. The Vineyard was an ordinary primary school in a Kent town but it was privileged in its building, a Georgian house, and took only girls.

The smell of damp sand and cold leaves, came back to Margaret so vividly as she read the advertisement in the paper that forty years dissolved and she might have been in "the shrubs" with her greatest treasure, an ostrich egg, crushed to chips of yellowish-white shell in her hands. Chestnut cases picked her fingers, the bitter taste of flat pale unripened fruit was in her mouth, and she remembered a girl called Jean Widdoes, who had scraped together a hovel in the dankest corner of the shrubs, where she dwelt alone in the long dinner hour.

Ronnie Sharples Reads From Her
Latest Bestseller
Flowers of Evil
At Dorothy's Bookshop, Flitcroft Court,
Charing Cross Road
Thursday 23 September 7:00
Ring to Reserve Signed Copies
Glass Of Wine Or Ale
Women Only

Veronica Sharples, her old classmate, whose books automatically shot straight into the number one slot of the Alternative Best Sellers.

Margaret rang Suzy at once, at work. They had been best friends at seven and were best friends still. Suzy, who had always ended up with at least ten extra stitches on her knitting, now had her own computer graphics company. When the class had started their tea cosies, Veronica, given first choice had picked "Camel and nigger, please Mrs. Lambie." Her words had stayed with Margaret all these years. All that remained when it came to Margaret's turn was dull orange and bottle green; the crimson lake and sea-green knitted fluted jelly that she had envisaged for as long as it took to distribute the wool, that would transform their broken-spouted teapot, was not to be; in fact it turned into a kettle-holder full of holes. She could hear Mrs. Lambie's voice now, striking terror along the desks in needlework:

"Unpick it!" "Unpick it!" "Unpick it!" "That's a lovely little run-and-fell seam, Veronica. You're developing into quite a nice little needlewoman." No terror in adult life would match that of double needlework with Mrs. Lambie.

"Are you sure we're ready for this?" Suzy asked. "I mean, Veronica Sharples . . . will we have to have our bodies pierced to pass ourselves off as fans? There's no way I'm paying out good money to feed her monstrous ego and you know her books are quite unreadable. Dennis Wheatley and The Girls of The Chalet School meet the Clan of the Cave Bear at The Well of Loneliness—no thanks. What would be the point of going? She'd only think we were impressed."

"This is the point," said Margaret, "we'll go in disguise. Surely you don't imagine she'd remember us anyway? Be in the Beaujolais at six on Thursday, and we can fortify ourselves for the fray. Bring your shinty stick."

She put the phone down without hearing Suzy's whine of, "It'll be just like school, everybody standing around watching Veronica showing off," but realized she was humming "The Dead-wood Stage" and was transported back to the washbasins, as the lavatories at the Vineyard were known, where Veronica leaped onto a toilet seat, breaking it, in her imitation of Calamity Jane. Whip crack away, whip crack away, whip crack away! "Do the 'Dying Swan,' Veronica," someone begged, and Veronica closed her eyes, assumed a doleful expression, clasped her hands in a coronet above her head, and died on the tiled floor, as a coterie of clumsy cygnets waited in the wings for tuition in the art of the arabesque.

Veronica was the arbiter of fashion and her dress code was as immutable as her social strictures. Jean "Fish-Face" Widdoes, whose mother by cruel chance was a widow, had once turned up, horror or horrors, in a knitted pixie-hood, and on another occasion in pink ankle socks edged with a blue stripe. "Baby's socks, 1/11 in Wool-worths," pronounced Veronica, who had spotted them at once. "Oh, look, your legs are going all blotchy to match your socks." It was extremely bad form, and dangerous, to admit to any home life—especially if like Linda Wells, you had a brother who was mental.

To bring to the classroom a faint reminder of the previous night's fried food was a serious offense, and one which did not endear Jean to the teachers either, although they did not grasp their noses at her approach, as the girls did. The Dolphin Fish Bar in Arbutus Road was a hundred yards downhill from the swimming baths, and on Saturdays, when Jean helped in the shop, there was always the threat that Veronica and her pals would appear in the queue, blue-lipped and red-eyed, reeking of chlorine, sleek-haired mobsters in cotton frocks and cardigans. Jean paid protection in extra chips and free pickled eggs. Once, when Margaret was in the Dolphin with her own mother, she heard Jean's mother suggesting that Jean might like to go swimming with her friends sometimes instead of serving in the shop. Jean shook her head so vehemently that the big white turban she wore slipped right down over her face. "Oh, go on, Jeannie, plee-ease, be a sport, we'll call for you tomorrow," pleaded Veronica, so eloquently that Jean was persuaded that she would not be *the* sport. Foolish little Fish-Face, forgetting about the diving board as she trotted along with her costume rolled in her towel. "It looks like a fish, it smells like a fish, but it sure don't swim like a fish," Veronica summed it up.

"Why don't you like Jean?" somebody challenged Veronica one day.

"Because she's got a big conk and she's smelly."

When Margaret told Suzy to arm herself with her shinty stick for the reading, she was making a reference to the half-moon shaped scar above Suzy's ankle, the memory of a wound inflicted when Veronica had tripped her up, making her fall on the sharp-edged tin that held the shinty balls. For reasons best known to Miss Short who taught Hygiene and PT, and presumably with the headmistress's, Miss Barnard's, approval, the Vineyard girls played shinty rather than hockey. Perhaps the smaller sticks made the playing field look larger. There was no gymnasium, and wet games and PT lessons took place in the cloakrooms. Miss Short was particularly fond of an activity called "duckwalking" wherein the girls had to crook their arms into wings and waddle at speed around the narrow benches and pegs hung with coats and shoebags. Quacking was forbidden. If there had been a Junior Olympic Duckwalking event, Veronica would have walked it, with her bony wings pumping from her blinding white vest—somebody's mom always used Persil—and jaunty little navy-blue bottom jerking from side to side over speedy plimsoles as she lapped the field. Veronica was Miss Short's pet duckling and Miss Short turned a blind eye to a wing winding a rival, as she did to wet netballs smacking an opponent's face or knees grazing asphalt in a heavy fall; but it was at shinty that Veronica really shone. Her own sharp shins, the blade bone of her nose, honed to a finer point that Jean's despised conk, cutting a swathe through the opposing team, although she was never a team player.

After speaking to Suzy, Margaret decided that the years which had passed since Veronica had seen her old schoolmates would provide sufficient disguise, and besides, Veronica had not watched them, as they had watched her, on the television, strutting her stuff on 01 For London. As is customary on that program, the interview took place in a restaurant of the guest's choice, and Veronica had opted for Bob's Eel and Pie House, an establishment in Smithfield which had repulsed trendiness, where, elbows on the formica tabletop, mouth full of jelly she had chomped on working-class solidarity while charting her progress from the rural and cultural poverty of her childhood to her present cult status. All had gone swimmingly until the interviewer had asked, in his affable Scottish way, "Are ye no not slumming it a wee bit the night through, Ronnie? I mean to say, rumor has it that you have your own special table in the Groucho, where you're to be found most evenings?"

The camera lingered on him as eels, mash, liquor and peas slid down his face from the plate upturned on his head, and then pursued Veronica as she wrenched open the door of the Ronniemobile parked outside and was chauffeured away at speed.

Margaret was no longer the plump child she had been when "Twice around the gasworks, once around the Maggot" had been Veronica's estimation of her size, but as she got ready for the evening's entertainment, her dress felt a little tight. How typical of Veronica to make her put on weight today. "Pooh! Can anybody smell gas?" Veronica would taunt when Margaret was out of favor. Home was number 5 Gasworks Cottages. Suzy lived in a tiny village, just a street with a shop, a pub and a church, a farm, a scattering of villas and cottages and a crescent of new council houses. She came to school on the bus.

When Margaret, dressed as herself, Margaret Jones, who had recently celebrated her silver wedding, mother of four grown-up children, regional director of a large housing association, arrived at the Beaujolais, she saw a black fedora waving at her through the smoke of the crowded room. Suzy had got herself up as a gangster in a wasp-waisted pinstripe suit, and as Margaret squeezed onto the chair she had managed to reserve, she flashed open her jacket to show the butt of a gun poking from her inside pocket.

"I was going to get a violin case but I thought it would be a bit obvious," she said.

"Mmm. That's *so* much more subtle. Sorry I'm late, there's been a bomb scare at Charing Cross and half the Strand's closed off. Bloody security alerts, it's probably just some jerk of a commuter who left his briefcase on the concourse." She poured herself a glass of wine from the bottle on the table.

"Sweet of you to save some for me. Cheers. That thing in your pocket is a toy, I hope?"

"Realistic, though, eh? What happened to your disguise, and where's my shinty stick?"

"Funnily enough, I couldn't find it—possibly because Veronica Sharples was the only girl who had her own shinty stick—and unbeknownst to you, there is a liberty bodice with rubber buttons concealed beneath this workaday print. I've come as Jean Widdoes." She had just remembered how Jean Widdoes had been the only girl in the school, perhaps the last girl in the world, to wear one of those obsolete padded vests.

"Jean Widdoes is dead," said Suzy.

"What? I don't believe you. When? Why didn't you tell me?"

"Sorry. It was while you were in France in the spring. My mother sent me a cutting from the local paper. Her car was hit by a train on a level crossing. It was an open verdict. I didn't send it on to you because you had enough troubles of your own, and then I suppose I just blocked it out. Couldn't bear to think about it."

"It doesn't bear thinking about."

She wished she had not brought up the liberty bodice. PT lessons had been made hell on its account until Jean learned to take it off beforehand and hide it in her shoebag.

"Remember that awful time her mother dragged her screaming into assembly and she was clinging to her in hysterics, and Miss Barnard said, 'I shall have my cane, Jean?'"

"Yes—they knew how to cure school phobia in them days—I wish we weren't doing this," Margaret said. "Shall we just go and have something to eat instead? It doesn't seem so amusing now, and you could do with some blotting paper."

"What, and waste this suit?"

Margaret wished herself miles away from bodies and braying laughter, and fumes of wine, smoke and charcuterie, in the heart of the Kent they had shared, a tumbledown place of old yellow-lichened red brick, sagging garden walls held up by old man's beard, old rabbit hutches and chicken runs, Virginia creeper and apples and rosehips against blue autumn sky, dark lacy cabbages, quinces and wasps, the bittersweet smell of hops.

But there was Legs Diamond waving two tickets at her and saying, "I made a special trip at lunchtime to get them. There are bound to be coachloads of Ronnie's little fans."

She took her ticket, drained her glass, stubbed out her cigarette and squeezed herself out of her chair to follow her friend.

"There she is!" Suzy clutched Margaret's arm outside the shop, whose window was dominated by a blown-up photograph of Ronnie surrounded by pyramids of her books. "No it isn't, it's a clone. My God, there are hundreds of them. Surrounded by Ronnie Sharples Wannabees, what a terrifying prospect. Do you think we'll be all right?"

"No," said Margaret.

"It was your idea, remember. Another nice mess you've got me into. . . ."

As that could not be denied there was nothing to say. Miss Barnard's voice came faintly through the ether, "Margaret Adams, you are a bad influence and you, Susan Smithers are weak and easily led. Together you make a deplorable pair. I am separating you for the rest of the term."

Apart from the chums, as Margaret christened herself and Suzy grimly, the audience was composed of young women and girls with short hair gelled back from their foreheads, dressed in polo shirts tucked into knee-length khaki shorts fastened with snake belts.

"Gott in Himmel! The Hitler Youth!" whispered Suzy.

"They've all copied exactly what she was wearing on 01 For London! What must it be like to have a following like that? The Michael Jackson of literature." Margaret whispered back, thinking that they looked like a troop of Boy Scouts that Baden-Powell wouldn't have touched with a tent-pole. Camp as a row of tents. Then she recalled Veronica, sleek-haired after the swimming baths, except that she had worn a cotton frock in those days. Each of the clones carried a copy of Ronnie's latest book, *Flowers of Evil*, and some of them carried six-packs of Thackray's Old Peculiar Ale.

"Original title . . ." Margaret commented, of the book.

A shop assistant was trying to hold the door open just wide enough for several of the scouts to evict an old wino woman who had managed to infiltrate, while repelling latecomers at the same time.

"So much for sisterhood," as Suzy remarked.

Dorothy, the bookshop's owner was looking worried at her watch. Ronnie Sharples had a reputation for unpredictability.

"She'll be here," her friend and business partner was soothing her, "Her girlfriend was on the phone again only an hour ago to confirm we'd got the right ale in."

"Did you reassure her that the dumb duck who shelved *Wicca and Willow* with the Craft Books was sacked on the spot as soon as she confessed?

If only Ronnie's sidekick hadn't spotted it when she was in checking the window display. The event had almost been canceled.

A small table held a jar of water, a bottle of red wine, half-empty, a similar bottle of white, some plastic cups, and a crate of Thackray's Old Peculiar, the extra-strong Northern ale which was all that Ronnie, despising the Kentish hopfields of her youth, would drink. More cans were stacked below.

"Our Ronnie was always heavily into uniforms, wasn't she?" said Suzy, as she paid for two cups of wine. Margaret felt a pang of shame remembering how she had cajoled her parents into buying a new blazer that they could ill afford. There was a Vineyard uniform of blue blazer, gymslip, white blouse and blue and white striped tie, but it was optional; a few girls, like Margaret whose was second-hand, wore blazers but that was as far as it went. Until the arrival of Veronica in the middle of the third year, in the full rig or fig. She even sported a blue pancake, with a badge. The force of Veronica's personality was such that Easterfield's the High Street Outfitters enjoyed an unprecedented boom, and the more berets there were on heads meant, to Veronica and the gang she had formed at once, the more berets to toss into tress and pull down over people's eyes. Strange though that she, the proponent of the Windsor knot in the school tie that was such a useful garotte, should have made Miss Harvey, who wore a collar and necktie with her tailored coat and skirt, the target of her scorn.

"Old Ma Harvey looks a right twerp in that tie," Veronica decreed, and it was so. Margaret, who loved Miss Harvey and yearned for a tweed or tartan tie, cried for Miss Harvey secretly in the washbasins. Her heart bled for Miss Harvey, knotting her tie in the mirror in the morning, sitting on her desk, swinging her legs as she read them "The Kon-Tiki Expedition," unaware that she had been diminished by Veronica calling her a right twerp. Veronica put up her hand.

"How did they go to the toilet, Miss Harvey?"

The class was shocked at the rudeness and audacity of Veronica's question, but Miss Harvey laughed like the good sport she was. Margaret longed for brogues like Miss Harvey's too, shiny brown and punched with interesting patterns of holes. "Old Ma Harvey," indeed. Veronica and her gang knew nothing of the real Miss Harvey.

"I bet she wears trousers at home," Margaret told Suzy. "She only has to wear a skirt at school because it's the law." Suzy agreed. They had lurked outside Miss Harvey's house one afternoon in the holidays in the hope of seeing her but a cross old lady in gardening trousers had advanced on them with a trowel as they passed the gate of Heronsmere Cottage for the tenth time, and they had run away. Cycling home from Miss Harvey's village, they wondered how someone as nice as Miss Harvey could have such a grumpy old mother.

"Remember how Veronica got the Grammer uniform before we'd even sat the scholarship?" Margaret asked, as they waited for her to appear.

"And wore it on Saturdays!"

"If only she hadn't passed. . . ."

"Jean Widdoes passed too didn't she? But she didn't go, for some reason."

"Do you think I should tell them that Ronnie didn't turn up as guest speaker at the Sevenoaks Soroptimists?" Suzy was saying as the audience grew restive on its seats, when the heavy glass door crashed open, flattening the assistant against a bookcase.

Twin Tontons Macoutes in mirror sunglasses swung in, followed by Ronnie, elfin in white T-shirt and black jeans. Scattered applause, whistles and disappointed sighs came from her fans, in their shorts and polo shirts. Sidling in as the door banged shut came a tall, drooping young woman in limp viscose, with long pale hair pushed behind her ears. Mog, Ronnie's latest partner and general factotum. Rumor had it that she had been bought as a slave in Camden Market. The crocodile Kelly bag that Mog carried suggested that Ronnie had tried to make something of her, but Quality Seconds had prevailed. A

Band-Aid was coming unstuck from one of her heels where her sandals had rubbed blisters.

"It's guts for garters time if we get clamped again," were the first words the faithful heard from their idol, and Mog's muttered reference to a disabled sticker was lost as she ripped the tab from the can of Thackray's handed to her by the genuflecting Dorothy, and gave it to Ronnie.

"I think we should make a start as soon as you're ready," Dorothy suggested timidly, "We are running a tad late . . . if you don't mind. I'll just give brief introduction . . ."

"A tad late?" Ronnie interrupted her. "Half of bloody London's closed off. Think yourself lucky we're here at all."

"Oh, we do, Ronnie. We do."

"Ronnie needs no introduction," put in Mog in a monotone as flat as her face.

"Shut up Mog, or I'll cancel the check for your assertiveness class."

Ronnie gave Mog an affectionate nudge which sprayed Old Peculiar over her frock. Mog gazed down on her adoringly and gratefully at this public display of intimacy. Margaret whispered into Suzy's ear a poem they had learned in school:

"Rufty and Tufty were two little elves
They lived in a hollow tree . . .
Rufty was clever and kept the accounts
While Tufty preferred to do cooking.
He could bake a cake without a mistake,
And eat it when no one was looking!"

"It's like the black hole of Calcutta in here. Haven't you got any air conditioning?" Ronnie demanded and at once a Tonton

Macoute switched on the electric fan that stood by the till sending a whirlwind of leaflets into the front row of the audience, as the police and ambulance sirens drowned Dorothy's apologies while she scrambled after the papers. Mog, flanked by the bodyguards, was seated in the front row, after reassurances that a thorough search of the premises for incendiary devices had been made, as ordered, earlier. Ronnie suspected that she was a prime target.

"It would be like the IRA's biggest coup ever if they got Ronnie," Mog explained. "We have to be like constantly vigilant. Security's a real hassle."

Dorothy, stained with shyness at the ordeal of public speaking, was motioning for silence in the ranks.

"OK, OK, let's 'ave a bit of 'ush. Right, well, we're really honored to have with us tonight someone who needs no introduction from me. Dorothy's is proud and privileged to welcome the writer who has been called variously 'the lodestar of lesbian literature' and the 'Anne Hathaway de nos jours.' So please put your hands together in a great big Dorothy's welcome for your own, your very own, RONNIE SHARPLES!!"

Suzy gave Margaret a questioning nudge under cover of the catcalls and whistles that broke out, as Dorothy sat down heavily after her lapse into the persona she had assumed for her role as mistress of ceremonies at the ill-starred Old Tyme Varieties at the Drill Hall one Christmas.

"Don't tell me you haven't read *Dyke Lady of The Sonnets,* or *Second Best Bard*, which proves Anne Hathaway wrote the plays," Margaret replied.

"Hi gang." Ronnie waited for silence to follow the return of her greeting, then snatched up the copy of *Flowers of Evil* that lay, bristling with bookmarks, in Mog's ample lap. She opened the book, and took a swig from her can.

"Hope you've all bought a copy, or three . . ."

Only two pairs of hands were still as a flock of books rose and flapped their pages in the air.

"Right then, we can all go home . . ."

Through the laughter came the sound of the door rattling and the Tonton Macoute posted there shouting, "Can't you read, dickhead? It says Wimmin Only!" She held the bulging door, calling over her shoulder, "Boss, some wanker says he's your dad!"

"Oh, for fuck's sake! Deal with it, Mog. Get rid of him. Take the bloody diary and see if I've got a window after Christmas. Just do it, you great waste of space!" Ronnie's lips were thin bloodless scars of fury in her livid face. Her eyes blazed as the front row squirmed in their seats. Before Mog made it to the door the gatecrasher disappeared and a megaphone was thrust in, and the bouncer stepped back to admit a uniformed policeman.

"Nobody is to leave the building until the police give clearance that it is safe to do so," he said, and backed out, pulling the door closed behind him. Yellow official tape sealed them in. Ronnie ran to the door, dragging it open.

"What is this, a police state, now?"

She was thrust courteously but ignominiously back inside as an explosion down the road erupted ale from cans and hurled books to the floor.

"Bye bye, Daddy. It was nice knowing you," Ronnie attempted to retrieve lost face. "Where d'you think you're going, Madam?" She grabbed Mog by the hair.

"People may be hurt, Ronnie. I've got my first-aid badge, I must go."

"They need paramedics not bloody Brownies, you dipstick!" But Mog twisted free, leaving a hank of pale hair wound round Ronnie's fingers, and escaped.

"You're fired! And I want that bloody ring back!"

A cluster of clones surrounded Ronnie, comforting, placating, tacitly offering themselves as replacements. She thrust them aside.

"Where's the loo in this dump? I need some space."

"This way Ronnie, I'll show you," Dorothy was saying soothingly, but Ronnie pushed past her and strode to the back of the shop and wrenched open a door. When it proved to be a cupboard holding cleaning materials, she shut herself in anyway, defying anybody to recognize a cliché of farce, sharing her space with a vileda mop and bucket.

Margaret turned to Suzy, and saw that she was crying.

"Her father was such a nice man," she sobbed. "He was really good fun. Remember when he bought us all ice cream after the pageant, the one when Ronnie was Elizabeth the First, and we were scullions?" She scrubbed at her eyes with a tissue. "Only that pathetic Mog had the guts to do anything."

"Look, the explosion was miles away, probably right down in Trafalgar Square. It sounded pretty feeble anyway, a small incendiary device. There's no way Mr. Sharples could have been in it."

Her own feelings of guilt at not having done as Mog had done, and uselessness, made her voice impatient. Instinct told her that people were not bleeding and dying yards away, but how could she be sure?

The cupboard door opened and Ronnie emerged, clinging to the mop handle looking ill.

"It's Mrs. Mop, the Cockney Treasure," said Margaret, trying to make Suzy laugh.

"What's *your* problem?" said a voice behind her.

Margaret turned, her smile withered by the hate on the face that was saying, "Sitting there sniggering in your Laura Ashley frigging frock. I suppose it offends your middle-class mores that someone like Ronnie should be a working-class gay icon. Some people just can't stand to see anybody from the wrong background succeed. "Why don't you piss off back to Hampstead. Lipstick Lesbian, and take your fashion victim girlfriend with you?"

"It isn't Laura Ashley," was all that Margaret could say. She was frightened, expecting a fist in her face. She turned around again, trembling, but Suzy had slewed around indignantly.

"Working class? You've got to be joking. If you believe that you'll believe any of Ronnie's hype and lies. Veronica Sharples was the first girl in our class to have a patio, *and* the first to have a car, one of those green jobs with woodwork, *and, and* she went on holiday to the Costa del Sol before it was even invented, so don't give me that underprivileged crap. *And* you should have seen her lunch—a big Oxo tin crammed with sandwiches, and that was just for playtime."

"Leave it, Suze," said Margaret.

"Leave it, Suze," her accuser imitated her.

"*And* your working-class icon went to Cambridge."

"So what?"

"So nothing, except Veronica Sharples is a fraud as well as a lousy writer. *And* they had their own chalet at Camber Sands!"

Margaret heard Veronica's childish voice pipe, "Anyway, *we've* got a vestibule!" and her own defiant retort "Well my dad's getting us one tomorrow, so there!"

She pulled Suzy to her feet. "Come on, we might as well get a drink, as we seem to be stuck here for the duration. Everybody else is helping herself."

A can of Thackray's was preferable to a necktie party, she

decided, noting the mirror shades of a Macoute reflecting the argument, even though Old Peculiar might not mix with the wine Suzy had drunk earlier.

"I suddenly realized I—I mean, all of us—might have been killed," they heard Ronnie say. "Somebody better deal with that bucket in there."

As they stood apart in a corner, drinking their ale, Margaret thought about her ostrich egg. When her father had brought it home from a Toc H jumble sale, she had begged to be allowed to take it to school. Her mother had relented at last, against her better judgment. Margaret had been standing in the playground, the center of an admiring circle, holding the big, frail, miraculous thing, when Veronica had come up behind her and grabbed Margaret's hands and clapped them together shattering the shell.

"Now look what you've been and gone and done! Oh" Veronica crowed "dear what a pity never mind. What will Mommy say now? Boo hoo."

That was what she always said when she made somebody cry: Oh dear what a pity never mind. But why had she wanted to make other children cry? Was it in rehearsal for her life as a writer, a testing of her power to move to tears? If so, art had failed to imitate life. Perhaps, then, Veronica had no choice, her character as predetermined as the blade of her nose. Margaret pictured a phrenologist's porcelain head with bulging prominences marked Spite, Ambition, Envy, and a tiny section just big enough to contain the blurred word Talent.

"There's something I never told you," Suzy said.

"Let me guess, you kissed Veronica in the bike shed?"

"I was her best friend for a day."

"What? You traitor! How could you?" Her childhood was cracking like an eggshell.

"No, she made me, it was awful. It was a Sunday and she just suddenly appeared at the top of our lane, and I was playing with that little girl Doreen, she was only about four, with her doll's pram, and I was wearing my mom's white peep-toes and one of her old dance frocks. Veronica said she'd tell everybody at school that I played with dollies if I wouldn't be her best friend. And the worst thing was, Keith Maxfield shouted out "Oo's that queer gink?" as she came down the lane, no, the worst thing was, my mother, mistaking her for a nice little school friend, invited her to tea. She pushed my baby sister down the stairs, accidentally on purpose. When I was walking her back to the bus stop the cows came down the lane and Veronica said, "I do pity you, Suzy, living in all this cows' muck.""

"Oh dear what a pity never mind."

"And she tried to hang my teddy from the apple tree with elastic. . . ."

"This catalog of crimes only makes your perfidy more indefensible. Why didn't you tell me?"

"I was going to—you must remember how scary she was—and anyway, on the Monday, that new girl Madeleine came, and Veronica forgot all about me. Natch. I was only ten, Margaret. . . ."

" 'Only obeying orders,' you mean."

A crash of glass might have been a damaged window of an adjacent shop leaving its moorings, or the sound of someone in a glass house throwing stones. As people converged on Dorothy's window to see what was happening in the street, her own little jagged lump of guilt began to cut. There was a girl named Angela Billings who had a slight speech impediment. One playtime stumbling over her words,

Margaret had produced an accidental approximation to Angela's diction.

"Hey, listen, Margaret's super at taking-off Angela Billings! Go on, Margaret, do it again!" called Ronnie.

Shamefaced after feeble protestations, Margaret had. And again, enjoying the brief warmth of Veronica's friends' laughter, Veronica's arm around her shoulder.

"She got bitten by a horse fly," Suzy was saying, "and she said it would be my fault if it went septic and she had to have her leg off. I was sick with fear."

Time passed. Dorothy looked increasingly desperate as people mulled aimlessly around her. Ronnie looked at her watch, as if she had another appointment.

"This is getting ridiculous. Get Scotland Yard or the Bomb Squad on the phone," she commanded. "They've no right to keep us cooped up in here like a load of bloody Bosnians under fire. Where's that Little Hitler with the loud hailer?"

"History was always Veronica's strong point," said Suzy, loud enough for Ronnie to whirl around and demand, "Do I know you?"

"Torture, wasn't it, that really turned you on? Medieval punishments? An early interest that was to bear fruit in your mature work. No, you don't know me. But I wonder if you'd do me the honor of signing this book for me?" She pulled a book off a shelf. Ronnie struck it away contemptuously.

"Are you out of your trees? Why should I sign somebody else's book? I don't even *read* other people's books!"

"Is it? Oh dear what a pity never mind, an easy mistake . . . ."

"The Old Bill wasn't very helpful, Boss," reported a twin.

"Look, Ronnie, in the circumstances, I'm prepared to double your fee—if you'll just give us a short reading . . . we're running out of booze . . ." Dorothy pleaded, as fans, following Suzy's lead, surrounded Ronnie waving books and pens.

As Margaret, her second can of Thackray's half-drunk, watched them, the scene dissolved into the washbasins where a little girl executed an arabesque against the snowlight of a winter afternoon. She was just a child, she thought, we were all only children. A muzzy mellow maternal benevolence suffused her, absolving her of her betrayal of Angela Billings; far away, made tiny by the perspective of the years, Ronnie danced, as fragile and guiltless as a ballerina pirou-etting atop a musical jewel casket to a tinkling tune. Margaret turned to Suzy, her eyes bright with unshed tears.

"School," she told her, "is a place for learning—"

"No! You don't say! I'd never have known."

"No, I mean—lessons in life. About ourselves, our limits and weaknesses, and how to overcome them . . ."

"No wonder they call this stuff Old Peculiar. And I thought you flunked that Open University Philosophy course . . ."

Margaret had to swallow her tears, just as if someone had given her the good playground pinch she had been tempted to inflict on her friend.

"What I'm trying to say is—Veronica can't be held respon-sible for Jean's suicide."

"Nobody suggested she could, just because she ruined the childhood of a short, and presumably unhappy life. 'Every child has the right to be happy,' that's what you've told me often enough, isn't it? Mummy?"

Margaret plonked down her drink, and made toward Ronnie, bursting with something, she didn't know what, that she had to say to her.

Ronnie was berating an abject Dorothy:

"Look, there's no way I'm giving a reading of any kind whatsoever at this shambles. The whole thing's a monumental cockup. You can give me a check for three, no make it four, times what we agreed, to compensate for my time and mental trauma and"—she looked around for something to add to the bill—"and the break-up of my relationship!"

"You aren't too complimentary about her thighs here," Suzy's voice was loud in the respectful silence cast by the reference to the departed Mog. She had got hold of a copy of *Flowers of Evil* and was stabbing her finger at the opening line.

Ronnie's face was white, the bone in her nose razor sharp, and two crimson patches blazed on her cheeks. Margaret knew that look, that dangerous painted doll face: something was about to get broken; a house of leaves kicked to pieces.

"Veronica," she said; as Ronnie ripped the cloth from the table and empties, the bottles and plastic cups and a jug of water crashed to the floor.

"How dare you make remarks about my lover's thighs!" she shouted at Suzy. "I do know you—you were at school with me! I know who you are, bitch, you're that Fish-Face creature aren't you? Who the hell let you in here to wreck my reading? My God, you've got a nerve! Get her out of here!"

The Tontons Macoutes were moving toward Suzy as Ronnie yelled, "Still stink of chips do you Fish-Face? Go on, give us a pickled egg!" The Macoutes closed in on Suzy. One of them twisted her arm behind her back.

"*And* there was something fishy about your mother! Wasn't she the local tart or something?"

Margaret grabbed at the other bodyguard's arm, her fingers

slipping in slick sweat, and was shrugged contemptuously off, bounced against a bookshelf.

"Freeze! Hold it right there!"

Suzy had scrabbled the gun from her pocket with her free hand and had it trained on Ronnie's head. Her attacker dropped her arm and stepped away.

"It's only a gun, you wimps!" Ronnie shrieked, "Get it off her!"

The entire audience, but for Margaret, and the bodyguards oozed backward against the windows and the sealed door.

"Do something! Kill her, put her in hospital! You're all pathetic, you're all fired, the lot of you! I forbid you to so much as open one of my books as long as you live! Give them all back!"

"Cool it, Veronica," said Suzy. "You know what this reminds me of? A wet PT lesson in the cloakroom. Shame we can't get out on the shinty field and hack each other's shins, isn't it? Still, never mind. Forgotten your plimsoles again, have you, or perhaps the truth is that you don't in fact possess any plimsoles? Take a pair out of the school box then, quick sharp—those khaki ones with no laces. Vests and knickers, everybody, and you can take off that ridiculous liberty bodice, Jean Widdoes, I don't care if your mother does say you've got a weak chest, it's your weak brain that concerns *me*. Buck up, you're like a lot of old ladies!"

A sycophantic titter came from the back. Suzy crossed the room and pressed the gun behind Ronnie's ear. She addressed the paralyzed fans.

"Right, form two teams, Reds and Greens, quick sharp! Margaret, give out the bands!"

Margaret almost stepped forward to distribute the rough red and green hessian bands but realized she was in a bookshop where

Suzy, with a gun, was imitating Miss Short. However, the fans, and Tontons were scrambling into two untidy lines, fighting not to be at the front. A couple of cravens had stripped to vests and knickers.

"Dorothy, you're Green Captain. You, Veronica, can be Captain of the Reds. Where's my whistle?"

"Here, miss, you can use mine."

A silver whistle was pulled from a polo-shirt pocket and an eager figure darted out, and dashed back to her place.

"Thank you dear, you can take a House Point."

Ronnie was marched at gunpoint to the head of one line. Half Dorothy's team defected at once.

"Back in your own line, you Greens quick sharp! Right, everybody squat down, hands on hips, elbows out. On the whistle, go! Duckwalk once right around the room, back to the end of the line, then bunnyhop a complete circuit again, and then, Captains only, duckwalk once around again. Got that? First team all home in a nice straight line is the winner!"

"I don't believe this," Ronnie was protesting when the gun forced her to her haunches. Suzy's finger tightened on the trigger. She blew the whistle and jabbed Ronnie behind the ear.

"OK, Sharples, Duckwalk till you drop."

Ten minutes later, the shop door opened and a policeman announced "All clear, ladies. You can come out now." But nobody heard him through the clamor and shouts of "Greens! Greens!" "Reds! Reds! Reds!" And "Cheat! Cheat!" as the two big ducklings slugged it out, scarlet-faced and panting, wings pumping, waddling for dear life over the chaos of torn books, spilled beer and crackling plastic cups.

THE LAUGHING ACADEMY

After he had closed the door of his mother's flat for the last time McCloud took a taxi to Glasgow airport to catch the shuttle back to London. The driver turned his head and said through the metal grille,

"I know you. You used to be that, ehh . . ." he broke off, not just because he couldn't remember the name but because the burly blond man in the back had his head in his hands and was greeting like a wean, or a boxer who had just lost a fight and knows it was his last. He concentrated on getting through the rush-hour traffic but when a holdup forced them to a crawl a glance in the mirror showed that the blond curls were tarnished and the cashmere coat had seen better days. As the smell of whisky filtered through, he recognized his passenger as Vincent McCloud the singer. "Looks like the end of the road for you, pal" he thought. "The end of the pier." Reruns of ancient *Celebrity Squares*, and guesting on some fellow fallen star's *This Is Your Life*; he could see it all, the blazers and slacks and brave Dentu-Creme smiles and jokes about Bernard Delfont and the golf course that only the old cronies in their ill-fitting toupees would get. Like veterans at the Cenotaph they were, their ranks a little thinner every year. That mandatory bit of business they all did, the bear-hugging, backslapping, look-at-you-you-old-rascal, isn't-he-wonderful-ladies-and-gentlemen finger-pointing routine—as if the milked applause could drown the tinkle of colored lightbulbs popping one by one against the darkness and the desolate swishing of the sea. As the taxi-driver pondered on the intrinsic sadness of English showbiz, he thought he remembered that McCloud had been in some bother. Fiddling the taxman, if he minded right. They were all at it.

McCloud was trying not to remember. He'd stood at his mother's bed in the ward, slapping the long thick envelope whose contents brought information about a *Readers' Digest* grand prize draw, that her eyes were too dim to read.

"Made it, Ma! Top of the world! This is it, the big yin! A recording contract and an American tour!"

He didn't want to recall all those black and white movies they'd watched together on the television, the smiles and tears of two-bit hoofers and over-the-hill vaudevillians and burlesque queens who were told, "You'll never play the Palace," and did. His mother had thought he'd be another Kenneth McKellar.

"That's you, Jimmy."

McCloud realized that the cab was standing at the airport and the driver was waiting to be paid. Old habits die hard, and McCloud was grateful that the man had failed to recognize him and had not proved to be of a philosophical bent. He gave him a handsome tip.

"Enjoy your flight!" the cabbie called out after him as McCloud went through the door carrying a heavy suitcase of his mother's things.

On his way to the plane McCloud bought a newspaper, a box of Edinburgh rock and a tartan tin of Soor Plooms, acidic boiled sweets which he used to buy in a paper poke when he was a boy. He felt like a tourist. There was nobody left in Scotland for him now.

"Do you mind?" said an indignant English voice.

It seemed he had barged into someone. He glowered. In his

heart he had been swinging his fist into the treacherous features of his former manager, Delves Winthrop, that nose that divided into two fat garlic cloves at the tip and the chin with the dark dimple that the razor couldn't penetrate.

"Don't be bitter, Vinny," Delves had counseled him on the telephone after the trial. "That's showbiz—you win some, you lose some. Swings and roundabouts. And you know what they say, no publicity is bad publicity. . . ."

In that, as in his management of McCloud's career, Delves had been wrong. The Sunday paper which had expressed interest in McCloud's story had gone cold on the idea, and his appearance on Wogan had been canceled at the last minute. Box Office Poison. McCloud, branded more fool than knave, had narrowly escaped prison and bankruptcy, and had, the taxi-driver's surmise had been correct, a guest appearance on a forgotten comedian's *This Is Your Life* to look forward to, and a one-night stand at the De La Warr Pavilion, Bexhill-On-Sea. The small amount of money he'd managed to hold onto was diminishing at a frightening rate.

While McCloud was homing through the gloaming to a flat with rusting green aluminum windows in a vast block in Streatham, Delves was soaking up the sun on the Costa Del Crime with some bikinied floozie. McCloud hoped it would snow on them. Bitter? You bet Vinny was bitter. He sat on the plane contemplating the English seaside in February, his heart a rotting oyster marinated in brackish seawater. Wormwood and gall, sloes, aloes, lemons were not so bitter. His teeth were set on edge as if by sour green plums. It came to him that Delves Winthrop owned a house on the south coast, not a million miles away from Bexhill.

∗   ∗   ∗

At Heathrow he lit a cigarette, great for a singer's throat, and telephoned his former wife, Roberta. She was friendly enough at first, and then he lost it.

"Is either of the weans with you? I'd like a word."

"The weans? What is this? Sorting out your mother's things, the perfect excuse to get legless and sentimental, eh Vinny? I might have known you'd come back lapsing into the Doric. I'm glad *we* flew straight back after the funeral."

"Is Catriona there, or Craig? Put them on, I've a right to speak to them. I'm their father, as far as I know."

"Ach, away'n bile yer heid, Tammy Troot!" Roberta put the phone down.

Tongue like a rusty razor blade, she'd always had it, since they'd met when he'd been a Redcoat at Butlins at Ayr, and she a holiday-maker hanging around the shows, Frank Codona's funfair it was, thinking herself in love with the greasy boy who worked the waltzer. The Billy Bigelow of Barassie. Well, at least he hadn't gone around to her house, as he'd half intended, the emissary from the Land O' Cakes standing on the doorstep in a tartan scarf to match his breath, with sweeties for his twenty-seven and twenty-eight-year-olds, the door opened by Roberta's husband. Of course he knew they'd left home years ago. He'd rung on the off chance that one of them might be there. They'd always been closer to their mother.

McCloud let himself into his stale and dusty fourth-floor flat and found two messages waiting on his machine, the first from his daughter Catriona sending love, the second from Stacey, a young dancer he'd been seeing for the past six months.

"Hiya darling, guess what? I got the job!!! Knew you'd be proud of me. Listen babes, we leave on Wednesday so I've got masses to get ready. Oh, hope everything went OK and you're not feeling blue. You know I'd be with you if I could. Call you later. Love you."

"Dazzle Them at Sea" the ad in the *Stage* had read. Royal Caribbean Cruises. He'd spoken to Stacey yesterday on the phone, just catching her before she trotted off to the audition at the Pineapple Studios in Covent Garden. He could tell from her voice, which sounded as if it were transmitted over miles of ocean by a ship's telephone, that in her heart she was already hoofing under sequined tropical stars.

Her neon-red words hung in the air, then faded as gray silence drifted and extinguished them.

McCloud stowed the bag of his mother's things on top of the wardrobe, feeling guilty at leaving them there but knowing it would be some time before he could bear to look at them. There were objects in that bag he had known all his life, pieces that were older than he was. Desolation suffused him as he stood on the strip of rented carpet. With mother gone, nobody would know who he really was ever again.

He found the copy of the *Stage* and the ad and read it again. Stacey had joined the company of Strong Female Dancers who Sing Well. McCloud could testify to her strength, he thought, but reserved judgment on the singing.

He sat in the living room with framed and unframed posters and playbills stacked against the wall, a glass of whisky in his hand, studying the Directory, the gallery of eccentrics like himself who lived on hope and disappointment: "Look at me!" they begged, "Let me entertain you!" Clowns, acrobats, stilt-walkers, magicians, belly-dancers, once-famous pop groups, one-hit wonders, reincarnated George Formbys still cleaning windows, fire-eaters, hilarious hypno-tists, Glenn Millers swinging yet and the Dagenham Girl Pipers defying time. Then there were the Look-alikes, fated to impersonate the famous and those whose tragedy lay in a true or imagined resemblance to somebody so faded or obscure that it was inconceivable that the most desperate supermarket manager or stagnight would dream of hiring them. McCloud read on, keeping at bay with little sips of whisky the thought that his own face would soon be grinning desperately there, until he came to the Apartments column.

"Sunny room in friendly Hastings house. Long or short stay. Full English breakfast, evening meal available. Owner in the profession."

A sunny room in February? McCloud was tempted, although there were three weeks to go before his Bexhill booking. The lime-green fluorescent flyers piled on the table filled him with fear every time they caught his eye, and he worried that his accompanist was going to let him down. The last time he'd seen Joe Ogilvy in the Pizza Express in Dean Street, the boiled blue yolks of his eyes and red-threaded filaments in the whites had not inspired confidence. He could go down and case the joint, get a bit of sea air. He put the thought of Sherry Winthrop, Delves's crazy wife out of his mind, and dialed the number.

However as he drove down the following morning, crawling along in the old red Cavalier with a windscreen starred by sleet, and Melody Radio, the taxi-drivers' friend, buzzing through the faulty speaker, he imagined Delves's house, to which he had never been invited. Neither had anybody else as far as he knew. It was common knowledge among those who knew Delves had a wife, that Sherry had been in the bin and she was never allowed to come to London or to be seen in public. She had been Delves's PA, but now he was ashamed of her. She was younger than Delves of course, and had been quite lively once. In McCloud's mind's eye the Sussex house was tile-hung, its old bricks mellowed with lichen and moss, standing in a sheltered walled garden with a prospect of the sea, and gray-green branches of the southernwood which gave it its name half-hiding the stone toadstools either side of its five-barred gate.

If you listened to Melody Radio, you'd think that love were all, that the world was full of people falling in love and the sky raining cupid's little arrows. And McCloud liked gutsy songs sung from the heart by people who'd been through the mill, that made you feel life was worth living despite everything. Take the rhinestone cowboy singing now, for example, he hadn't a hope in hell of riding a horse in that star-spangled rodeo, but there he was with his subway token and dollar in his shoe, bloody but unbowed. Tragic if you thought about his future, but it cheered you up, the song. It was not in McCloud's repertoire, he was expected to wester home via the low road to Marie's wedding and his ain folk, but he sang along lustily.

His spirits lifted as he left London's suburbs behind. "Seagull House, Rock-A-Nore Road, Hastings;" the address had a carefree, striped-candy, rock-a-bye, holiday look about it, and he felt almost as if he were going on holiday with a painted tin spade and pail. The memory of his mother, holding her dress bunched above her bare knees, laughing and running back from the frill of foam at the tide's edge, pulling him with her was more bittersweet than painful, and he resolved to remember only happy times. That was the best he could do for her now. She had told him a poem about fairies who "live on crispy pancakes of yellow tide-foam," and he'd tried to remember it for his own children, Catriona and Craig, with their little legs, paddling in their wee stripey pants. Catriona worked in a building society now, and had assured him that it had been for the best, really, that she'd had to leave the Arts Educational Trust when he couldn't find the fees. Craig hadn't found his niche yet and was employed on a casual basis behind the scenes at the National. Great kids, the pair of them. McCloud was not ready yet to admit that whatever he had done as a father was done for good or ill and he was now peripheral to their lives, and the thought of his little girl out in the dark in a dangerous city was too painful to dwell on. He was eager to hit the coast, and so hungry that he could have eaten a pile of those crispy pancakes.

Sherry Winthrop stood at the lounge window of the 1930s bungalow, "Southernwood." Flanked by two tall dogs, in her pale-green fluted nightdress with her short auburn hair she might have been a figurine of the period. She was watching the sails of the model windmill on the lawn whirling and whirling in the icy wind, and old gnomes skulking under the shivering bushes. Beyond the front garden's high chain-link fence was a tangle of sloes and briars on a stretch of frostbitten cliff top, narrower every year as boulders of chalk broke off and fell, and beyond that, the sea. A hand on each Dobermann's head, she stood, her mind whirring as purposely as the windmill's sails in the crashing sound of the waves. At length, knowing that she must get dressed and take Duke and Prince for a run, she went to make a cup of coffee. The kitchen, modernized by previous owners and untouched since, was decorated and furnished in late-fifties contemporary style. Sherry would have preferred to go back to bed and lose herself in the murder mystery she was reading but she felt guilty about the dogs' dull lives with her and would force herself for their sakes. Was she not afraid, living alone as she did, to read, late into the night, those gruesome accounts of the fates of solitary women? The dogs were her guards, although some-times she imagined they might tire of their hostage and kill her, and sometimes she felt it would be almost a relief when the actual murderer turned up at last. There was never one around when you needed him, she had learned. Like plumbers. She just hoped that when he did show up he'd only drug the dogs not hurt them, and it would be quick and the contents of her stomach not too embarrassing at the autopsy. Had Sherry cared to watch them, her husband's stack of videos would have shown her deeds done to women and children beyond her worst nightmares.

She was conscious of the thin skin of her ankles and her bare feet as she unlocked the back door and let the dogs into the garden. There was a freezer packed with shins and shanks and plastic bags of meat in the garage. Crime novels apart, Sherry was quite partial to stories about nobby people who were always cutting up the dogs' meat and visiting rectors with worn carpets in their studies, and American fiction where they drank orange juice and black coffee in kitchens with very white surfaces.

The time she had needed a murderer most was after she'd lost the baby in an early miscarriage. Delves hadn't wanted children anyway, so he didn't care, and she'd ended up in the bin. It had taken her years to get off the tranquillizers but she was all right now, just half-dead. Sometimes, for no reason, she'd get a peculiar smell in her nose, a sort of stale amyl-nitratey whiff, a sniff of sad, sour institutional air or a thick meaty odor that frightened her. She had woken with it this morning, a taint in the air that made her afraid to open her wardrobe and find it full of stained dressing gowns.

She would have done something about her life ages ago, if it hadn't been for the dogs. When Delves had brought them home as svelte one-year-olds, they had spied on her and reported her every movement to Delves on portable telephones hidden in their leather muzzles, but Delves had lost all interest in her long since and her relationship with Duke and Prince was much better. It was just that it would be impossible to leave with two great Dobermanns in tow, or towing her. Delves had no wish to remarry—why should he when there was always some girl stupid enough to give him what he wanted—and he said it was cheaper to keep her than divorce her.

There was nothing of the thirties figurine about her when, in boots and padded jacket, she crunched the gravel path past "Spindrift," "South Wind," "Trade Winds," "Kittiwakes," and "Miramar," with Duke and Prince setting off the dogs in each bungalow in turn.

It was three o'clock when McCloud, having found a parking space, walked up the steep path, through wintry plants on either side and past a rockery where snowdrops bloomed among flints and shells, and rang the bell of Seagull House. It was tall, painted gray with white windows, a deeper gray door, bare wisteria stems, and a sea gull shrieking from one of the chimneys. He felt some trepidation now, wishing he'd checked into an anonymous B and B or a sleazy hotel with a scumbag who didn't know him from Adam behind the desk. His fears proved groundless. The ageing Phil Everly look-alike who opened the door showed no sign of recognition. Later, McCloud would learn that he was the remaining half of an Everly Brothers duo whose partner had died recently from AIDS, but for the present Phil simply showed him to a pleasant attic room and asked if he would be in for the evening meal. McCloud decided that he might as well. Left alone, looking out over the jumbled slate and tiled roofs, a few lighted windows and roosting gulls, he wondered what he was doing here. Then he unpacked and walked down to the front and ate a bag of chips in the cold wind among the fishing debris that littered the ground around the old, tall tarred net shops along the Stade. Not very far away, Sherry Winthrop was drifting around Superdrug with an empty basket to the muzak of "The Girl From Ipanema," avoiding her reflection in the mirror behind the display of sunglasses.

★   ★   ★

The following day McCloud drove over to Bexhill. Bexhill Bexhill, so good they named it twice. McCloud sat nursing a cup of bitter tea in the cafeteria of the De La Warr Pavilion. He had opened the doors of the theater and taken a quick look, at the rows of seats and the wooden stage and his throat had constricted, his heart flung itself around in his tight chest and his skin crawled with fear. He had closed the doors quickly on the scene, shabby and terrifying in the February daylight. Then, like the fool he was, clammily he'd asked the woman in the box office how the tickets for the Vincent McCloud show were going.

"Oh, well it's early days yet. Everything's slow just now. Mind you, we were turning people away for Norman Wisdom, but that's different. Anyhow, we can usually rely on a few regulars who'll turn out for anything. Did you want to book some seats?" she concluded hopefully.

McCloud sat among the scattering of elderly tea–drinkers, his prospective audience if he were lucky, with *Let's call the whole thing off* going through his head. The woman in the box office must have taken him for a loony. Maybe he was. Maybe that's where he was headed, the Funny Farm. He saw the inmates racing around a farmyard in big papier-mâché animal heads, butting each other mirthlessly and falling over waving their legs in the air. Or the Laughing Academy. He'd heard the bin called that too, a grander establishment obviously, and then he remembered reading of someone setting up a school for clowns. He pictured the Laughing Academy as a white classical building with columns, and saw its pupils sitting at rows of desks in a classroom with their red noses, all going "Ha ha ha ha, ho ho ho" like those sinister mechanical clowns at funfairs. He cursed Delves Winthrop for all the bookings not made, the poor publicity, the wasted opportunities, the wonky contracts, the criminally negligent financial management, and he cursed himself for not having broken away while his voice and his hair were still golden. He thought about Norman Wisdom who traveled with his entourage in a forty-seater luxury coach, with a cardboard cutout of himself propped up in one of them, and he remembered the child, a mini-Norman look-alike in a "gump suit" who followed Norman around the country with his parents, and speculated on their weird family life; father driving, mother stitching a new urchin cap for the boy's expanding head and the kid in the back working on his dimples, mentally rehearsing a comic pratfall; a star waiting to be born. The hell with it. He was down, but not out yet. McCloud finished his tea, stubbed out his cigarette and went out into the sea fog which had swirled up suddenly, and found a ticket on his windscreen. He had forgotten to pay and display.

When he had arrived he had been momentarily cheered by the De La Warr Pavilion, that Futurist gem rising above the shingle with its splendor damaged but not entirely gone, the white colonnade and the odd houses with their little domes and minarets and gardens and white-painted wooden steps, but now he saw that Bexhill-on-Sea was a town without pity. He bought a bottle of whisky and drove back to Hastings.

Phil was in the hall of Seagull House talking to a woman with a little dog.

"Let me introduce you" he said. "Mr. McCloud—Miss Bowser, and her schnauzer Towser. Miss Bowser has the flatlet on the first floor."

Beatrix Bowser, a gaunt grizzled girl in her sixties with hair like a wind-bitten coastal shrub, wearing a skirt and jersey, held out a rough, shy hand.

"I did so enjoy hearing you sing that lovely old Tom Moore

song on Desert Island Discs recently, Mr. McCloud" she said gruffly, and fled upstairs with the little grinning brindled chap at her heels.

"Is she in the profession?" asked McCloud, imagining a novelty act with Towser wearing a paper ruff and pierrot cap whizzing around the stage accompanied by Miss Bowser on the accordion.

"Retired schoolmistress. Classics. Beatrix is one of the old school. I'm sorry, should I have recognized you?"

"No," McCloud said. "I'm out for dinner, by the way."

On the way to his room he took a glass from the bathroom, and he poured himself a shot and lay on his bed thinking about the grip of Stacey's strong dancer's legs.

The sea fog seeped through "Southernwood's" windows and the dogs were restless in the dank, chilly air, making Sherry uneasy with their pacing, clinking claws on the lino as she lay in bed reading.

"Settle down, you two!" she commanded. "Come on, up on the bed with Mommy!"

She patted the old peach-colored eiderdown. As she did, the dogs hurled themselves towards the front door barking dementedly. Sherry froze in terror. The doorbell rang. The dogs were going mad, leaping and battering the door. The murderer had come and she didn't want him. The bell sent another charge through her rigid body. Unable to move, to creep to the telephone, she sat upright, praying that the dogs would frighten him off.

A man's voice came through the door, distorted by the barking. Sherry looked around wildly for a weapon, her mind lurching towards the back door, the garden fence and the flight through darkness to "Spindrift," seeing herself beating on its door while its inhabitants, as she had done, cowered in fear, refusing to open. Feeling the hands around her throat.

"Vincent McCloud—" The voice was snapped off by the letterbox and dogs' teeth.

Half-aware of feeling like someone in a film, Sherry slid her legs to the floor, and slipped on her dressing gown. The front door was unlocked and opened a crack. McCloud saw a bit of her face, a brass poker, two thrusting muzzles with the upper lip lifted over snarling teeth.

"I'm terribly sorry to disturb you. Can I come in a minute?"

"Friend!" said Sherry, keeping the dogs, who had no conception of the word, at bay with the poker. "Lie down!"

Slavering, they sank growling to the floor.

"Delves isn't here," Sherry said. "In fact he's hardly ever here. What do you want?"

"Oh—I was just passing." McCloud attempted a disarming grin.

"Pull the other one," said Sherry, tightening the belt of her dressing gown. "If you're hoping to get at Delves by doing anything to me, forget it. I'm his least valued possession."

"I wasn't, I swear. Look, the truth is, I had to be in Bexhill and I thought I'd look you up. And take a look at the Winthrop lifestyle, I must admit."

"Well, now you've seen it. Bit different from what you expected, eh? The heart of the evil empire. You might have telephoned first."

"And you'd have told me not to come. Look, here's my bona fides." He took a lime-green flyer announcing his concert from his pocket.

Sherry studied it and handed it back without comment. She was beginning to experience an odd, long-forgotten sense of having the upper hand, and enjoying it.

"Do you want a drink?" she asked. "Before you go. Another drink, perhaps I should say."

They were sitting in the front room, Sherry with her feet tucked up under her on the sofa, and McCloud in a chair. A bottle of Cloudy Bay stood opened on the table, a rectangular slice of onyx on curlicued gilt legs. McCloud put out a tentative hand to Prince, who didn't bite it off.

"This is Delves's wine," Sherry said. "I don't often touch his precious cellar. It's too dangerous, living on your own. And it's horrible replacing it. I feel so guilty that I'm sure they think I'm an alcky, and if they think you really need the stuff, they just fling it at you without even a bit of colored tissue around it. That blue tissue always makes me think of fireworks—light the blue touchpaper and retire. Sorry, I'm rabbitting on. I'm not used to having anyone to talk to and I got a bit carried away."

"It's nice to hear you talk. We never got a chance to get to know each other, did we?"

"No. But I never get the chance to know anybody. People around here keep themselves to themselves, well, I suppose I do too. I've sort of lost touch with my family. After I was ill, you know, after I—my baby—well, I think they were embarrassed, didn't know what to say to me. And they never liked Delves. Or vice versa."

As Vincent clicked the table-lighter, an onyx ball, at a cigarette, Sherry was thinking that she might get in touch now. Suddenly she missed them dreadfully. McCloud was thinking how pretty she looked, now that the wine and the gas fire had flushed her pale face. He was thinking too that if he drank any more, he wouldn't be able to drive. He'd had a good snort or two before setting out, as Sherry had noticed.

"May I?" He refilled their glasses.

"Do you want some stale nuts or crisps?"

"That would be nice. I am a bit hungry."

"I could make you a sandwich. It will have to be Marmite."

"My favorite," said McCloud.

"Vincent," she said, as he ate his sandwiches, "Are you on your own? I mean, is there anybody in your, you know, life?"

He shook his head. "There was, a girl, a dancer. She was young enough to be my daughter. I don't know what she saw in me. Well, not much, evidently."

Sherry's dislike of the glamorous nubile cavorter, was appeased when Vincent added, "A two-bit hoofer who'll never play the Palace."

He found himself telling Sherry about his mother, and how he had deceived her about the recording contract.

"I wanted to make her happy. Or proud of me. I don't really know for whose sake I did it. Anyway, either she can see me and know the truth, or she can't."

"She would just want you to be happy. And I bet she *was* proud of you."

Vincent saw his young self against a painted backdrop of loch and mountains. "Och, aye," he said flatly. "Look, Sherry, I ought to be going. After all, I got you out of bed." A deep blush overtook the rosy flush on her face. Motes of embarrassment swarmed in the air around them, settling on her dressing gown.

"You shouldn't really be driving. You must be over the limit."

"Probably.

"There is a spare room. Only we'd have to air some sheets. Everything gets really damp here. I think it's the sea. Everything rusts." Including me, she thought, not knowing if she wanted him to make a move towards her. She knew she was lousy in bed. Delves had told her.

"May I really stay? Thank you. Please don't worry about the sheets, I'm sure I've slept in worse."

"I could give you a hot-water bottle."

"Real men don't use hot-water bottles. Have you got any music? The night's still young."

He flicked through the few albums. Tapes and CDs had not arrived at "Southernwood." He held out his arms. They danced awkwardly, to "La vie en rose," watched by the dogs with Duke howling along to the song.

"They think we've gone mad," said Sherry, invoking a memory of the bin, and remembering her own inadequacy. She broke away from Vincent and sat down abruptly.

"Look, Sherry, I don't know what upset you but I'm sorry." He was disturbed by the feel of her body through the dressing gown and nightdress. She shivered at the loss of his body close to her.

"If you think I was trying to use you to get back at Delves, you're quite, quite wrong. This is nothing whatsoever to do with him." He knelt beside her and took her hand. "We'll leave it for tonight. Maybe we can go out somewhere tomorrow. Would you like that?"

Sherry nodded. Then remembered that she had started out calling the shots and said, "We'll take the dogs to Camber and give them a good run over the sands. OK?" she added a little uncertainly.

"Fine. And I'll take you out to lunch."

He dismissed the thought of his dwindling bank balance, and realized he should call Seagull House, to let them know he hadn't done a runner or gone over a cliff.

Sometime later, lying wakefully with his cold hot-water bottle in sheets that smelled faintly mildewed, having refused a pair of Delves's damp

pajamas and wearing the tartan boxer shorts Stacey had given him—
"Tartan breath" was one of her names for him—he sensed his door
opening slowly. Sherry? Two shapes leaped through the gloom and
landed on the bed and made themselves comfortable on either side of
him.

"Thanks, boys. You're pals."

He eased himself out and padded to Sherry's room. "The dogs
have taken over my bed," he said, shutting the door behind him.

She was soft and warm as he took her in his arms, and inert.
He kissed her gently and then harder when a fluttering response came
from her lips.

"I don't do this . . ." she struggled to say.

"No. Only with me."

"I've forgotten how. Rusty . . ." she was saying into his
mouth, feeling herself to be as attractive as an old gate. She was warm and
soft. His lips grazed breasts like little seashells just visible in the darkness.
They made love gently. It was nothing like being in bed with Stacey he
thought, which sometimes felt more like an aerobics session than passion.

"I thought you'd forgotten how," he teased her, and said,
"You are quite wonderful, and beautiful."

After a late breakfast of toast and Marmite they drove to
Camber. A pair of firecrests flashed past them, bright against dun
tangles as they climbed the path between prickly bushes to the dunes.

"Oh look, aren't they pretty!" said Sherry. Then she
screamed. She saw a dead bird impaled on the thorns, and then another
and another. All around them hundreds of little birds were stuck on the
thorns, netted in the wire diamonds of a broken fence; gray-brown
sodden masses of feathers glued and pinned to every bush.

"What's the matter?"

She was paralyzed with horror. "We've got to go back!"

"Why?"

"Can't you see them? Look! Everywhere. Songbirds. Trapped. Please, please, we've got to get out of here!" She was crying, tugging his arm violently.

As he saw them it flashed through Vincent's mind that this was some horrible local custom perpetrated by the people who owned the closed pub they had passed and he felt that they were in an evil, barren place. Then he looked harder as the dogs came bounding back to find them.

"They're not birds, darling! Look! They're some sort of, of natural, vegetable phenomenon. Cast up by the sea perhaps, just bits of—matter, dead foliage or something."

Sherry was not convinced. The shape and color of them were so dead-birdlike. Vincent pulled one off a bush.

"See?"

It lay, disgusting, in his hand. She did see now that the matted hanks had never been birds, but still the place seemed the scene of a thousand crucifixions. She was trembling with the thorny impact of it. Vincent wrapped the two sides of his coat around her, pulling tightly to his chest.

" 'Come, rest in this bosom, my owns stricken deer, Though the herd have fled from thee, thy home is still here.' " Then he said, "You're frozen. Come back to Seagull House with me. There are some kind people there, and then we can decide what we're going to do next."

And there's a little dog, he realized, but decided to worry about that when they got there. They walked back past the shuttered chalets and beach shops to the car, Vincent trying not to think about the De La Warr Pavilion, shuddering at the image of himself on the stage, hanging onto the mike for support, belting out "My Way."

"'Regrets, I've had a few . . .'" and a heckling voice shouting "More than a few, mate!" Maybe he would give the rest of the whisky to Phil or Miss Bowser. Sherry was suddenly reminded of an afternoon near Christmas two years ago when she had delivered some presents to her sister's house. The three children had been sitting in a row on the sofa with a big bowl on the low table in front of them, threading popcorn on string for the birds. Like children in a storybook, except they were watching television. The picture of them made her happy.

ACKNOWLEDGMENTS

"Soft Volcano" was first published in *New Review,* 1974.

"Curry at the Laburnums" was first published in *New Review,* 1976.

"The Stained-Glass Door" was first published in *Encounter Magazine,* 1981, and was read on BBC Radio 3, 1980.

"Bananas" was read on BBC Radio 3, 1982.

"The Thirty-first of October" first appeared in *Woman's Journal,* in October 1986.

"A Pair of Spoons" was first published in slightly different form in *Critical Quarterly,* vol. 32, no. 1, spring 1990, and subsequently in *Best Short Stories 1991* (ed. Giles Gordon and David Hughes), William Heinemann, 1991.

"The Curtain with the Knot In It" was first published in *Midwinter Mysteries* (ed. Hilary Hale), Little, Brown & Co., 1992.

"Two Sleepy People" by Hogey Carmichael and Frank Loesser © 1938 Famous Music Corp. USA. Famous Chappell/International Music Publications. Used by permission.

"For All We Know" by Samuel Lewis and Fred Coots used by kind permission Redwood Music Ltd., Iron Bridge House, 3 Bridge Approach, Chalk Farm, London NWI 8BD.